××××××× SCARLET PASSION ×××××××

James and Nesta looked across the saloon at one another and their glances locked. The noise and smoke and hubbub in the room seemed to vanish. Icy spirals of delight coursed up Nesta's spine, and her palms grew cold, then hot. Had she been aware of others in the room, she would have noticed that they were staring at her, seeing how scarlet were her cheeks.

James had not come under any pretense of playing at the tables or of visiting one of the girls. He had come to see her. As if destiny itself were manipulating her, she walked across the crowded room toward him, her face alight.

Within a matter of minutes they were ensconced in her private quarters . . .

Also by Julia Fitzgerald:

ROYAL SLAVE

We will send you a free catalog on request. Any titles not in your local book store can be purchased by mail. Send the price of the book plus 50¢ shipping charge to Leisure Books, P.O. Box 270, Norwalk, Connecticut 06852.

Titles currently in print are available for industrial and sales promotion at reduced rates. Address inquiries to Nordon Publications, Inc., Two Park Avenue, New York, New York 10016, Attention: Premium Sales Department.

SCARLET WOMAN

Julia Fitzgerald

LEISURE BOOKS   NEW YORK CITY

A LEISURE BOOK

Published by

Nordon Publications, Inc.
Two Park Avenue
New York, N.Y. 10016

Copyright © 1979 by Julia Watson

All rights reserved
Printed in the United States

Published by arrangement with Futura Publications Ltd.

*For Rosemary De Courcy
With Love and Thanks*

"If you prick us, do we not bleed? If you poison us, do we not die? And if you wrong us, shall we not revenge?"
William Shakespeare, *The Merchant of Venice*

"A man that studieth revenge keeps his own wounds green."
Francis Bacon (1561-1626)

PART ONE

CHAPTER ONE

London 1860

To the children of rich parents, it was the equivalent of hell. Nannies would say, 'If you don't mind your manners, little one, you will end up in Rats' Castle,' and, momentarily, the child being admonished would pay heed.

The Peelers had long given up hope of gaining some control over the Rookery. Although the building of New Oxford Street a few years earlier had broken up its immense, sprawling size, it was still a maze of filthy, disease-riddled hovels, beneath which lay a warren of secret underground passages so intricate that a man could use them for years and still get lost in them. The entrances to the passages were carefully concealed. A bundle of rags alive with lice would hide one entry, a mattress solid with dirt another. Unless entire hovels were to be wrenched apart, screaming babies torn from their rag nests and spitting women manhandled, how could a Peeler find where thugs and criminals hid? The Peelers were hardy but not invincible.

In the corner of one hovel, Meggie Blunt squatted, her thin bare legs drawn up under her chin, her eyes dilated, her fingers pinched together. Beads of terror spattered her brow. She was listening to her mother being raped by her father.

Jack Blunt had come home drunk again. Not bluff drunk, nor helpless drunk, but blind, savage, raging drunk. At these times, his fists became rocks which he would let fly at his wife and daughter; his face would turn magenta, his eyes bulge and his lips draw back to show the stumps of five rotting teeth.

Meggie would cower when he turned on her. The coldness of fear shrouding her like a cloak was born not only of terror but also of the knowledge that he, her father, loathed her and wished her harm. Demon Jack they called him in Rats' Castle; it was a place where demons abounded, where it was in no way unusual to be brutish, yet Jack was bad enough to be called Demon even here. When he was sober, he was treated with a cautious deference which tried the wits of many a resident of the Rookery; when he was drunk, men ran.

In the curtained-off corner of the hovel, Meggie tried to bunch herself into the tiniest of shapes. She and her mother couldn't run away like others could: this was their home. Jenny, her mam, had been beaten up more times than Meggie could remember. Her arm had been twisted until it broke, her nose had been smashed more than once, her eyes were more often black and bruised than not; once the bones in her left foot had been deliberately crushed by Blunt's boot. Meggie thought of those horrors as she listened in terror now. Why didn't somebody come and help her mam? Surely others heard her screams? But if they did, no one dared to come. Demon Jack would kill any intruder with his huge fists.

Jack Blunt didn't make love, he waged war. A woman was something to use, like the painted dollymops, the amateur prostitutes who hung around street corners. He used them, too, when he had spare coins, and if they would not do as he ordered, he would beat them, cobbing his hands into fists and slamming them into their painted faces, gouging out their eyes with his massive thumbs and biting their breasts until they fainted from the pain. The women were accustomed to all kinds of treatment, but only ignorant newcomers would let Demon Jack take them in the back alleys now.

'Mam, Mam, don't fight him, don't!' Meggie sobbed into her hands. 'Let him finish, then he'll leave you alone!'

Still the battle raged behind the curtain. She heard her mother's indrawn breath and then the sound of smashing china. Her mother's most prized possession, the flowered china bowl: had her mam thrown it, or her da? Either way, she knew its loss would break her mam's heart.

After the noise, there was a short silence before her

mother cried out. Her father roared angrily, then her mother cried out again, a long, thin wail of pain.

Icy with dread, Meggie cried out, 'No, Mam, no! Don't! Please, please, don't!'

Finally there was silence. Somehow that was even more frightening to the little girl. She curled up more tightly, trying to make herself invisible, delving into the mound of rags which was her bed, her heart beating wildly.

Her mam was dead. Demon Jack had killed her mam! The thing she had always feared had happened at last. Her mam, her lovely mam was dead!

At that moment the curtains were flung roughly to one side and her father staggered into view, panting heavily, tugging his shabby breeches together as he lurched towards the door. Meggie stared at him, wanting to kill her father yet too frozen in sick dismay to move. Blunt saw her eyes on him, gazing, as he thought, at his naked chest and stomach, and he stopped, his hand loosening its hold on his breeches so that more of the bulging, matted stomach was revealed.

How old was the brat now? he pondered. Past ten, wasn't she, and tall for her age. Ten. There were girls of eight and nine out on the streets bringing in money for their fathers. Why shouldn't she be doing the same? She sat around doing nothing, eating his food sleeping in the bed he provided for her, but she brought not so much as sixpence into the home. What was more her sharp eyes saw and noted everything, and he did not like being watched. Worst of all, her mother doted on her, spoiling the brat shamelessly, and he had never condoned that. How had he stood it all these years? That cold stubborn creature he had married, who had to have sense knocked into her at every turn, and this hostile, silent chit who never took her bright dark eyes off him. He felt somehow ashamed when she looked at him, as if she could see his sins and was silently accusing him. She had no right to treat him with so little respect. He was her father, wasn't he? She should be grateful to him.

A groan from behind the curtain told him that his wife

was regaining consciousness. Hastily he finished tying up his breeches. He would go to The Sun God and try and forget this hovel and its hostile occupants, damn them both to hell. After a swill of Geneva and a pie he would feel more like himself again.

As the rickety door closed behind him, Meggie heard her mother groan again. Her spirits leapt. Uncurling, the little girl sprang to the pallet where her mother lay, bone white except for a red welt which covered one side of her face and a rapidly swelling eye.

'Water, *cariad*, water, please,' her mother moaned.

Meggie hurried to obey. 'Just you lie there and rest, Mam. Don't move. I'll look after you.'

Meggie ran in the direction of the flowered china bowl where Jenny kept the water and then remembered that it had been shattered. She reached for her own tin mug and filled it with water.

Jenny drank greedily, then sank back amongst the tattered rags which covered her pallet. She was quite for so long that Meggie grew afraid and reached out to touch her soft, pale skin. Her mother's eyes flew open at once. Years ago, they had been a rich hyacinth-blue in colour, but strain and malnutrition had robbed them of their brightness.

'Don't fret for me, *cariad*,' she whispered in her lilting Welsh voice. 'I had to throw the bowl at him. I had to. There was nothing else left to throw. But I was foolish thinking that it would stop him. I should have known better.' She sighed and drank again. 'I recall the day I got it. Old Tab had it on his cart. It was covered in dirt and it took me days to clean it. He said he'd found it buried and that was why it was so dirty, but I always thought that sounded a bit strange. Who'd want to bury a pretty bowl like that? Anyway, he gave it to me in exchange for a shawl of mine he'd had his eye on for his missis.' Jenny sighed again. 'I knew afterwards that I'd done a stupid thing, parting with a good warm shawl for a useless bowl, but I couldn't resist it. Those big fat roses . . . . There was

a garden once, with roses like that. I shall never forget it.'
Jenny closed her eyes again, tears rolling down her cheeks.

'Don't cry, Mam,' Meggie pleaded, clasping her mother's cold hands in her own. 'I'll get you another bowl.'

'There won't be another like that for me, *cariad*,' Jenny whispered. 'I was lucky to have had that.'

"Course there'll be another for you, Mam. I'll get it for you, I promise!'

Meggie clung tightly to her mother, a wave of determination coursing through her frail body. Her love for her mother had sustained her for as long as she could remember. She knew she was fortunate. Mothers and fathers in the Rookery usually cared more for their Geneva than for their children. Toddlers were taught to thieve; babies were stuck with pins to make them cry so that their sisters and brothers could say they were crying from starvation to beg larger sums of money for them; young girls were put on the streets and told not to come home until they had filled their pockets or else they would be beaten.

Only Jenny's protection had saved Meggie from such a fate. Jenny took in sewing from her friends, for she was a good seamstress, having once been a lady's maid before her fortunes had changed. Even amongst the tattered inmates of Rats' Castle there were women who liked a new dress now and then, and they hired Jenny to sew for them. She could make hats, too, and would sell these when she could find buyers. If Demon Jack had been helpful and less oppressive, she might have built up a nice little business, but how could she work in such surroundings and with a man around whose brutal nature upset the family day after day?

There was also the difficulty of keeping the money she earned out of his hands. Jenny was not one to lie, but she had lied to her husband about the hats she sold; when he demanded her earnings, he got less than half, and she gave the rest to Meggie to buy fruit in secret. Their conspiracy brought mother and daughter even closer together but only served to enrage Demon Jack.

Love had made Meggie promise her mother a new bowl, and it was love and her desire to protect Jenny that made her watch her father so carefully. Whenever she heard Jack Blunt's boots outside on the cobbles and the door to their hovel crash open against the wall, that love was endangered. Her mother would suffer and so would she, but what were her own sufferings compared to those of Jenny?

There had been baby brothers: four of them, all dead now. None had lived for long. How could a baby survive in this place? Jenny's milk had dried up quickly, from her fear of Demon Jack's attacking the baby; without milk, the baby had wasted away. Meggie had been as heartbroken as her mother at the loss of the babies, but Demon Jack had not grieved for his sons, only for the lack of money to spend on drink.

Meggie herself had helped to deliver the baby boys; tiny little scraps, one was born stiff and blue, another ceased to cry after only a few hours of life, the others survived for a few weeks until Jenny's milk dried up.

Jack Blunt had said it was what Jenny deserved. She was a stupid, witless bitch, he said, and God knew she should be punished. It seemed odd to hear him speaking as if he believed in God. Meggie did not think her father was a believer, but when it suited him he would bring God into the conversation. God had known what He was doing when He had let the babies die. God knew who was fit to look after babies and who was not.

Meggie could be forgiven for thinking that he had no feelings other than anger. She had learned a lot for a ten-year-old, things which sheltered young ladies would never know. She had learned that men did not love women, that they only kept them to satisfy their own lusts; that when a woman was ill, her husband beat her; that when she was pregnant, he beat her; that if she disagreed with him, he beat her; that if she did anything, however small, which he did not like, he beat her. Meggie had decided long ago that she would never marry.

Life seemed to be intolerable yet somehow they endured it. Meggie's only knowledge of love was what she received from her mother and returned: always plentiful, constant, steady, reassuring.

Meggie bathed her mother's face, gently smoothing it with a piece of damp rag until the scarlet streaks of dried blood had been removed, and then placed the damp rag over the swollen eye. As she worked, she thought about how she was going to keep that promise to her mother. Somewhere there had to be another flowered china bowl; she had to find it, even if she had to search the whole of Rats' Castle – the whole of the Rookery. She would not tell her mother what she was going to do, or where she was going, because it would only worry her.

After she gave her mother more water to drink, Meggie waited until she fell asleep and then slipped out to look for the new bowl. She thought about going to Old Tab, who was a regular sight with his shabby cart piled high with junk, but realized that was all he usually carried: just junk.

It was cold outside. Meggie's feet were bare and her ragged dress was far too small for her: she shivered with cold. For a time she wandered, thinking about possible places where she could find china ware. Near St Giles's church she saw a tiny pawnshop and peered through its grimy window. Inside, there were leather boots, a top hat, a shabby moth-eaten fur pelisse, a tiny evening purse with glittering beads and a few dozen dusty old books – but no china at all. Even if she did find a bowl with roses on it, where would she get the money to buy it? Her shoulders slumped.

Two ragged urchins passed by, bowling an enormous hoop they had just stolen from a boy in a sailor suit in the park. Turning, one of the boys made a rude gesture at her; then, cackling, both boys ran off. Meggie ignored them. There were hundreds of their kind here. Growing numb with cold, she wandered down a side alley, where a dollymop was standing. The woman's painted face twisted and her eyes bulged with anger when she spotted Meggie.

'What yer doin' 'ere, gel?' she screeched. 'Gerroutta 'ere, this 'ere's me road. *Gerrout!*'

Meggie stopped in her tracks, hands clenched by her sides. Did this woman think she was *like her*? Hastily, she turned on her heel and ran off. The woman would probably have a burly male protector nearby, and Meggie had no wish to be beaten up. The dollymops guarded their territory fiercely; no one else was allowed on it unless she happened to be a very good friend, and good friends were rare in this business.

Meggie glanced back over her shoulder. The dollymop was all smiles now, for she had a customer, whose hand was pushing up her skirts. She was grinning at him coquettishly, as if he were some sort of god. What she really worshipped, of course, was the money in his hand. They proceeded to couple, there in the street, seemingly unafraid of being caught by the Peelers.

Meggie was not shocked. She had seen it all before, if not out in the streets then in her own home.

Ahead were half a dozen alleys. There was another pawnshop, but it was even poorer than the one she had just seen, and dealt mainly in ragged clothes. Was there any way she could borrow some money? It did not seem likely. Her friends were even poorer than she was – if she could call them friends; they would tear her dress off her if they could, and steal from her purse.

A stumbling figure approached her. From a distance it looked like a bundle of animated rags, but closer up she saw the brown, wizened face of Old Katie. Old Katie was notorious round here. It was said that she had been drunk longer than anyone else in Rats' Castle, and certainly, for as long as she could recall, Meggie had seen the old woman stumbling around and heard her slurring her words. Sometimes Old Katie collapsed in a heap and stayed where she lay for hours until she revived or a kinder than usual friend helped her to her hovel.

'What yer doin', gel? Yer should be wiv yer ma.'

Everyone who knew Jenny knew that she kept a close watch on her daughter.

'Mam's asleep,' Meggie replied. 'She – she's been beat again.'

Old Katie shrugged. 'Thass 'ow it goes, dunnit? Keeps a man comin' back to 'is 'ome if'n 'e got someone ter knock roun' there, dunnit?' she cackled.

'It would be better if he didn't come home, wouldn't it? He never brings us any money.'

'Times is 'ard, duckie. 'Ard fer aller us. Can't blame a man fer that, can yer?'

'I can blame him for hitting my mam!' Meggie retorted hotly.

'If'n 'e knew what yer sayin' 'bout 'im now, 'e'd set in ter yer, wouldn' 'e, an' that would 'it yer ma 'arder than if'n she were 'it, I reckons.'

Old Katie had spoken the truth, and Meggie knew it. Sucking on the stumps of her rotting teeth, the old woman watched the girl. This young miss would have more than a few beatings in her own lifetime. Girls with spirit always came to a bad end, sooner or later.

"Ow is yer ma, anyways?'

'Fine, apart from being beaten up, bruised and covered in blood,' Meggie replied caustically.

Old Katie's eyes tried to focus on the little girl. 'Yer sound bitter fer a chile. Worse'n that 'as 'appened ter others, yer know.'

'I suppose I got to believe you,' Meggie shrugged, 'but there are some families that don't live in fear of their man.'

'An' 'ow would yer know, a little chit like yer?' Old Katie snorted. 'The way yer speaks yer'd think yer was ownin' some big knowledge no one else got.'

'Mebbe I have,' Meggie said, but without conviction for she had only been guessing that there were happy families elsewhere. She could not think of one family in the Rookery where the man did not beat his kinfolk.

'Don' look so mis'rable, gel. Tek yer ma a jug o' Geneva; that'll brighten 'er up an' mek her fergit 'er pains.'

'She's not keen on it.'

Old Katie's mouth fell open. 'Not keen on it? She don' like gin? Tell me another 'un, do!' The old woman hiccoughed loudly, a scraggy hand pressed to her sagging stomach.

'Mam's never liked it. She's not a drinker. She prefers tea if she can get it.'

'Tea, do she?' Old Katie put on a haughty accent. 'Thinks she's a leddy, do she? An' arter all these years in the Rookery, eh? Got a strong guardi'n angel, 'as she?' Chortles ended this remark. Finally, Old Katie collected herself. 'Well, where yer gonna git 'er a cuppa tea, gel?'

'That's just it, I'm not, am I?' retorted Meggie, who was well aware of her shortcomings. 'But I wanted to get her something. That's why I came out while she was asleep.'

'Yer should tek 'er some Geneva. 'Twould please me more'n anyfink. Cheer 'er up an' make 'er smile, it would.'

'But I ain't even got a penny,' Meggie said.

'Well, that do spoil things a bit, dunnit? I ain't got a penny nivver.' Old Katie hiccoughed. Then, creasing her already furrowed brow, she said, 'Yer go back ter yer ma, 'old 'er 'and an' smile at 'er. Ain't much more yer can do if'n yer ain't got no money.'

Having passed on what she viewed as wise advice, Old Katie folded her arms; a self-congratulatory smile crossed her wrinkled face.

Meggie nodded. Her eyes softened with the memory of all the times she had done just that for her mother, holding her hand and looking at her adoringly.

'Tell yer ma I'll come an' see 'er when I gits the time,' Old Katie said, moving off.

Meggie watched her go. From the back she looked like a bundle of rags with sticks poking out from them. Perhaps one day, she, Meggie, would be like that, too, having drowned her miseries in Geneva? In the Rookery, there seemed little chance of better.

It was getting dark now and Meggie was hungry. Snow had begun to fall again. Meggie knew that her mother would probably have woken by now, and she would be hungry, too. Better to get back home before Jenny became anxious.

She wondered what they could have for tea. There was half that stale loaf left – if her father had not eaten it – and some sour milk. There would have been a hunk of mildewed cheese only the rats had got it the previous night. How could she make stale bread and sour milk into a tasty meal for her mam? As she turned on her heel for home, the impossibility of it weighed her down.

Thinking of the milk made her remember the little kitten with thick black fur and brilliant green eyes. It had strayed into their hovel a few weeks ago and had refused to leave. She and Jenny had kept it hidden when Demon Jack was at home, for he hated animals and would have crushed the kitten with his boot as he had done to a little puppy which Jenny had got her daughter two or three years earlier. They knew they were taking a risk not forcing the kitten to go, but it was a darling and had won their tender hearts. One day Demon Jack had come home unexpectedly, and before they could stop it, the kitten had jumped up at him, eager to be friendly. He had roared with fury at the sight of it, then grasped it in his massive fists and strangled it before their eyes.

Meggie swallowed with difficulty. Her father was a madman; he had been born a monster.

Tears gathered behind her lids. The kitten's death had been one more horror to be added to the list of nightmares which filled her life.

When Meggie reached home, she slipped inside silently. Jenny was still asleep. She seemed not to have moved. Her breathing was laboured, and her chest seemed to rattle. With sinking heart Meggie recognized the symptoms. Her mother's cough came and went with unerring regularity; sometimes Jenny had been able to throw it off, at other times she had grown feverish and weak.

When Jack returned and saw Jenny was ill again, it would mean another beating for them both. Meggie fought back tears, the familiar coldness of dread creeping over her as she made bread and milk for herself and her mother. There were rats' droppings on the shelf by the bread, and she swept them off with a practised hand. They should have a metal box to keep their food in so the rats could not eat it.

Meggie went to her mother's bed.

'Mam, Mam, here's your supper,' she said, repeating her words in a louder voice when Jenny did not at first respond.

Jenny's lids fluttered, and she opened her eyes slowly to see her daughter standing there anxiously.

'Oh, you're a good girl!' she said. 'Aren't I lucky having a good girl like you to look after me?' Carefully, for she was bruised and aching, Jenny struggled to sit up. She was wheezing, and coughed weakly. 'It's back, that dratted cough. As if I haven't got enough troubles.'

'Don't worry, Mam, I'll look after you!' Meggie said valiantly.

'I know you will, *cariad*. I know.'

Jenny began to eat the sour milk and bread. She had eaten similar food so often before that she no longer grimaced. When you were hungry, any food was manna.

It was cosy sitting there together, even if the hovel was cold and the food foul. Meggie felt a glow of happiness. Nothing could be better than sitting down with your mam. They knew Jack Blunt wouldn't be back for hours. He would be down at The Sun God, drinking. With luck, he would drink himself insensible and sleep the night through in the street somewhere.

Handing her empty dish to her daughter, Jenny sighed. 'You are a lovely girl, Meggie. I've been so lucky with you; no one needs to tell me that.'

Meggie beamed, warmth flowing through her. Putting the dishes to one side, she snuggled into bed beside her mother, who cradled her in her arms lovingly and stroked her forehead.

'You're a dear girl, Meggie, and I wish I could give you more. You deserve a better life than this. If you only knew.'

'Only knew what, Mam?' Meggie asked.

'If you only knew the things I'd like to give you, *cariad*.'

Meggie closed her eyes, putting her arms round her mother to squeeze her tight. 'All I want's you, Mam. Nothing else, just you.'

They fell asleep together on the bed. Outside the night grew blacker and snow billowed down in huge soft flakes. The Thames was frozen hard, and those who had the spirit for it were skating and skidding about, eating hot chestnuts cooked on the braziers, buying wares at the stalls set up so boldly on frozen water. For those who had money, life was full and exciting.

Jenny took a long time to recover from the beating. Her face was deathly pale, her eyes dull with fever. Maggie worried about her constantly. Her sneezing filled the room, and she complained of pain in her chest. Helpless, Meggie nursed her as ably as she could, wishing that she had some money to get a doctor and buy her proper food. The only good thing was that Demon Jack hadn't come back that first night; he had stayed away for nearly five days, giving Jenny some time to rest and recover.

Meggie had heard of an old woman who was said to be good at curing illness, but she, too, would expect to be paid. If you could not afford to pay a doctor, how could you pay anyone else? Besides, Meggie did not know where the woman lived.

When Blunt returned, he swore loudly at the sight of his sick wife. Kicking over their sticks of furniture and ripping down the dividing curtain which Jenny had put up, he spat at her and the child, calling them good-for-nothings and saying that he would put an end to them both.

Meggie huddled in her corner, not daring to breathe, praying that he would go soon, and without touching her mam. After about half an hour of ranting and raving, Demon Jack did indeed leave, saying that he would not come back while his wife was lolling about in bed like a duchess.

When he had gone, Jenny laughed hysterically. 'If only I could believe him, it would mean he might never come back!' Her laughter turned to tears as Meggie hugged her.

Meggie tried to console her mother, but she was remembering the way her father had looked at her before he left. It was not the first time he had looked at her like that, in that new, searching sort of way. It frightened her far more than when he lost his temper or raised his fist to her. It was as if he were weighing her up for some reason; as if she weren't his daughter anymore but a stranger to him. She had said nothing to Jenny; she did not know how to express what she felt.

Meggie knew that whatever she said or did, her father hated her for it. If she answered his questions, he said she was cheeky. If she stayed silent, he said she was sullen. Either way, she got a cuff on the head. That had been bad enough, but now to have his eyes fixed upon her face and body in this new way. . . . She did not know how to cope with it.

As the days passed, Jenny's cough grew worse and her feverishness increased. 'It's just the cold,' she said. 'By spring, I'll be well again, *cariad*.'

Meggie failed to be comforted. She had never seen Jenny so weak nor felt her brow so hot. She barely slept now for the coughing. A feeling of dread was taking hold of Meggie. She thought of all the other people she had known whose illnesses had started with coughs. All of them were dead now. They had needed fruit and milk and sunshine, things they could never get in the Rookery.

All she could do was pray to God, Whom Jenny had always encouraged her to worship in secret, mindful of her own strict Chapel upbringing in Bangor before she had left to get work in London to help her impoverished parents.

'Please, God, please make Mam get well. Please look after her and make her cough go away. *Please*.'

A few hours later, a customer dropped by to collect a hat which Jenny had made for her. Jenny had thought the woman had forgotten, but now here she was, with money in her hand. It was like a miracle.

'Give her the hat,' Jenny whispered to her daughter.

Meggie went to the secret niche where her mother hid her sewing so that Demon Jack would not get his fists on it. The hat glowed in the gloom of the hovel. It was a gaudy emerald green with an orange ribbon, just as the woman, a worker at Bryant and May's factory, had ordered. The match-girls were renowned for their peacock-coloured finery. The woman grinned at the sight of it and set it on her brown, frizzled curls. She had on a magenta dress with black trim but that did not deter her from keeping on the gaudy hat. She handed the payment to Jenny and then swaggered out.

After she had gone, Jenny said, 'All her spare money goes on clothes. Her father is an invalid, but she doesn't look after him properly. Still, we've got money for food now, *cariad*.'

Jenny gave a tremulous smile.

'Here, take this money, *cariad*, and get the best bargain you can with the costermongers. Bread, fruit, anything you fancy, and if you see your da, whatever you do, don't let him know you've got money!'

Meggie scuttled off, grinning, sure that her prayers had been answered.

CHAPTER TWO

The costermonger had a flat, ruddy face and cauliflower ears which intrigued Meggie. She stared at them longer than was polite, until the man's rough voice brought her out of her reverie.

'Come on now, me gel. Ain't got all day, yer know. People's waitin' ter be served.'

Hastily she proferred her money, asking for whatever fruit the man had to sell, and some vegetables, too. If the man thought she had what seemed like a lot of coins for a ragged urchin, he said nothing. It wasn't his business to pry or to turn away a good customer. Next, Meggie bought a loaf and some cheese; then, her purchases looped up into her skirt, she headed for home. She felt triumphant being able to take home good food like this; before, she had never had more than a loaf or a few scraps tucked in her skirt.

Her mother's face lit up at the sight of the fruit. They tore hunks off the fresh soft bread and devoured it hungrily.

'I should have got some tea and now there's no money left,' Meggie said regretfully.

'This is lovely, *cariad*, more than enough. Oh, I have enjoyed this feast. It's taken me right back to when I was a girl, when me and my family'd have a tea just like this round the parlour table. Nain would sit in the corner, nodding over her mug and pretending to be wide awake if anyone spoke to her, and Taid would ramble on about when he was a boy. He didn't half have some tales to tell, my Taid. There was the time he went to visit the lighthouse at Holyhead, South Stack 'tis called, and he slipped on the steps leading down to it. Dozens of those steps there were, and he fell down with a mighty crash. Everyone thought he'd be dead, but he got up and grinned and said he was all right. Two hours later, he keeled over and they couldn't rouse him whatever they did. When he finally came round, he couldn't recall one thing about the lighthouse. Didn't even know he'd been there!' Jenny smiled at the memory. 'Quite a lad he was before he settled down with Nain. She kept him under her thumb.'

Meggie had heard these stories before, but she never grew bored with them. The family who lived in Bangor, and whom she had never met, were as real to her as Jenny. Her mother had often talked of going home, back to Bangor, but they had never been able to save up enough money for the long journey.

That day was one of the last of the happy ones. Demon Jack's rages seemed to be growing more frequent. He grumbled about everything now, but especially about Jenny's coughing during the night.

'Doin' it o' purpose ter spoil me sleep, thass what yer doin'!' he stormed at his wife, who shrank from his waving fists. 'Cough, cough, cough, thass all I 'ear, all night, 'our after 'our....'

'Mam can't help it,' Meggie said bravely, standing up to her father with a courage she did not feel.

'An' who told yer ter interrupt, eh?' Jack whirled on his heel, snarling in anger.

Meggie cringed, waiting for the blow, but Jenny intervened. 'Please, Jack, she didn't mean any harm. She's said the truth. I can't help the coughing. Don't hit her, please don't hit her!'

For once, Jack seemed as if he would obey his wife, for he let his arm drop, but the furious expression did not leave his craggy features. 'I knows what yer two's up ter. Trickery, thass what. Yer thinks yer can keep me awake all night so's I'll be too tired ter go out ter drink. Well, yer thinks wrong, yer does, 'cos nothin' ain't gonna stop me goin' out when I wants ter, see!' He stabbed at the air with one huge, black-nailed finger. 'If I wants ter go out I'll go, see!'

Jenny struggled to get up into a sitting position, the little colour she had ebbing from her cheeks. 'If you want to go out, Jack, don't let us stop you.'

'*Yer* stop *me*? Hah!' her husband sneered. 'Whinin' bitches both o' yer!'

Demon Jack spat across the room, narrowly missing Jenny, just to show what he thought of women, and then he stormed out of the house, slamming the door behind him.

'Oh, Mam, you shouldn't have spoke up to him! He might have hit you again.' Meggie ran to her mother to hug her.

'It's not easy staying silent, as you know, *cariad*. Sometimes it's easier to risk being beaten. Oh how I rue the day I ever met him. But if you'd known him when he was young, *cariad*. . . . So handsome and cheery he was.

thought he was the answer to my prayers, and it seemed like he was – for a time.' Jenny sighed heartrendingly.

'What changed him, Mam?' Meggie asked.

'Who knows? Drink perhaps? Marriage? Seems like a lot of men never grow up and they can't adjust to being wed. Stupid and childish they are. It wasn't always like this you know, *cariad*. We had a nice little cottage at the start, and some good pieces of furniture when your da used to work. All of it sold to keep us in food long ago. Then he didn't pay the rent on the cottage so we lost that, too, and I couldn't get a job by then 'cos I had you to care for.'

'That must have broke your heart, Mam.' Meggie stroked her mother's hair gently.

'I've got every reason to be angry, *cariad*, and I just wish I could get up and knock him around like he's done with us. Years and years we've suffered from his beatings. Where will it all end, that's what I'd like to know.'

'Mam, don't upset yourself. Lie back, and we'll talk about what we'll do in the summer. You can take me to the park and we'll look at the lake and the swans, and the sun'll be hot on our faces. We can take some bread to eat, and sit on the grass and sunbathe. You'd like that, wouldn't you, Mam?'

Jenny nodded. 'It seems like ten years since I stood in the sunshine. This has been such a long, cold winter. It's robbed me of my strength.'

Meggie said nothing, pressing her head against her mother's breast and longing with all her heart that Jenny would soon be well.

The weather grew colder and Meggie spent hours searching for twigs, bits of wood, rags, worm-eaten old boards, anything she could find to keep the fire burning in the hovel. Jenny huddled by the flames, face pinched, teeth chattering, thinking longingly of the shawl she had exchanged for the now broken rose bowl.

Old Katie made her promised visit, cackling at them, smelling of Geneva and rotting teeth.

'Whass wrong wiv yer two?' she said. 'Yer look like Death's got yer both in 'is grip, yer do.' She sucked on her decaying teeth as she held out a bottle of ale. 'Brung this I did. 'Eat it fer yer ma, Meggie, an' it'll warm 'er 'eart up good an' proper.'

Jenny hated ale, but she was grateful for Old Katie's thoughtfulness, and, after Meggie had put it in a mug and dipped in a hot nail to warm it, she sipped at it cautiously.

'Mmmn, that's good, Katie. You're a dear to remember me.'

'Say nuffink of it, Jenny. Shoulda come before but I bin a bit sickly meself.' To illustrate, Katie slapped her chest with a clawed, sepia hand and forced a cough. 'An' I got sumfink else an' all – ' From out of the folds of her wrinkled gown, Katie drew a coarse brown loaf.

Soon they were all eating, squatting round the fire and exchanging snippets of gossip.

'Tizzy Allan's gittin' married. No choice,' Katie cackled. 'Got 'er filled up. An' Gawd knows who's the father, but 'Arry Melts is willin' ter claim it. More fool 'im! An' Annie Cooper's 'ad 'er twelfth but it don' look like it'll live, poor little sod. Did yer 'ear that Gerrid Cooper's got a fancy piece over at Seven Dials? Know what 'es after there, I does – ' Katie made a sweeping shape in the air, to illustrate what had attracted Gerard Cooper.

Jenny was always a little nonplussed by Old Katie's heartiness, but today it was cheering, so she welcomed it. Meggie looked brighter, too. The mere fact of the old woman's incorrigible spirit had a heartening effect on her. Also, the reassuring knowledge that, despite a long life of drinking too much and never eating the right food, Old Katie was still hale and in possession of her wits. If she could do it, why not others?

After a few minutes of silence, Katie cleared her throat loudly and then said, as if she were uttering something forbidden, 'Where's the Demon?'

'Need you ask,' Jenny replied. 'At The Sun God, where else?'

'Should 'ave a bed made up fer 'isself there, 'e should,' Katie rasped. 'Not that I'm one ter talk, an' thass a fact. Still, better the devil yer know than the devil yer don' know, eh, Jenny?'

'Why know any devil at all?' Jenny replied, with a little of her old fire.

'Yer needs a man roun' the 'ouse, 'specially now yer ill. Aller us needs a man roun'.' That was Old Katie's belief and she was sticking to it.

'A man, yes,' Jenny agreed, 'but I thought we were talking about my husband.'

Katie narrowed her eyes, as if weighing up what the Welsh woman had said, and then she let out a roar of laughter.

'I sees yer ain't lost none o' yer old spirit, gel. Thass a comfort an' no mistake.'

The food had all gone, and their stomachs were comfortably full. Old Katie stretched and said she had better be getting back home, although they all knew she meant back to The Sun God, which was her real home.

'If'n I sees yer old man I'll give 'im a kick in the ankles an' tell 'im ter git back 'ere where 'e belongs.'

'Don't you dare!' Jenny retorted. 'Say nothing. The longer he's out the better.'

'Tell 'im ter stay away then, eh?' Katie teased.

'No, say nothing, Katie. Words are like blows to him. Whatever you say, he takes it the wrong way. If he didn't come home and hit us, he'd hit you.'

'Don't fret yerself, Jenny. I'll say nothin', yer can be sure o' that. Now look after yerself, an' yer, Meggie, keep yer eye on yer ma an' be a good gel.'

'She always is,' Jenny smiled, resting her thin hand on Meggie's arm.

'Demon Jack can't find it easy livin' wiv two angels, can 'e?' was Katie's parting remark.

When Old Katie had gone, Meggie looked at her mother. Did she really have some of her old spirit back or

28

had Old Katie been imagining it? Once, Jenny's ready response to life had been marvellous, or so Old Katie had said long ago. Now much of that had been crushed out of her by Demon Jack's brutality and the lack of nourishing food. But Jenny looked pale and thin to her daughter, and Meggie felt the now familiar resurgence of depression sweep over her. Jenny insisted, however, that she was feeling much stronger, and she did indeed begin to move around again, and even to go out, although the cold weather made her coughing attacks much harsher and she would return from her short outings with an almost greenish pallor, her eyes sunken. She looked as if she had barely survived a terribly tragedy. Meggie's fears for her grew daily. There was sadness in her eyes, poverty in her gaunt cheekbones, fear in her tense body.

It was just not fair that her mam had to suffer like this, Meggie thought for the hundredth time. Why did Old Katie stay so strong, when all she lived for was gin, while her mam, who was so good and kind, went down so quickly when she was ill? It was just not fair. But what could she *do* to help her?

Jack Blunt stomped back to his hovel, a red mist before his eyes. He was raging drunk, an insane fury pounding in his head. He had delayed long enough, putting up with those two bitches who thought of no one but themselves. Was he a man or a weakling? It was time he showed them both who was master at home. More than ten years he had fed and housed that cold-faced brat and never seen anything by way of return. Well, that was all about to end, and no mistake. He was going to get his payment now, and no one was going to stop him.

Blunt was slow-witted for a brutal man, with his anger being the only sharp thing about him, and so he had not realized what to do immediately. But since the night when he had looked at Meggie and seen her as a girl of all but eleven years and thought of all the girls on the streets bringing in good money at a younger age than she, he had been planning this moment. It had to be when Jenny was out, he knew that. If he tried it when she was at home, he would have two bitches to fend off, and one with the strength of a lioness in defence of her young. He wanted it to go smoothly, without hindrance. Afterwards, the brat would be ready for the sailors and other men eager to couple with a young wench in the back alleys. Men who would be willing to pay handsomely for the experience.

He himself had used many young creatures at one time or another. He liked young girls. They were filled with awe at his advances and would look at him with big, wide eyes. Just the thought excited him. Now he wanted to add Meggie to his list. If Jenny would just get well and leave the hovel for an hour or two. That Welsh bitch had fussed and pampered Meggie from the hour she was born. It disgusted him, filling him with a blind, ungovernable jealousy. When he felt like this, he wanted to strangle both the woman and the girl until their faces turned blue and their tongues stuck out, until their last breaths rasped and they fell limply to the floor. They were lucky he had such good control of himself.

He thought of Meggie; of her slender pale limbs and white face, of her big eyes, such a strange colour they were, like her ma's. Purple. Who'd own to purple eyes? And all that long black hair, like her ma's, too. But men were fond of variety. They would like her in a pretty dress and with a few frills and feathers in her hair. Pay well they would for a chit with such a pure face. He chortled at the thought of her purity. When he finished with her she wouldn't be innocent! If only her ma would get out of the house for an hour or two . . . .

Years ago, Jenny had looked at him in the same loving way she now looked at her daughter. She had doted on him at first. A shudder of revulsion shook his burly frame. Once that brat had sat up, it was good-bye to him. All she had thought of, night and day, from that time on was the brat. It was Meggie this and Meggie that, and don't wake the babe, and mind where you're stepping or you'll crush her hands, Jack Blunt. Nag nag nag all day, and then at night when he wanted a little comfort and his husbandly rights, she was too tired to please him. He'd never asked much, had he? Been a good provider when they were first wed. Hadn't been his fault that he'd been laid off from his job and they'd had to sell their furniture and lose the cottage. Couldn't blame a man for things he wasn't responsible for, could you? Well, some could. Her, for example. His thoughts continued to fester, as they had for years, all his malice revolving round the woman and her child and their special relationship which totally excluded him.

Jenny was teaching the brat to hate him; she had no right to do that. Meggie should respect and look up to him, not cheek him and interfere in his dealings with Jenny. That was wrong, bad, and he had to fix it.

Jenny had dragged herself up from her sickbed to silence his angry taunting, struggling to do her usual daily tasks until her head whirled with dizziness. Today, she had gone out to visit Old Katie, and so Demon Jack pounced. Meggie barely had time to look up from the bed she was making before he had her shoulders in his iron grip, his foul breath gusting in her face. She looked up at him in horror, anticipating a beating, and then, to her stunned dismay, she saw his hand drop to his breeches to open them.

'*No!*' The word hissed from her throat. She thought her eyes would burst from their sockets. Her head pounded with dread. Her father – her own father – he – he was going to – A wave of dizziness gripping her, she swayed, hearing Demon Jack's raucous laughter echoing round the hovel as he pushed her down onto the bed and climbed on top of her.

He was breaking her in, making her ready for the streets and the sailors who would lust after her. When she made a few coppers, she could get a red dress, or a green one, and a big hat, and stand on the street corners like the dollymops to entice men. He would have a fine time. He would watch them, watch them having the brat, and, if he felt inclined, he would have her afterwards as well.

Blunt pushed down on Meggie's thin arms and legs, ignoring her screams and struggles, cuffing her across the head, once, twice, telling her to shut up or he would kill her, until finally she lay still, eyes closed. Whether she was stunned or just pretending, he did not know or care. At this moment, all he cared about was his own increasing lust and the need to use this child's body, this little virgin's body....

Blunt shouted at her, tugging at her chin. 'Look at me, brat, look at me!' Again he gripped her, one hamfist round her tiny throat, cutting off her breath. She spluttered, trying to free herself from his grasp, but she might as well have tried to move a mountain. Six feet of brutal, heavily muscled man was Demon Jack, and a woman had no chance against him.

Meggie struggled until her strength had drained; then, aching and stunned, she began to sink into unconsciousness, unable to endure the trauma of the onslaught. Her head rolled back limply and her arms fell to her sides; a long sigh escaped her lips.

It was at that moment that Jenny stepped into the hovel, breathing raspingly from the effects of the icy air, her fingers and nose blue with cold. Fighting back waves of faintness, she took in the scene with horror. Was she really seeing what she thought or was she fevered? Was it some terrible nightmare like the ones she had had when she was ill? But no . . . Jack, and Meggie – He –

Jenny screamed, then screamed again, throwing herself at Blunt, scrabbling to pull him off the child. He had killed her little girl! He had killed her!

'You swine, you monster, get off, get away!' Jenny screamed, tearing at her husband's jacket, beating at his back with her clenched fists.

Sneering, Blunt pushed her away as if she were made of straw.

'Be off, bitch, an' about yer business. This ain't none o'

yer affair. Git away or it'll be the worse fer yer an' the brat.'

Jenny continued to hit him, screaming at him to get off her child. Finally, incensed, he lashed out with his arm, catching her a stunning blow which flung her across the room to land with a sickening thud against the opposite wall.

Regaining consciousness at that moment, Meggie saw her mother crash to the floor and lie still.

'Mam, *Mam*!' she yelled, bunching her little fists and beating them against Blunt's face. 'Get away, *get away*!' she yelled. 'What have you done to me mam, you pig, you *pig*!' She screamed until her throat was raw.

'Ferget 'er,' Blunt bellowed. "Ere, yer bitch!' His iron fingers gripped Meggie and he pinned her down on the bed.

What happened next was to scar Meggie's subconscious for years, too terrible to be faced openly. All the pain, the shame and fear hidden away where she would not have to look at them but doing her no less harm because they were hidden. She would be haunted by it, dream of it in dreams which she would be unable to remember on waking.

When Blunt had finished, he rearranged his clothing and left the hovel in his accustomed fashion, heavy footed, slamming the door behind him with a resounding crash. The two women were forgotten as if they had never existed.

Meggie lay where he had left her, eyes staring sightlessly at the ceiling, one hand twitching spasmodically. Her mind was a blank, but her body was on fire with pain. For a time she was too drained to get up and see to Jenny.

Jenny groaned as she began to come round, memory returning to her. '*Cariad*,' she whispered hoarsely, '*cariad*?'

Meggie slowly sat up. Then, moved to tears by the sight of her ashen-faced mother on the floor, she went to her and cradled her in her arms, tears beading her lashes. They wept together, but there was no comfort in their tears.

'*Cariad*, did – what happened, are you – did he – ?' Jenny stopped, unable to continue, emotion constricting her throat.

Meggie buried her face against her mother's hair. 'Don't ask me what happened, Mam. Never. Don't ever ask me. Pretend nothing happened.' A sob ended her words.

Now Meggie became the patient and Jenny the nurse as mother cared for shocked child. Jenny was stricken with guilt. If she hadn't married Jack Blunt, this would never have happened. It was all her fault for taking up with him – she should have known better. She should never have got involved with him! She would get her revenge on him if it killed her, she vowed.

Jenny's coughing began to get worse again, after the temporary reprieve, and now there was blood on the rags she held against her lips. In the night, she would wake drenched with sweat, even in the icy weather, and then one morning she woke to find she was soaked in blood from a haemorrhage. She knew that she was not going to live much longer, and she was filled with trepidation. What would happen to Meggie after she was gone? Blunt had said he was going to put her on the streets, that he already had customers lined up for her. The decimating horror of it all robbed Jenny of the little spark of vitality which was all she had left now.

In the next few days, Blunt spoke boastingly of all the money he was going to make from putting the child on the streets, and when Jenny tried to plead with him, he pushed his face sneeringly into hers and uttered a stream of obscenities which made her blanch.

Meggie hid when Blunt was about. She lived on a razor's edge of tension, running at the sound of his heavy footsteps, dreading that he would come home and catch her unexpectedly. Once when this had happened, Jenny bravely drew his attention to her to give her daughter time to escape. He fell on his wife like a starving man while she submitted meekly, to save her daughter.

When it was over, Blunt prodded his wife's breast with a hard finger.

'Where's the brat, eh? Can't keep 'er 'idden from me ferever, yer know. No right ter keep 'er 'idden, yer 'aven't. I'm 'er da an' I gots rights, I 'ave. Yer wait 'til yer sees what I gots in store fer 'er. Yer just wait,' he leered. 'She'll be a smasher in a new dress wiv' 'er 'air done up an' a few frills. The men don' know whass comin' their way, lucky buggers.'

Feeling nausea rise, Jenny clamped a hand over her mouth while stars flashed out of the corners of her vision. 'You can't mean it?' she whispered haltingly.

'Oh, can't I?' Blunt retorted. 'We'll soon see whevver I means it, yer bitch. Wait 'til ternight.' He guffawed.

'Wh-what do you mean, "Wait 'til tonight?"' Jenny whispered.

'It's 'er big night ternight, it is. Gots some fine men comin' roun' ter break 'er in, I 'ave. Been lickin' their lips at the describin' of 'er, they 'ave. Goin' ter 'ave a fine celebration we are, them an' me. Yes, me an' all,' he leered. 'So yer make sure the brat's 'ere ternight or it'll be the worse fer yer an' fer 'er. Unnerstan'?'

Clamping a hand over Jenny's throat, he pressed until blackness threatened.

'Yes – I – understand,' she croaked, tears flooding her eyes.

Blunt went then, leaving Jenny weak and numb on the bed. As the worst of the pain receded, fear for her daughter took its place, the sheer weight of their dilemma crushing her as heavily as Jack's body had done only minutes before. In God's name, what was she going to do?

CHAPTER THREE

When Meggie returned, her mother took her in her arms, as if she were hugging her for the last time. Tears poured down her cheeks. She was sure they would never meet again. Her little girl, who had always been such a comfort to her, the one she loved most in all the world, would have to be sent away. Her Meggie was not going to be a dollymop, even if she had to send her away to prevent it.

'Meggie,' she began, her voice breaking. The child looked at her expectantly. 'Meggie, if you stay here something dreadful is going to happen to you, something really terrible. I – I can't explain it, it – it's – well, you will have to trust me when I tell you it is bad. You're in danger, great danger, and you've *got* to get away from here. Do you understand?' A sob rose in her throat. She could not meet her daughter's gaze.

'It's da, isn't it? He's got plans for me, hasn't he? I heard him boasting to some of his cronies. Drunk he was, and loud-mouthed, and he was telling them to come here tonight.' A shudder shook the girl's slender frame.

'You – you heard? Oh my God!' Feeling her courage drain, Jenny clutched at her daughter for support. '*Cariad*, you've got to get away before tonight! Right away, in secret. Hide yourself, and don't come back – not *ever*!'

'I won't go, Mam! I won't leave you, not ever!' Meggie gasped.

'You must, *cariad*! If I have to see you – given to – to men like your – like Jack plans, it'll kill me. You must get away, now, *now*!' Urgency made her voice crack. She had never been so brave nor so scared in her whole life.

'Yes, Mam.'

Meggie's eyes were dulled, her lips wooden. Her mam was sending her away, and although she knew it was for her own good, how could she bear to go? What would her mam do without her?

Mother and daughter clung together weeping uncontrollably, kissing and hugging, trying to prolong the moment of parting for ever.

Finally, Jenny pushed her daughter to the door. 'Go, go, *cariad*, while this heavy snow gives you some cover. Stay out of sight. If you're in trouble, go to Old Katie. She's got a kind heart. I wish I had some money to give you, but I've nothing. Oh, *cariad*, *cariad*, go, *now* –' Dragging open the door, Jenny pushed her daughter out into the snow.

Meggie turned for one last look at her, but her tears blotted out the sight of the frail, ragged woman at the door. Then she began to run, trying to stifle her sobs so that no one would hear them and take notice of her.

Jenny sank down onto her pallet, shaking like an old woman, her teeth chattering together. What had she done? Oh God, what had she done? How could she have sent Meggie away? Curving her arms round her waist to try and still the pain, she bent low, moaning her daughter's name over and over again.

Meggie had to run as far away as possible. Although people hated Demon Jack, there were many who would be all too willing to let her father know where she had gone. Some took great delight in calamity. There were those who had been jealous of Jenny's wild Celtic beauty when she had first arrived at Rats' Castle. There were always people willing to spite you. The fact that you had done nothing to deserve their malice did not matter to them.

A deep icing of snow lay on the streets. The clouds were heavy: more snow was to come. Meggie's feet were blue; they had often been blue, it was nothing new to her. What really mattered to her now was that she had had to run away from home, that she had had to leave her mother. She could never go back, yet her mother needed her – they needed each other. They had never been apart for more than a few hours in all her ten years. It was snowing in her heart. It was more than the coldness of winter, more than the coldness of rags and bare feet: it was the coldness of complete, desperate isolation.

The streets were empty; everyone had gone inside to keep warm. She could imagine people sitting by their firesides, drinking mulled ale, eating pies, hunks of cheese and bread. Her stomach felt empty, but she could not eat even if someone gave her a plate of the most appetising food. Nothing could get past her lips at this moment. She thought she would never eat again. She wondered when her mother would eat next, who would get Jenny's meals, who would bring her the food from the costermonger's? Who would look out for the extra tasty morsels for her, making her meals and feeding them to her when the coughing got really bad and she was too weak to move? There would be nobody to do that now. Jack Blunt would never do it. He would kick out at Jenny and go off to drink.

She slept that night, a bundle of rags, under the awning of a shop. Nobody saw her, the street was quite empty. No drunks walked past, no dollymops.

When Meggie woke, it was dawn. She was paralysed from the cold, unable to feel her fingers. Her feet felt swollen and yet, at the same time, pinched. She looked around her: why was she out here, in this street? What was she doing here? She had never slept away from home before. Slowly, memory flooded back. Tears pressed behind her eyes but she did not shed them. Only weaklings cried out in the streets in Rats' Castle. Ravenously hungry, Meggie could have eaten anything at that moment, but there was nothing to be found, not even a crust lying in the gutter. What was she going to do for food? She thought of Old Katie. Old Katie would give her some, even though she would have little to spare.

Meggie stood up, rubbing her hands together, stamping her numb feet on the ground. She did not recognize this street. It was quiet, even at dawn. The rest of the Rookery would be waking now. People who had been out all night thieving, picking pockets, would be tip-toeing back home, but, for most, it would be time to get up and go about their usual tasks. Their hunger, for food, for drink, for love, would never be satisfied.

Meggie was nearly at Old Katie's and was just about to turn the corner to her hovel when she thought of Jack Blunt. People knew her in Old Katie's street. If Jack Blunt came asking questions they'd say, 'Meggie was 'ere, she was 'ere. She went into Old Katie's. Old Katie will tell yer where she is.' Then Jack Blunt would storm into the old woman's hovel, pick her up by the shoulders and shake her until her teeth rattled. He might beat her, as he had beaten Jenny, and Old Katie could not survive that. Meggie stopped in her tracks, dismayed. Where was she going to go?

She hurried away from Old Katie's, as far away as she could get, right across Rats' Castle, until she was out of the slums and into the Rookery itself. It wasn't quite so filthy here, although the streets were still crammed together and the stench was intolerable. She passed a dead rat in the gutter. Cats and dogs lay piled high in heaps, decaying. If it had been summer, their bodies would have been veneered with blow flies buzzing thickly in a black cloud.

In the city she knew there was a place called Houndsditch, so named because for centuries everyone had flung their litter, dead cats and rats, horses and sewage, into it. At one time it was said that it was piled so high with bodies that the people had complained of the stench. The Rookery was like a huge Houndsditch, every street, every alley, every gulley crammed with filth and ordure, so nobody thought twice about gutters filled with dead animals. Meggie was used to it, for that was all she had ever known. Now she would have to leave here, to get far away from Jack Blunt. Even though the place was hell, it was home to her and where she wanted to stay.

A noisy crowd of drunken revellers passed her, and she watched them, feeling her loneliness increase. They were on their way home to bed, singing a bawdy ballad, their arms around one another's shoulders.

'If you'd seduce a maid, you must swear an' sigh an' flatter, but if you'd win a widow you must down with your breeches an' at her,' one of the men was singing hoarsely.

The others joined in the chorus: *'Fol-de-rol, fol-de-rol hey, fol-de-rol, fol-de-rol ho.'*

They didn't notice Meggie in the shadows of the alley,

but she noticed them, envying their comradeship. She walked on, numb with cold and misery. If she went back home it would only make things worse. Jenny would die of the horror of having to watch Jack Blunt and his friends make use of her daughter. She could not go back. She could do nothing now but walk on, hour after hour, in a daze, feeling colder and colder, longing for her mother.

Meggie still did not know where she was going. With a start, she realized it was night-time again and she'd have to sleep out. She would wake up with frost bite, if she did not die of cold in the night. The heavy clouds had begun to unburden their weight. Snow was coming down in huge, soft flakes which fell on her cheeks like tickling fingers. All she could hope for now was that her mother would be left in peace.

She had wandered into a part of London she did not know. The streets were empty of decent people. People who cared for their lives, their money, and their reputations would be in front of their own firesides by now, safely out of harm's way.

It was time for the revellers, the dollymops, the prostitutes, the drunks, the pick-pockets and thieves, the cut-throats and cut-purses. Night, which brought more than one kind of darkness.

Hearing the sound of feet on cobbles, Meggie looked up to see a gentleman coming her way, lorgnette held before his eyes, gleaming black topper perched on his head. He wore beige kid trousers and a smart black jacket. An evening cloak hung jauntily over his shoulders. He seemed not to notice the little girl, but others had noticed him.

Meggie crouched back, well into the shadows, flattening herself against the wall, as she saw a gang of ragged boys dart out of a side alley ahead. One of the boys jumped up behind the gentleman, thrusting out his bare foot to catch the man's ankle so that he lurched, trying to maintain his balance. That was the signal for four other boys to attack. One darted a hand under his cloak, snatching his purse; another rifled his inner pockets with a speedy, experienced hand. Before the man knew what had happened he had lost his topper, his cloak and all his money. Even his lorgnette had disappeared, along with the gang of street urchins.

Meggie remained pressed against the wall, dreading the roar of anger the man would emit if his eyes fell upon her, for he would surely blame her in some way for what had taken place. But the man looked stunned, seeming not to know what he should do next. She crept away silently, still pressed against the wall, her heart thudding wildly.

Rounding a corner, Meggie saw what looked like a body in the gutter. It was a drunk, his red flushed face and gaping mouth reminding her horribly of her father. Sickened, she hurried past. She knew what to expect at night: hadn't her mother warned her often enough? Girls were not safe in the streets of London after dark, however young they were. There would always be someone out preying on females. Gentlemen with perverted tastes, slum-dwellers reeling home drunkenly, needing only the sight of a skirt to inflame their passions. Meggie dreaded being caught by such as these. In the past, more than one acquaintance of hers had been brutally attacked, returning home wretched and bruised, with blacked eyes. It was something Jenny had wanted her daughter to escape at all costs, keeping her inside the house at night. How ironic that she had been in her own home when this fate had befallen her. Meggie shivered. Her lids felt leaden and she desperately wanted to sleep. She was approaching that moment when she would have to curl up in the gutter, never mind how cold the coming hours.

A burst of noisy laughter alerted her to a building which stood half-hidden by its overhanging roof, a red lamp glowing outside its door. Some women were standing in the doorway flirting with a group of men, encouraging them to come inside. One of the women had a huge, mustard-coloured hat pulled low over her thickly painted face, and her breasts hung out of a gauzy black gown on which she had pinned a multitude of brooches, all of them cheap and glittery.

'Come on inside, dearie, do,' she was cajoling one of the men. 'I can see yer a real big feller what needs a good swivin' else yer gits gloomy. An' I'm jus' the gel ter give it ter yer. Come on in, yer ain't seen nuffink like yer'll see 'ere at Bella's Brothel!'

Meggie watched the crowd enviously. How healthy they were, plump and rosy-cheeked. The men were burly, the women full blown: none of them looked as if they had ever known starvation. How she ached to be able to go in through that lighted doorway to ask for food, to eat all that she could find in there until she could not move.

'Come in, love, come in,' they would say to her. 'Yer 'ungry? Well, 'ere, 'ave this 'ere big veal pie, 'ave these oranges an' apples an' this 'ere cheese. An' what about some white bread an' some mulled wine ter warm yer innards? 'Tis lovely an' spicy; warm yer up from top ter bottom it will!'

The group at the doorway parted to let a man out. He looked very pleased with himself, smug and superior. On his head was a very tall black topper, and his cloak was immaculate, his boots gleaming. Stepping through the crowd, he walked towards the little girl. The sight of her seemed to disturb him in some way. Was he thinking of all the money he had recently spent enjoying himself inside Bella's Brothel? Possibly this was the reason why he put his hand into his pocket and pulled out a sovereign, which he then threw to the child. Meggie gaped at the glittering gold on the cobbles, her eyes wide.

'Take it. Take it, child, and be off with you,' the man barked, before turning on his heel and disappearing into the night.

Meggie snatched up the coin before anyone else could get his hands on it, for the prostitutes and their customers were staring at her.

She ran off, not stopping until shortness of breath pulled her to a halt. A sovereign! One whole sovereign for herself! Now she could buy food.

Farther on she came to a street corner where tables were laid out in readiness for the workers who would pass by in the morning and purchase their breakfasts there. An old man snored nearby. Meggie wondered if he stayed on guard all night, for if he did he would surely be frozen solid. He was completely bald, his face magenta-coloured, and his loud snores ricocheted off the opposite wall and bounced back at him. Even this did not rouse him from his sleep.

Meggie stood uncertainly. Should she wake him? There was a tiny brazier alight beside him. That would be where he would heat the drinks for his morning customers. Men going to and from work would be grateful for a steaming mug of broth or tea. She wondered if the man would heat something up for her and whether she could have one of the pies now. She was so hungry that she almost snatched the cloth off the pies, but she knew that would be asking for trouble. The man would surely waken and strike her, either with his fists or with the big stick which was tucked in the crook of his arm.

'Sir, sir,' she said, then repeated her words, for the snores continued unabated. 'Sir, sir, can I buy a pie, can I buy a drink?' she asked more loudly.

'Eh, eh?' the man grunted. 'Gerrout, gerrout,' he said, his voice blurred with sleep. "Tain't morning yet, gerrout.'

'Sir, sir, can I buy a pie and a drink *now*? I'm starving,' Meggie shouted, desperation making her voice crack. 'Please, sir, *please*, I've got a sovereign, a whole sovereign!'

The man grunted, unlinking his arms, opening his bloodshot eyes.

'Sovereign, sovereign, eh, eh? Yer can buy more'n one pie wiv a sovereign, gel.'

'Can I have two then, please?' said Meggie, having no idea of the value of a sovereign or how much she could get for it.

"Course yer can 'ave two fer it,' the man said, smirking to himself.

He whisked back the corner of the cloth to reveal a pile of the most succulent, appetising pastries Meggie had ever seen. They were golden brown, their crusts thick, and she longed to sink her teeth into them right this minute. She could not wait a moment longer. Thrusting the sovereign at the man she took two of the pies and devoured them ravenously.

The man watched her, bloodshot eyes half-closed, the sovereign now tucked away in his jacket. She was not going to see it again. If she was ignorant enough to think that two pies were worth a whole sovereign then that was her look-out, not his.

After eating she was overcome by extreme weariness and knew that she had to find some place safe to sleep. The high walls of the narrow alleys were closing in around her. Glancing up, she saw that the sky looked black and starless. Some dogs shot past her legs, barking wildly. They were chasing a rat . . . .

Finding a doorway which leaned back from its neighbours, Meggie curled up on the step, dragging her skirt down over her bare feet, resting her head on her knees, curving her arms round her face. Anyone passing would not have seen her in the shadows. Her exhaustion was so complete that she slept until dawn when the cries of the street hawkers woke her. She was stiff, aching, numb with cold, and it took her some time to uncurl and stand up straight. Stamping her bare feet on the cobbles, she clapped her hands together and shook her arms to try and bring some feeling back into them.

The street-hawkers' cries were growing louder. Hungry, Meggie listened to their words, her stomach rumbling.

'Ripe chestnuts, ripe walnuts, ripe small nuts!'

'Hot apple pies, hot pudding pies, hot mutton pies!'

'A good sausage roasted! Will yer buy a good sausage roasted?'

Interspersed with these were the cries of the chimney sweeps and others who were selling non-edible merchandise.

'Sweep, chimney sweep! From bottom ter the top! Chimney sweep! Then shall no soot fall in yer porridge pot! Sweep, chimney sweep!'

'Very fine writing ink, very fine bright ink. Buy any ink! Will yer buy any ink?'

The ink-seller walked close by where Meggie stood rubbing her hands together. He carried a little barrel full of ink, a measure and a funnel, and, in one hand, a bunch of new goose quills. Meggie wished that she could write so that she could buy some ink and send her mother a message. The longing to do that distracted her from her hunger for some moments.

An old woman shuffled past with a huge tray crammed high with hot spice cakes, and she called out to Meggie when she walked within a few inches of her.

Her sight must be bad if she thinks I have money for her cakes, thought Meggie, longing to shoot out an arm and snatch one of the steaming, scented buns, her strict upbringing preventing her. Jenny would be heartbroken finding her daughter a thief.

Looking up, the old woman saw the ragged child and curled her lip at her as if she could read her mind.

'Git yer gone, baggage!' the cake-seller spat.

Meggie stepped back quickly, her cheeks flushed.

'We don' wan' the likes o' yer 'ere!' the old woman added. 'Git yer gone afore I calls a Peeler!'

Stung into retorting, Meggie said, 'I'm not hurting anyone!'

''Eard that afore I 'ave,' sneered the old woman. 'Git off wiv yer! Go on, git!'

Regretfully, Meggie turned her back on the thriving street, the sellers of wares, the stalls packed with fish, pies, the gleaming churns of fresh frothing milk, the chestnuts popping over burning braziers.

A group of match-girls wove their way past her, giggling and shouting. The were willing to part with a generous share of their money in exchange for a decent breakfast. Most of the girls were young, fresh-faced and high-spirited. Two of them were older women who had worked in the match factory all their lives. One had a horribly rotted jaw; her mouth was crooked, her face twisted.

Meggie knew what was wrong with her. She had phossy jaw. Old Katie had told her about that. It affected girls who had worked for years amongst the phosphorous in the match factories. First they got toothache, which was so common that they did not take much notice; then their cheeks swelled up and the girls would rush to have all their teeth pulled out in the hope of averting disaster. But by then it was too late: the phosphorous used in the matches had gone to work in the girls' jaws, and eventually the entire jaw would be affected. It was just one unavoidable consequence of their work, or so they considered it.

The match-girls were well dressed, for it was said they were the smartest factory girls in London. They loved big hats and gaudy colours, and indeed Jenny had made many hats for them over the years. But they paid dearly for the wages which brought them their fine feathers. In summer, they worked from 6 in the morning to 6 at night and, in the winter, from 8 to 6, with only one hour for dinner and half an hour for breakfast. They were lucky if they earned four shillings a week.

Strict discipline was maintained in the match factories, with penalties for the slightest breach in the regulations. If a girl arrived five minutes late, she would be shut out of the factory for half a day, losing her pay for that time. For untidiness or for forgetting to clear the litter under her bench, she would be fined.

Meggie knew all this because Old Katie's daughter had been a match-girl, and she had died of phossy jaw when she was twenty-five.

Nonetheless, despite knowing how hard the work was and how terrible the penalties, Meggie thought how fortunate they were having work to go to, and money to buy food and pretty clothes. She was too young to work in the factories, but she could be making match boxes at home, if Jack Blunt would leave her possessions alone and not wreck them during his drunken frenzies. Bryant and May's paid twopence, three farthings per gross for large matchboxes made by their homeworkers. But she was not at home, nor was she going to be. Heavy hearted, she began to walk away from the noisy girls, from the food and the hubbub, retracing her steps.

After a while she realized that she was near the river. You could not mistake being near the river. Its stench hung on the air, a heavy shroud throughout the night, and even when it was buoyed up by the morning mists it did not lose its foulness. The Thames was nothing more than an open sewer. When water closets had been introduced into houses, making them more pleasant, it had made the Thames even more offensive, for now everybody's household waste gushed into the river. People of a genteel disposition, or those who had delicate stomachs, kept well away from the river. It was only two years since the scorching summer of 1858, which had been known as the Great Stink. Then, the smell had been so overpowering that the curtains of the Houses of Parliament had been dipped in chloride of lime. Even the Serpentine in Hyde Park, where people went to boat and walk, had been fouled by sewage.

Meggie was almost in sight of the Thames when suddenly the slam of metal on cobbles startled her. A man appeared before her, having apparently leapt out of the ground like a genie. Terrified, she jumped back before realizing it was a tosher. These were men who scoured the underground sewers searching for coins, rings, bits of jewellery or any treasure which had found its way downwards. They carried a lantern and a stout stick to fight off rats. Old Katie's husband had been a tosher; he had died of cholera during the summer of the Great Stink, his face turned greenish-black in colour, his cries heard throughout Rats' Castle.

The tosher who now stood before Meggie was filthy black from head to foot, and she could barely make out his face. There was no colour about him except for the whites of his eyes. In his left hand he held an old rusted lantern, and a gnarled stick was in his right. Sharp nails had been driven into the end of the stick to punish any rats who thought they could get the better of him. His feet were bare, and he wore an old top hat on his head. But it was his smell which was most apparent. It was sickening.

Meggie made as if to run off, but the man shouted to her, his voice rasping.

"Elp me, gel, 'elp me! Me mate's still in the sewers. 'E's took bad, fainted away 'e 'as. Can yer fetch some 'elp? An' some Geneva ter pour down 'is gullet? I can't leave 'im else the rats'll gnaw 'im.'

'I – I don't know anyone here,' Meggie replied hesitantly.

'Strangers'll do, gel. Look, I gots money, see!'

He held out his hand. Meggie looked at the gleaming gold coin on his palm wonderingly.

"Urry, gel, 'urry. I gots ter go back down afore me mate's attacked!'

Snatching the coin, Meggie hurried away, hearing the man shout out behind her, "Ey, yer come back, gel, an' soon! Don' yer mek off wiv that gold or I'll chase after yer an' screw yer neck!'

'I'll be back!' Meggie shouted over her shoulder. 'Go down and look after your mate!'

Meggie headed for the street where the breakfast tables stood. The match-girls had gone, and there were few people there now. A crone sat on a bench, a jug of rum in her fist, a pipe in her mouth, clouds of evil black smoke issuing from it. Her chest whistled loudly when she breathed.

'There's a man what needs help down there!' Meggie said, pointing. 'Do you know a strong man what'll help him? He can pay. And can I buy some of your rum? I got a coin.' She held out her hand to show that she spoke the truth.

Immediately the crone's look of disinterest became one of rapt concern. It seemed to Meggie that a person's entire character could be altered in seconds at the sight of gold.

With the mug of rum safely in her had, Meggie returned to the tosher as speedily as possible. The crone was sending help behind her.

Seeing the mug, the tosher snatched it from Meggie and disappeared back down the dark passage beneath the

48

street. Meggie crouched over the manhole listening to the sounds which floated up in a ghostly manner. She heard squeaks, the tosher's foul curses, the scuttering of tiny feet, the splashing of water.

'Gel, gel!' the man's voice came up from out of the hole. 'Did yer ask someone ter come an' 'elp me? Did yer?'

'Yes!' Meggie shouted down. 'Someone's coming soon!'

'Yer gimme a 'and now, gel.'

'What do you want me to do?'

Leaning over the hole and fighting nausea, Meggie looked down into the stinking blackness, just making out the whites of the tosher's eyes in the gloom below.

'Gimme a 'and up, gel, can yer?'

Gritting her teeth, Meggie lowered her arm. First her fingers and then her palm were gripped by the slippery, filthy hand of the tosher. His first pull almost yanked her down into the sewer, and she screamed.

'I can't hold you! I'm not strong enough. You'll have to wait for the men. They won't be long. An old crone sent her grandson to fetch his da and uncle.'

The tosher cursed by way of reply, and Meggie sank back onto her heels wondering how he had got out of the hole before without her help. Perhaps the terrible smell had now made him weak as well. She was not far from the truth. Only a certain length of time could be spent in the sewers before the deadly gases took their toll.

Hours seemed to pass before Meggie heard the sound of boots on cobbles and saw the crone's grandson, accompanied by two burly, shirt-sleeved men.

'Where's 'e? Where's the man what needs 'elp?' asked one of the men as the grandson gestured towards Meggie.

Meggie pointed at the hole. The two men peered down it with grim faces. At first she thought they were going to refuse to help, but the tosher called up that he'd pay them generously, and with *gold*. His voice sounded weaker, and he urged the men to make haste.

It was a long, painful business, but when the tosher and his mate were finally up on the cobbles, everyone seemed relieved. The tosher's mate looked near death and did not move. He just lay there, a ghastly pallor on his face, and Meggie shuddered.

The tosher coughed a lot and breathed noisily. 'Thanks, mates!' he rasped to the two men who had helped him. "Ere's yer money what I promised yer.' Digging into the pocket of his filthy jacket, he pulled out a gold sovereign for each of the men. They looked very happy indeed, grinning widely, glancing at one another as if to say, That was a job well done. The tosher coughed again, then continued. 'First time me mate's been took bad down there. Can't unnerstan' it. 'Is missis'll be proper upset. Got eight little 'uns she 'as. Gawd 'elp 'er.'

Having decided that the tosher's mate was beyond help, the men threw a rag over his face. Meggie looked at the body, feeling a deep pity for the poor widow and her eight children.

The tosher asked the men to help him home, and to carry his mate's body with them. When he promised them more gold, they readily agreed.

Meggie watched them go. They had forgotten her. None of them said good-bye. When they were out of sight, Meggie continued on towards the river. Although the streets were filling up, they still seemed empty to Meggie, who was accustomed to the crush of humanity in the Rookery.

She thought of the sovereign which had passed through her hands that day, and yet she had not so much as sipped at the rum she had bought for the tosher. She wished now that she had taken something for herself, but Jenny had always said, 'No daughter of mine will ever steal.' What else *could* she do if she did not want to starve? Who would employ a skinny, ragged, barefoot urchin? There was not enough work for children who had shoes and warm coats!

She thought of dying out in the cold street, her stomach shrunken from hunger, and the snow falling over her until she was totally covered. Her corpse would not be found until the spring thaws; then it would be carried away on a cart and flung into a pauper's grave. This doom-laden thought brought tears to her eyes. But the instinct to survive was a driving force within her. Think of dying she might, but she had no intention of doing so. She was going to see her mother again one day and rescue her from that terrible life. She would make some money, somehow, to rent a little house for them both.

If only she could secretly get a message to her mother, to tell her she would come back for her someday, as soon as she could. If only Jenny had taught her to write, but there had been little opportunity and no spare money to buy quill and ink. Jenny herself could read and write, for she had been to school in Bangor.

'We didn't have to be too good at writing,' Jenny had told her. 'Only good enough to make ourselves understood.'

'Can you teach me, then, Mam?' Meggie has asked.

'I wish I could,' Jenny had replied gently, 'but where would we get the ink and quill and paper?'

Meggie had learned some things though – how to speak properly, and how to write her name, with a bit of charred stick on a scrap of white cloth. Before Jenny could teach her anything else, Blunt had found out what she was doing. He had burnt the stick and the cloth, thereby closing that door for Meggie.

It might have been some distant memory which brought her to St Thomas's Wharf, where she saw a gaggle of people queuing up, shuffling their feet and looking expectant but cold. A fine veiling of snow was falling again, and children were gripping their mothers' knees for warmth. Meggie wondered why they were there, dozens of them – men, women and children of all ages, all sizes. She had walked halfway along the queue when a voice called out to her.

"Ey, gel, tryin' ter jump this queue are yer? Git back there.'

Meggie turned but could not identify the speaker. Other voices called out to her to get back and take her proper place and so she obeyed. She heard those around her talking of bread and soup and realized this was the soup-kitchen on St Thomas's Wharf. There were others, but she

51

had heard someone in Rats' Castle speak of this one by name. A feeling of excitement gripped her. She was going to have food! Hot soup and bread. She felt faint: it seemed a month since she had last eaten. Clasping her arms tightly round her thin waist to quell her stomach growls, she waited as patiently as she could.

The doors to the old warehouse slowly swung inwards and the crowd at once shuffled forwards, with Meggie following. The rich scent of mutton broth billowed out into the cold air. It seemed to take an age for those first in the queue to be served with their bowls of broth and hunks of bread, and Meggie was almost desperate by the time her turn came.

She looked up in surprise at the woman who was serving her, for she was beautiful, totally unlike what Meggie had expected. Her eyes were a bright, rich blue, and they glowed in a strongly-featured but classically lovely face. Her hair was dark and swept back into intricate whorls and loops beneath a handsome velvet hat on top of which a brightly-coloured stuffed bird was perched, its feathers gold and green. The bird looked alive, and Meggie half-expected it to flap its wings suddenly and take to the air. The woman's gown was soft green velvet. In her ears hung gold and emerald earrings; an emerald flashed on her left hand, and in a brooch at her neck.

The woman noticed Meggie gaping and gave her a little smile.

Meggie's mouth had fallen open as she noticed the jewels, the velvet, the exotic bird on the woman's hat, but she was not too dazzled to smile back, nervously. The woman filled her bowl right to the brim and gave her two hunks of the soft white bread instead of the regulation one. Meggie's eyes glowed her thanks, and then she went to one of the tables to sit down and eat.

The broth was very hot, and spicy, too; she had to sip carefully for fear of burning her mouth. Even so, her tongue was hurting after a few mouthfuls, but it was bliss to hold the hot bowl in her hands to warm herself. She had never tasted such fine, light bread. It seemed to melt in her mouth. She could have sat there all day eating that meal but unfortunately the other paupers were beginning to leave. She could hardly sit there after they had gone, but she lingered, wishing she could stay. For a short time, this place had been her home, bleak and draughty though it was, and she had grown fond of it.

She saw the lady in the green gown glance across at her. Her helpers were whispering amongst themselves. Were they talking about her?

The woman called out. 'Haven't you anywhere to go, dear?' Her voice of melodious and smooth. Meggie savoured the sound of it.

'I – I ain't got no home,' she replied hesitantly, wondering if she ought to add 'Your Ladyship'. With those rich clothes, the woman must be a great lady.

The woman looked unhappy at her reply. Yet surely, Meggie thought, she was accustomed to seeing homeless paupers, for she had obviously worked here for a long time – she even knew some of them by name.

Meggie was startled as the woman headed towards her, so she rose hurriedly, glancing at the doors as if to find a way of escape. Now she'd done it! She was going to be flung out.

The woman opened her mouth to speak, but Meggie would never know what it was she had been going to say for at that moment a young man entered the warehouse.

'Mama, Mama, are you ready?' he called out, directing his words at the woman in the green gown who looked up, her face alight. If she had been beautiful before, she was radiant now.

'Darling, you are here already and we are not yet finished. Can you help the ladies put away the chairs?'

'Better still, I will come later with some of my friends to clear away everything so that we can all go home now. You have guests coming this afternoon, do you not?'

The lady nodded. 'You are a dear boy,' she smiled, calling out to her helpers that they could leave now.

Bidding her good-bye, they left, while Meggie continued to stare at the young man. As she watched him, she felt something coming to life inside her. He had glossy golden hair that shone even in the dimness of the warehouse and his eyes were the same clear, dazzling blue as his mother's. His face was kindly, genial. He was immaculately, expensively dressed, in a grey morning coat and black trousers, and a black cloak was flung carelessly over his broad shoulders.

Meggie was aware that something had happened inside her. Before the young man had come into the warehouse, she had been Meggie, Meggie Blunt, a homeless pauper girl. Now she was someone else. She could not have explained what had happened for it had begun of its own accord. It had started when the young man called out to his mother, as Meggie saw him for the first time – tall, strong, wide-shouldered, with that mass of gleaming golden hair and the kind blue eyes. And as his mother answered him, it was as if something of the love between mother and son had enveloped Meggie, making her a part of them, bringing her into the nucleus of their feelings for one another.

For those few moments during which she was close to the young man, the coldness which had gripped her receded. She felt warm, comforted, safe. It was like the summer sun's shining suddenly on a frosty winter's day, which perhaps was what *had* happened: Meggie's sun had begun to shine at the sight of this young Sun God with his gilded hair and smiling eyes.

Mother and son seemed oblivious of Meggie's scrutiny; the young man was helping his mother on with her sable-lined cape, and she lightly touched his hands as they rested momentarily on her shoulders. As she was pulling on immaculate white kid gloves, she remembered the child was still present.

'We have to close the doors now, dear, otherwise all our chairs and tables and cooking utensils will be stolen.' She smiled at her son. 'The keys are in my reticule, darling.' Turning again to the girl, she said, 'I would so much like to leave you here, so that you can keep warm, but it would not be possible, my dear.'

'That's all right, missis,' Meggie said, then she flushed a brilliant scarlet as she realized that she should have said 'Your Ladyship', as the other helpers had done as they were bidding the beautiful woman good-bye. 'I got to go anyway,' she added hoarsely, wishing that the young man was not there to see her embarrassment.

'Come again tomorrow, my dear.'

'I will if I can,' Meggie said, as if she had somewhere more important to go than here. She stood up, taking a last look at the young man. He must be about eighteen, she thought; the same age as Old Katie's grandson – but there the comparison ended. This young man was every inch the gentleman. Handsome, assured, he had grown up amongst rich and titled people who owned luxurious houses and had carriages and horses at their beck and call. His power was absolute compared with that of Katie's grandson, Lennie, who drank too much and who had worn the same old coat and baggy breeches for as long as Meggie could remember. Lennie swore and spat, too, and all he thought about was gin.

She wished that she could ask the young Sun God his name, or where he lived. She expected his own house would be a fine mansion with vast gardens. Servants would wait on him from morning until bedtime, and he would have an endless supply of sovereigns to spend.

Now he and his mother were staring at her curiously, and she knew it was time to go. Slowly, unwillingly, she walked out of the warehouse, stopping at the door to glance back once. The warm glow was receding rapidly, reminding her again that it was winter, that her feet were bare, that she had no home, that she was now a motherless child.

CHAPTER FOUR

Meggie had one comfort: she could go back to St Thomas's Wharf every morning and have her dish of soup and her pieces of bread handed to her by the Sun God's mother. That thought brought a wintry smile to her lips as she walked along. Maybe she would see *him* again – perhaps he came every day to fetch his mother in their fine carriage? Her spirits rose.

The rest of that day hardly mattered. She trailed round the alleys, not noticing the cold, thinking of the next morning and her return visit to the wharf. That night, she curled up in a sheltered alley whose ramshackle houses leaned towards one another as if in drunken greeting. She was near the soup-kitchen, for she intended to be first in the queue.

Next morning she reached the soup-kitchen before anyone else had arrived. The queue was long and straggly within an hour, but it was even longer and the people waiting were becoming ill-tempered when the two men came on the scene. Both were burly and dressed in gaudy checkered jackets and dark bowlers. They had ruddy faces and bristly chins, but one was very tall and so thin he looked as if the wind might snap him in two. His companion was small and ball-shaped.

Meggie watched to see what they intended to do – did they think they could join the queue? They were not dressed like beggars. But the men seemed not to notice the waiting men and women. One had a rolled notice under his arm; the other drew a hammer and some nails out of his pocket. Without exchanging a word, they approached the doors to the warehouse and proceeded to nail up the notice.

Having done this, they began to move away but were stopped by angry howls from the hungry paupers.

'What do it say, eh?' a man asked in a rasping voice.

'Tell us, man. We can't read, yer know!' screeched an old woman, shaking her scrawny fist at the men.

Meggie waited, barely daring to breathe, while the men conferred. She heard one say, 'O' course – daft it were 'avin' a notice put up fer these dullards. They ain't nivver been ter school, Sid!'

Sid answered with a snort, 'Crikey, yer right, Bert. None 'as thought o' that, 'ave they? Read it out ter 'em.'

Bert nodded, bracing his shoulders self-importantly before clearing his throat to read out the notice in booming, sergeant-major tones. As he spoke, Meggie felt all hope leaving her. Wilting, she clasped her arms round her waist, suddenly aware of a piercing hunger.

'Owing to unexpected illness, St Thomas's soup-kitchen will be closed until further notice.'

Then the two men went on their way, ignorant of the effect the notice was having on the paupers, who barely managed to survive even with the help of one dish of soup each day.

Meggie wanted to sob out loud, to scream, 'Come back! Come back! Tell me who is ill? Is *he* ill?' but she did not even know the young man's name. And if she started asking such questions, the men would think her mad – if they paid any attention to her at all.

Shocked, she stood there, her legs wooden. She wasn't going to see her Sun God today, or his mother. She might not see either of them ever again! Tears bruised her lids, but she refused to cry in front of the slowly dispersing crowd. Everyone else seemed to have some destination, but after this great disappointment Meggie had nowhere to go. After a little while, her numbed mind began to function again. She put one stiff leg in front of the other and set off in the direction of the city centre. She had no idea where she was heading or what she was going to do next.

Martin, Lord Chanleigh, was bowling along in his shiny black carriage on the look-out for pauper girls. He had a definite purpose in mind, and if he did not achieve it, he would return home morose and foul-tempered. Failure was a rarity, however, for pauper girls roamed the streets in their hundreds. He was not easily satisfied, for he knew exactly what he was looking for: girls of a certain age, a certain build, with bright eyes and a healthy air about them. He had a pathological fear of illness; however much he might be drawn to a pretty child, he would not approach her if she looked sickly.

Chanleigh was feeling somewhat desperate today, for his latest plaything, Rosetta, had died. He was accustomed to his girls dying sooner or later, but her death had been very sudden, taking him by surprise. He had been unprepared for it and needed a replacement badly.

Wealthy and titled, Chanleigh had both the money and the time to indulge himself. He felt no shame about his predilection for little girls, for he was not alone in this. One after the other, his playthings had brought him pleasure down the years; pretty children with pale skins and golden curls, or chestnut hair, straight and fine, accompanying hazel or green eyes. He had no particular preference for any colouring, as long as each child was healthy and different in some way, either with a dimpled smile or a straight back, or pretty hands and feet, or eyes which sparkled at him when he addressed her. One, he recalled, had been dappled with pale golden freckles; how he had loved those freckles, until he had tired of the child – as he always tired of them in the end, however attractive he had found them at the outset.

His interest in each girl was brief but intense. From the age of about eight and a half until they reached eleven or thereabouts, when they began to show a womanly shape, the girls would receive every care from him; he would shower them with gifts and gewgaws, clothes, ribbons and, of course, his physical attentions. Only when he tired of his current favourite would he rid himself of her. Usually *he* decided when to rid himself of a plaything, but Rosetta's death had caught him unawares, making him feel vulnerable, almost frightened. He would not feel his usual self until he replaced Rosetta with a girl who glowed with health and liveliness.

Chanleigh knew that Rosetta's death of consumption had been foreshadowed by her early life in the slums, and yet the slums were the safest source of playthings for him.

Pauper parents often sold their children so that they could buy Geneva; he had obtained many bedmates in this way. If a pauper girl went missing while out in London's back alleys, who cared, who would inform the Peelers? Certainly not the thieving, drunken, immoral wretches who were likely to be her mother and father.

Chanleigh was nearing fifty now, and he had had a steady stream of little girls ever since his thirty-fifth birthday. Once, when he was far too young, he had been unsuccessfully married, a match arranged by his parents. He had not liked his wife nor had she liked him. Her warmth and gaiety had made him feel like a cold fish, and he had hated her for it. They had agreed to live apart, but discreetly, of course, for London society viewed such separations with a jaundiced eye.

Chanleigh had no heir, but in this, too, he was different from other titled gentlemen for he had no wish to ensure that his title survived. Because he had no interest whatsoever in the future but only in the way he spent his hours – by day and by night – the thought of trying to get his wife with child filled him with the severest repugnance; as she was in good health and therefore not likely to die soon, he was unable to marry a younger, more pleasing creature. He preferred his life of freedom, however, for a wife would soon put a stop to his main interest – and without his little girls he knew he would go mad.

The first child was called Joan; the last, Rosetta, who had died in his arms only hours before, without his having realized she was ill. Had he known, he would not have gone near her: he would have had her bundled out of the back kitchens in all haste. But she had concealed her sickness cleverly – how, he could not guess, for he had never heard her coughing. He thought of her large, pale eyes fixed on his, and beads of sweat started to appear on his brow. What if she had passed her illness on to him? He shuddered, knowing that it would be rough justice indeed if such a thing happened, for, while he could no more prevent himself from doing what he did than stop eating, inwardly he knew he was a fiend.

59

It would have been a touching death-bed scene to remember had he not been prickling with horror at the thought of the child's breath rising to contaminate him. She had been lying on the floor when he found her, and he thought she had fallen. By the time he picked her up, it was too late for him to protect himself.

Immediately Rosetta's limp body had been carried out in a rough wooden coffin, he had dressed in his immaculate evening clothes and sable-lined cloak, picked up his carved, silver-topped ebony cane and then summoned his carriage for this expedition. But it was failing miserably – he had not seen any suitable child. Suddenly, he felt old, and feeble. He had never felt so dispirited before. Everything was turning against him, and he had never been capable of handling failure.

He gritted his teeth until his jaw throbbed with pain. Just then a young girl caught his eye through the carriage window. Breathing heavily, he peered out from behind the concealment of the drapery and viewed her critically, then slumped back onto the seat. From the back she had looked like a child, but when she turned round, he could see that she had breasts. His mouth turned down at the corners with distaste.

Time was passing. He dreaded the thought of having to sleep alone again: he had terrible dreams, sometimes believing that he was awake but paralysed and that an avenging demon was spearing him in the loins with a pitchfork. The proximity of a warm, sweet-breathed child usually kept the nightmares at bay.

The carriage bowled along through the back alleys and slum streets, while Chanleigh crouched in his seat, ashen faced, his hands trembling.

Meggie's fortunes that day had been of a minor variety. She had earned a penny fetching a mug of rum for an old flower-woman; then the flower-girls, having seen her willingness, had also sent her on errands. She had earned quite a few pennies that way, and with these she had bought herself a good lunch. For a few hours she had been so busy and in such cheery company that she had been able to put out of her mind her disappointment about not seeing the Sun God and his mother.

Despite the cold weather, business was brisk for the flower-girls. There were snowdrops to sell, and evergreens; someone had brought some early crocuses up from the south and these were selling at a great rate. Meggie ended up sitting beside one of the flower-girls and helping her to sell her snowdrops, for which she received sixpence. She asked the girl if she could come back every day to help her, but the girl grinned, saying that she was packing up her job in two days to get married.

Just my luck, thought Meggie, to find a kind person and then to hear that she's giving up her work. She was beginning to think that fate was against her.

Nonetheless, she enjoyed the flower-girls' hearty chatter and jokes. Even when it was snowing and business was poor, they had a laugh at the ready. Today, the girls were full of stories about the antics of the Prince of Wales – young Edward, or Bertie as his family called him. Apparently, he was in great trouble with his parents for having an *affaire* with an actress. Even though he was twenty, Queen Victoria and Prince Albert, her consort, kept a tight rein on their son. They had attempted to raise him to be a highly moral, dignified and deeply religious man, but they had not allowed for his developing personality.

Nellie Clifden, the young actress involved, had captivated him, and he had behaved without caution, Meggie heard the girls saying. She listened with wide eyes. What a marvellous figure Prince Edward sounded – imagine being the son of the Queen! One day he would be King of England!

The flower-girls seemed to know everything about the Prince's *affaire* – even the most intimate facts. Faced with his parents' wrath, Edward had said that he had been tempted and unable to resist but that the *affaire* was now over. But the girls said he was lying, and good for him: a young man needed to sow his wild oats even if his mother was the Queen. Now that the Queen and Prince Albert thought their son was behaving himself, he'd be able to see Nellie in secret, and good luck to them both!

The Prince of Wales, the Queen's own son, was having a secret *affaire* with a commoner like herself! Imagine having a Queen's son in your bed! Meggie marvelled.

'Prince Albert warned 'im, 'e did. 'Ee said, "Yer mustn't see 'er agin, m'lad",' one of the flower-girls said. ' "Yer mustn', yer dare not be lost. The consequences fer the country, fer the whole world, would be too dreadful." Thass what 'e said.'

'Well, so they might, but why shouldn' the young 'un 'ave 'is fling like what we do? Can't keep it under wraps, can yer?' one of the others retorted testily.

'Yeah, Mavis, give the lad a chance,' one of the other girls said. "E's 'uman like the rest of us, ain't 'e? Give the poor blighter a chance. 'E ain't a bleedin' monk!'

'What do yer know about it?' Mavis snorted. "E's a Queen's son an' 'eir, ain't 'e? What if'n 'e got it – yer know, what yer can git from loose women? That'd be a fine how d'yer do, wouldn' it, when 'e came ter choose a princess ter marry! What a scandal there'd be then, an' no mistake!' Mavis nodded her head vigorously. "E's the Queen's son an' it ain't right that 'e beds wiv common girls like us.'

'Who're yer callin' common?' Meggie's flower-girl retorted but when Meggie looked at her, she saw the girl was grinning and nowhere near as outraged as she sounded.

Not to be outdone, Mavis said, 'Well, we is common, ain't we? Look, there's flower-girls all roun' this square, ain't there? That means we's common, don' it!'

'Ssh, Mavis, yer gots a customer!' Meggie's flower-girl, Annie, hissed sibilantly.

Immediately, the girls stopped their banter, while a tall distinguished-looking gentleman strolled towards them, purchased two bunches of flowers and strolled nonchalantly away. At once, the banter sprang up again.

'A fine 'andsome young fellow, the Prince o' Wales. Wouldn' look at yer, Annie. Rather 'ave a dollymop 'e would!' Mavis got her own back.

Annie seemed unaffected by this remark. 'Can yer see me goin' up ter the Palace ter meet me new ma an' pa?' She roared with laughter. 'There'd be a bleedin' riot – an' it'd be me what started it! I'm 'appy wiv me Reggie what I'm wedding in two days' time.'

Mavis fell silent, but she was not beaten. She'd bide her time and wait to spike Annie with her tongue if she had to wait a month.

'Yeah,' said one of the girls who had stayed out of the conversation until now. 'If'n 'e can look at actresses, 'e can look at us, can't 'e? An' why not, eh? I wouldn' 'alf fancy havin' a prince in me bed! Coo! I bet 'e knows a fing or two, that lad.'

'But nuffink yer don' know already, Maisie!' Annie grinned, and Maisie hooted with laughter.

'Well, p'haps I could teach the little bugger a fing or two, eh?' Maisie smirked.

Raucous laughter greeted this remark, for Maisie was quite a one with the boys, priding herself on her reputation.

"Twouldn' tek much, yer know, ter git 'im interested if'n 'e 'appened along,' Mavis continued. 'If'n 'e came 'ere ter buy some flowers fer one o' 'is lady loves, what'd 'e do but look up from our flowers an' inter our faces. Then 'e'd say ter 'isself, "Well, there's a fine 'andsome gel an' no mistake!" Arter that, it'd be inter bed wiv 'im afore yer could say chimney sweep!'

The girls tittered, imagining the Prince of Wales happening along, as Mavis had said, and dragging one of them into his bed. It was a colourful fantasy, but they were level-headed girls and unlikely to be swept away by such dreams.

'Prince o' Wales tek yer 'ome wiv 'im? What'd 'is ma

say? Yer'd be kicked out! They got soldiers an' guards all roun' 'em, protectin' 'em night an' day wiv guns.'

'Don' be silly, 'course they 'aven' got guns!' Annie retorted.

'Oh yes they 'ave! 'Ow do yer think they keep all the robbers an' thieves out o' the Palace if'n they ain't got guns?' another girl sneered.

'Don' be daft! They don' 'ave robbers an' thieves tryin' ter git in the Palace! They wouldn' go near it!'

'I know – 'cos the guards 'ave big guns, thass why!' replied the first girl victoriously.

So the argument went on. Meggie was fascinated by the spirited rejoinders. What she understood from that afternoon's exchange was that the Queen was very stern with her heir and that popular opinion said he should be allowed to sow his oats as he pleased. He was a winsome young man, and very good looking, the girls agreed – even if they could not agree on other points. The younger girls would have given everything for an evening with him, even knowing there could be no future in it.

Thinking of the young Prince of Wales naturally brought Meggie's thoughts back to her young Sun God. He had been like a prince; tall, golden-haired, assured. In his presence, she had felt as she imagined a real princess must, and it was a feeling she longed to recapture. She wondered what he would be doing now, for she knew little of the manner in which the rich spent their time. Riding round and round in their carriages probably, through the parks, the avenues and gardens, their beautiful horses glossy-coated and proud-necked. They would spend a lot of their time ordering their servants about, while they sat back in their jewels, furs and silks. She wouldn't mind having a life like that. All that money to spend, purses which never emptied. . . . Was her Sun God spending money at this very minute? Perhaps choosing a fine new cloak or a carved ebony cane?

The chatter of the flower-girls receded as her memory conjured up her Sun God, and she longed with all her heart for him to appear now in the square so that she could see him again. After all, there was no reason why he should not come here to buy flowers for his mother, unless, of course, it was he who was ill and he was still confined to bed. She had not thought of that. Her Sun God ill . . . . Meggie's mouth turned down at the corners and she hunched her shoulders as if she were feeling an inner pain. She didn't want him to be ill, or helpless; she wanted him to be strong and vigorous, taking her by the hand and saying, 'Come with me, little one; come to my home and live with me and my mother. You will be like my sister, and you will have everything you could wish for, and servants to do as you bid.'

But instead of her Sun God sauntering into the square, it was Martin, Lord Chanleigh, who came. Having alighted from his carriage a little way from the square, he approached the flower-girls with a casual air. Once before he had picked up a little flower-girl, Sally Bruton; he might be fortunate again today. He was feeling desperate but concealing this expertly – the flower-girls were his final resort. If there were no child here to attract him, then he would have to risk his reputation by going to one of the child brothels. That he did not wish to do: there, not only would he be laying himself open to blackmail, scandal and censure, but there was the terrible risk of disease, even from child prostitutes.

Looking every inch the gentleman as he surveyed the girls' wares, Chanleigh raised each one's hopes by appearing about to buy before losing interest and passing on to the next girl. With his brows arched, his dark eyes half-closed, a silver-topped cane in his hand, he gave every appearance of being very rich. No one would have suspected the nature of his secret life or the dreadful crimes he committed. Much of his smugness was due to the façade he carefully and expertly displayed.

He showed little interest in the first few girls, old as they were, thick woolly shawls round their sloping shoulders and crossed across their chests to keep out the cold. Rough woollen mittens encased their hands, leaving their fingertips bare to handle the flowers and the customers' payments. How ungainly they were with their big, pointed feet and red-tipped, dripping noses, thought Chanleigh, withdrawing inwardly in distaste. Some of them were as burly as men, an added repugnance. What little beauty these girls had was soon dissipated with the effects of gin and their outdoor work.

Chanleigh headed in the direction of Annie and Meggie, coming to a halt before one of the other sellers and glancing down at her box of snowdrops, his expression fixed. He seemed to reject the flowers. They obviously did not meet with his satisfaction. Going to the next girl, he glanced similarly at her wares. He then moved round from one girl to another, until finally, having made no purchases, he came to a halt before Annie and Meggie. His glance at their snowdrops was brief, and then his eyes travelled from the box to Meggie's feet and ankles, to her legs, her face. She must have looked a sorry sight – her nose was red and she was hugging herself to keep warm – nonetheless, Chanleigh's bright black eyes caught and held hers. As if mesmerized, Meggie could not drag her eyes from his.

Chanleigh was not unused to this reaction from slum girls. After all, he was a gentleman, rich and powerful. This child was a bedraggled sight at the moment – blue with cold, skinny and wretched, her hair tangled – but her eyes were bright and shining, and there was spirit in them. Her hands were tiny and well formed, her feet shapely. Tiny hands and feet had a special attraction for him. He tried to subdue the sudden beating of his heart, but he was already a master at keeping his expression stony. She would never be able to read his mind.

If the flower-girls thought the prolonged scrutiny of Meggie was unusual, they did not show it. They were worldly girls who had seen all types and had heard all kinds of stories. Very little could shock them. Perhaps none of them actually realized why the man was looking at the girl. Perhaps they thought he was looking for pupils for a ragged school of which he was the governor?

Chanleigh stood for some time wondering what to do,

an unexpected wave of nervousness gripping him. He wanted to take the girl away now, but the square was full; there were flower-girls everywhere, and customers moving about.

He kept his gaze on the girl, and her eyes returned his look steadily. They were beautiful eyes; violet, he now realized, whereas before he had thought they were dark brown. A deep velvety violet. Once she had been put in different clothes, she would be a charmer. After a few good meals, she would take on the glow of health which he liked his little girls to have.

Meggie did not know what to make of the man. She had never been studied so closely before, except when her mother had looked at her dotingly, as mothers do. That, of course, had been delightful. This – well, she could not decide what this was. The man had such a hard expression on his face; his features were strong, almost frighteningly severe. His eyes were very dark, like two black gimlets, his mouth set, his nostrils curved outwards, his skin very white, almost clay-like. She could not see his hands, for he wore kid gloves, but his fingers appeared to be long and thin. A shiver ran through her for she had an uncomfortable thought of those long thin fingers touching her. She wanted to get away from this man. Yet to do so would mean leaving Annie, who had been so kind to her, and she might lose Annie's friendship. She had been hoping to talk one of the other girls into letting her come back the next day to help, and if she went away now, that opportunity would be lost.

'Do you go to school, child?' the man asked suddenly, his words uttered in a stream with barely a breath between each. They seemed to spurt out from his mouth, and she could almost feel them striking against her body.

'No,' she replied.

'Would you like to?'

'No,' she said frankly.

'But school is a good place where you learn a great deal, where you can become a young lady. You're given good meals and cared for. If you are ill, you are put in a cosy bed and looked after by a nurse.'

Meggie did not reply. She did not trust the man. Before she said any more she wanted to know what he wanted. But she was not going to ask the question. Let him reveal himself first. She might only be ten years old, but her shrewdness was marked.

The man sighed, shuffling his feet a little. He seemed restless. 'When do you finish work, child?' he asked.

'When there are no more messages for me to run,' Meggie said sedately.

'And when will that be?'

'I cannot say,' replied Meggie.

'Would you like a ride in a fine carriage, child?'

'How would I get that?'

'Why, if I allowed it,' said the man. 'What if I brought my coach nearer the square so you could see it, and my fine horses and the beautiful emblem painted on the coach's door? Would you not like to see those, child? Would you not like to get into the carriage and take a ride?'

Meggie did not reply. Her lower lip jutted out a little. The more the man tried to draw her out the more she withdrew inside herself.

Putting caution aside, Chanleigh said, 'I'll give you a shilling.'

Meggie pushed down a wave of excitement. 'Only a shilling?' she said coldly.

Chanleigh wavered. She was sharper than she looked.

'That would be only the beginning.' He lowered his voice. 'Look, child, why are you so wary of me? I have done you no harm. Will you not come with me and ride in my fine carriage? I will give you a shilling or more if you wish it, and cakes, and perhaps a pretty dress or a feathered fan. Would you not like a feathered fan?'

Meggie clamped her lips together. It sounded marvellous, and very like the dream she had been having only a little while ago about the Sun God and his mother. Yet this man was old. He was no laughing sun god, but oh! how fine were his clothes.

A customer was busy choosing snowdrops from Annie's tray, and while the girl's attention was elsewhere Chanleigh leaned closer to Meggie, hissing in her ear. 'Look, child, I have no time to stand here arguing with you. I tell you that I have money, more money than you have ever dreamed of, and it can all be yours if you will come with me and ride in my carriage.'

Meggie's caution wavered a little. A warm carriage, money, clothes! Money was what she needed, so that she could send some back to Jenny, so that she could get a letter to her. And of course she needed money just to survive. If she were careful, if she remained cautious, she might get all the money she needed and come to no harm. The more she thought about it, the more she realized she really had no choice. As far as she knew there was no work for her here with the flower-girls, and the one who had given her sixpence had only been in a happy, generous mood because of her coming wedding. Who else would be as generous? She might linger here in the freezing cold and earn only a penny a week, if that.

Here was this fine gentleman offering her a shilling or more, and clothes, food. How she longed to accept! Yet something was preventing her. She had no knowledge of intuition, but she recognized the feeling inside her which said, 'Stay here, it's safer here.' But this man was rich, and wasn't money what she needed most in all the world? Wouldn't that solve all her problems and her mother's problems, too? If she sent money to her mother, Jenny could buy oranges and milk and bread to regain her health, to cure her cough.

Meggie thought hard. To make her mother better, that was her dearest wish. Firmly putting intuition aside, she said to the man, 'Show me your carriage, then.'

Chanleigh had not realized how tense he was, waiting for the child's reply. But now that she had said 'Yes', he shrugged a little with relief. Nonchalantly, as if having nothing to do with her, he strolled out of the square, Meggie following him.

The flower-girl looked up, calling, "Ey, gel! 'Ey! Where yer goin'?"

Meggie waved. 'I'll be back,' she said. 'I hope your marriage goes all right.'

"Ey – " the flower-girl called.

If Meggie heard her, she did not show it, for she was already across the square, following the fine gentleman down the street towards his carriage.

Chanleigh walked on as if he were alone. He did not look back. If the child were to stop now, he would say nothing, do nothing. He had no intention of revealing his plans to anyone; not here, not in public. He had already behaved more carelessly than he had ever done before.

The carriage was in sight; the coachman had spotted him and now jumped down from his seat to open the door for his master. Chanleigh climbed in. The coachman shut the door, awaiting his master's orders, but Chanleigh did not speak, so he returned to his seat on the box. He sat there waiting obediently, while Chanleigh sat inside waiting, saying nothing, barely breathing.

Meggie had seen him get into the carriage, and now as she walked up to it she was unsure of what to do. Should she call out? But what could she say except 'Sir!' or 'Lord! My Lord!' Perhaps he was a lord. She saw the beautiful painted coat-of-arms on the carriage door; he had told her about that, and the horses were fine, with glossy coats. She raised her hand to tap on the coach door, but slowly, for coldness was gripping her. Her feelings of doubt were increasing. If she got into this carriage, that would be it; she wouldn't be able to get out. Why should she put that fear aside? For money. She needed money. Jenny needed money. She wasn't going to get any shillings wandering around the streets, starving and cold. She must look upon this chance as the most golden, heaven-sent opportunity of her life. This man had been sent to save her, to help her.

Summoning her courage, Meggie tapped on the coach

door. It swung open instantly; a hand helped her inside. Within a few moments the coach was bowling briskly towards Lord Chanleigh's London home.

CHAPTER FIVE

Number 4, Pattingham Court had an imposing Georgian façade, the smooth red brick offset by the gleaming white window sills and the carved front door. There were beautiful wrough-iron railings round the front garden, which looked out onto a little park, and across the park was another similar house. But Meggie was not looking there today. She was looking at the house outside which the carriage had come to a halt. The journey had been short and they had said little. Meggie had asked about the coat-of-arms on the door, and Chanleigh had begun to tell her what it meant and then had stopped abruptly, as if he did not wish to speak. She was too ill at ease to ask him anything else.

A gloomy-faced major-domo opened the front door, stepping forward and bowing low. On his chest was a coat-of-arms exactly like the one on the carriage door. But it was his face which caught and held Meggie's attention. It was a dour, grim face; cold, with tiny, screwed-up eyes and a down-curving mouth. The man said nothing but continued bowing.

Chanleigh took Meggie by the hand, leading her up the gleaming marble steps and into the great hall. He glanced at the major-domo briefly – there seemed to be no need for him to say anything; the man obviously knew this ritual well. He clicked his fingers at another servant, who brought a soft, blanket-like material, which was put round Meggie's shoulders.

Behind them a small but grossly fat woman waddled into the hall. Her face was so fat and shiny that the skin looked ready to burst. Long, coarse black hairs were growing on her chin, and her eyes were lost in the ruts of fat which enfolded them. Her clothes were none too clean but that was nothing to Meggie and so she did not notice it. The woman wore a voluminous mob cap, the frill of which was grey and straggly, looking as if it had been dipped in grease and left to dry. Her ample bosom was swathed in a moth-eaten shawl of some mysterious brown material which might once have been wool, and her dress was much creased and of a faded blue colour.

Meggie stared up at her. Was she to go with this woman?

Glancing down at Meggie, the woman gave a throaty chuckle. 'Me name's Aggie. Come wiv me, little 'un, an' I'll show yer comforts yer ain't nivver known before.'

Meggie glanced at Lord Chanleigh, who was having his cloak removed by the major-domo. She wanted to ask if she should go with her, but when Chanleigh had that cold look on his face she felt inhibited. Meggie mutely followed the woman, who waddled along at a snail's pace, the boulders of her flesh slapping together as she walked, and panted and huffed as they went down corridor after corridor and up winding staircases.

They finally came to a huge, echoing room. It had marble floors and marble walls, and in one corner was the most enormous, white, hollowed-out object Meggie had ever seen. It was cumbersome and ugly; indeed, everything in the room was ugly. The washstand and towel-rails were made of heavy wood, and, at the foot of the bath, a strange kidney-shaped white pottery bowl stood on its own stand of heavy wood. There was a water closet of Delft china, blue and white, and there were blue and white flowers and little figurines on one of the walls.

Aggie, having closed the door behind her, said, 'Well, get 'em off, girl. We ain't come here ter admire your clothes, yer know.'

'Get them off?' Meggie repeated hesitantly.

'Yes, dearie. This here's the bathroom, in case yer don't know it. Clothes come off in here. The big thing there be a bath an' in it yer going.'

Aggie proceeded to turn on the huge ugly metal taps, and steaming hot water poured into the bath.

'Yer be lucky, we gots aller comforts here. This here's the newest water system yer can get. No heaving of heavy bowls here. Yer just turns on the tap an' out comes the water like magic.'

Meggie looked nervously at the steaming water. Was she really meant to sit in that? It looked dangerously hot. Slowly she took off her ragged, dirty clothes.

Aggie bent over, huffing as she picked them up gingerly with her forefinger and thumb to drop them into a woven willow box in the corner of the bathroom. 'They'll be burnt, an' that's no doubt,' she said.

'But they're my clothes,' Meggie stammered.

'Clothes? They're just dirty old rags.' Aggie shuddered, although Aggie herself and her own clothes were none too clean. Now that she was closer, Meggie could smell her breath. It smelt of strong tobacco, and her teeth were stained black.

'Get yer more pretty clothes, the master will,' Aggie went on. 'Yer don't know what yer going ter get, me girl,' she tittered. 'Yer don't know what yer going ter get! The master's got everything, an' more. Now come into this here bath an' get all that muck off yer.'

'But the water's steaming,' Meggie protested.

"Course it's steaming. Don't get dirt off with cold water! In yer gets.'

Meggie put her hands on the edge of the bath, feeling the water with one toe. It was indeed piping hot. 'If I get in there I'll boil!'

"Course yer won't. Ah, but I ain't got all day ter stand round here. I'll puts some more cold in fer yer.'

Aggie turned on the cold tap. In a few minutes, when the water had cooled down a little, Meggie slowly slipped into it. It was the strangest sensation: the water pressed against her skin and yet at the same time almost seemed to be invisible. It was there and yet it wasn't there. When she moved about, little waves of water bobbed up and down against her skin.

Aggie waddled over to a corner and brought back some scented soap, pink and shaped like a rose. She took a little packet of pink crystals and dropped these into the water. Instantly the water become the most beautiful deep rose-pink. Meggie sighed seeing the beautiful colour.

There was a vast pale yellow loofah at the foot of the bath. It was about two feet long and it felt rough to the touch. Aggie passed it to her, saying, 'Come on now, me girl, get this here scrubbing against yer skin or I'll do it fer yer, and I's bin known ter bring up the blood, I has!'

'What do I do?' Meggie said.

'What do yer do? Yer ignorant, girl, ain't yer?'

Aggie showed her how to soap the loofah and then to rub the loofah against her skin. Meggie did as she was instructed. Soon, the pink water became murky grey as the dirt and grime came off her skin, and she saw for the first time that her flesh was really quite a delicate ivory colour and not the beigey-grey she had thought it was.

'An' as fer yer hair,' Aggie said, 'well, we has ter wash that first with soap a few times ter get off all that mire.'

'My hair?' Meggie looked startled.

"Course! Can't wash yer body an' leave yer hair filthy, can yer? That just ain't proper!'

Meggie shrugged and let Aggie lather the pink soap into her hair. Once, twice, three times her hair was shampooed and still the dirt poured out. Her hair had to be shampooed six times before Aggie said it was clean enough.

Meggie realized that she was enjoying the bath. She felt cozy and warm, and the scent of the soap was delicious, but she knew that there was something else pressing at the back of her mind along with the trepidation about what was going to happen after the bath – hunger. She looked at Aggie, wondering if she could ask for some food but decided against it. The fat old woman seemed agreeable enough but who knew what her temper might be if she were asked to do something by someone other than her master.

'Do we have dinner?' Meggie asked instead.

'Indeed we do! Indeed we do, the best part of the day!' Aggie grinned, folding her huge, fat arms across her huge, fat breasts. 'There'll be food ternight like yer nivver known it! There'll be ham an' there'll be capon an' turkey an' there'll be iced pudding. Iced pudding! Mmmn!' She licked her big pink lips and rubbed her stomach with one broad hand. 'Now, come, girl, I gots the towel ready here fer yer. Out yer steps.'

Meggie got out of the bath cautiously because she was wet and the bath was slippery. Aggie helped her down onto the floor, swathing her in a thick white towel, and began to rub the skin so briskly that she had to beg her to go more gently. Her hair was wrapped in a turban, and another dry towel was wrapped round her shoulders. Then Aggie opened the door and led her out along the landing to a room with a dark oak door. Inside the room a huge fire was roaring in the grate. There was a massive bed with curtains hanging at its sides, and on the bed was a bright ginger cat wrapped in the tightest ball imaginable.

By the fire was a chest with the lid thrown back, and from the chest issued the fragrant scent of cedarwood. On closer inspection, Meggie saw that it was full of the most beautiful clothes she had ever seen: lace and velvet, silk and satin, brocade, tiny little slippers with jewelled toes, a shawl so lacy and fragile it was almost invisible. Even little caps with bows.

'For me?' she asked incredulously.

'Yes, me dearie. Rosetta, she – ' Aggie stopped suddenly, coughing loudly.

Meggie seemed not to have heard Aggie, for the beautiful clothes in the chest were taking up all her attention now. She lifted them out, excited beyond belief. She had been right to come to this house. Yes, this man had been sent by Providence. She had had the most marvellous bath, and now she was going to wear beautiful clothes. Then she would have the most enormous meal she had ever eaten in her whole life, and soon, very soon, she would have some money to send to her mother. If only Jenny could be here with her now to share this cosy bedroom and eat a big supper with her, to curl up in the huge comfortable bed. The pang of longing for her mother was sharp, cutting through her.

'Well, which are yer going ter choose, child?' Aggie's voice disturbed her thoughts. 'The pretty blue dress? That pink 'un? The yellow with the rose buds? Mighty pretty, ain't they? Rosetta – ' Again the old woman paused, her cheeks reddening. Hastily she turned away, as if involved with delving into the chest to bring out more treasures.

Meggie's eyes had fallen on the dresses, fluffy, frothy creations of lace and rosebuds and silk; they were unbelievably soft to the touch. She caressed the material, holding it against her cheek, revelling in the softness, the satiny feeling.

'Well, child?' Aggie prompted her. 'Which one is it ter be?'

'I think the pink one, Aggie. It's lovely. It's so pretty and the colour is so fresh.'

'Suits yer, it does, with that black hair of yern. See how nice yer hair is now it's clean!'

Aggie reached in front of the mantelpiece and brought down a hand-mirror of tortoiseshell. Taking the mirror, Meggie looked into it and saw her face for the first time.

Her hair was fluffed up after its washing and had dried in strong waves, glossy and black with blue lights. Her face seemed quite white, whiter than she had ever imagined skin could be, and her eyes were bluish-purple, just like her mother's. She was thin; she already knew that. Her cheekbones were too sharp and her chin too pointed, but her mouth smiled, and her nose was not unattractive. Her black eyebrows were narrow and high, and she touched them lingeringly with her finger. They, too, were as soft and silky as her hair, and her thick black eyelashes were long and swept across her cheeks when she half-closed her eyes.

Aggie stood watching her, hands on hips. 'Yes, yer a fine handsome girl,' she nodded. 'No wonder His Lordship brought yer in. He knows a good thing when he sees 'un.'

Meggie was still entranced by her reflection, but Aggie was in a hurry to get the child dressed and down to supper, where her master would be waiting for his guest.

Under the flouncing pink dress went an ivory silk chemise and numerous white silk petticoats edged with lace. There were silk stockings and pretty little slippers of white satin with big pink rosettes on the toes. The garters which held up the stockings quite captivated Meggie. They were intricately sewn with a design of roses and irises in pink, blue and white. They were a little loose on her slim legs, so she had to roll the tops of the stockings over to pad out the garters. Then it was time for the pink dress. It was slipped over her shoulders, to grip snugly round the waist.

Aggie twitched the dress into place and buttoned it down the back. She brushed out the glossy black hair, told Meggie to pinch her cheeks to bring some colour into them and then stood back to survey her handiwork. Indeed the child was adorable, a picture, the prettiest the master had ever brought into the house.

Aggie had no conscience about her master's predilection for little girls. She knew she was lucky to be in such a good household. If she wanted to snore in her chair or put her feet up and smoke her pipe, her master never said a word. As long as she did her job, he said nothing. Her job, of course, was to care for the little girls when they were not with him. It was easy work, and apart from the odd child who proved truculent, she had had a remarkably good time of it. Other masters would have complained about her: her slovenliness, her slow walk, the smoking, the state of her clothes, a thousand other little things about which employers were apt to complain. But Chanleigh had never said a word to her, as long as she did what she was supposed to do.

Aggie had been with him now for ten years, coming to him a poor sobbing widow on his doorstep, to beg. He had seen she was in dire straits, the sort of woman who was desperate enough to do anything for a meal. He had taken her in, fed her, told her what her duties would be and given her the opportunity to walk out if she had a conscience, but she seemed to have been born without one. Widowhood, or any other sorrow, was not likely to give her that. Survival was all she cared about, and in that she was like the people in Rats' Castle with whom Meggie had grown up.

Aggie had had a hard life. Married when very young to a man she had thought was perfect, she had doted on him, worshipped him almost, and for some years had lived in a fog of rosy delight, not seeing the truth until it hit her full hard. The man she adored, for whom she had cared so much and so well, had another woman in a neighbouring town and had given her a family. Indeed, in that town, he was known as her husband. And the woman had not even known that he had been married first to Aggie. . . .

Aggie had no children; it had been something which had never troubled her. Indeed, her husband had never said he wanted children. But the other woman had seven children, and when the time had come for him to choose between his real wife and her, he had chosen her! Small comfort to Aggie that he had died two months later of an apoplectic fit.

By that time, she was desperate for money; she had lost her home and had sold all her belongings. She had been unable to find work of any kind since she could not read or write; she was untrained, for she had married very young. The day she had come to Lord Chanleigh's door had been a turning point in her life. She had never looked back from that moment. She was the only woman in the household, for Chanleigh knew that few women would tolerate what he did. Anyway, he preferred male servants who were less likely to gossip.

Aggie, being the only woman, and of a rough diamond variety, had soon begun to dominate the household – except for her master, of course. The others went somewhat in fear of her, for her temper could be a venomous thing when it was roused. But to the child this evening, she was all sweetness and smiles. Indeed, it was possible that Meggie would never see the other side of Aggie.

Meggie was now dressed and ready. Aggie led the child down the stairs to the dining-room where Chanleigh awaited her, standing at the sideboard and pouring himself a second glass of port. He was elegantly dressed, smelling of pomade, and with not a hair out of place. When they entered the room his black gimlet eyes fixed on Meggie and remained on her as he gestured to the old woman to leave them alone.

The first course had already been set. Chanleigh ushered the child to the table to sit her beside him on a high carved chair. He himself draped a fine white linen napkin on her knee and showed her which spoon, knife and fork to use as the meal progressed. He poured her some wine, a light rosé, sweet enough for a child and disarmingly pleasant. She would never guess the effect it would have on her until it was too late.

Chanleigh was cunning in his methods, and greatly experienced. If the child did not grow sleepy and bemused after two glasses of this rosé, he would slip a powder into it. It was one which he had used before and it had never failed to work. It would put her to sleep instantly, after which she would know nothing until the morning. But that would only be a last result, of course, for he preferred his victims to be alert and responsive. An unconscious, limp child was not as diverting as one who was sufficiently awake to display every facet of her personality – whatever that proved to be in the heat of the moment.

Meggie was dazzled by the glistening crystal, the sparkling pink wine, the sumptuous food, course after course brought in by silent, obsequious servants : delicious creamy soup, pâté, fish, then capon, ham and turkey in succulent sauces.

Chanleigh was eager to explain the names of all the foods she was eating and how they were prepared. When it was time for the sweet course, no less than four dishes were borne in, much to Meggie's delight: fresh fruit chopped into tiny pieces, rich fruit pudding, a luscious trifle thick with cream and a huge fruit cake layered with marzipan. She longed to be able to taste all of them but knew that it would be rude to do this. Jenny had always been strict about her daughter's table manners, even when they had no table left on which to put their food, for Jenny had once worked in a great household and had learned there the proper way to do things. Jack Blunt had done his utmost to interfere, of course, raging that the child would never have need of such affected ways in Rats' Castle. Finally Jenny had ceased to teach her daughter the refinements which she herself had been taught long ago, but, by that time, Meggie knew the essentials. In remembering her table manners now, she was also remembering her mother; to forget what Jenny had taught her would be to forget Jenny herself.

Meggie wished her mother was here with her at this table, because then everything would be all right. She knew with certainty that her misgivings would vanish and she could relax and be happy. With her mother's approval, she could be content again. She had always needed Jenny's approval, more so than other children. Now, alone, she was floundering, almost having to relearn how to live.

Meggie felt that she had done the right thing in making the decision to come here. It was surely better than starving and being cold and homeless? But now that her stomach was filled and she was warm, she was beginning to realize that she had acted in haste, that she might well regret what she had done. Those black gimlet eyes were boring into her again as Chanleigh refilled her goblet, urging her to drink. She smiled at him, thanking him politely for the meal and telling him how much she had enjoyed it. If he was startled by her good manners, he did not show it. Smiling back at her, he said that she was indeed very welcome in his house.

She was ignorant of the thronging passions behind his tranquil gaze, for, much as she believed she was a wise little creature of the world and knew all there was to know of life, her knowledge was in actuality severely limited, as much by her immaturity as by Jenny's having kept careful watch over her. If she had heard about men who preyed on little girls, she did not recall it at this moment.

As the servants cleared away the dishes and silver, removing the remains of the most sumptuous feast Meggie had ever enjoyed, she watched them being carried out and felt a pang at their going. Secretly she would have liked to start the meal all over again.

Chanleigh handed his little guest a gleaming silver comfit dish full of sweetmeats. Mouth dropping open, she stared at them, unable to choose. Marchpane, sugared cherries, sugared plums, crystallized fruits, crystallized ginger, peppermint lumps: he said all their names until her ears rang with them. When he pressed her to try as many as she liked, she did so, but not in a greedy fashion. She chose slowly and chewed delicately, hoping that she would not offend him.

Meggie found that the sweetmeats were making her very thirsty, and she hardly noticed as Chanleigh refilled her goblet for the fourth time, so intent was she upon the different, delicious flavours she was tasting. Nor did she notice his eyes running up and down her body, lingering on her hands and feet, her ankles, slender neck and girlish shape. By the time she realized that she had eaten far too much and was beginning to feel sick, it was too late. She groaned, holding a hand to her stomach and looking apologetically at her host.

Chanleigh leaned over her solicitously, thinking that she was merely expressing a pleasant repleteness. Then he saw her colour change, the pink fading out of her cheeks, and a grimace of pain cross her face.

'Do you not feel well, my dear?' he asked, brushing her cheek with his hand. 'Do you have a pain?'

'I – think I have eaten too much, sir,' Meggie admitted. 'It was lovely food and I do not want to appear rude, but I ate too quick.'

Her host smiled down at her tolerantly. This he could deal with; he was accustomed to little girls and their greedy ways, their penchant for gobbling food and their lying groaning in bed afterwards. She would soon recover – with the right treatment.

'May I carry you to bed, my dear?' he said.

Meggie was not at all sure about being carried, for no one had ever done that for her since she was an infant, but she thought that bed would be a good idea.

Helping her to her feet, his thin but wiry hand grasping hers, Chanleigh led her across the dining-room to the large, gleaming hall with its spotless tiled floor and glossy linenfold panelling. Up the stairway they went, Meggie clinging to the carved balustrade while Chanleigh's wiry fingers gripped hers.

Meggie was glad of his support for the stairs were wide and seemed to rise endlessly. When they reached the door to her room, she looked up enquiringly at her host. She wanted him to go away as soon as possible, for she was now feeling very queasy and did not wish him to see her in such a state.

'I'll be all right now, sir,' she said. 'Thank you.'

'I would not dream of leaving you alone while you are ill.'

Chanleigh smiled down at her benevolently, feeling a rising excitement at entering the bedroom with her. That petite body, those luminous violet-blue eyes, the slender but shapely ankles which he longed to hold against his face and kiss, over and over. . . . There were other things which he wanted to do to her, too, and as he thought of them, his cheeks became florid and pearls of sweat broke out on his brow. Swallowing, he made as if to open the bedroom door.

'Let me assist you to your bed, my dear,' he said insistently.

Feeling even more nauseous with every passing moment, Meggie had not the energy to resist. The door now open before her, she stepped into the bedroom. Chanleigh followed her, breathing strangely. She wondered if he had something wrong with his chest.

With thudding heart, he shut the door behind them, running his tongue across arid lips. Surreptitiously, he locked the door and pocketed the key. This was the room where he had brought all the others. Merely to walk into this room with a child was enough to excite him.

'Take off your dress,' he said, striving to keep his voice steady. 'You do not want to crush it.'

Meggie did not know which feeling was most distressing her, nausea or embarrassment. Chanleigh did not appear about to leave. He was staring at her intently, his face flushed, his tongue darting across his lips so that they looked wet and shiny. She felt a shudder of revulsion but did not recognize it for what it was. The nausea increasing, she put her hand across her stomach and groaned.

Expectantly, Chanleigh handed her the fragile lace nightrobe which lay in readiness across the bed. He then strolled across to the window and lifted the heavy velvet drapes, appearing to be interested in what was going on outside in the park. Hastily, before he turned round, Meggie slipped out of the dress, fumbling with its many buttons and laces. Her haste was her undoing. She thought she would be very sick indeed within the next few minutes, for her head was already swirling. She slipped into the bed with relief, to lie back on the soft white pillows, the scent of fresh lavender filling her nostrils.

'I think I shall soon be well, sir,' she whispered, striving in her discomfort to be polite. If only the woman – Aggie – would come; she could ask her for a bowl. Meggie dared not stain these immaculate sheets.

Chanleigh walked to her bedside and took her tiny hands in his. The way he looked at her made her feel like an insect speared on a stick, the way she had seen pauper boys treat helpless creatures.

'I will sit with you for a little while,' he said, doing just that, his thighs pressed against her with only the coverlets between them.

Chanleigh felt wildly excited now, barely able to control himself. He wanted to tear aside the sheets and her nightrobe to see the slender, pale limbs beneath, to kiss her everywhere, to run his hands across her breasts and thighs .... A moan escaped from his lips.

Meggie, who was struggling not to vomit on the bed, heard the groan but did not realize what it meant. If only he would go!

'Are you not the prettiest little girl I have ever seen?' Chanleigh murmured. 'How shiny is your hair now that it is clean, and how beautiful are your eyes.'

As Meggie did not reply, he went on, 'You are a very fortunate little girl being invited to my house, you know. If I had left you out in the cold streets, you would have starved to death. You owe your life to me, do you realize that? You should be very grateful to me, my dear.'

'But I am, sir,' Meggie replied hoarsely.

'So you are going to show your gratitude?'

'If I can, sir.'

Chanleigh leaned forward, his body blocking out her view, hands outstretched to grasp her in an embrace.

It was at that moment that Meggie knew she was going to vomit. Clamping a hand across her mouth, she looked up at Chanleigh pleadingly, her chest convulsed.

Chanleigh, who had been imagining untold sexual delights, leapt to his feet in horror. The child really was ill! She had a fever – see how flushed her cheeks were – and she was going to vomit all over his fine clothes! He saw again in his mind's eye little Rosetta's coughing up blood from the haemorrhage which had killed her. He should have been more careful, picking this slum-child out of the streets – his desperation had made him foolish. Yet she had looked so sturdy despite her slenderness. . . . What if

– what if she had typhus, or one of the other fatal slum fevers?

Blanching, he backed away, making for the door, fumbling in his pocket for the key. His fingers were clumsy and refused at first to respond. He was almost sobbing by the time he had found the key, fitted it into the lock, turned it, and shot outside into the safety of the corridor.

Meggie heard the door slamming behind him but paid scant notice. She was now being very sick indeed.

CHAPTER SIX

Outside, in comparative safety, Chanleigh bellowed for Aggie. She came as quickly as she was able, rolls of fat juddering, face crimson with the effort of carrying her great bulk. She had been so startled by his roaring tones that she still had her clay pipe in her mouth.

Glancing once at her master's ashen face and staring eyes, Aggie imagined all the worst things possible. The child had tried to kill him, the child was threatening to expose him in some way, the child was malformed....

'In – there – ' Chanleigh rasped. 'The – the typhus! The child has – the – typhus!' Then, having imparted this information, he made his way to his own quarters to strip off his clothes and plunge into a scalding bath laced with vinegar to protect himself from the dreaded disease.

Aggie was stunned. The child had looked so clean, neat and healthy when she had last seen her. Could the typhus happen so suddenly? She doubted it. Hesitating only momentarily, she entered Meggie's room, where she saw a greedy child, unused to rich food, being very sick on the counterpane.

'Help me, please!' Meggied begged.

Aggie responded immediately. 'Yer poor chick!' she said, whipping off the soiled bedding and the child's stained nightrobe, and placing a damp cloth on her forehead. When she had bathed her and moistened her lips with water, she dressed Meggie again, in a clean robe, and then smiled down at her.

'Too much good food, lovey,' she said cautioningly. 'Gotta eat careful 'til yer stomach's accustomed ter meat an' such like. Not had much more'n bread an' sops before, I'll wager?' Meggie nodded. 'Well, yer stomach ain't used ter richness, yer see. Gotta take it slow.'

Meggie nodded again, her eyes filled with mute gratitude. She had been terrified that she would be beaten for soiling the bed, but instead this huge, ugly woman had been as gentle as her own mother. Meggie felt much better now; in fact, lying back in the sweet-scented bed, she felt almost at home.

Aggie was experiencing the strangest sensations. This little girl was so touchingly grateful to her, so polite – unlike all the others who had come into the house – that it moved her. Unused to such feelings, she did not at first recognize them for what they were. Something was being woken inside her, something which she had not known she could feel, and it was ushering out the long-repressed maternal instinct along with a warmth few had ever evoked in her before.

As Aggie was about to go, leaving the child to sleep, Meggie whispered her apologies again.

'That's all right, dearie. Don't yer fret. Could have happened ter anyone. Go ter sleep now. Do yer good it will.'

Meggie gave her a grateful smile, then sighed and settled down to sleep.

Aggie went back to her room, a few doors away from Meggie. She had a small room, which she had chosen for herself. It was cosy and contained a massive bed heaped with down quilts, for she felt the cold at night. A table and stool stood in one corner, and there was a vast, shabby armchair into which she sank when her legs ached and where she would smoke her pipe and stare out of the window at nothing. An embroidered footstool which she had filched from one of the main sitting-rooms was near the armchair, awaiting her huge, booted feet.

Aggie heaved her bulk into the armchair, placed her

feet on the stool and lit her pipe. Soon she was shrouded by smoke so that, from behind, one might have been forgiven for imagining that the chair was on fire. Her thoughts rambled for some time, as they frequently did when she first sucked on her pipe and then they settled down into a more comfortable pattern. Meggie. Little pretty Meggie, like a daisy she was.

In her room, Meggie sank into blissful sleep – her first sleep ever in a proper bed. Her body seemed weightless; she felt as if she were floating away on swansdown.

On the far side of the house, Chanleigh huddled in his bed, cold and shivering, his skin stinging painfully from the acidic bath and the scrubbing he had given it. He had gargled with a foul-tasting medicine and had swallowed a strong purgative; he suspected that he had overdone the latter, for he was already beginning to feel its effects. Groaning as the first lancing pain struck him, he flung himself out of bed and raced to the water closet.

Meggie's reprieve came next morning. At dawn a messenger arrived, having galloped overnight across the country, to tell His Lordship that his uncle was dying and that he must make all haste to his bedside. His uncle had a last message for him and wished to see him before he died.

Chanleigh was out of the house by mid-morning, accompanied by a small cortège of servants, his face suitably grim, his spirits secretly high as he contemplated a sudden and welcome inheritance. He did not stop to say good-bye to Meggie or even to ask how she fared.

Days passed and still Chanleigh did not return. Uncle Bertrand had rallied, keeping his nephew and other relatives at his home, waiting for him to die. Chanleigh cursed beneath his breath as he paced up and down, thinking of the adorable child waiting for him at his home.

Aggie, left so long without her master's eagle eyes upon her, began drinking heavily; port, ale, beer, wine, sherry, anything which came to hand. Some days she barely stirred from the great armchair in her room, where she would slump, snoring and twitching, occasionally crying out loud during a violent dream. Her snores could be heard down the corridor. When she was in a stupor, Meggie could not rouse her, and during these times, the child grew exceedingly bored, thinking of her early life and seeing it in a far more agreeable light.

By the tenth day Meggie would have done anything to alleviate the boredom. She had searched through the trunks of clothes, had examined the jewels, had looked at the small books and the larger ones, had admired the ornaments and had stroked the cat – and she had eaten so much food that she was beginning to plump out already.

She dressed and undressed dozens of times in all the clothes, draping herself with jewels and scenting herself with perfume, rouging her cheeks and putting feathers in her hair, dancing up and down in satin or velvet slippers, waving a fan in front of her face and admiring herself in all the mirrors which the house possessed. Finally, she asked Aggie when the master would be back, but Aggie said she had no notion; he came and went as he pleased, she said, and it was not up to her to say when or how he would return.

If only Jenny were here, thought Meggie, how different everything would be. They would laugh and tease one another, make jokes and hug and reminisce, looking at each other with love-filled eyes.

Aggie, after another bout of heavy drinking, had fallen asleep again. Suddenly she made a loud grunting noise, then gasped and woke abruptly.

'Eh? Eh? What was that, what was that?' she spluttered.

Going to her side, Meggie knelt down by her chair. 'You were dreaming, Aggie; that's all, just dreaming.'

'Dreaming! Dreaming, was I? . . . Poor little girl. Yer a right pretty 'un, prettiest he's ever had. 'Tis a shame, a great shame. Shouldn't be allowed, it shouldn't.' She hiccoughed.

'What shouldn't be allowed, Aggie?' Meggie wanted to know.

Aggie gave a huge sigh which seemed to rumble down to her very depths. 'Little 'un, when he gets back, when the master gets back an' he wants ter play his little games with yer, don't fight him, will yer? Yer can get hurt, hurt real bad if yer fight him.'

Meggie's scalp prickled. 'Fight him? Why should I want to fight him?' she asked.

Aggie's cheeks darkened. She squirmed uncomfortably. 'Well, I didn't mean *fight*, did I? Not fight, no.'

'Well, what word do you mean then, Aggie?'

Aggie looked down at the little girl in her beautiful pink flowered dress, her face with its big amethyst eyes framed by glossy black curls. None of the other children had affected her like this, but there was something about this child, something that twisted her heart. She was beginning to realize that she did not want this little one to end up like all the others.

How to aid the little one was another matter. How could she help Meggie to escape without incurring her master's wrath? Dare she endanger her own position for the sake of this child whom she had not known existed a fortnight ago? Risk all that she had worked so hard for, all these years; risk her safety, her security and the roof over her head for a *child*?

Meggie waited in vain for an answer to her question.

Later that day a messenger arrived: Lord Chanleigh, his uncle having died, hoped to return within the week, although he could not as yet state the day of his arrival.

Aggie felt a leap of alarm. Within the week! Turning away from the messenger and biting her lips, Aggie felt a cold sweat breaking out on her wrinkled brow. What was the matter with her? Here she was, wanting to protect this little girl as if she were her own. That was it! She felt as if Meggie were her own daughter!

Although her memory was blurry from too much drink,

Aggie could not help thinking about the other young girls who had come into this household, all of them dead now. At the time, she had closed her eyes to it. In truth, she had not grown fond of any of the others. None of them had had the sweet charm of Meggie Blunt. They had been spoilt brats, petulant and sulky, who had demanded instead of asked, turning the whole household upsidedown with their tantrums. But Meggie was different – although it was obvious that she was strongminded and had spirit. Someone had taught her good manners. She had a genteel air about her, which Aggie found both touching and attractive; it involved her feelings in a way in which they had never been involved before, not even by her husband. This pretty, innocent girl must not become another one of Chanleigh's helpless victims. Aggie began to plan in earnest how Meggie was going to be saved.

CHAPTER SEVEN

Each of Lord Chanleigh's previous playthings had left the house, sooner or later, in a little, rough wooden coffin, hurried out the scullery door and through the stables at the darkest hour of night; Meggie would apparently leave the same way, but, unlike the others, she would leave alive. This Aggie decided over another glass of port. She would tell Lord Chanleigh upon his return that the child had indeed had typhus and that, despite all efforts to nurse her through, she had finally succumbed to the dreaded disease and had been smuggled out of the house and buried late one night in the same way as all the others. . . .

But it would be a box of stones that old Andrew, the gardener, and she would carry out to Josh Brownlee's cart to be driven off and buried in some remote piece of waste ground where no one, neither Peeler nor parent, would ever find it.

Aggie knew that she had to act quickly. She shuddered

at the thought of the child she had begun to love becoming another victim of Chanleigh's lusts or of one of his demented furies. She marvelled now at how she had been an accomplice to the foul crimes he committed and yet had never before looked inside herself, never once felt a twinge of conscience about the poor creatures – not until this moment. She had begun to glow at the thought of saving this child; it must be done now – at once, before the master returned.

Meggie was startled when Aggie came towards her, weeping noisily, putting her arms round her and hugging her tightly, mumbling beneath her breath as if she were intoning a prayer.

'What's wrong? What's wrong? Please tell me. You're frightening me, Aggie,' Meggie cried.

Nameless fears rushed upon the child, pushing out the comfort and warmth which Aggie's presence usually gave her. Memories of coldness and pain gathered in her mind until she shivered. There seemed to be an icy draught in the room, sweeping past her legs, buoying her up with merciless force. She didn't want anything to go wrong now; she didn't want this life to change, not until she could go back to her mother with money to help her. She didn't want this cosy, comforting cocoon to be shattered.

Aggie was now shuffling about the room, her vast arms looped round her waist. Meggie stared at her in mystification, wondering what had taken hold of her. Suddenly Aggie stopped shuffling; she heaved her great bulk into her armchair and pulled the child onto her knee.

'Meggie, dearie,' she said, her voice hoarse, 'there's something I gots ter tell yer. An' yer gots to listen good. Ternight we're going away from here. It's got ter end fer yer. I don't know how ter tell yer. I'm not a good one at words, but I gots me feelings.' She banged one clenched fist against her bosom. 'I wish yer could stay here ferever an' be me little girl, but there's things here what yer don't understand, dearie, terrible things. I knows, I seen 'em, and I – I don't want yer to suffer 'em. This household ain't what yer thinks, an' Chanleigh, well, he ain't what yer thinks either. Yer thinks he's kind an' wants ter look after yer, an' in his twisted way I suppose he does want ter, but it'll change, love. I seen it all before. Yer'll be safe if yer listens ter me.'

Meggie stared at her, mouth hanging open, the coldness creeping up her until she was enclosed in ice. She tried to speak but her tongue was frozen. Aggie did not notice. She was rambling on, and now that she had begun talking, it seemed impossible to stop her.

'Yer'll be safe, lovey, where I'll take yer. I'll get yer away from here before anything dreadful happens ter yer, like it has fer the others. I's some money fer yer, enough ter feed yer until yer finds a place to rest. Go back to yer ma an' show her yer gots some money. She'll welcome yer with open arms if she be like most of the mothers I knows.'

Finally Meggie found her tongue. 'Go back home! Go away and not see you any more? But why? *Why?*'

Aggie clenched her jaw. "Cause I say. Yer gots ter go an' that's that. Yer *gots* ter go. Yer stays here an' all sorts of terrible things'll happen ter yer an' yer leaves here in a way yer wasn't imagining.'

'I don't understand!' Meggie whimpered.

'Yer not meant ter understand!'

Aggie's cheeks and nose were scarlet, the bristles on her chin seeming to stick out like a beard, but there was love in her eyes as she looked down at the little girl, trying to sound as stern as she could, and failing. Instead she sounded harsh in a way Meggie knew she could never be, not to her anyway. Was Aggie trying to deceive her?

But if Meggie thought at first that Aggie was not speaking the truth about her going, she was soon to learn that the old woman meant what she said. Displaying a new briskness, Aggie bustled about, adding one or two oddments to the parcel of food she was making. Every time Meggie tried to speak, she was treated to a barrage of angry words.

'Yer gots ter go an' that's that. Best thing,' Aggie kept repeating. Then, pausing in her mindless activity – for that was what it was, she was doing it to keep from breaking down – she looked at the white-faced child in her lace and frills, the unsuitable satin slippers and immaculate white stockings. An outfit like that would do her no good out in the back alleys she was going to! Somewhere there was a brown worsted dress and a pair of shabby old shoes which a servant-girl had left behind years ago. Where were they now? At last she remembered they were in the old trunk in the kitchens. She instructed Meggie to stay where she was while she went to fetch them.

In the kitchen, Aggie received only scowls and grunts as she waddled past the cook and her assistants. Without saying a word, she flung open the lid of the trunk and rummaged inside until she found what she sought. She also kept her own old cloak and shoes in there, so no one was surprised at what she was doing. Draping her cloak over the smaller clothes, she waddled out of the kitchens and back upstairs to Meggie.

The child was sitting on the edge of the huge armchair, looking like a tiny doll. Tears fought to escape Aggie's eyes as she ordered the girl to undress and then helped her into the worsted gown, which was sizes too large for her, as were the shoes. String – they needed string! She found some and tied it round Meggie's insteps so that the shoes would not fall off her feet. More string went round the waist of the voluminous dress. Then, picking up the packages of food in one hand, Aggie took Meggie by the arm with the other.

'Sssh, now, no one must hear us or there'll be ructions. Follow me, lovey, down the backstairs an' out through the stables. I knows a secret way.'

Ashen, Meggie obeyed, her legs moving like those of a puppet. Along shadowy corridors and down narrow backstairs they went, then through a heavy studded door and into a room which smelled strongly of animals. The rooms became larger, lighter, and more malodorous as they neared the stables.

Aggie gripped her hand more tightly. 'Not a sound!' she hissed. 'Tiptoe like the devil might hear yer!'

Nodding, Meggie crept along until they came out onto

a stretch of waste ground. It was almost dark now, and no one saw them. The waste ground stretched for quite a distance, then a copse appeared, and then clumps of trees to conceal their passage.

Aggie was breathing very loudly now, her face puce, her eyes bulging. She hadn't walked so far in years and she knew she was going to be very stiff the next day. Not only stiff. She glanced down at the silent, obedient child, imagining the rest of her life without Meggie. It would be a punishment; yes, a punishment for all her crimes, God help her.

'Nearly there now,' Aggie puffed.

'Nearly where?' Meggie's voice was toneless. The ill-fitting shoes had rubbed her heels and blisters were beginning to form. She did not feel the pain in her feet, only the void inside.

'Hangman's Common, lovey. That's where I has ter leave yer. Aggie's not good at walking far. But yer has the food an' the money ter take back ter yer ma. Go straight home, lovey, never mind what's happened ter yer. An' don't yer nivver come back here. Promise?'

Meggie promised, asking no more questions, her spirit crushed.

Finally, Aggie stopped, gasping for breath, and pushed the food into Meggie's hand. 'There's plenty in there ter give yer a real good feed; yer ma, too. An' enough money ter keep yer going months, if yer careful. Now, lovey – '

Aggie fell silent, drinking in her last sight of the adored child. She had forgotten about the white satin ribbon in the glossy ringlets; untying it, she tucked it in her apron pocket. How could she be so cruel as to send the child away like this? For a moment, she considered taking her back, but only for a moment.

Swallowing, Aggie said, 'Home, get home, an' quick. See yer ma an' give her the loot. She'll be right glad ter see yer. It won't be as bad as yer thinks. Now be a good girl and get off wiv yer. An' – an' don't ferget I – ' her voice broke – 'I loves yer!'

At that, Aggie turned on her heel and set off walking

as quickly as she was able, not looking back, tears streaming down her cheeks and into the bristles on her chin. The child *did* have the typhus, she would tell the master just as soon as he entered the house; she could imagine how he would pale and back away. Then, with luck, he would head off to his club in the city while his house was being scrubbed and fumigated. But before that, Aggie would fill the wooden coffin with stones and get the men to help her carry it out and bury it, so she could prove she had told the truth.

By the time Aggie returned to the house, she had stopped crying and was able to tell the servants that the child had typhus and they must stay away from her room. Once she put her plan into action, she'd have something to grip onto, something to keep her from breaking down. . . .

After seeing the servants, Aggie went up to Meggie's room and placed the white satin ribbon on the pillow beside one of the child's favourite dolls. Then she sat on the edge of the bed and started to talk to the doll, just as if Meggie were there. Now and again, she'd laugh, almost wildly, while the splitting pain in her head doubled and pulsed and her feet throbbed from the unaccustomed exercise all the walking across waste ground had forced on them.

CHAPTER EIGHT

Meggie had stood on Hangman's Common watching Aggie waddle away, her vast, pneumatic figure growing smaller and smaller in the distance. It was like part of herself vanishing forever: a part of herself which she had not even known existed. It was her mother, too, who was walking away, and the grief of her earlier parting from Jenny was revived, making the parting from Aggie doubly painful.

I am alone, all alone. She's gone away for ever, Meggie

thought as she watched Aggie disappear. She didn't love me, she doesn't care about me, she never did. Her feeling of abandonment increased as Meggie slowly turned round, away from the direction in which she had been facing, Hangman's Common now behind her. There was nothing in the landscape to catch her eye or attract her. It was bare, plain and cold, and she felt pain and cold, too. She must be ugly and pathetic, repulsive even, to have been deserted by Aggie, who had professed to love her.

So Meggie's youthful thoughts went, for she was unable to put into words what had happened and how she felt about it. There are no words for such pain. She wanted to scream out loud, to make her throat raw, but all her life she had been forced to be quiet, to repress her feelings out of fear of a beating from her father. Old habits die hard; besides, at this moment she had not the courage nor the confidence to make such an arrogant gesture.

Then something inside Meggie stirred: the voice of instinct telling her to move or she would freeze to death. She realized that she must have stood there for a long time, for it was dark now. She moved one foot woodenly, the chink of coins reminding her of the money that Aggie had given her; money, the most sought-after possession: surely money brought happiness? Her mind registered that distant memory and then expelled it, confused, for in her short life she had once held two gold sovereigns in her hand and neither of them had brought her any happiness at all. Now here she was with a bag of food and the coins that Aggie had given her, yet she had never felt more desperately miserable in her life.

Mam, she wanted her mam, and that thought was to be Meggie's saviour. She wasn't really alone; she had her mother, hadn't she? That was why Aggie had brought her here.

Meggie began to stumble forwards on wooden feet, stiff and cold, shivering. In the distance there was a glow of light: London. She had a considerable way to walk before she could get to her mother, and now that it was night there were other things to think of, like thieves and footpads and all the horrors which fell upon people foolish enough to be out after dark. Hadn't Jenny always warned her about them and said to stay indoors where it was safe? Tears fell from Meggie's eyes as she remembered this. She thought of the last three months of her life, during which she had been out night after night in the terrifying London darkness, at the mercy of anyone who wished to prey on her. She stumbled on for some time, barely seeing where she was walking but heading toward the glow in the sky. Torches, gas lamps – she could not recall what caused the lights but there were lights, and where they were was London, and this made her happy in a strange, poignant way.

Meggie's legs were beginning to ache painfully as life flowed back into them. Thankfully she sank down onto a boulder where she fumbled with the corners of the napkin Aggie had given her. Inside, the food, slung together hastily, was somewhat crushed and battered. More tears rolled down Meggie's cheeks as she plunged her fingers into it and greedily devoured handfuls. She ate for some time but failed to feel satisfied. Putting the napkin of food down, she stood up to stamp her feet on the ground and rub her hands together. She seemed to have lost all sensation: she couldn't feel the food in her stomach nor the blood in her veins. She did not seem to be really there. Meggie was frightened now. It was so dark, and she was so alone; she wanted to feel warm again, full of food, and be snug and cosy in her mother's arms.

Whether occasioned by the food or the burst of activity she didn't know, but suddenly memory came back piercingly. Jenny, her lovely mam, sitting with her, laughing with her, putting her arms round her. Talking about when she was a child in Bangor: about Nain and Taid, her grandmother and grandfather; about Chapel days when all the village would dress up to go to church, and then afterwards the jolly chattering and feasting, eating *Bara Brith* and Welsh cakes and drinking hot, strong, sweet tea. Such blissful thoughts of togetherness, and quickly repressed. She knotted the napkin again, ensured that the bundle of coins was safely hidden underneath the food and then continued on her way.

As she headed towards the lights of London, there was a new feeling in her heart. Longing, yes, but she knew that soon she would be with her mother, that things would be all right once she was back with Jenny. It was as near to happiness as she was going to feel.

Meggie seemed to have been walking for hours and knew she was going to have to rest soon. The wind had got up and was howling through the thin, scraggy trees and the shrubs at the edge of the common. There seemed to be a copse ahead; she could vaguely distinguish the trees' black shapes against the sky. She wished there was a moon out, but it was one of those black nights when everything seems dead, even the heavens. She found a stretch of dry bracken and, hearing it crackle as she lay down on it, curled up into a tight ball, clutching the napkin holding her food and money against her chest. Pulling her knees up under her chin she tugged down the vast worsted skirt of the too-big dress and closed her eyes. For a time, her body shivered violently as it adjusted to the cold, but she was soon asleep, utterly exhausted, her desire for oblivion obliterating everything else.

When Meggie woke it was past dawn. The copse appeared to be cultivated: it must be somebody's parkland, or perhaps part of a garden. She did not want to come into contact with any fine gentleman or anyone else who guarded their gardens and estates carrying guns to keep away trespassers. She knew she could not cope with any more difficulties at this moment, for she had reached the end of her strength. But Meggie's yearning to be back with her mother was acute enough to carry her over the ground, past the trees, through copse, parkland and grassland, round waste ground, across the stream where, parched, she bent down to drink; across a small moor, through the first mists of a fine veiling of snow and onwards to the edge of the city. The journey would have taken but a short time in a coach, or even on a farmer's cart, but on foot it had taken several hours. Again, it was growing dark.

Meggie's first scent of London was the river, putrid and decaying, but it meant home to her and her spirits rose. She felt excited now, despite the cold and her exhaustion. 'Mam,' she whispered under her breath, 'oh, mam, I'll be with you soon!'

Suddenly a twirl of thick fluffy snow hurled itself against her, completely drowning her vision. She kept to the track, occasionally glancing upwards, following the lights of the houses to the right. She stumbled over something in the dark and, glancing down, saw a dead cat or a little dog, frozen to death. Shuddering, she pressed on; through the alleys, barely noticing St Thomas's Wharf as she passed it; past the place where the tosher had given her the sovereign to fetch help for him; through the streets where the match-girls had stopped to buy their breakfast; past Bella's Brothel – she saw nothing but, in her mind's eye, her mother's face.

Absorbed in her thoughts, Meggie did not hear the clump of boots or realize what was happening until two large hands gripped her by the shoulders and a great red face pushed into hers. She froze like a terrified animal while a man tried to kiss her, slobbering over her, trying to pry her arms open. She didn't know whether he wanted to steal her bundle or whether he wanted something else, but whatever it was, she was not going to let him have it; she struggled and fought like a wild creature. Nothing was going to keep her from getting back home again with this money for Jenny.

At first the man was startled by her reaction, for he had not met with resistance like this before. He thought she was a dollymop or one of those street urchins who sold their bodies.

'Hey, hey!' he growled. 'I got money. Look, I got money. Don't fight, kid. I got money – look.'

Fumbling in his pocket to draw out some coins to prove his point, the man relaxed his grip, and in that moment

Meggie snatched up her skirts and ran like the wind down the passage. Growling and cursing, the man crashed after her, stumbling, half-falling, then picking himself up to continue his noisy pursuit. His curses made her flinch as she ran, but she need not have worried for he was drunk and within a few minutes would collapse, overcome by exhaustion.

Meggie stopped running the minute the noise of his pursuit ceased. She had no wish to arrive home gasping for breath and in a state of collapse herself. That might frighten her mother.

The big, flapping shoes that Aggie had given her were working themselves loose. One of the strings had burst during her flight; Meggie paused now to remove it and to throw the old shoes away. Now she was barefoot again, as she had been when she left home. Somehow it seemed only right that she should return barefoot.

The sagging, voluminous dress annoyed her, so Meggie hitched it up, tucking in the folds. She looked plumper – and indeed she was in this dress – heavier than when she had left home. Weeks of eating good food and doing little but wandering round Chanleigh's house with Aggie had put flesh on her bones. Even her slender legs had some shape now. Her cheeks had filled out, her eyes sparkled even more than before and her hair had a new, lustrous gloss. Her nails had grown – they had never been long before; now they curved, white semi-circles beyond the tips of her fingers, and they were clean.

Mam, Mam – the word went through her head repeatedly as she approached the street where her home was. Would her mam be getting a meal together or sitting on the old jumble of rags in the corner? Would she be sewing a hat for a customer? Would she have her face turned towards the door or away from it?

Meggie pondered these things as her front door came into view, and then, as she stood some two or three feet away, she was gripped by such an attack of nerves that she felt ill. Home meant safety, didn't it? She was very young and had forgotten many things that were too terrible to remember. Ups and downs confuse a child, and Meggie felt confused now. All she had thought of for so long was her mother, and yet now that she was returning to her she had a premonition of tragedy. She should not be here: it was dangerous. Because she could not understand this feeling, she pushed it away, like other feelings which had confused her.

Why was she standing outside in the cold when she could be inside, in Jenny's arms? Smiling to herself, Meggie approached the door. She turned the old, rickety handle slowly and pushed open the door.

Not even one candle was lit. For a moment she thought the room was empty, and her heart sank. But then she heard the sound of breathing and a faint sigh echoing eerily.

'Mam?' she whispered. 'Mam?'

Her reply was a stifled gasp from across the room.

The hairs on Meggie's scalp prickled; coldness gripped her. When her eyes had grown accustomed to the gloom, she could see the shape of a body on the bed.

'Mam?' she whispered again.

'Meggie – ' The faint, ghostly voice came again as a hand rose from the bundle of rags on the bed: a thin, white hand, little more than five spikes of bone.

Meggie knew now, without a doubt, that it was her mother, and she wasn't afraid any more. She crossed the room in two bounds, desperate to hug and kiss Jenny, wanting to see her face. She fumbled for the box of matches on the shelf, and the candle stubs kept beside them, but her hands were shaking so much that she had to strike several matches before she could finally light a candle.

Looking down at her mother Meggie nearly dropped the candle amongst the rags. She could not believe this was Jenny, so frighteningly thin, her cheeks sunken, her eyes two black holes, and her hair – it looked as if chunks had fallen out; only a few colourless wisps remained.

'*Mam!*' Meggie cried. 'What's happened to you! Has

he done this to you? Has he? I'll kill him! I will, I'll kill him!'

Jenny sobbed, 'No, *cariad*, no one did this to me. I'm ill – I'm – I'm dying.'

'*Dying?* No, no, you can't be dying! You're wrong, you *must* be wrong,' Meggie wailed, tears pouring down her face. 'I've come back to make you well, Mam. Look, I've got food here, lots of food to make you strong again – everything you could want to eat – and money, yes, money – Look!'

Tearing open the napkin with shaking hands, Meggie held out the money and a handful of crumbed cake to show Jenny.

Tears rolled out of Jenny's eyes, trickling down the sides of her face. She had waited for what seemed like years, desperate to see her daughter again, and now here she was – but too late, too late. Lying here alone on her bed of rags, deserted by Jack Blunt who had left as soon as he knew Meggie had escaped, she had slowly been starving to death. How she had prayed; at first she had raged at God, but later she had been penitent, longing for her little girl whom she believed she would never see again. Sometimes her longing had been so acute that she had seemed to float out of the hovel, away from the sordid, filthy bed and up into the sky, into paradise or whatever was there. Then, after all too short a time, she would return, becoming aware again of her surroundings and of the gnawing hunger inside her.

Before Blunt had left furious at being made to look a fool in front of his cronies, he had vented his rage on Jenny. She had been cruelly beaten, kicked, punched in the face, and then flung bodily across the room. Afterwards Blunt had stormed out, slamming the door behind him. She had not seen him since, and for that she thanked God.

The shock of having to send her daughter away and the brutality of the beating had hastened Jenny's end. Something had happened in her chest: she had felt bones crack when Jack punched her, and within an hour she had begun to spit blood almost continuously. She had crawled to her bed and slept, then woke only to fall asleep again. She was so ill that she did not even dread Jack's return but drifted into feverishness, losing touch with reality. At times she had thought that Meggie had come back home – or that she had never gone. She had even spoken to the little girl and held out her arms to her. Meggie had replied and hugged her, but, every time, she turned her face away, as if rejecting Jenny. Then Jenny would try to speak again, saying, 'Why do you look away from me, *cariad*? What have I done to hurt you? You *know* I love you.' But the little girl's back had remained turned towards her, and Jenny had begun to sob heart-brokenly, thinking that she had truly offended her daughter, that the child no longer loved her.

Jenny's fever had seemed to pass after a few days, but it left her very weak and with almost constant pain in her chest. She longed for someone to come and visit her – Old Katie perhaps – but no one came, and she wondered what had happened to them all. No sounds reached her in the hovel; it was as if Rats' Castle had faded away, and all its people with it. She did not know that Old Katie had fallen one night in a drunken stupor and had hit her head on somebody's doorstep, only to die later as a result. She could only think, lying there helplessly in her bed, growing weaker and thinner by the hour, that she had been deserted by everyone – even by the child she adored and the friend who had rallied round to her in the past.

Jenny could not remember when she had last eaten. There had been a little water left in the cracked jug by the bed and she had drunk that, trying to make it last. It was stagnant and had made her gag. After being a few days without food, she stopped feeling hungry and experienced a strange, drifting sensation, as if she were floating away from her body. Sometimes this became so acute that she seemed to be way above herself, looking down at the tangled, filthy rags on the bed and the body of an emaciated, deathly-white woman with black and hollow eyes. A dying woman, she now knew, one for whom there was no hope.

When Meggie had burst through the door, Jenny had thought it was another delusion, part of the fever, but shortly, due to the immediacy of her daughter's responses, she realized that this truly was her child come back to her. Once she had begun to cry she could not stop.

'Mam, Mam, don't cry!' Meggie pleaded, putting her arms round her mother, horrified at the feeling of fleshless bones where Jenny had once been soft and round. 'Mam, Mam, I've come home. I'm going to look after you! I'm not going to leave you again. Look, we've got money now, and food. *Lots* of money! A kind old lady gave it to me; she gave it to me to bring to you, Mam. *Please* don't cry.'

'Money,' sobbed Jenny, 'what's money? It can't buy me health; it can't buy me life. Can't you see how ill I am, child? I've been like this for weeks. Blunt went away, soon as he knew you'd gone. I haven't seen anyone for days. I've just been lying here, getting weaker and weaker, too ill even to get to the door to call for help. But if I had, it would have been worse. People would have burst in here if they'd known I was too sick to fend them off. They'd have stolen what little we have. Oh, I've been so lonely without you, *cariad*!'

'Me, too, Mam,' Meggie whispered. 'Come now, Mam, sit up a little. I'll make a pillow for you, and you can sit up and have something to eat.'

But Jenny was too weak to move; even the effort of trying to push herself up on her elbows was too much for her. She burst into a coughing fit, and blood began to ooze out of her mouth in a continuous stream. Meggie, staring in horror, tried to quench her fear. She realized what the smell in the room was. It was the smell of death, of decay. Her mother was going to die!

Meggie was determined not to faint. Gritting her teeth, she resolved to help her mother in every way she could.

She had come back to look after Jenny, and that was what she was going to do.

'*Cariad*,' Jenny said, her voice a rasp, 'there's something I've got to tell you. There is something you must know before I die. It will make all the difference to how you feel, *cariad*. Yes, yes, it will, and I must tell you now.'

'Don't speak, Mam,' Meggie said. 'Don't speak – save your strength. Here, have some of this food.'

She held a piece of cake out for her mother, who could only manage to eat a few crumbs at a time for her teeth were loose and it was difficult to chew.

'No time for that,' Jenny gasped after a while. 'No time to eat. Listen, *cariad*, you *must* listen.'

There was such a fierce, burning intensity in Jenny's eyes that Meggie sank down on the bed beside her, holding her hands, and listened.

Jenny began. 'Jack Blunt, he isn't – well, he isn't what you think, *cariad*.'

She paused and swallowed, acutely distressed, for she was going to confess something that she had hidden even from herself for years, something terrible in the light of her strict Chapel upbringing.

'*Cariad*, Jack Blunt *isn't* your father. If you have ever wondered why he was so cruel to you, why he's treated you so badly, it's because *you aren't his child*. I met him a few months after you were born. I was destitute. I had nothing. I had lost my job – I had been thrown out of the house where I'd worked as a maid. As soon as they knew I was pregnant, they threw me out. I lived from hand to mouth for months until you were born. You – you were born in a meadow the other side of the river. I was alone – I remember weeping – I remember the pain. Somehow we survived, you and I. I really don't know how.'

Meggie, who had been listening, stunned, her mouth dropping open, barely able to believe what she was hearing, at last found her voice. 'Not my da?' she stammered. 'Jack Blunt's *not* my da, but how can that be?' Slowly, realization filled her eyes. 'If he's not my da, who is?'

Jenny closed her eyes, as if to reply would be too much

agony, but she knew that she had to speak because her time was short. She must tell this child the whole truth so that she would know, so that she could climb from the abyss where she was now living and reach up to the sky – the sky which was represented by her real father, the heir to the dukedom of Malgrave.

For years, Jenny had repressed all memory of her *affaire* for it had seemed a time of bewitchment. Roses, she would always remember those fat cabbage roses with the sweet verbena scent, late blossom on the trees and the chamomile lawn at her lover's home. When she had walked on the chamomile it had smelled like sweet new-mown hay.

She had loved him, the Duke's heir; she had been totally enchanted by him. He was a few years older than she, dark-haired, dark-eyed, straight and tall. His smile alone had captivated her, broad, open and honest as it was. His eyes had shone with sincerity. Those who had held the title before him had been soldiers, men renowned for their courage and indomitable tenacity in the face of every known offensive, but her lover, Michael, was different: he was known for his intelligence.

It was Jenny's purity that had attracted him; her fresh, innocent country face, glossy black hair and violet eyes. He had been intrigued by her, accustomed as he was to world-weary women whose social advancement was the foremost consideration in their lives. Jenny asked nothing of him but his love, and they had come together as if they had been created solely for that moment.

On the chamomile lawn, concealed by shrubs and bushes, amidst the scent of cabbage roses, they had made love, *been* love, swept away by their emotions. They had met only a few times, swearing to love one another devotedly until the end of time, as young lovers do, believing in what they said with all their hearts, never imagining that they could break their word. Then Michael had been sent away, to relatives on the Continent. When they had kissed good-bye, they had sworn to be faithful to one another. Jenny had had tears in her eyes, and so had Michael.

'I won't forget you,' he had said, kissing her face, her neck, her fingers. 'I'll never forget you. I've had some of my happiest hours with you, Jenny. When I get back – and I won't be long, just a few months, I promise – I'll marry you. There's no doubt of that. I don't care what Mama and Papa say, we *will* be married. You're going to be my wife, Jenny.' They had kissed again, rapturously. 'This visit to the Continent is a cursed nuisance, but it's expected – to finish off my education, you know. But I'll write to you every day, without fail.'

Jenny had wept silently, feeling that the end of her world had come, and Michael had cocooned her in his arms. Twice before he had warned her about the trip, that his mother's cousins were awaiting him, that they had planned many social events in his honour. She knew that these travels were the way in which young gentlemen finished off their schooling, and that her lover was looking forward to it, but she knew she would be desolate without him. At least he would write – and they would marry when he returned.

When Jenny had known she was pregnant she tried her best to conceal it, wanting to get word to Michael. He had given her his address and she had hidden it away in the little chest of drawers in her room, but when she searched for it she could not find it. She had looked everywhere, turning the room upside down, but the slip of paper with his address on it had gone. She knew then that someone had found out about their *affaire*, someone who did not want them to correspond. With a sinking heart she had fallen onto her bed and wept.

Soon, she had become so ill that she could not carry on her work. Getting up at six every morning was difficult for her. She began to be sick in the mornings; pale and weak, she tried to do her work but found it beyond her. When she was summoned to the drawing-room by her mistress, she had a premonition of disaster. Now, she would have to confess everything. She was bringing disgrace on Michael and his family. This was not what they had planned when they had been making sweet love on the chamomile lawn.

Adelaide, Duchess of Malgrave, had never looked more stern or more forbidding as she gestured to the young maid to be seated. The Duchess was a handsome woman, with forbidding black eyes, yellow skin and crisp black hair which she had long ceased to try and control. She wore a severely-cut cream lace gown, flounced and tiered, which heightened the sallowness of her skin; wearing it, she looked almost sickly. Her hands on the silver-topped cane, which she held in front of her knees, were like claws, heavily beringed, the rings so loose on her fingers that they had slipped to the side.

Jenny's eyes settled on the jewels, then rose slowly to the pitch-black pupils of her mistress's eyes. Her heart was thumping. There were beads of sweat on her brow and the palms of her hands. She was rigid with fear.

'Your degenerate behaviour has come to my notice,' spat the Duchess, her lip curling. 'Your disgusting, depraved and *immoral* behaviour has been brought to my notice. You were selected, young woman, for your respectable upbringing. I believed that I could trust you, but instead you have behaved appallingly beneath my roof. You have *seduced* my young boy! You have given me hours of anguish, which I shall never forget.' The Duchess paused, shuddering, her eyes closed for a few moments as if she were suffering intolerable pain.

Jenny's mouth had fallen open. She could not believe her ears. *She*, behaving immorally? *She*, seducing Michael? That was not how it had been at all! They were in love, so much in love! She realized that the Duchess had a totally wrong picture of their love, and that it was going to be difficult to change her mind. When she tried to protest, the Duchess told her that she was dismissed, that she had to leave within one hour or her family in Bangor would be contacted and told what had been happening – that their daughter had been behaving like a jade. Her name would be disgraced. She would never dare to go home again.

Jenny had tried to explain, had tried to say that she and Michael were in love, that they were going to marry as soon as Michael got back from the Continent, but the Duchess continued to hurl abuse and finally Jenny's nerve gave way. Feebly, she tried to explain about the coming baby but could not get the words out. Then, after stumbling to the door, she had turned at the last moment and managed to stammer that she was going to have a child, Michael's child – his heir.

The Duchess's eyes had seemed to bulge, and she made an odd choking noise in her throat. 'Expecting a *bastard*, are you? Well, what else can you expect if you behave like a dirty whore?'

Jenny had shaken so much that she had had to hang onto the door knob for support. Could she really be hearing her mistress speaking such words, and she always so respectable, so decent before this?

'It – the baby – is – *is* – Michael's. . . .' Jenny insisted.

'But how are we to *know* that?' the Duchess sneered. 'Could it not be *anybody's*?'

Jenny's fingers lost their strength; she relinquished her hold on the door knob. Fighting to stay upright, she stammered that Michael had been her only love – *was* her only love, and that he had vowed to marry her –

'Get out, you filthy little *whore*!' hissed the Duchess, her face suffused with crimson. 'Get out before I strangle you with my own hands for what you have done to my son!'

How she managed to get up the stairs to her tiny attic room Jenny never knew. Pain swirled in her mind; she felt as if she was going to vomit and her heart was pounding. She collapsed on her narrow bed, lying inert for more than an hour, unable to gather her thoughts together. She could not make any plans while she was in this shocked frame of mind, nor could she even try to find out how the Duchess had learned of her relationship with Michael. Perhaps one of the other maids had seen them together and the Duchess had waited until Michael was safely out of the way before dismissing her?

That vicious old harridan downstairs had twisted the story of their sweet loving and made it sound dirty. If only she had Michael's address – he was somewhere in France, she thought – she could write and tell him to come home for her. If only he were here, he would look after her.

Jenny had still been in a shocked frame of mind as she gathered together her few simple belongings, putting them into the old carpet bag in which she had brought them from North Wales. Her morning dress, her Sunday bonnet, a spare pair of shoes, her Bible and prayer book, letters sent by her family, some history books which Michael had given her. She had not wanted to appear too stupid beside him, although he had repeatedly told her that what he was interested in was her sweet nature, her gentle face. She had believed him. She had glanced about the room, not seeing the narrow hard bed or the little chest of drawers in one corner; her tears had clouded her vision as she slowly went down the stairs and out through the servants' entrance. She had reached the nadir of despair – she could say nothing, do nothing. The Duchess had known how to immobilize her, and immobilized she was and continued to be for months afterwards, stumbling around, sometimes weeping, sometimes staring ahead sightlessly. She could not even remember how she had managed during those days.

As Meggie listened with tears in her eyes, Jenny told her story of love and betrayal. When the story was finished, Meggie was experiencing a feeling which she had never had before. It grew stronger as she listened, as she looked at her mother and thought about who had brought her to this state. Jack Blunt, ignorant and brutal as he was, knew no better, and still did not, but this unknown duchess, this great lady who had employed her mother – ! If that woman had been nearby, Meggie would have gripped her by the neck and choked the life out of her for all the misery she had caused them.

As Jenny continued her story, saying how she had met Jack Blunt when Meggie was four months old, her daughter listened numbly. She had heard all she wanted to hear. She had found out the name of the people who had so mistreated her mother; who had thrown her out when she was expecting a child; who had not cared if she starved to death; who had accused her of being immoral. Later, another realization would come to her: she was the daughter of a duke's heir – she was the granddaughter of a duke!

'Jack Blunt met me when I was down, as low as anyone could get,' Jenny went on. 'I had given birth to you in a meadow. I can remember now the pain and the tears. I didn't expect you to live, but you did. You have a great capacity for life, *cariad*; don't ever lose that, *whatever* happens.

'He was charming enough, Jack Blunt, when I met him. He took pity on me. He gave me things I hadn't had for months: attention, warmth, affection. We married, but whatever I had expected did not happen, for life did not change on the surface, although we seemed to have more to eat and I did not have to worry about going out to find food for Jack did that. He had work for a time and that at least seemed good, taking one worry from me.

'He could be charming in his own way, even after we were wed. He had his good times, when we would talk, and he'd even play with you once in a while, though mostly he would complain about smelly, noisy babies, seeming to have no notion of what babies are really like. I used to tell him his own baby would be just the same, but he wouldn't listen to that. No, *cariad*, he didn't listen to anything except what he wanted to hear. His mind would not admit anything that didn't suit him,' Jenny sighed sadly.

Meggie was listening, stunned by this information. She had known something about her parents' early years together, for Jenny had never hidden any secrets from her

– or so she had thought until now – but the biggest secret of all had been kept from her: *Jack Blunt was not her father!*

Meggie thought she knew now why she had received such ill treatment at his hands, why he had cursed and kicked her and been so harsh with her all these years. He was a man who could not accept someone else's child; it was as simple as that. Had she been his daughter perhaps he might have been gentler with her – if he knew that gentleness was, but she doubted that. Other matters became clear as the knowledge filtered through her mind, many things seeming to straighten themselves out in her thoughts, but the worst thing that had happened to her when she had thought Jack Blunt was her father had by now done its damage. There was no way of reversing it; it had happened. Although she knew now that she was not his daughter, not a blood relative, her mind and her heart were still seared by the pain of his assault upon her fragile body. The suffering she had endured had changed her dramatically.

All these years Jenny had kept this secret from her for she was ashamed that she had borne a child out of wedlock. Meggie felt no anger towards her. Whatever her mother said or did, she would support her as she always had done.

Jenny was coughing feebly, seeming almost too frail to make the effort. A little colour stained her cheeks, then just as rapidly died away. Meggie clasped her mother's hands tightly, looking down into the much-loved face. She could almost see the white bones beneath the taut skin. Tears gushed from her eyes as if from a dam, as if it were raining in her mind and in her heart.

Jenny was deeply distressed, watching the child's grief yet unable to reassure her. She coughed once or twice, trying to swallow although her parched, aching throat was raw with pain. The pounding sensation in her lungs – the result of malnutrition and Jack's beating – was growing more insistent. Lately she had not even been conscious of hunger, so serious was her illness, but Meggie, having recovered a little, was talking of going to fetch her some milk as she could not manage to chew more than a few crumbs of cake.

At once, Jenny gripped Meggie's hand and pleaded with her not to go.

'Please, *cariad*, don't go! Stay here with me. Don't leave me. I feel so strange. I seem to be floating away from here – I – I can't understand it. I feel so light, as if my body has no weight.'

Meggie bit on her lower lip, trying to stifle a cry. She knew what was going to happen. A sensation of loss was stealing over her, a feeling long familiar to her and yet it was deeper now, colder, more terrible than any she had felt before. She held her mother tightly, cradling the bony body to hers, kissing the hollow, chilled cheeks, shocked at how cold Jenny felt. She remained fixed in that position, cradling her mother, whispering words of love. As soon as Jenny was well, they would get away from this place, far away where Jack Blunt would never find them again. Then Meggie stopped speaking. The room seemed darker, the shadows menacing. Jenny was dead.

Meggie lay cradling her mother throughout the night. She was oblivious to everything except the iciness which had enshrouded her when Jenny had drawn her last breath. If there was a God, the God of Whom Jenny had spoken, the God she had continued to believe in, despite everything, then He must be receiving Jenny's spirit at this very moment, welcoming her in His loving arms. The thought brought Meggie some small comfort.

The body in Meggie's arms grew colder and seemed to shrink. She could not look at the thin, shadowed face, the blue lips, the sunken eyes. This was not her mother any more, now that Jenny's spirit had departed.

It was dawn when Meggie gently removed herself from Jenny's arms, stifling a sob as she laid the thin, light arms gently across her mother's breast.

'I've got to leave you now, Mam,' she said, her voice

barely audible. 'I've got to go now. I can't stay here. This isn't my home, not when you're not here. Jack Blunt might come back, and then – well you know what would happen then, Mam. . . .' Her voice caught in her throat. 'I don't know what I'll do without you, Mam. I hope that where you've gone you'll be happy, happier than you were here.'

Tears rolled down her face unchecked as she backed slowly to the door. She was afraid of Jack Blunt's coming back and finding her, but she also wanted her mother to have a good burial. She had enough to pay for it, she was sure. There was plenty of money wrapped in the handkerchief. She would go to Old Katie and give the money to her, to see that Jenny was decently buried. She opened the door and looked out, for the last thing she wanted was to be caught by Jack Blunt. Then she headed for Old Katie's house.

As Meggie walked along, she thought about her stepfather. Blunt was not her real father, he never had been. He was her step-father, that cruel brute of a man, not of her blood at all. She need never fear that any of his brutality would come out in her. And that other terrible thing which had happened to her – the thing which came and went in her mind like a bad dream – perhaps that was not quite so bad now that she knew it was not her real father who had done it but her step-father.

Meggie knew something else now as well: Jack Blunt was not entirely to blame for the dreadful way her mother had lived these past years. Had that family, the Malgraves, looked after her decently, had she been allowed to marry their son or had they given her money to take care of herself, to find somewhere to live, Jenny would never have fallen into the clutches of someone like Jack Blunt. *The Duke and Duchess of Malgrave and their son Michael*: as her numbness and grief slowly lessened over the next few weeks, when she could think sanely again about her mother's death, that powerful, wealthy family who had everything yet who had mistreated her mother was to dominate Meggie's thoughts night and day. And the fact that she was their granddaughter.

When Meggie reached Old Katie's house she cautiously tapped at the door, then tapped again, and again. When no one answered, she tried the handle. Inside she saw a woman whom she did not know; her face was not unlike Old Katie's, but much younger. Her upper teeth were missing, and her hair was skewered on top of her head with what looked like a meat hook. Her dress was brown and ragged, and seemed to have been flung together from bits of sacking. She was smoking a clay pipe, and her broad, dirty feet were bare.

'Is – is Old Katie about?' Meggie asked.

'She be dead, ain't yer 'eard?' The woman sucked noisily on her pipe.

'*Dead?*' gasped Meggie. 'But what happened? How did she die?'

'Fell in a drunken stupor, she did. Knocked 'er 'ead on someone's doorstep. Stupid thing ter do but there y'are. Told 'er fer years I did that she'd be dyin' in 'er drink someday. Old 'ag.'

Meggie did not know what to do. The things she could have asked of Old Katie she could not ask of a stranger.

'Are you a friend of Old Katie's?' Meggie asked.

'I'm 'er sister. Didn' she nivver speak o' me?'

'No. I didn't know she had a sister. I knew about her other relatives, but she never spoke of a sister.'

The woman cackled. 'That's unnerstan'able. She 'ated me, she did. Nivver liked me at all, not since we was chil'ren. Still, I've got 'er stuff now. *I'm* livin' 'ere now.' The woman sounded triumphant.

Meggie glanced round the room. It was rank and bare, less comfortable than where her mother now lay. How could this woman rejoice at inheriting such a slum? Yet Old Katie herself had often said to her, 'One man's rubbish is another man's fortune.'

Meggie conveyed her sympathy, at which Katie's sister cackled again and spat a mouthful of tobacco-stained saliva onto the floor, and then took her leave, closing the door quietly behind her. She made her way down the side street into the dark shadows. Reaching a place where an old market stall had collapsed and been left to decay, she crouched under the shabby, rotted awning, placed her hands over her face and sobbed. One hour, perhaps two passed, and still she continued to weep until her throat was raw and her eyes swollen and gritty. There was no one she could trust now to give her mother a proper burial. Even as she had been going towards Old Katie's house, she realized the possibility that the old woman would spend the money given to her for the funeral on drink; even so, there would have been a fair chance that Jenny would be buried properly, with a name-plate over her grave, for Old Katie had been a good friend to her in her own way. Now there was not even that possibility, for Meggie herself did not know how to arrange her mother's burial.

Meggie continued to weep until she had no tears left, then she fell into an exhausted sleep. When she awoke it was daylight. She felt stiff and bruised, and ached from head to foot; her throat was raspingly dry, her eyes blistered from crying. Much of her grief had gone, but there was another feeling inside her breast now, and she marvelled at it. She had awakened with the name of Malgrave on her lips and a yearning for revenge in her heart.

CHAPTER NINE

It was an older, stronger Meggie, in more ways than one, who faced the coming day. Her eleventh birthday had even passed without her noticing it!

Meggie was not going to let her mother lie on that bed unburied. She walked through the Rookery, ignoring the aches and pains in her body, wondering what to do.

Across the street stood a shop where a man made signs. With purpose in her stride, she went up to him to ask how much a name-plate would cost, just a simple wooden name-plate for a grave. He answered her brusquely, and if he was puzzled at this ragged child's asking such a question he did not show it.

'Would you please carve on the plate the name Jenny Blunt, and then a date?'

With a feeling of rising panic she realized she could not remember the year her mother was born, nor could she remember how old she was, but if today's date were put on it surely that would be adequate?

'When will the sign be ready?'

'Come back this afternoon,' the man said. 'It will be ready then.'

Lest the man think she might trick him in some way, she paid him in advance. Her heart felt lighter after ordering the sign. Now she had to find somebody to bury her mother.

On the outskirts of the Rookery lay the paupers' graveyard. It was nothing more than a massive hole where bodies were flung without ceremony and then hastily covered over with a few shovel loads of soil. She knew that she would feel sick for the rest of her life if Jenny were flung in there, and she also knew that she was afraid of going back to get her mother's body in broad daylight. If Jack Blunt should come back – she shuddered at the thought. Finally, she selected a half-screened spot sheltered by trees a few yards from the paupers' grave. One of the trees she knew as a blossom tree, for she had seen it in summer. The thought that its pretty flowers would form a canopy over her mother's grave brought her a little comfort.

Meggie realized that she was going to be hard driven to make the grave, and she did not wish to be seen by anyone. Scrabbling at the earth with her hands, she found that it was soft and loose; nevertheless, she tore her nails and gave herself an aching back before she had dug little more than a foot into the ground. She needed something to help her dig. A few rotting old planks and some sharp sticks were piled up nearby. Picking up one of the sturdier sticks, she tried prodding the soil with it; the digging was a little easier going now, but it was still back-breaking work.

Snow began to fall. It was mid-day now, and Meggie realized that she would be here for hours, working at this speed. She needed help, not only to finish digging the grave. Jenny might have been thin when she died but her body would surely be heavy and difficult to get to this grave. Meggie would need a cart and a blanket to put over her mother's body, for the rags on her bed were not large enough to cover her. She would have to do it during the night, for if she were to be seen burying someone people would immediately think that a murder had occurred.

Finally, Meggie went in search of a spade, back to the street where the sign-writer had his store. At the ironmonger's she bought a spade, saying little to the man in the shop and behaving as courteously as she was able. Returning to the shallow grave, she began to dig again, working quickly; then she heard voices and saw a group of people approaching. They were coming towards the paupers' grave. Picking up the shovel, Meggie ran for the shelter of the trees, where she prayed that she would not be seen.

The group of officials remained, talking for what seemed like hours, discussing every aspect of the paupers' graveyard. They seemed to be unhappy about this method of mass burial and yet none presented any more reasonable suggestions. No one wanted to spend money on having paupers buried properly, although one man who seemed to be a churchman said in ringing tones that it was an abomination for people to be buried in unidentified graves without some sort of service.

Meggie listened to them, not understanding half of what they were saying and longing for them to go so that she could continue with her digging. She wanted the grave to be ready for her mother by nightfall. Silently, she cursed the men for blethering on through the afternoon without coming to some meaningful conclusions; not one of them seemed to agree with any other.

Suddenly Meggie remembered her mother's nameplate; it would be ready by now, for it was late afternoon. She hid the shovel under some rotting planks and then tiptoed away to the sign-writer's shop.

The sign was ready as promised. Meggie looked at it with pride, knowing that the letters on it spelt out her mother's name and, beneath it, today's date. Thanking the man, she tucked the sign beneath her arm and set out again for the graveyard.

By the time Meggie returned, it was dusk and the officials had gone. The place looked eerie in the half-light. Prickles coursed up and down her spine as she thought of all the corpses just a few feet away from her, concealed by merely a thin layer of soil. Quickly, without looking round, she began to dig. She toiled until her back was screaming with pain and she was ready to collapse. She paused only long enough to wipe her forehead with the back of her hand and then resumed working until she had dug a hole large enough to contain her mother's body. Only then did she allow herself to sink to the ground, half-weeping with weariness. When her strength had returned, she hid the shovel again and then walked back to her home.

As before Meggie moved cautiously, ducking into side passages when she heard voices, keeping an eagle eye open for anyone she knew, but most especially for Blunt himself. At the door she paused, reluctant to enter, even though she knew her dead mother was inside. It took all of her courage for her to enter the house. Inside, everything was as she had left it; her mother was still lying on the bed, whiter now, her hands still crossed on her breast. Her face looked peaceful. A little sigh escaped Meggie's lips as she looked down on her. She wished she could give Jenny a proper burial, with a service and mourners to pray over her body. Jenny would have liked that.

Reaching down, Meggie pulled her mother into a sitting position, curling her arms underneath her back and sides to feel how heavy she was, to find out if it would indeed be possible for her to carry her. As she had feared, the body was too heavy. She might make it to the door, perhaps a few feet beyond, but after that she knew that there would be an embarrassing half-dragging, half-staggering struggle to get her mother to the grave. People would see them and send word to Blunt if he was drinking at The Sun God. To avoid that risk, she took another. She thought of the man down the street whose son had a cart. The son went round shouting, 'Rags, I'll buy yer rags,' and in exchange for rags and tattered bits of cloth he would give broken biscuits or a screw of tea.

Meggie dashed off to the man's door. He had been ill for some years and never went out of the house. The son answered her knock as she had hoped, and she breathlessly put her case to him.

'I need to borrow your cart for an hour or two,' she explained, trying to look as calm as possible. 'I can pay,' she added.

The boy stared down at her, sucking on his decayed teeth and scratching his head with one filthy, black-nailed hand. Meggie saw lice crawling in his hair, just above each ear.

'Borry me cart, eh? What yer want ter borry me cart fer, eh?' he said, sounding exceedingly stupid, which perhaps he was.

'I just need to borrow it for an hour or two,' Meggie said. 'I shall be very careful with it, and I will have it back here later this evening, I can promise you that – and I can pay.'

She held out her hand, in which lay several coins, enough to gratify the boy.

'Tek it,' he shrugged. 'That be enough ter buy me a new 'un, if yer didn' come back.'

'Where is it?' Meggie asked, relief washing over her.

'Roun' back. Chained it is, can' trust no one. I'll come roun' with yer an' unlock it.'

The boy did as he promised, and shortly Meggie was on her way towards the graveyard with her mother concealed in the cart. She had not been able to find a decent blanket to cover the body and so had piled all the rags from her mother's bed and from other corners of the room on top of Jenny; to anyone who might see her, it would appear that Meggie was trundling a load of rags to some unknown destination.

For the rest of her life Meggie would remember the struggle to get her mother's body onto the cart. How cold Jenny had felt; how heavy her body had seemed to be. It had been an effort which had taken her longer than she had expected, and all the time she had felt like apologizing to Jenny. Tears had spilled out of her eyes, for this undignified treatment was the last thing she had wanted for her mother.

The graveyard was even eerier now that it was dark, and, thankfully, there was no one about. Steering the cart towards the freshly dug grave, Meggie lifted the rags off Jenny's body, and, as gently as she was able, lowered the body onto the soil at the side of the grave. Then, with tears rolling down her cheeks, she lowered her mother's legs into the grave, then her arms and head. Gently, she packed the rags on top of her.

'Forgive me, Mam, please forgive me,' she whispered through her tears as she shovelled the soil on top of the body. Meggie knew that neither Jack Blunt nor any of his cronies could read, so none of them would notice that the name on the freshly-dug grave said Jenny Blunt.

Kneeling beside the grave Meggie tried to say a prayer for her mother, but she was so weary and yet so relieved that her ordeal was over that her mind was a jumble of feelings which blocked out words. Finally she gave up, knowing that she must sleep before she collapsed on top of the grave. In the morning, perhaps, she would be able to think more clearly. Reluctantly, Meggie went behind the trees where she had hidden herself and the spade earlier and curled up, concealed by the piles of decaying wood planks, to sleep the sleep of total exhaustion.

Next morning Meggie found her mother's grave covered with fresh snow and knelt beside it to say her good-byes. She felt stronger than she had the previous day, more capable of dealing with any eventualities. After all, had she not experienced in her few short years more tragedies than those of many people who had lived to be four times her age? She knew but one prayer, half-remembered sentences which Jenny had taught her years ago; just simple words, but she felt a great deal happier after she had said them. At the end, she added something of her own devising: 'Please God, keep my mam safe and make her happy. I'm sorry it had to be this way.'

Then she stood up, biting her lips hard and brushing away her tears. Drawing the empty cart behind her, she walked away from the paupers' grave with no particular direction in mind, just wanting to get away as quickly as possible.

Spring came and went, and then it was high summer. By now Meggie had found somewhere to sleep at night and a place to hide her money. Although she was living from hand to mouth, she had no intention of spending any of the money Aggie had given her. She had concealed it at dead of night, and only she knew where the secret cache was, in a little copse in one of London's vast central parks. After hiding the money deep in the ground, she never returned to that spot. She would walk past it and sit by it on one of the park benches, but never would she by any gesture betray that hiding place. It was the money with which she had been going to save Jenny; herself, too. If she could not spend it for Jenny's sake then she would not spend it at all.

Thinking about the money seemed to give Meggie the strength she sorely needed. If she had considered herself alone before, that was nothing compared with the feelings which were gripping her now. Such bleakness had taken hold of her that she seemed not to be Meggie any more but merely a puppet. She spent her days wandering, hardly seeing anything, dropping into a deep sleep at night and sleeping sometimes until quite late in the morning now that the nights were warmer. No one noticed her; she was just one of the thousands of ragged children who roamed the streets of London.

The streets were always crammed with a multitude of people. There were many children both older and younger than she, and besides these there were some 80,000 prostitutes plying their trade. Sometimes, as she strolled through the park, she would see lords and ladies riding in their splendid coaches drawn by fine prancing horses, or ladies sitting side-saddle on their magnificent mounts – ladies who sat with their backs straight, in immaculate riding habits with hats perched jauntily on their glossy heads; their eyes wide, skins smooth and unblemished, their beautiful white hands, fragile as ferns, on the horses' reins. Meggie saw them all as she wandered about London that summer, but she was so benumbed with grief and loneliness that she had no energy left even to envy them.

As her mind slowly healed, with autumn drawing in, Meggie began to *feel* again. The first snows brought tears to her eyes, tears she had not shed for months, as she thought of the previous winter and of Jenny and of the snow on her mother's grave. She wept through the night, curled in the nest of bracken and rotting wood where she had been sleeping for some time now, at the edge of the park; then, at dawn, she looked out at the world feeling more like the Meggie she had once been. She knew that the worst of her mourning period was over, but she also realized that before winter came she had to stir herself; nights would be freezing cold from now on.

Meggie was approaching her twelfth birthday. She had grown to be a tall girl, despite the meagreness of her diet. Her hair was no longer glossy, as it had been when Aggie had shampooed it regularly; it hung lank and limp, with months of dirt congealed in it, and her face and hands were begrimed, her feet filthy after months of walking barefoot through the dusty streets. She knew from men's glances that she was attractive, and she knew from her contact with street beggars what possibilities might lie ahead for her if she did not want to starve to death this winter.

Although Meggie was a solitary figure by choice, she had made friends with a girl called Cathy. Cathy was already a professional prostitute, and only fourteen years old. She was a kind-hearted girl, in a rumbustious fashion. Since she had been on the streets from an early age, she considered herself worldly wise: she thought she knew everything and had done and seen everything in her lifetime. Cathy had taken Meggie under her wing, but that was as much intimacy as Meggie would allow: she put a barrier between her heart and other people. Meggie was fully aware of her lack of forthcomingness; consciously, she maintained that barrier for she had no intention of getting close to anybody again only to be hurt later – as she had been at the loss of her mother and Aggie.

Cathy had been put out on the streets by her brother when she was nine. She had come from a large family of fourteen children and the alternative to working the streets had been to starve. When the fourteenth baby had arrived, her mother had nodded to her brother, the signal to push Cathy out on her own. Her mother had never liked her. The other children she had birthed as easily as walking from one side of the room to the other, but Cathy had caused her a great deal of pain, which her mother would not forget – nor forgive.

Fortunately Cathy had an ebullient nature. She soon made friends with other young street girls and showed by her cheerful manner that she had no wish to steal their customers or to trespass on territory they considered to be their own. Her big heart had made her many friends, and no enemies of which she knew. She was probably the only person in London who could befriend Meggie.

It was Cathy who, gradually, during the autumn weeks, had prepared Meggie for what must come next if she wanted to survive the winter. She gave good, sound advice – as she saw it – but to Meggie it meant forgetting everything Jenny had ever told her about sinning, and taking on not only a new life but a new personality. She did not think she could ever bridge the gap between her mother's teachings and Cathy's sometimes ruthless common sense. She knew she had survived hunger before, and cold, but what she did not realize was that her appetite for food was greater than it had been a year ago : she seemed to be continually ravenous these days, however much food Cathy gave her or she pilfered from the barrows when no one was looking. And she had grown a lot in just a year : the voluminous dress which Aggie had given her was now far too small; her shoulders had burst out of the seams and the hem reached half-way down her legs instead of trailing on the floor as it had once done.

Meggie was quite adept at thieving now, but she stole only small things, which to her way of thinking meant that her self-respect was still intact. She did not want to do anything that would shame Jenny's memory. She could not bear to think of her mother's looking down at her, shocked and horrified at the way her daughter was sinking into a life of crime.

'Come on, Meggie, you've got to take it seriously, you've *got* to see the right in it,' said Cathy, exasperated. 'You don't really want to go on living like this, do you? Sleeping in the dirt an' half-starved most of the time. You could make a fortune, stash away a real lot of money, I reckon. You gotta pretty face. Look what *I* got out of my customers! You could do the same. Come on now, you can *see* I'm telling the truth, can't you?'

Meggie nodded, for Cathy dressed smartly, even if gaudily. Feathers bobbed on her wide-brimmed hat, and she had frilly underwear which she loved to display when she sat down, crossing one leg over the other in a most unladylike fashion to reveal her dainty ankles and the flounces of her petticoats. Sometimes she wore flashy jewellery which her men-friends had given her : large, glittering rings and brooches, ear-bobs, necklaces. One day one of her customers had given her a pretty fan, painted in blues and pinks, depicting fat cherubims and roses. Meggie had held the fan carefully in her hands, staring at it with delighted eyes.

'You could have one, too,' Cathy had said persuasively. 'All you gotta do is what I do. Come on, girl, you know what it's all about, *sure* you do; you been living from hand to mouth for a year now, eh?'

'My mother – ' Meggie began her story, at which Cathy scoffed.

'What good are mothers? What use are they to anybody, hard-faced bitches, all they ever thinks about is theirselves. You should have met my mother – oh, what a bitch she was! Fourteen kids – *fourteen* kids, can you believe that? An' she not thirty-eight.

'She never liked me . . . told my brother to kick me out she did, an' said, "Don't come here no more!" But I ain't regretted it. Look what I got now. . . . Look at all the good clothes an' money I got now. Fine, ain't it? I gotta bed to sleep on. I share it with another girl what's doing the same work. We're not complaining – why should we complain? Everything's fine, ain't it? Men won't pay to have worse conditions than they get at home, y'know.'

'But there are other men apart from men who work and who are poorly paid, aren't there?' Meggie said, raising her eyebrows.

'Yes,' said Cathy doubtfully, 'but except for the odd type of gentleman who prefers a low-class girl like us, how're we going to attract 'em?'

Meggie remembered walking past Bella's Brothel what seemed like a whole lifetime ago.

'But I've seen gentlemen being entertained by girls like you and me,' she said, although she did not tell Cathy that her own father was a gentleman. She did not feel this was the right moment, nor did she think the girls would believe her. They would call her a tale-teller and laugh. Who would believe that her grandparents were a duke and duchess? Sometimes, she could hardly believe it herself, and yet she knew that one day she was going to come face to face with that family and get her revenge on them.

Amy, Cathy's partner, put her hands on her hips and grinned. 'A finer class of gentleman, now that's a good thought, Meggie. Seems like you did the right thing bringing this young 'un into our room, Cathy. A finer class of gentleman – that would mean more money, you know; more gifts, more jewels, more fun an' a better time. Might get round to drinking champagne, we might, you never know – anything's possible, it seems, when we take our Meggie on!'

She poked Meggie in the ribs and grinned at her, her lettuce-green eyes twinkling.

Meggie looked closely at Amy, noticing the unusual pale green of her eyes and her bright carrot-red hair. She realized how horribly they clashed with the lurid orange dress which Amy was wearing. Perhaps she wore the bright orange to attract her customers, but all it did was detract from the unusual colour of her hair and the pretty colour of her eyes. Meggie thought back to her days with Aggie when she had had a choice of so many different colours and so many beautiful gowns – she knew instinctively that Amy would be a different person altogether if she wore clothes of more tasteful colour. In a white dress, she would look like a water nymph; in a pale green dress, which would bring out the colour of her eyes, she would be captivating.

Meggie thought about this, looking Amy up and down until Amy was forced to say, 'You're looking at me so close-like, lovey, what are you thinking?'

Meggie looked her in the face, almost boldly. 'I was thinking about the colour of your dress, Amy. That bright orange don't do nothing for your hair. I think your hair is a most unusual colour – it would catch a man's eye all by itself. You don't need to wear a bright orange dress or any other bright colour. What you need is cool, simple colours; quite ordinary colours, until they are put next to you with that bright-coloured hair and those lovely green eyes you got.'

Amy sat down on the bed. 'Huh, you've got a fine 'un here, Cathy. Wants to change us already an' she ain't been here a minute. From what you told me last night, you brought her here to change *her* an' here she is altering *us* afore she's in for a second.'

But Amy was quite good natured and was taking Meggie's suggestions in good spirit. She had no intention of being annoyed by the young waif's criticism.

Cathy, who was wearing a bright blue dress, looked at Meggie with new eyes. 'What do you think I ought to wear then, Meggie?' she said.

'I like that blue,' Meggie said, looking at her friend. 'Blue suits you very much.'

'That's nice to know,' Cathy said, grinning. 'Very nice to know. Thanks, Meggie.'

The girls looked at one another and then at their new friend. Whatever they had imagined would come about from this meeting, it was not this.

Meggie was looking round the room. 'I like your room,' she said. 'You're very lucky having a bed to sleep in, I haven't slept in a bed in my whole life.'

'Not ever?' Cathy asked. 'Sure, you must have had a bed at some time?'

'No, never, not as far as I can remember. My mam might have had one when I was little and I might have slept in it with her, but all we had in our home was just a pile of rags on the floor what we called a bed, and I just slept in a pile of rags in the corner.'

Meggie had chosen to say nothing to her friends about Chanleigh and Aggie; she did not think they had anything to do with what was going to happen in her future. She always spoke and behaved as if her interlude at Chanleighs' townhouse had never occurred.

'Try the bed then,' Amy said. 'You'll see it's right nice an' soft. Go on, try it.'

Meggie sat on the bed and then bounced up and down once or twice. Indeed it was the softest bed she had ever imagined; how she would love to sleep on it.

Cathy and Amy exchanged glances. They were seriously thinking about taking Meggie in with them, letting her share their bed or perhaps getting a little bed for her in the corner, but they had to remember their customers. One room was just not large enough to accommodate three girls. As it was, they had to take turns bringing their customers back. Each girl occupied the room for perhaps half an hour or more, depending on which customer she had with her, how much he could pay and how much she liked him. Sometimes, of course, their stays were even shorter than that, but usually they took time to build up a good relationship with a man, knowing that clients who grew fond of them would come back regularly.

Meggie seemed to have guessed their thoughts, for she said, 'I know you want me to join in with you, but where is there going to be room for me? There's only one bed here, and I guess you can only bring back one customer at a time, can't you?'

'That's right,' Cathy said. 'Actually we been thinking of putting a little bed in the corner for you to sleep in nights.'

Meggie's face lit up. 'For me? Oh, you are so kind! But,' she added hesitantly, 'what about the customers? I can't interfere with your work . . . that wouldn't be right.'

Amy put her hands on her hips. 'Oh, we'll sort something out, Meggie, that we'll do, don't you worry. Don't you fret yourself, we'll sort something out.'

During the weeks that followed, Meggie returned to Cathy and Amy's room virtually every day, to be taught the rudiments of their trade and to discover how they spoke and behaved with their customers. She also learned what to do should a customer turn nasty. But neither girl had spoken again about getting her a truckle bed nor had they invited her to share their room, so she continued sleeping out in the rough. After a time, she began to wonder if she would ever join them.

Amy and Cathy wanted Meggie to be with them; they liked her and realized that she had as much to offer them as they had to offer her, but they were continually trapped, whichever way they looked, by having just one room between them and not the means to get anything else. If Meggie proved as popular as they with their customers, and brought home fresh clients, they would be able to afford perhaps two rooms, or even, with luck, a little house. But that would take time, and meanwhile they could not spare the money needed for larger rooms. The problem seemed insurmountable to the girls, who were very kind-hearted but who had not been accustomed to solving anything but the simplest dilemmas.

What did happen was that, on an off-day, when Meggie went back to their room they brought out a hip-bath, an old battered relic, and sat Meggie in it. Then they proceeded to scrub her with soap and water, and shampooed her hair, rinsing it with herbs. Whilst Meggie was in the bath, Amy washed her one dress and pressed it with a flat iron, which did little to improve it but at least it was clean. Meggie still looked like a ragged urchin when she donned the clean dress, but she was a whiter, more sparkling urchin now. When damp, her hair curled into large glossy ringlets, which Amy envied because they were so manageable; Cathy loaned her a blue satin ribbon to tie up her curls.

It was after one of many such sessions, when she had been newly bathed and her hair was tied up with the satin ribbon, that Meggie noticed a man following her through the park. She glanced over her shoulder, somewhat nervously, as the creak of boots pursued her for some yards, but what she saw cheered her. This was no aged lecher with red face and stertorous breathing; he was a young fellow, not much older than Meggie herself, with a ruddy face and pale ginger hair. He even had a little ginger moustache, which must have taken him weeks to grow, and his eyes were a pale, almost watery blue. He wore a neat checked jacket and plain trousers and black shiny boots.

Meggie slowed her steps and then took a seat on one of the park benches. The young man, colour flushing his cheeks, sat down beside her. For a moment she pretended not to see him and stared out across the lake at the dipping and diving birds.

After a little while, the man coughed and then coughed again, at which Meggie slowly turned her head to look at him. Meggie felt rather sorry for him – he looked as if he had been pushed into this. She could imagine his older friends saying, 'Time you took your first dip, Charlie' – or whatever his name was – and poor Charlie feeling that he could never be calling himself a man until he had lain with one of the park girls. But Meggie was not a park girl – perhaps he did not know that? The park girls were, on the whole, a ragged and verminous lot, who would lie with any man, however foul and diseased.

The man coughed again, then said, his voice croaking, 'How do. Nice day, ain't it, fer the time o' year?'

Meggie nodded, marvelling at his healthy skin.

'I, I ain't seen you here before,' the man said, adjusting his collar, which seemed to be too tight for him, causing him a little discomfort.

'Haven't you?' Meggie said innocently. 'I'm often here. I walk through here at least once a day.'

'So do I,' said the young man eagerly. 'Then why haven't I seen you before? Surely I'd a noticed you, your hair's lovely.'

'Thank you,' Meggie said pertly.

The young man seemed unsure of what to do next, and Meggie was sure now that it was the first time he had ever approached a girl. She did not know what to say herself or what to do next under these circumstances, for all she had been taught by Cathy and Amy happened with men who came willingly to their room, or men whom they themselves had gone out to find. This man had found her.

Where was she to take him, if things should go *that way*? There were bushes and shrubs in plenty, and places where you could hide, but those were for the park women and Meggie did not want to behave like them. Her pride would not allow it, and yet what alternative did she have? If she made enough money, then she would be able to bear her share of Amy and Cathy's expenses and pull her lot with them; then she would feel happier and safer.

These thoughts flitted through her head as she smiled attentively at the young man. Finally he put his hand on hers and freely admitted that he did not know what to do next, that this was his first time with a girl.

Meggie wanted to say, 'And it's my first time, too,' but she knew that she would be misunderstood.

They stood up, hand in hand, and walked round the perimeter of the lake, watching the water birds. The willow fronds which had looked like lush green hair now looked like fingers dipping into the water's glassy depths. Beneath the willow's shade, the air was cool and damp, and there was a feel of winter in the air despite the late afternoon sun. It was this feel of winter which reminded Meggie of what was to come if she did not find a decent place to sleep, and it was this as much as anything which made her grip the young man's hand tightly and proceed to lead him round the corner to a more secluded place where they would be screened by shrubs and trees.

As they lay down on the patch of grass, the young man's cheeks flushed bright pink. He loosened his collar and tie, swallowing repeatedly as if something were lodged in his throat. Meggie lay back, looking up at him and wondering who would make the next move. It seemed that they moved together, for her arms went up as his lips came down and his body covered hers. As he kissed her face, her neck, her lips, his mouth felt smooth and cool, and his tongue darted in between her teeth, the sensation causing a flush of heat to score through her body. He held her tightly but did not hurt her, and when his knee fell across her legs, she pushed herself against him responsively, sighing.

'You're a lovely girl,' the young man said. 'Real lovely. I ain't seen anyone else in the park as pretty as you.'

His breath came more heavily; in fact, he seemed to be having trouble with it. Meggie could hear it rasping in his throat as his chest rose and fell rapidly. He moved his hand inside her dress to touch her little breasts, sliding his hands over her nipples and back again as heat continued to soar through her body in great blankets of warmth. Then he touched her leg, her thighs, inching his hand upwards until it touched the most secret part of her, causing her body to quiver unrestrainedly. As another sigh escaped her mouth, he crushed it into silence with his lips, and Meggie felt the most intense sensation she had ever experienced. It seemed to take her breath away. Almost as suddenly as it had begun, it ended, subsiding until she was left with nothing.

Meggie was alarmed at first, not understanding, but by now her young man was so carried away that nothing could stop him. Within a few brief spasmodic seconds he was finished with her. Then he lay back, gasping, while Meggie stared up at the sky, feeling empty, abandoned, wondering what had happened to that build-up of sensation which had seemed so promising, so exciting.

The young man knelt beside her, quickly adjusting his clothing, licking his lips nervously. He seemed about to apologize and then realized how foolish he would sound apologizing to the likes of her; instead, he reached into his pocket, grabbed the first coins which came to hand and flung them down beside her. Then, scarlet, and still breathing heavily, he ran off hastily, as if he had committed a crime.

Tears filled Meggie's eyes as she lay limp and dejected on the grass. She did not even look at the money. What had gone wrong? Why had she been abandoned like this? Had it been the change in her emotions which had embarrassed the young man and scared him off, or would he have behaved like that anyway? Now she would never know.

When her tears subsided Meggie straightened her dress and gathered up the coins. From what Cathy and Amy had told her she had received three times as much as she ought. Perhaps the young man was not so ignorant and this was not his first time? It was very good payment indeed if he had thought her a park girl.

CHAPTER TEN

Meggie had been especially careful about hiding her money. Whenever she went near the hiding place, she always made sure that no one could see her; she had been equally careful the previous night when she had buried the little bunch of coins she had earned, adding them to Aggie's savings. Although she knew the girls wanted her to put forth some money and join them, she did not want to touch Aggie's hoard, not the money which had been intended to save Jenny's life.

When she stored away her earnings, Meggie was acting like her mother, although she did not realize it at the time. Over the years, she had watched Jenny hide the money she had earned from hat-making, money which Jack Blunt would have spent on drink had he found it. Meggie knew that it was wise to save; without a sizeable sum she would never be able to rise above her present life of degradation and poverty. Meggie needed a nest egg for another reason. One day, she vowed, she would have her mother reburied properly, in a decent grave, with a beautiful memorial stone at its head with the name of Jenny Blunt and loving words written on it to show passers-by that she had been the dearest, most cherished mother. Over the grave she would have a marble angel, specially ordered if need be. Perhaps when that day came, Meggie would be a little happier and would be able to think about Jenny without the knifing pain of memory and remorse which beset her even now, over one year after her loss.

The secret hoard was being added to daily, until the time came when Meggie realized it was no longer safe to go on hiding her earnings this way. She had been going to that place too often now, and on every visit her chances of being seen increased.

Two weeks passed, and Meggie knew she would soon have enough money to buy a truckle bed to put in Cathy and Amy's room. The last time she had concealed some coins, she had thought that someone had followed her part of the way. She had looked round carefully, slowing down, and then had sat on one of the park benches for a time, as if admiring the scenery; finally, assured that she was not being spied upon, she had gone ahead and buried her latest earnings.

Now, as she came to her secret place again, a bag of money twisted beneath her waistband, she caught a flicker of movement out of the corner of her eye. Somebody was there! Somebody had seen her. Somebody had been spying on her all this time!

It was late evening. Storm clouds were gathering, and the parkland was shadowed with great black patches where anything could happen to her and no one would see and come to her aid. Suddenly feeling very vulnerable, Meggie turned away from her secret place, but as she did so she heard the snap of a twig, the crunching of a boot on stones, rasping breathing growing louder as a man approached her. He looked massive in the darkness, with great hunched shoulders pulled up almost to his ears, his arms quite short and thick, his hands balled into fists. She tried in vain to make out his face in the dark but saw nothing but a stubble of hair around the thick, square head.

Struggling for composure, determined to look relaxed as if she were doing nothing more than taking an evening stroll through the park, Meggie turned, making to walk away from that burly, gorilla-like figure.

"Ey,' he growled, 'come here, you!'

Meggie did not stop to answer but took to her heels, running like the wind. But she was not fast enough for him; she would have been had she not tripped over a coiled tree root and crashed to the ground, breath shaken out of her. Dazed, she heard the man close in upon her.

No past experience, no worldly armour gained in her short life could have protected Meggie from what was to happen next. The burly, crazed animal who launched himself on top of her little body was a fiend, a demon. In the ensuing moments, as she struggled, screaming and gasping, half-choking, the great ham hands held her down against the dead leaves.

When he was finished with her, when his panting, heaving, hairy body fell away from her, collapsing into a gasping mass by her side, Meggie began to scream hysterically. Her entire body was convulsed in horror. It was her helplessness that had been the worst thing of it, her having no choice in the matter, being forced to submit to the man's lust.

Swaying, Meggie managed to get to her feet. Panting, she began to run, but her steps were unsteady. She had to pause and lean against a tree-trunk to recover her breath; her lungs hurt but that was no matter: all she was worried about was the man's reviving and coming after her again. She glanced back once, terrified of what she would see, but he was still lying there, apparently in a deep sleep; his head was slung back and his mouth opened wide, and snores were rattling in his throat. What a fool, she thought; what a fool – but her thoughts were so jumbled that she did not know to whom she referred, the man or herself.

Meggie realized that this was a moment too good to miss. Glancing over her shoulder every few moments lest he wake up, she scrabbled at the earth, lifting up the rocks, bits of twigs and dead leaves with which she had so carefully camouflaged her hiding place. Drawing out the handkerchief containing her money, she thrust it beneath her skirt and then ran back into the crowded streets, filled with people out to enjoy the night time. More frightened than she had been for a long time, she made straight for Cathy and Amy's room; she would beg them, if she had to, to let her share their room tonight.

Meggie realized that the girls might well be out getting customers now, if not in the room actually entertaining them. She paused outside their room, biting her lip, and then leaned against the door, pressing her ear against the flaking wood. She could hear nothing. Perhaps they were both out?

Inside, the empty room was dark and quiet. She would rest here for a while, until the girls came back and perhaps shooed her out. Shaking with relief and the aftereffects of the shock, Meggie lurched towards the bed, tears rolling down her face. The bed looked soft and inviting. Thankfully, she slipped between the covers and rested her head against the rough cotton pillow.

Before she knew it, Meggie was asleep, lost in a dark, jumbled dream of fearful flight and unknown horrors which suddenly sharpened into focus as men's brutal fingers prodding her body. She woke with a start, drenched in sweat; a sound outside the door had alerted her. She waited, not sure what to do. Her first instinct was to hide under the bed, for it had been Cathy's voice she had heard and she did not want to keep her from going about her business. But she had no time to move before the door opened.

'Come in, dearie, come in. We got a nice cosy room here,' Cathy was saying as she lit the gas-lamp and ushered in her customer. He looked like a working-class man, red-faced and ill at ease, his bowler hat in his hands, as he glanced around the room and flushed even redder in the face.

'Come in, dearie. Don't be shy, don't be shy,' Cathy continued. Then, turning into the now lighted room, she noticed a little mound in the bed, beneath the blankets, and drew her hand to her mouth.

'Meggie!' she cried. 'Meggie, are you ill?'

At the word 'ill' the man, who had seen the wild unkempt hair on the pillow, stepped back out of the room in a flash, his eyes bulging.

'Got a fever has she; got a fever? 'Ere, look, I got kids back 'ome, I don't want to take the fever ter them,' he stammered.

Cathy made a decision at that moment, out of the goodness of her heart. She turned to the man and gave him a mouthful, telling him what she thought of his reaction.

Then she slammed the door in his astonished face and hurried over to the bed to Meggie.

'Are you sick, lovey? Have you got a fever? Tell Cathy, come on, do; tell Cathy.'

Meggie looked up at the girl, knowing what a sacrifice she had made, and, for a few rare moments, she was a little girl again. Tears streamed from her eyes and she was helpless, broken-hearted, sobbing in Cathy's loving arms, telling her all that had happened that evening. Cathy was shocked at first, then horrified and finally angered at what had happened to her friend. It seemed appalling that this should have happened to her now, just as she was getting back on her feet. If she herself had met the man she would have given him a dose of her tongue and a few hard, well-aimed kicks. That would have put paid to his lust, the dirty devil.

Cathy didn't regret turning her customer away; she hadn't relished the look of him. She usually had a rest period this time of the day, but the man had stopped her in the street on her way home. He seemed clean and decent, but she hadn't liked the shifty look of his eyes. She was glad now that Meggie's being ill in her room was an excuse to send the man away, because her instincts were telling her that there had been something odd about him, too. It was a constant worry in her line of business: men who looked so handsome and seemed charming and so eager to please could turn nasty the minute they got a girl alone in her room, venting repressed hostility on some poor girl they knew but for a few minutes. That was why she and Amy were usually so careful, getting to know their customers and having the affable ones back time and again rather than going out in search of new ones. A girl down the road had her eye put out by a man who had gone berserk when he got her alone in her room. She'd never recovered from that beating; she'd had to give up her business, of course, and go back home to her parents – and what man was ever going to want her, with one eye missing?

'I'm sorry, Cathy, really I am,' Meggie sobbed. 'I've

lost you money now, haven't I? It's all my fault, I shouldn't have come back here. Oh, but I was so scared and th-there was something else – I wanted to hide it.'

'Hide what, lovey?' Cathy said, her voice sympathetic. Then Meggie moved and she heard the clink of coins. Her eyes fell on the money at the same time as Meggie's. 'Where in Gawd's name did you get all that?' Cathy gasped. 'You ain't stolen it, have you? Oh, Meggie, what have you done?'

'Oh no, no, I haven't stolen it,' Meggie explained. 'I've had this a *long* time. It was given to me months and months ago by an old woman. She was fond of me, and she gave me this money and told me to take it home to look after my mam, but my mam died and so I've had the money hidden ever since. That man, that man in the park, I thought he knew about it and I was scared. I managed to get it out of its hiding place while he wasn't looking and I brought it with me here. I've got nowhere to hide it now. I don't know what to do.' Fresh tears welled in her amethyst eyes.

'Oh, you poor lamb,' Cathy said with a sigh. 'What are we going to do? All that money. Why didn't you tell us before, Meggie? It would have been the answer to all our troubles. You needn't have slept out when you had money like this.'

'But I didn't want to *spend* any. I still don't want to,' Meggie said. 'You see, this money was given to me by Aggie, that old woman I told you about, and she gave me the money to look after my mam. I thought the money was going to make my mam better and give us a nice house and good food and things like that, so we could live proper. But it didn't, did it? It was too late to save my mam, and I vowed that I'd never touch a coin of it after that. It's Jenny's money really. Jenny was my mam. It's really *her* money; it was meant for her, but it just came too late.'

There were tears in Cathy's eyes now. Meggie certainly knew how to twist her heart strings with those soulful, deep purple eyes of hers. All three of them had had a rough life, of course, but there was something about this girl, something different. Beneath all that grime and tangled hair she had pride, she carried herself well. She had such healthy shining eyes, and the times when Cathy had seen her spanking clean, just out of the bathtub, her skin had been as white as the roses in the park, smooth and soft, just asking to be decked out in satins and silks.

Amy had said once, out of Meggie's hearing, that she was like a little princess, with her straight back and glowing eyes, and Cathy had agreed. If anyone said that she, in her ragged clothes and tangled hair, with her feet bare, carried herself like royalty, people would laugh. You had to see her to know what was meant.

At that moment the door opened and Amy stepped in. She looked tired but pleased with herself. When she saw Cathy and Meggie sitting on the bed, Meggie's face grubby and tear-streaked, and tear marks on Cathy's face, too, she immediately thought something terrible had happened.

'What you two been up to? What's happened? Not had some trouble with a fella, have you?' she cried in alarm.

'Oh no, Amy. Well, that is, I haven't,' Cathy said. 'But our Meggie here, well, she's had a spot of bother with a gent in the park, but she got away from him. Brute he was from the sound of it.'

'Oh, you poor little mite,' Amy said, sitting down on the other side of Meggie and taking her hand and squeezing it. 'You poor little mite. What a thing to happen to you. A bad start that is. Still, you got us now, ain't you, so you don't have to worry no more. You don't have to go out in the park like that with them strange gents. You can stay here safe with us an' only go with men what we all know. Then you're safe, see?'

Meggie looked from one to the other, her eyes bubbling with grateful tears. 'I don't deserve you,' she said. 'You've been so kind to me.'

"Course you deserve us, lovey,' Cathy said, warmly. 'Look how good you've been to us. You cheer us up, an' look what you've done for our clothes. Look at all that

140

good advice you've given us on colours and such like. See how smart we are these days an' it's all 'cause of you. Cheered us up you have, given us something good to think about, something to be interested in apart from ourselves – an' that's always a good thing, ain't it, Amy?'

Amy agreed, nodding her head vigorously.

Meggie gave a tremulous smile. 'I wish you were my sisters,' she said.

'We can be, lovey. You just pretend we're your sisters an' we'll *be* your sisters. That's better than your real sisters, 'cause we ain't going to be jealous of you, see,' Amy grinned.

Cathy didn't want to mention the money Meggie now had in her possession. She wasn't interested in Meggie's money except for its being able to better all their lives, nor did she want to give her what might be bad advice. Meggie must be tired of having people getting after her for one thing or another. Cathy knew that feeling well herself, that of being driven to your limits where even the smallest request was enough to drive you to screaming point.

Nonetheless, something would have to be done about her money; they couldn't just leave it lying around here, it wasn't safe. She did not want to discuss the money in front of Amy, so she said, 'Look now, lovey, you're still pale, how about a nice night's sleep tucked up in our bed, eh? Amy will make you a nice hot cup of tea an' you'll feel real good after that.'

Amy set about boiling the kettle on the old spirit stove they kept in the corner of the room. Soon its merry bubbling and the hiss of steam was declaring its readiness and then Amy was passing round battered mugs full of steaming hot, very strong tea.

'You haven't put sugar in it, have you?' Meggie asked as she took her mug from Amy.

'Oh no, lovey, I remembered you don't like it so I didn't put none in,' Amy winked.

When her tea was drunk, its heat having flushed her cheeks to the colour of roses, Meggie lay back on the pillows while Cathy pulled the blankets round her and tucked her in, just as if she were a baby.

'Sleep now, Meggie. We'll leave you in peace. We've got some shopping to do, ain't we, Amy? We'll come back later. You'll feel much better after you've had a good sleep.'

The room seemed very quiet and empty without their colourful presence. Fingering the coins still tucked in bed with her, Meggie began to think about Jenny, but she was very tired. Within a few moments her breathing came evenly and she was fast asleep.

Autumn leaves swirling down in the park coated the earth bronze, tan and ochre. It was the coldest day they'd had this autumn; a day which reminded everybody that winter was not far behind. It was also the day that Meggie's truckle bed was delivered to the girls' room, along with a good stout mattress, thick blankets and a pillow. Meggie had paid for them herself, and now she stood staring at the bed in the corner of the room. She had made it up herself and it looked very cosy.

She had bought a screen, too; quite a large one, which completely concealed her bed from anyone on the opposite side of the room. It was a bamboo screen and she had found it in a pawnshop. It looked foreign; there were figures on it which Amy said were Japanese, but they were faded and the material was threadbare in places and sagging on its bamboo frame. Nonetheless, it did its job, affording the girls some privacy.

Meggie had also bought herself a box. A strong, wooden box with a lock. Although she had not much to put in it as yet, she intended to keep her treasures there: whatever she accumulated over the weeks, valuable or not, would go inside and be locked safely away. At the moment her money was in it. She did not know where else safer to put it, without questions being asked.

Meggie was wearing a plain, dark blue dress, frilled with white lace. She had also bought herself a warm cloak, thick gloves and a dark blue bonnet, edged with white. She did not think it wise to put on too much of a show or people would notice the change in her and would ask questions. That was something she always dreaded – questions being asked. People would say she had been stealing or had come upon money illegally, and there were always people willing to report to the Peelers. She had also got herself stout boots and thick black stockings to keep her legs warm.

Although she had revelled in her purchases, joyful at the thought that she would be cosily dressed this winter for the first time in her life, she was also deeply sad about having bought things which were, after all, fripperies compared with what the money might have bought had it come in time to save Jenny. She spoke to her mother in her mind, sending up a little prayer, saying, '*Please* understand what I'm doing, Mam, and why I'm doing it. I know if you were here you'd want me to be warm and snug, and winter *is* coming, Mam. I can't bear another cold winter like I had in the past . . .'

Meggie was sure that Jenny heard her wherever she was, and that she did forgive her; nonetheless, the anguish of her sinful life took its toll on her, and she suffered regular and debilitating headaches.

As to what she planned to do now that she was safe with Cathy and Amy, Meggie never mentioned that in her prayers to Jenny; nor did she contemplate it. It was simply a means to an end: she wanted money, she wanted success and power; anything to enable her to keep her vow of revenge on the Malgraves.

After weeks of making discreet enquiries, Meggie found out the address of their London home. Now that everything was safely sorted out and her bed in its place, feeling that she had a proper home again, Meggie determined to see what kind of place her grandparents lived in. She wanted to look at it and find out everything she could about them. She wanted to know how their servants behaved, what the house's windows and doors, and the flowers in their garden, looked like, if they had a fence or a wall round the house, and a coat-of-arms on their carriage. She must know *all* of it.

With the donning of her new clothes Meggie gained confidence. She was older, wiser, and she had a home at last. Somewhere to go, people to care about her. What was more, she knew that her grandparents were a duke and duchess, cruel though they had been to her mother.

When the day came that she would make her first proper contact with the Malgraves everything had to be just right; she must meet them on their own terms, as their equal. Not for her to go to them unprepared, to be beaten back by their cruel words, by their hostility and their hatred. She had no intention of cringing in their presence as Jenny had done. She was going to face them boldly.

She would tell them what they had done to her mother, what had happened to Jenny because of *their* wickedness. And she would ask to see her father. She would say, 'Where is *my father* – Michael? I wish to see him now.' He would come into the room, and they would say, 'This is Jenny's daughter – do you remember Jenny? Jenny's daughter – *your* daughter, too, Michael.' His face would brighten and he would take her in his arms, saying, 'My daughter! My own sweet daughter! I never knew you existed. God forgive me for my ignorance! Let me make amends to you!' Then she would discover that he had had no son, that she was his only child; he would love her all the more for that. She would make them all love her; perhaps it would be an easy thing to do, for they would be very old now, the Duke and Duchess, and ready to take her to their hearts: ready to forgive and forget. Then, when they loved her desperately, when they had told her that she was everything they had ever wanted – when she was part of their family – she would go, slipping away in the night. Before she even met them she would have learned how to write, and so she would leave them a letter on the dresser in her room. The letter which would say that they did not deserve her love, that they did not deserve *her*, that they had killed her mother as surely as if they had stuck a knife into her back and that she, Meggie, did not love them, had never loved them, because of what they had done to her mother.

She imagined their tears and grief and heart-ache, their feelings of desperation and helplessness, and she knew that at that moment her revenge would be complete.

This fantasy brought Meggie immense comfort.

Meggie was still an ignorant child; she could not read and she could barely write. There was so much she had to learn. She must also know how to walk and talk properly, how to carry the fine clothes that she intended to wear one day. She must learn how to make up her face so that her rouge was not obvious; she must learn how to look ravishingly beautiful whilst giving the impression that she took only the minimum of care about her appearance, for it was thought shocking that a lady should paint her face. She must learn how to carry her gloves, her reticule; she must learn the language of the fan, for by moving a fan in a certain way across her face a lady might, in the most genteel fashion, let her wishes and desires be known to the gentleman most attractive to her.

For a few moments Meggie thought about her grandparents and their society friends, and of the life they must lead. How tranquil their lives must be, enlivened only by enjoyment and pleasure, never by shock and grief as hers had been. She tried to imagine herself gowned in satins and furs, living a pampered and cossetted life, the granddaughter of a duke and duchess, at the centre of London society, a frequent visitor to the Queen and her family, going to parties and balls where only the aristocracy gathered.

If she were already accustomed to that kind of life, would she be standing here now a stronger, better person, more confident, more courageous, her head higher, her back straighter, her eyes bolder? Meggie wished she knew the answer. She assumed a pose which she imagined she might well display had she been rich. Throwing back her head, straightening her shoulders, walking with an easy, fluid grace, she began to move again, heading for that avenue where her grandparents lived.

Meggie passed rows of handsome Georgian houses, their gardens immaculate. They were vast edifices possessing dozens of rooms; rooms in the attic and below-stairs for the servants and large, luxurious rooms in between for their owners. She wondered if titled people lived here. At the end of the Georgian street she came to the crescent at the bottom of the avenue where Malgrave Manor stood.

She had no difficulty in recognizing the manor when she stood a few yards from it. It was built in Palladian style, its handsome façade a brilliant white. A massive house, larger than those around it, it stood in its own little parkland. On each of its ornate, seemingly fragile, wrought-iron gates like carefully woven lace suspended in the air was fashioned a large letter 'M' for Malgrave. The gate-posts were huge colonnades on top of which rested snarling lions' heads carved out of white stone. Meggie felt a tingle of fear and anticipation as she looked at them and then beyond, through the gate, to the elegant and beautifully-tended manor house and its gardens.

As Meggie stood staring, there came the noise of movement from the house. A beautiful carriage emerged from the rear of the building, pulled by two jet black horses, proud and high-necked. A servant pulled them right round to the front of the house. The carriage was of glossy rosewood; on its side was what she imagined must be the Malgraves' coat-of-arms, a lion's head and two doves, and the intricately scrolled 'M' which was also on the gates.

A lion and two doves, she thought, what did it mean? Did it mean that the Malgraves were ferocious and would eat anything gentler than they? Or that despite their ferocity they could be tamed?

The servant who had brought the carriage round to the front of the house stood with his hands on the horses' reins. He wore brilliant gold and green livery, and on his chest was the letter 'M.' He had a scowling face, and Meggie did not like the look of him.

At that moment the massive, gleaming wooden doors of the manor began to open. Two more liveried servants hurried down the steps carrying valises, or boxes of some sort, which they proceeded to load into the coach. A silence fell, and it seemed that the men were waiting. Then Meggie's mouth fell open. Was she imagining it? Was she really seeing what her heart wished her to see?

There, standing in the open doorway of Malgrave Manor, was her Sun God.

Meggie's legs seemed to melt. She felt sick and faint and weak all at the same time and had to grip the wrought-iron bars of the gate to keep herself steady. He couldn't really be there, not her Sun God! She had dreamed about him so often, both sleeping and awake. She had thought of him when she was at her lowest moments, seeing over and over again that scene at St Thomas's Wharf when he had come to collect his mother.

Now he stood there, so tall, so imposing, the glossy gold hair she remembered so well swept back carelessly from his handsome brow. She was too far away to be able to see his eyes, but she could remember them. He wore what she knew must be an expensive suit, in the softest grey colour. His black boots were glossy and gleaming, and on his shoulders rested a wide, swinging black cloak, lined with fur. He must be very rich.

It was not the thought of all his wealth which compelled Meggie to continue gazing at him; it was the memory of her Sun God, the kind, gloriously handsome Sun God of her childhood. Had it been only a year, two years ago? She could not remember exactly when she had first met him. She seemed always to have known him, always to have basked in the glow of his smile and his eyes. More than anything else on earth she wanted to meet him.

Meggie was older now, of course. Looking back in time, she realized what a gawky, skinny, gubby child she had been: a pauper child. He could not have looked at her without thinking that she was filthy, impoverished, not worth remembering. She recalled the message that had been written on the door to the soup-kitchen the following day. Due to illness the soup-kitchen was closed. It had never opened again. She wondered whose illness it had been.

How Meggie wanted to have answers for all her questions. How she desired the courage to push open the great wrought-iron gates and walk down the drive towards Malgrave Manor, towards her Sun God, to greet him, smiling and speaking as if they knew each other well. She could almost feel herself walking down the drive towards him, going up the steps and past the scowling servant, to hold out her hands to her Sun God, who would grasp them in his own and smile down at her, perhaps even pull her close to him and kiss her, on each cheek or on the lips. The thought of that made her weak with joy.

As her senses steadied, Meggie saw her Sun God begin to descend the steps. One of the liveried footmen opened the door of the carriage for him to step inside, and then the door was closed. Another man appeared, dressed in a heavy greatcoat, with a thick woollen scarf swathed round his neck and a hat pulled down over his eyes; he climbed into the driving seat of the carriage and whipped up the horses, who snorted and stamped excitedly, eager to be away. The coach wheeled around and faced the drive, at the end of which Meggie stood, staring.

Meggie realized with a start that there was someone close to her. From out of a little cottage nearby a man had appeared, and he was hurrying towards the gates to open them. Her heart pounding, she stepped behind one of the thick stone pillars. What if he had seen her? What if he began to shout at her, asking her what she was doing, why she was staring? Sweat sprang out on her forehead and her palms as she stood, shaking, while the gates creaked, and then the carriage bowled out between the beautiful stone pillars, past the shivering girl and on down the avenue, the horses prancing, the coach swinging from side to side.

Her Sun God was gone. As before, Meggie felt as if the light had gone out of her life; as if blackness had gripped her or a cloak had been thrown over her head.

Numbly, Meggie walked back home, oblivious of the cold and the flakes of snow patting her cheeks and settling on her clothes. Was he a visitor to Malgrave Manor, her Sun God? A friend? A relation? Had the Malgraves lent him their carriage to go wherever he wished?

How could he be a relative? She knew that Michael, her own father, was tall and slender, with jet black hair like her own. Could he be Michael's brother? But had Jenny not said that Michael was an only child and that his mother was past the child-bearing years? No, her Sun God must be a visitor; he had borrowed the Malgrave coach for an outing.

Meggie felt drained and exhausted by the time she got back home. All spirit seemed to have gone out of her. She sat down in the creaking old armchair in the corner of their room and warmed her hands by the fire. It was only a little fireplace, but it burned well when they had fuel for it. The room seemed hot and stale after her long walk in the brisk air but she sat there, letting the baking heat of the fire relax her, while she thought of her Sun God in his beautiful carriage. Where was he going? What would he be doing for the rest of that day, for all the rest of his days?

Now Meggie had an even stronger reason for getting money to make her rich and powerful in order to get to know the Malgrave family. When she presented herself to her grandparents she would, she hoped, meet her Sun God. By then, of course, she would be much older, for she knew it would not be an easy task to accumulate money even if she worked very hard at the business she, Amy and Cathy had set up together. She would not only be older, sixteen at least – a woman, in fact – but she would have to know how to speak and move like a lady. She must know what to do in any circumstance, for it was unthinkable that she might make a fool of herself. She was going to have to work hard in the coming months, very hard indeed. . . .

Meggie remembered Bella's Brothel, and its association with gold sovereigns was very strong in her mind. One day, she vowed, she was going to have a similar establishment, only hers would be far superior. A place where gentlemen came; titled gentlemen, she hoped. It might seem a very ambitious dream for a girl so young, but in her brief life she had already learned much. She had found out there was only one source of money for a girl in her position: men. Men in need of women. And the richer the man, the more money he would pay. It was as simple as that.

The time she had spent at her mother's knee now seemed like more than a lifetime away. In all good conscience she could not nurture those memories and embark on the life she planned. She intended not only to survive but to be successful. She knew she was extremely young, but she was also strongly determined.

She had so much to do and so little time to accomplish it all. Meggie felt impatient to begin.

PART TWO

CHAPTER ELEVEN

The Crimson Club was not only crimson in name; it was lushly furnished and decorated in sumptuous red plush. Even the lamps had red shades. The colour flattered everyone, especially women. Not that the women at the Crimson Club needed embellishment, for they were all young, beautiful, unblemished.

In summer, magnificent silver bowls of crimson and pink roses filled the club with their heady scent. In winter, the blossoms were replaced by flowers exquisitely sewn from the most sumptuous satins and velvets.

Many paintings lined the walls, depicting famous ladies of the demi-monde. There was a famous portrait of Agnes Sorel, mistress of the King of France centuries ago. She wore a modest head-dress, similar to that worn by a nun, but, below, one voluptuous breast was exposed. Another portrait showed Nell Gwynn, completely naked, her glossy auburn curls framing her face with its pretty baby features. Barbara Castlemaine, too, was represented. Her red hair was darker than Nell's but, unlike Nell, she was attired in brocade with an ermine cloak about her shoulders. Many and varied were the portraits of Emma, Lady Hamilton, mistress of Nelson. Smiling, serious, laughing, clothed and unclothed, she decorated many rooms in the Crimson Club, both downstairs in the salon and upstairs in the private boudoirs.

Not surprisingly, the owner of the Crimson Club herself was frequently to be seen wearing every shade of red, all of which suited her to perfection for she had porcelain skin, fragile and delicate, and glossy black hair which needed no artifice to highlight it. Her beautiful amethyst eyes seemed dark and slumbrous in the rosy lighting of the club's rooms.

She was very young to be a madam; some said she was only seventeen, but others said nineteen or twenty was nearer the truth. Not that her age mattered. What did matter was that she had built up her club from a tiny, virtually one-roomed establishment into the splendid and famed bordello that it now was. An astute mind, a sound business head and imagination had all combined to give the young Madam her early success, although she had been helped by close friends on whose loyalty she could depend. She was somebody who, at one and the same time, appreciated and cultivated her few intimate friends and yet cherished solitude above all things. Although her clients would never know it, she read extensively; not only the classics, but romantic novels and books on far-distant countries, history, the lives of famous people. Her appetite for knowledge was voracious.

Few knew the truth of Nesta Bellingham's origins or what had motivated her to found the Crimson Club. Nor did Nesta intend that anyone should ever find out. She wanted her club to be a success, her girls to be famous and her own life to be smoothly ordered; she had a deep need for peace, and the only thing that would bring her peace was security. There was nothing at present disturbing her except for a group of people who had visited her once before and who were about to visit her again, people whom she had dismissed as arrogant do-gooders; society people born to wealth and indolence, who had never had to struggle as she had once done, as she was doing even now.

She could not imagine anything more ludicrous and unnecessary than a group of expensively-dressed, highly-educated but nonetheless empty-headed reformers crossing swords with her in her sumptuous crimson lounge. Speaking to her of evil, of immorality and debauchery, beseeching her to mend her ways.

How dared they invade her premises? How dared they consider themselves better than she? What made them think they had the right to intrude upon her life, to attempt to change what she was doing?

At that moment a bell sounded at the front of the house. Nesta Bellingham glimpsed her face briefly in the beautifully-wrought mirror hanging on one wall of her drawing-room. She knew that face well; the immaculate complexion, white as clouds; the deep purple eyes, midnight blue in certain lights; the arched eyebrows, beautifully sculpted; the glossy black hair winging its way back from her smooth brow, and, at the centre of her forehead, the deeply-curved point of hair which was called a widow's peak adding even more drama to her aloof but compelling beauty.

Whatever the invaders might think of her morals they could not quibble about her taste. Her gown was of the warmest shade of rose-pink, fashioned from a fine, rich satin. It had a decorous neckline, which revealed her beautiful white swan neck but very little else. A smile flitted across Nesta's mouth as she thought of them now grouping to attack; she knew their eyes would dart to her bosom. They were going to be disappointed this visit! The last time she had met them wearing her peignoir, with very little beneath it, and took great delight in their discomfiture. This time there would be nothing to mark her as the madam of a high-class brothel.

Smoothing the deep pink ruches at the front of her skirt and straightening the glossy, fat pink pearls that hung round her neck, Nesta waited for her drawing-room door to open. A few moments later, Betsy, her little maid, bobbed a curtsy.

'They're here, ma'am. Shall I show 'em in?' Betsy chewed on her lips, not knowing whether to blush or pale.

Nesta Bellingham, with a cool wave of her hand, instructed Betsy to show them in. When they appeared she was standing by the window, framed against the light like a beautiful painting. Slowly she turned to greet them, her expression immutable. This time there seemed to be more of them. There had been only three or four the last time, if she remembered correctly; now, six people faced her.

Had she been anyone else the sight of that sixth person would have struck her dumb, stripping her of both confidence and pride. For a moment she thought, no, it's not possible; then, as her eyes raked him from head to foot, she realized that it *was* he. The years vanished. She was a little girl again, in the soup-kitchen at St Thomas's Wharf, glowing in the warmth of the smile from her Sun God and then she was standing at the gateway to a beautiful mansion, watching him getting into his carriage. Yes, it really was her Sun God.

Nesta's blood seemed to throb in her veins, her heart pounded and sweat broke out on her palms. She fought for composure, breathing deeply, waiting for anyone in the group to speak before she did. Not one of them, staring hard at her as they were, could guess the struggle for self-control she was undergoing.

He was every bit as handsome as she remembered him; a few years older now, but that hardly showed. He would be about twenty-six, she guessed; his glossy golden hair was as abundant and silky as ever, and his eyes the same intense blue. Did she imagine it or was he supporting her? She glanced at the other faces grouped with his, all of them stony, cold, hostile, and then looked back to his. Yes, he *was* supporting her. Silent words seemed to spring between them. He seemed to be saying, 'I'm only here on sufferance; this is really none of my business. I came to keep these people company. We're adults, aren't we, my dear? We know that all of this is nonsense.'

A slight, blonde girl was the first to speak, as she had done the previous visit. Jane, Lady Finchley-Clark. Little more than Nesta's age, she had originated the attack on the Crimson Club and on other clubs in the area. It was all her idea. She had been raised with a rigidly puritan background. Her father, the younger son of a nobleman, was also a man of the Church; for him, there was no guiding word but God's, no book to be read but the Bible, and he had raised his daughter, Jane, to uphold his beliefs.

Lady Finchley-Clark stepped forward a little, as if to take a closer look at Nesta Bellingham. Only very briefly was Nesta again little Meggie Blunt, frightened and naïve.

'Madam,' Lady Finchley-Clark began, her voice as thin and high as her brows, 'madam, we are here because we feel that we did not get anywhere during our last visit.

We feel that we have much more to say to you. We are concerned about the moral health of the young girls who work in your establishment. *Deeply* concerned. We feel that they are in *great* danger of losing their souls.'

Nesta threw back her head and laughed boldly. 'Souls? You are concerned about their *souls*? Where were you when they came to me cold and starving? What about the ragged children and young girls on the streets of London at this very moment? Do you not feel that you might be better occupied caring for *them*?'

Lady Finchley-Clark swallowed hard, as if her throat were constricted, her baby-blue eyes bulging slightly. She seemed to have difficulty in finding words to reply to this rebuke.

'Madam, it is, for the moment anyway, with the girls in this establishment that we are concerned. We feel that they are in a greater moral danger than any of those out in the streets of London.'

Nesta laughed again, remembering herself as a child and all the dangers she had faced alone, half-starved, desperate for love. She was not going to allude to her past, because she almost never thought of it now, not wanting to remember, steeling herself when she thought of how helpless she had been during those terrible years, not realizing that in repressing those memories she was hardening her heart.

'You laugh, madam. You seem not at all concerned about the girls who work here. In fact, madam, I would say that you are heartless!'

And then the Sun God spoke. 'Perhaps we have come at the wrong time, Jane. Perhaps we should come again another day.'

Jane turned to him, her eyes flashing. 'This *is* the right time! Anytime is *the right time* to come here!' she cried, and then, as if chastened by her outburst, she lowered her eyes, appearing contrite for rebuking the young man.

Nesta seemed hardly aware of anything except the fact that her Sun God had spoken, that his eyes were now looking at her. He was half-smiling, seeming silently to beg her forgiveness for the golden-haired girl's wrath. Time was suspended. She waited, aware that very soon she would discover his name – who he was – and that she wanted to know *now*. Too many years had gone by with her knowing next to nothing about him.

'James – ' Lady Finchley-Clark began, and then she seemed to reconsider, glancing round at the others who were present.

One man was dressed very sombrely; perhaps he was a man of the cloth? The three other ladies were of varying indeterminate ages; dumpy and overdressed, all had tight-lipped mouths and cold eyes. Had they come out of the same do-gooder mould? Nesta wondered.

Lady Finchley-Clark seemed to be poised, waiting for someone to speak, but nobody did. They all looked at her, then at James, finally at Nesta herself. Everyone seemed to be waiting; it was one of those uncomfortable moments when no one wishes to speak first.

Nesta had little desire to dismiss them now; she might never see her Sun God again, never discover his full name. James, that was his Christian name. She liked it; it was strong and masculine. But what was his surname, and was he titled?

Suddenly the only two people in the room who were truly alive were staring at one another as if no one else were present!

Lady Finchley-Clark panicked. She had not come here to have her future husband stare covetously at the black-haired whore they had planned to save. When she had asked James to accompany her she had wanted him present for moral strength, to take her side, to help and encourage her. She had never expected him to stand transfixed, gawking at the whore as if she had hexed him, as if he could not draw his eyes away from hers.

This woman is a witch! She has evil powers – Jane could feel them from across the room, and she blanched, praying silently beneath her breath, struggling to ward off their pull. By now her cheeks were scarlet and her hands in their pale-grey gloves clasped and unclasped as if she had no control over them; indeed, that was how she felt, for she had entirely lost control of the situation. She could do nothing, say nothing, while she watched her James being enchanted by the woman. The black-haired whore was bewitching her fiancé! She wanted to scream to break the spell but could do nothing. Her tongue seemed clamped to the roof of her mouth, her lips were wooden.

Was no one else aware of what was happening? She tried to look round but her neck felt stiff. Had she been paralysed by the witch? Yes, that must be it: the witch had paralysed them all. No one could move while *she* was inexorably drawing James to herself!

Finally Lady Finchley-Clark found her voice. She stepped back two, three paces, her legs quivering. 'We will go,' she said, her voice hoarse. 'We will go now.'

The little group turned as one man, all save James. He departed in his own good time, trailing behind the group. He glanced back once at Nesta as she stood framed by the window. Was she smiling at him? Were those magnificent purple eyes softening? He thought she was, they were, and the ghost of a smile drifted across his own face and then was gone. This encounter had caught him by surprise, but he knew one thing as he followed his fiancée and her friends down the hallway and out into the square: he would be back – and next time he would come alone.

'James, James, how *could* you?' Jane sobbed, beating her bird-like hands frantically against his broad chest. 'How *could* you have behaved like that? Why did you not support me? Why did you not back me up? I took you along because I *needed* your support! You did not help me, James. Oh, James, James, *why?*'

James looked down at her petulant face, at the baby-blue eyes wide with accusation. What could he say? He had been as surprised by events as she. Whatever had taken place in the drawing-room of the Crimson Club had been entirely beyond his control.

Now he felt different somehow. The fair, slim Jane to

whom he had been promised since they were children was now no longer the mate for him. He felt as if he had come to a watershed; as if everything had suddenly become clarified in his mind. But this new realization raised problems. Her family was delighted with the match. For months they had been preparing for their marriage. Jane was about to leave for Paris to choose the material for her wedding gown and to have it made by a leading couturière. He had chosen his best man. They had decided upon the church where the ceremony would be held. But now he no longer wanted to make her his wife. . . .

Looking down at Jane, James realized he was no longer willing to be led by Jane's managing parents, who had coaxed, cajoled and perhaps forced them both into hastening their union, for which they were temperamentally unsuited. Jane's stern, rigid upbringing had crushed any liveliness she had begun to show as a child. He had received a freer, almost indulgent and certainly very loving upbringing, before his parents had died.

He realized now that he had never actually contemplated taking Jane to bed, that he had done little more than kiss her cheek. She always withdrew into a shell when he wanted to clasp her to him; she blushed if he so much as glanced at her bosom. He saw now how intolerable their life together would be.

It was not only himself he was saving; he was saving Jane, too. Eventually she would realize that he had saved them both from making a terrible mistake. She was an heiress; there would be countless suitable young gentlemen, with backgrounds similar to her own, who would jump at the chance to marry her.

He would return to Malgrave Manor and think about the Crimson Club and its handsome, passionate mistress. He would imagine taking her in his arms and the wave of emotion which would encompass them both as his lips came down on hers. She would be pliable in his arms; sweet hours of passion and love would follow.

He would think about her until he could wait no longer

and then he would go to the Crimson Club, calling there like any of its regular clientele, asking not to see one of the young ladies of the establishment but Miss Bellingham herself. He had heard from his friends of the club's delights; of the sumptuous rooms, the expensively draped boudoirs, the antiques and pictures and beautiful *objets d'art* all carefully chosen by Miss Bellingham herself. He had heard of the girls who could cater for every taste imaginable, and he had heard, too, of the mystery surrounding Nesta Bellingham.

No one knew where she had come from or how she had become so successful. There was much conjecture about her origins. Indeed, he had not been interested in the truth until he had heard Jane mention the Crimson Club and its mistress, until she had asked him to accompany her there. Then he had done a little homework.

But he, who had thought himself mature and worldly-wise, immune to all feminine blandishments, had not been prepared for the meeting which had just taken place, nor for the change it had wrought in him.

Jane was weeping now. 'You're not listening to me, James! You do not hear what I am saying. You do not *care* for me!'

'That is not true, my dear,' he said gently. 'I do care for you, as I care about all my friends. We have been friends for many years, how could I not care what happens to you?'

'Then why do you stare into space like that, blankly? Why do you not heed what I say?'

'Forgive me,' he said, contrite. 'I was unaware of it.'

'But you were *not listening*! How can you deny it? Your face has gone all stony and cold. It is as if I am a stranger, a beggar-woman in the street trying to obtain money from you.'

'You exaggerate, Jane.'

'I do not exaggerate!' Giving a great sob, she plunged her face into her hands, causing him to feel totally helpless.

What could he do or say under such circumstances? He

must get away from her; go home, sit quietly and think. When he had gathered his thoughts, then would be the time for him to speak, but not until then.

'James, you will come back with me?'

'Back?' he said, perplexed.

'Yes, back. Back to the Crimson Club. We must finish the work we have begun. I will not have any peace until it is finished. All those girls, those poor girls, in such great moral danger! I cannot sleep at night for thinking of them.'

James was speechless. How could she consider going back? Had she not met her match in Nesta Bellingham? Had they not all, in different ways, been made to look foolish? And yet she could speak of going back – and of taking him! One thing he knew for certain: he could never face Nesta Bellingham again in Jane's presence.

Asking Jane to pardon his seemingly abrupt departure, James offered the excuse that he must return home for he was expecting a visitor to discuss some business concerning the estate. She looked at him reproachfully, tears dewing her gold-lashed eyes, but said nothing.

Once in the privacy of his carriage, James's thoughts returned to Nesta Bellingham. Her very name rang in his head. He could not help but recall her lustrous amethyst eyes, her glossy black hair. What would that hair look like when pulled free of its pins to sweep down over her naked white body?

Was it infatuation he was experiencing? He found that a hard question to answer, for he had never been infatuated before. He only knew that he wanted to be back in her company, to talk to her, hold her hands, kiss her. . . . The thought of taking her to bed made his blood pound.

At the Crimson Club, Betsy was giggling with her mistress. 'Did you ever see the likes of that snobby lot?' she was saying. 'Noses in the air so high 'tis a wonder they didn't trip over the rugs! What they wants is a good kick up the pants, that's what.'

'You could be right, Betsy.'

'Left their visiting cards they did, ma'am. Do you want 'em,' Betsy asked, 'or shall I chuck 'em in the fire where they belongs?'

'Their cards?'

Nesta's face paled. Of course, they would have left their cards! Why had she not thought of it?

'Betsy, how many times have I told you that when people give you their visiting cards, you are to bring them *straight* to me so that I know exactly to whom I am speaking!'

'Yes, ma'am,' Betsy said, chastened.

'Now where are the cards?'

'Over here, ma'am.'

Betsy delved into the capacious pockets of her apron, drawing out a bunch of cards and handing them to her mistress before bobbing a curtsy and departing.

With shaking hands, Nesta glanced through them. No, that was not the one, she was sure of that. That card belonged to that stubby little man in the sombre clothes. Four more cards, all of them belonging to ladies, and then – she looked down at the sixth card, her blood freezing in her veins, her heart pausing in its beat. *Malgrave*!

No, no, there was some mistake, it could not be. *Malgrave*!

She did not know whether to laugh hysterically or to sob. *James, Duke of Malgrave*. She read the name again: James, Duke of Malgrave. And the address: Malgrave Manor. How well she knew it. At least once a week she went to gaze at the manor and to think of the revenge that she had promised herself – when the time was right. And now James, Duke of Malgrave, had come to her. But who exactly *was* he? Not her father, whose name was Michael; besides, her father would now be twice this man's age. Nesta's thoughts seemed such a jumble that she had difficulty getting a grip on them.

Was he Michael's young brother? Nesta's throat tightened; she felt faint as the room spun round her. Maybe her Sun God was her own uncle?

The following day seemed to pass in a haze. Nesta felt spiritless, devoid of emotion; she had to work extra hard to push to the back of her mind thoughts of her Sun God, who had haunted her for years. If he were her uncle – Michael's brother – then she would have to change the way in which she had regarded him for so very long – but could she do it?

Nesta was perturbed by this new turn of events, but by the end of the afternoon she already understood that nothing could alter her feelings for her Sun God. But there was still the matter of her vow of revenge on the Malgraves. Obviously the old Duke was dead, but his wife might still be alive, and she was the one who had cast the pregnant Jenny out on the streets; she was the one whom Nesta must punish.

Nightfall came, and with it the Crimson Club's regular customers. Nesta looked breathtakingly lovely in an ivory tulle dress beaded with silver spangles, an outfit totally unlike those which she normally wore. Round her neck was a string of moonstones, their pristine beauty no rival for her complexion.

Nesta could not forget the way James Malgrave had looked at her the previous afternoon. Her experience of men being what it was, she felt certain that he would come again. When he did arrive, he came alone.

James and Nesta looked across the salon at one another and their glances locked. The noise and smoke and hubbub in the room seemed to vanish. Icy spirals of delight coursed up Nesta's spine, and her palms grew cold, then hot. Had she been aware of others in the room, she would have noticed that they were staring at her, seeing how scarlet were her cheeks.

James had not come under any pretence of playing at the tables or of visiting one of the girls. He had come to see her. . . . As if destiny itself were manipulating her, she walked across the crowded room towards him, her face alight.

Within a matter of minutes they were ensconced in her private quarters. They had still not spoken to each other.

When the door closed and was locked behind them, they found one another's arms as if they had lived their lives solely as a prelude to this meeting.

'Nesta,' James whispered into her hair, crushing her against his powerful chest. 'I had to return – I couldn't stay away. It was as if I were being pulled here by some invisible force. . . . I tried to fight it, but not for long. You have my heart, I swear it, but how you took it I do not know. . . .'

Nesta smiled. There was no need for her to reply. Words were superfluous when lovers such as they were at last together. If he only knew that she had been a ragged urchin who had taken soup from his mother all those years ago . . . but she would never willingly tell him that. She was too proud. What did her past matter? If he loved her, he would be concerned only with the present – and *their* future together. With that thought thrilling deliciously in her mind, she gave herself up to his embrace.

'James – ' she moaned, as he began to press hard kisses against her mouth and throat, crushing all feeling from her lips.

He led her to the bed and then, scooping her up in his powerful arms as though she were thistledown, placed her gently on the coverlet. For a few moments he stood over her, raking her face and body with his sapphirine gaze; then, slowly, he began to strip off his black broadcloth jacket and white silk stock until he stood before her clad only in an unbuttoned shirt and trousers. When he sat down beside her on the bed, she smiled up at him languorously, silently urging him to make haste and undress her, too.

As if he heard her thoughts, James reached out to unfasten her tulle gown, pushing it open so that her creamy breasts sprang out, as if eager for his caresses. He smiled, lowering his face to them and gently nipped at the velvet flesh until she moaned and squirmed rapturously. His tongue flicked at her nipples, wet and warm and incredibly stimulating, making her moan again and pull him closer. In her eagerness, she parted the skirts of her petticoats herself and placed his hand on her stomach.

Stroking the smooth alabaster skin, he encircled her navel with his finger and then darted his tongue inside, making her writhe uncontrollably. Heat raced to her cheeks as he rose to strip off his shirt, revealing broad muscular shoulders, trim waist and a thicket of gilded hairs on his chest.

Dazed by his beauty, Nesta placed a hand across her mouth, watching as he discarded his trousers, flinging them aside in his haste. She could barely contain her longing – she wanted to tear at him, to pull him on top of her, to force him into her body and never allow him to stop making love to her. . . .

The *frisson* between them as their naked bodies came together was like an electric spark, almost painful in its intensity. Nesta wanted to close her eyes and float away on the blissful cloud that James was creating for her, but she could not bear to shut her lids on the glorious sight of her Sun God. . . .

'My love,' he groaned against her cheek, and she caged him tightly in her arms, entwining her fingers so that he could never escape.

He did not have to open her thighs, for they were wide and waiting for him. Her breath was his, his hers, as their lips merged while he sought and found the entrance to her womanhood and thrust inside her. She writhed, throwing back her head, tossing it from side to side while he drove again and again inside her, filling her with his love, laying siege to her very soul. Then the singing started, deep in the pit of her stomach; low at first, like half-heard angel song in a dream, then louder, more insistent, until she could no longer deny it. Her every nerve cell, every fibre, was alive and tingling; the fiery, darting flames leapt into furious life, scorching her thighs and higher, to her mind and back again, until she screamed out loud in her passion while James looked down on her, watching her ecstasy until his own began.

Later, satiated, lying entwined, they slept; the distant clamour of the club's customers did not disturb them. At an hour or two past midnight, outside a carriage bowled into a hansom cab, waking them. Nesta exulted to find herself caged in her Sun God's arms and to see him smiling down at her as she opened her eyes.

'Is it dawn?' she whispered, not really caring what time of day it was. Time could go to perdition when he was with her.

'It is two in the morning, my dove, my little jet and ivory dove. . . .'

James began to kiss her gently, then with a wildly rising passion so that she had no wish to say anything more but only to spend every moment responding to his love-making. The other men who had made love to her were as empty manikins compared to James. She had been emotionally dead with them compared with how she was with him. Her senses rioted with a delicious joy to be so near, so beloved by her Sun God. . . .

If she died in his arms, she would die the happiest woman on earth. She asked no more than to lie beneath him, totally submissive to his kisses and his thrusting body. He was so tender and yet so strong; she had never known any man like this before. The cupidity of fate was extraordinary, but she would ponder on that later. For now, she need not think of anything but James's ardour, of his need for her, and hers for him. . . .

Before James left, late the following afternoon, he made it clear to Nesta that he would be back, and soon. Kissing the palms of her hands, he bade her good-bye, then left slowly, glancing back at her twice where she stood smiling in the doorway.

Nesta spent the rest of that day as excited as a child anticipating Christmas. He loved her – her Sun God loved her! Together, they wrought perfection, ecstasy, rapture. He would be back soon, he had promised. How would she survive until he came?

Looking back on the past few years, it seemed to Nesta that, unbeknownst to her, destiny had been moving her towards the moment when she and James would find one another. She was no longer poor but had a reasonably large sum of money banked. She had been very successful with her investments of late, aided by her financial advisor, William Temple, who said that she had gold fingers when her instincts had proved to be correct time and time again. The Crimson Club was flourishing. Customers who had frequented other clubs in London were now habitués of her establishment, and their money poured into her coffers. She had bought property, two handsome terraces of houses on the city's outskirts, which she rented out to respectable, working-class families.

There was an air of opulence about his office; the rich rosewood desk, the elegant Louis Quatorze clock, the Ming dynasty vases which held lilies and what looked like exotic orchids with ornately-speckled petals. The carpets on the floors were of a luxuriant Turkey weave in rich purples and blues, which made the cream-painted walls look cool and temple-like, the white lilies almost waxen in their purity. Temple himself was always expensively dressed, his shirt and cravat of silk, his suit of fine black broadcloth; framing his plump cheeks were the most lavish Dundreary whiskers Nesta had ever seen.

Nesta had been suitably impressed by William Temple and the *décor* of his office. She had liked his face; he wasn't handsome but he had a good look about him, not exactly benevolent but genial. She had liked his twinkling eyes, his neat little dark beard, carefully fashioned into a spade shape. She had liked his glossy dark hair, although there wasn't much of it left. Most of all, she had liked the way he treated her, as if she had common sense, intelligence. It was all too rare to find a man who treated a woman in such a way and she revelled in it, realizing all the same that it was his business manner, that she must not let it go to her head. She had reminded herself that he was a businessman, that he was there to make money out of her as much as he was to make it for her.

When, of late, the healthy gold-ringed hands touched hers a little longer than was necessary as he bade her goodbye she pretended not to notice, and when the twinkling, genial, rich brown eyes gazed more than was circumspect upon her face and figure, that too she ignored. She could never forget how vulnerable she was; it was dangerous to forget even for so much as a minute how assailable she was, a woman and alone.

Nesta had had a long, hard struggle, hampered by her acute sense of isolation and her realization that she was behaving in a way which would have horrified Jenny had she known. Chapel-reared, her mother had been determined that Meggie would not fall by the wayside like other poor girls. Over and over again, she had told Meggie not to let men touch her, nor give her money, for this was far worse than stealing. She must save herself for her husband; only he was to kiss and hold her. How could Meggie forget those teachings at her mother's knee? And yet, to survive, she had been forced to push them aside, but she could never truly erase from her mind what her mother had instructed.

The tranquil, confident façade which Nesta showed to the world was totally at variance with her inner conflict, the anxiety which haunted her private moments. She had betrayed her mother, not once but repeatedly during the past several years. She had taken money from men, and clothes and jewels; even a cottage, from one doting admirer. But she had also learned to read and write, and she had saved her pennies so that she could advance herself and further her ambitions.

Everything she had possessed had gone into the Crimson Club, but at what cost to her peace of mind! Sometimes, she dreamed that Jenny was begging her to give up her life of prostitution, and she would awaken with tears streaming down her face. But she was driven by a determination which outweighed everything else, although she suffered for it with fits of nervousness and blinding headaches, for she was behaving in a way alien to her childhood upbringing and she knew that Jenny would have wept had she known.

Nesta believed that she might have succeeded in keeping her guilt at bay had not Lady Finchley-Clark and her fellow do-gooders appeared on her doorstep. Had she been without a conscience, or raised differently, she would not have felt threatened by them. For months now they had been calling, assailing her with accusations and pleas to close down the Crimson Club and put her girls and herself into decent, moral occupations.

She had no intention of heeding them, but they did not know the price she paid for her apparent disregard of their arguments. Every time one of them spoke, it was as if Jenny herself were doing the talking, saying, 'Leave this terrible life, *cariad*. Go away from this place and be a good girl, like you used to be.' Inwardly, Nesta was being tortured, but she had little alternative save to put on a hard face and answer them coldly. To agree would mean facing herself and her past life in all its harsh reality. To do so would destroy her, so she fought, sharply and boldly, but each time, after they left, she would suffer debilitating headaches and her hands would shake.

Nesta had seen the likes of Lady Finchley-Clark before; women who had been brought up by strict parents, tightly corsetted in heavy, voluminous clothes, never let out of the sight of their nannies, watched carefully for any transgressions and beaten should they commit any error, however slight. There were children like that amongst the poor, of course; boys and girls who were thrashed soundly by parents who were consumed by frustration. For wealthy children it was a different matter; when they were punished or chastised it was said to be for their own good.

No doubt Lady Finchley-Clark had had her every whim checked, her every intention subjected to such scrutiny that she dare not express any emotion other than those rooted in the most strait-laced virtue. Certainly that was apparent in her manner. Would the virtuous Jane ever unlace her stays, let down her hair, smile and laugh and warm to a lover's arms? Nesta doubted it. Women like that were a danger. Not only to themselves but to the men whose lives they ruined and to the children whom they reared in the same prudish, loveless fashion; indeed, to everyone whose lives they tried to alter by advancing their rigid beliefs in the name of Christianity.

Nesta believed, as her mother had, that to save people one had to love them unstintingly, not accuse and reprimand them. She thought the reformers' outlook was acutely selfish, for they taught that one must be mindful of one's soul in order to attain a personal reward in the afterlife. Surely good deeds should be done without thought of any reward? Or so Jenny had always told her. Was that not what made a person quintessentially good? She decided that she would have to say as much to Lady Finchley-Clark and her friends the next time they visited.

Thinking of them brought her thoughts sharply back to her Sun God – not that her thoughts of him had ever strayed. Their night together seemed like a dream now – had it really happened? But yes; her body ached and was deliciously bruised. How she wished that he was still with her, so that they could begin their lovemaking all over again. . . .

Two days passed, then three; it seemed an eternity. Would James never visit her again? She had felt so sure when he had been beside her, positive that he, too, had felt more than just sexual attraction. But when five days had elapsed and he had not even sent her a note, Nesta felt deep despair. She toyed with the idea of contacting him but decided against it. Any overture must come from him. If only he would call or write, send flowers, *anything*.

Nesta could not settle her thoughts; her appetite vanished; she woke every morning at dawn and could not get back to sleep. Trying to calm her nerves, she paced up and down her room endlessly. Nothing seemed to calm her. She was in love; oh, how she was in love. She tried to distract her thoughts, but every line she came across seemed to reflect her own yearning.

> *And yet I love the looks that made me blind,*
> *And like to kiss the lips that fret my life,*
> *In heat of fire an ease of heat I find,*
> *And greater peace of mind in greater strife.*
> *That if my choice were now to make again,*
> *I would not have this joy without this pain.*
> *My true love hath my heart and I have his,*
> *By just exchange one for another given:*
> *I hold his dear, and mine he cannot miss,*
> *There never was a better bargain driven.*

Sir Philip Sidney's words only served to make her feel more insecure. She had no proof at all that James had even considered her heart. . . .

If only he would come! Surely he had guessed her feelings when they had made love? They had seemed to appear so obvious to her, as if they were in some way being transmitted to him. He must know – he *must*.

She had plumbed the darkness of total rejection and then had regained her equilibrium when the letter was brought by one of the Duke's valets. Nesta opened it with trembling fingers, almost forgetting to breathe.

James wanted to see her again! He would come that night at ten if the time was not inconvenient for her. . . .

After despatching her reply, Nesta tried to cope with the rest of the day. It was not easy. She was as impatient as a child before Christmas; how could she endure the long, lonely hours until he arrived? She was so desperate for his loving that she could concentrate on little else. Tonight, no vow of revenge, no past tragedy was going to interfere with their happiness! Later, if necessary, she would pay the price. . . .

An idea fluttered through her mind and was gone. It would return later, but, for tonight, she would not think of it again.

When the time arrived, Nesta was ready to greet James

in a flowing gown of watered green and blue silk, virtually transparent. At first glance she seemed to be naked beneath it; however, closer scrutiny revealed that underneath the gown she was wearing a flesh-coloured tube-style robe, figure hugging and delicate, also of silk. Neither article, of course, was in the current fashion, but Nesta did not want to be hampered by a crinoline, not tonight of all nights. She wore her hair loose, a black waterfall down her back, hoping that he would entwine his fingers in it and hold it against his face, as he had done before.

Nesta was just about to settle down to await her visitor's arrival when Betsy came bursting into the room, bobbing a curtsy, her cheeks scarlet as she stammered her words.

'Ma'am, ma'am! A terrible thing has happened. A terrible thing! Oh, oh, oh!' she gasped, throwing up her hands.

'Get on with it, Betsy. What has happened? Tell me quickly, quickly.' Nesta was on her feet, her eyes bright. Was the house on fire?

By now Betsy had been joined by one of the girls, who was sobbing, her hands held to her ears as if she had heard something so terrible that she must shut out the noise.

'Oh! Oh! Miss Bellingham, Miss Bellingham, something terrible has happened! Poor Carlotta. Oh, oh, do come quickly!'

The girl turned on her heel, still crying. Nesta hurried after her. They went up the wide, carved stairway. Carlotta's room was a shambles; it looked as if some wild beast had gone berserk in it. Carlotta lay quite still, half-on, half-off the bed, face down.

'Oh my God, is she dead?' Nesta cried, rushing to the bed.

Carlotta was not dead, only stunned by the brutal beating she had received. Her back was lacerated, her skin bloodied, her *négligée* torn. As Nesta slowly, gently, turned her over she groaned.

'Lord Trenton – Lord Trenton. He – he did this.'

'That pig! He'll never come in here again!' Nesta cried, furious.

Carlotta was one of her best workers. A tall, beautiful girl; strong, too. The man must have been insane in his rage for him to get the better of her. Now Carlotta's beautiful, pale flaxen hair was bloodied and her eyes bruised. She was very pale indeed. As Nesta tried to prop her head up with a pillow she tried to say something.

'Don't speak,' Nesta said immediately. 'Save your strength. Lie back and we'll make you comfortable. We'll take care of you, don't worry, my dear.'

Charlotta was determined to say what she must, although her voice was faint and hoarse, as if she were choking.

'He – he – hasn't gone yet,' she managed to whisper. 'He – he is still here.'

A shudder coursed through Nesta. She straightened up, her eyes flitting round the room. There seemed to be no intruders lurking in it. Turning to the girls who were grouped behind her, she said, 'Girls, search the room. Look behind the screen over there. Look in the dressing-room.'

The girls obeyed her immediately, but there was no one there.

Nesta turned back to Carlotta with a smile. 'Rest now, my dear. He's gone. Don't you trouble yourself. We'll take care of you.' Turning again, she issued fresh orders to the girls. 'Bring hot water and linen and towels, and some of that medicament out of my store-cupboard, Annette, please.'

Tears flowed unchecked out of Carlotta's swollen eyes. 'He hasn't gone,' she whispered hoarsely. 'He's still here ... I know it, I can feel it. He's still here. Oh, you've no idea what it was like,' she said haltingly. The words seemed to be torn from her.

Nesta's anger gave way to compassion. The girl was suffering badly.

This was the first time such an outrage had occurred at the Crimson Club. Nesta had always prided herself on having the most genteel and refined clientele. Lord Trenton was a spade-chinned man, with shaggy light-grey hair and bright, black eyes; broad-shouldered, quite tall, with a wide, full-lipped mouth and deep lines from nose to chin. She had never imagined for one moment that he could become violent and beat a young girl. She wished Cathy or Amy were here for support, but they were both away visiting relatives and she was suddenly conscious of how very alone she felt.

Nesta bathed Carlotta's striped back and spread medicament into the wounds; then she helped her into a cool clean nightshift and tucked her into bed with a smile when a scream rang out from a distant part of the club. Immediately Carlotta's eyes flew open, her pupils wide with horror.

'He's still here, he's still here! I told you he was, I told you. Oh, take care, take care!'

'Get the coachmen,' Nesta snapped to one of the girls. 'Tell them to come immediately – we need help.'

The screams continued, joined by other screams of a different timbre. Nesta felt herself stiffen. Before the coachmen could arrive from the rear out-building, James Malgrave appeared. Betsy had shown him straight up the stairs, knowing that her mistress would be more than pleased to see such a solid looking man at this moment. Nesta whirled round as the door opened, her mouth falling open a little.

'Am I intruding? Pray forgive me if I am,' he said, 'but your maid told me to come upstairs. She said that there was trouble.'

Nesta clasped her hands together. 'Oh, indeed there is trouble. Grave trouble. This poor girl here,' she gestured to Carlotta, 'has been badly beaten by Lord Trenton.'

Malgrave frowned. 'Trenton? My God – he always seemed to me to be a normal sort of fellow.'

'And to me,' Nesta said, 'but he has done this, and a few moments ago we heard screams. I sent down for the coachmen.'

'Trenton is still here, in the building?'

'Yes!'

'Wait here. Lock your doors,' Malgrave rapped out his orders. 'Do not open it for anyone except myself.'

'But my girls! What of my girls?' Nesta cried.

'I shall take care of everything. Now do as I say. Stay in this room with this poor girl and lock this door. Let no one in. I repeat, open it for no one but myself.' With that he whirled on his heel and was gone.

Nesta did as she was bid. Then she sank down on the bed to take Charlotta's hands and try to comfort the poor girl. Nesta spent the next quarter hour trying to soothe her while she wondered what was going on outside the room. How different this was from what she had planned to happen when James arrived!

Nesta heard feet scurrying to and fro, a scuffling sound, then deadly silence, while she waited, hardly daring to breathe. Doors slammed in far parts of the building. She heard a gruff voice, then another, and realized that the coachmen had arrived at last; they had certainly taken their time in coming. She determined to speak sternly to them and, if she deemed it necessary, to dismiss them and engage others who would be quicker to respond when emergencies arose.

Time ticked by slowly and then the most dreadful din arose; a sound like a mad animal's bellowing, and shouting, the smashing of delicate furniture, the splintering of crystal chandeliers. Nesta held her hands to her ears, hunching forward, thinking of her James fighting the crazed beast who had been an apparently sober Lord Trenton only an hour or so ago. She was experiencing a wash of emotions – dread, panic, fear, anxiety; they were warring within her, and all the time she was trying to quell them, trying to pretend that she did not really care what happened to James, reminding herself that she had only made love with him once and that she barely knew him. She tried to make this a truth she could accept but finally had to admit failure.

If James were being beaten, attacked by that maniac Trenton, she must be with him, helping him, although she realized that she would be a weak thing in the face of such a monster as Trenton. She stood up, unable to bear the suspense any longer; she must know what was happening. She was at the door, turning the key, when she heard James's voice outside.

'Open the door, Nesta. It is I, James.'

Immediately she obeyed him, terrified of what she would see. She had no idea how white and frightened she looked, how large and velvet-dark her eyes appeared as she stood there, trembling.

James was anything but pale and his thick golden hair was awry. His neat black suit was torn, his cravat wrenched loose. He had a graze on his forehead and a cut on one cheek, and beads of blood were dropping down onto his immaculate white shirt.

'Oh my God – ' Nesta gasped, her hands at her cheeks. 'Are you hurt? Has that beast . . .?'

'No,' he interrupted, 'not hurt. I've just had the very devil of a fight, that's all. The man's crazed, quite crazed, but we've got him trussed up now in one of the rooms, and he's not going to get out of that in a hurry, I can promise you. Your coachmen are standing guard over him, just in case, and we've sent for the Peelers.'

'Come inside . . . sit down,' Nesta cried.

When she had James seated on the chair Nesta bathed the cut on his face and the graze on his forehead, smoothing back the golden hair so that she could clean the wound more thoroughly. How soft and silken his hair was, and how she longed for him to be kissing her again. . . .

She finished bathing the wounds and put on some of the medicament she had applied to Carlotta's back. Then she poured out whisky for them both; she sipped hers as he downed his in one gulp. Then she glanced across at the bed to see if Carlotta, too, wanted a drink, but the girl appeared to have fallen asleep, totally exhausted but relieved now that everything was over. They spoke in lowered voices so as not to disturb the girl.

Nesta whispered, 'I always dreaded something like this happening, but I have taken such care. I've always been aware of men like this.'

'Being aware isn't enough,' Malgrave said severely. 'You can't control everybody. Perhaps he himself didn't know this morning when he woke up that he would go berserk like this. Who's to forecast such a thing? Obviously such men don't go around behaving like crazed lunatics all the time or they would be locked up. There comes a time when anyone is apt to lose his control suddenly and go over the edge. That's a dangerous time, and I'm sure you know, Miss Bellingham, that where sex is concerned it is, indeed, a very dangerous time for a man who is even so much as slightly abnormal.'

To her astonishment, Nesta found herself blushing as if she were a coy young virgin.

He seemed so wise. His knowledge astonished her; she had never pictured him knowing about such things, thinking that only she and others like herself, who had learned the hard way, knew of the darker depths of human nature.

'You are right,' she said humbly, 'and yet we have not had trouble like this before.'

'And with good fortune you will not have it again,' he said, smiling up at her, 'but do take care. Worse than this might have happened; your girl might have been murdered, and others harmed as well.'

'I know,' she said, biting her lip. 'Fortunately Carlotta is a strong girl. Had it been one of the more fragile ones I dread to think what might have happened. But thank you for your help, James. Thank you so much. I don't know what I'd have done without you.'

He smiled again, and his blue eyes were full of the twinkling kindness she remembered so well from all those years ago.

When Trenton had been borne away, the club was settled down for the night. One of the girls, Annette, would attend Carlotta until morning. Nesta and James retired to her private drawing-room, which was gently illuminated by the light of one lamp. A silver tray stood nearby, and on it were a flask of Madeira and two delicate crystal glasses. Food had been prepared for their supper, but neither was hungry.

As they talked, almost ill at ease now that they were alone, Nesta began to feel bitter disappointment. He was behaving so formally, making no advances towards her. Had he regretted coming? How could she bear it if he left without making love to her? What could she do to encourage him? When she poured him more Madeira, she let her fingers brush against his and their eyes met. Immediately, she blushed, astonished at how nervous he always made her feel.

'You are very beautiful, Nesta,' he said, his voice husky. 'I've thought about you a great deal in the past week. In fact, I haven't been able to get you out of my mind.' He caught her hand and kissed it. 'Your skin is so fragrant, and it feels like polished silk – did you know that? I suppose you are used to compliments.' It was a statement, not a question.

Nesta lowered her eyes almost demurely, her heart beating fast. Before she could reply, he caught her in his arms and was crushing her mouth with his, making her lips throb.

'Nesta, darling, can we not go somewhere more comfortable?'

'Of course.'

She led him into her bedroom, his hand in hers, her heart pounding, almost painfully. She thrilled with delight at having him close to her again.

James lifted her up and placed her gently against the pillows while he took off his clothes and she removed hers. Then they were naked in each other's arms, kissing wildly, clinging to one another fiercely. When Nesta closed her eyes in ecstasy, she saw brilliant stars amidst the darkness, as if she were gazing up into the moonlit night sky; stars sparkled deep within her, too, glittering with a fiery radiance. He loved her! Her beautiful, adored Sun God was really here in bed with her again. . . .

She could not wait for his further caresses but urged him inside her, gasping at his strength and hardness. How could she endure such rapture without losing consciousness? As he began to move in and out of her body, she entwined her legs behind his back to pull him closer, moaning his name. He paused for a moment to look deep into her eyes, but she begged him not to stop; so he began again, with ever more power, until they truly seemed to be as one, welded together. To be in his arms was to know all the secrets of life, to have a reason for having been born. How she had yearned for him, for half her life, and now he was aching for her. . . .

'Nesta,' he groaned, 'how have I existed without you, my darling? My God, what I've been missing all these years! Darling, you're beautiful – I wish I could go on longer but I don't think I can hold out – '

By way of reply, Nesta hugged him closer, slanting her hips against his so that he gasped. Then, feeling him convulse inside her, she smiled joyfully at his passion.

Satiated, they lay close, his head on her breasts. They slept for some time before waking to make love once more.

'Tell me how you came to own the Crimson Club?' James asked afterwards, as they watched the dawn light filtering into the room. 'You are so very young. . . .' He paused, as if to choose his words. 'You must have known many men.'

Nesta should have recognized the danger signals then, but she did not. Mellow after his loving, she told him a little of her origins while he listened intently. In the half-light, she did not see the expression on his face nor the way his mouth had tightened.

'Tell me about the men you have slept with.'

'There's nothing to tell. They have meant nothing to me. I have never loved any of them.'

'What of me?'

Nesta bit her lip. 'You are not to be compared with them.'

'How do you think of me, then?'

'I have dreamed of being in bed with you – '

'In bed only?' His fingers tightened round her wrist.

'Anywhere. I'd be grateful for any time, anything you might choose to give me,' she admitted.

'Are you quite sure of that?'

'Absolutely, James.'

'What if it turns out to be nothing?'

She guessed that he was testing her. 'Then I would accept it – and let my heart be broken.'

'You feel that strongly about me?'

'I could not care for you more than I do now.'

'Then I really mean more to you than just another client?'

'I told you that you have never been that. You have always been special to me.'

'Always? You speak as if you have known me for years.'

'Perhaps I have.'

'You sound very mysterious, my darling, but it is true that I feel as if I have known you a long time.' He kissed her forehead, then her nose. 'Do you like that?'

'How could I not?'

Their kisses grew wilder; they made love for a third time, and it was just as blissful as the first.

James left at eleven the next morning, kissing Nesta good-bye as she reclined amongst the pillows, her hair a raven cloud, her cheeks a rosy pink.

It was only after he had gone that Nesta realized that he had said nothing about seeing her again.

The following weeks seemed to drag by, and James did not call or write. Experienced as she was, Nesta should have been able to deal with this, to laugh it off, but she could not. He was no ordinary man, no ordinary love. She was barely sleeping, and eating only a few mouthfuls of food; already she had begun to look ill.

'You are looking peaky, lovey, an' that's no mistake,' Amy said to her, concerned.

'Yes, Nesta, it's true. Now don't go on denying it. Amy an' I've both been watchin' you. It's that Malgrave bloke, ain't it? You've gone an' fallen for him, ain't you?' Cathy said.

'An' he don't want to know, that's it, ain't it?'

Nesta nodded gloomily, feeling more tears threatening.

'Look, lovey, you been here all this time, an' it's just been work, work, work for you. You know how you live on your nerves an' fret over every little thing. What you need is a holiday away.'

Nesta managed a smile, grateful for their concern. They were dears, and she was very fond of them. When they were in her company they were all three of them relaxed. Nesta always listened to their advice – had they not been dealing it out to her for years now, and always motivated by affection?

Yes, she did need a holiday, and badly. She would get as far away as possible from London, somewhere entirely different. She needed solitude. When the girls had gone, she took out her atlas and opened it at a map of Great Britain. Lifting one hand, she closed her eyes and circled her finger round and round the page, then let it land where it wished.

Her finger pointed to York.

CHAPTER TWELVE

Thanks to the swift development of the railroads the journey was completed in a comparatively short time. Had Nesta been travelling in the previous century, it would have taken her no less than six days to get from London to York. Not that she was aware of the length of the journey or, indeed, anything else for that matter: she seemed to be in an emotional limbo, all feelings and sensations drained from her.

Betsy, sitting beside her on the seat in the first-class compartment, glanced at her now and again, worried. She had never seen her mistress so lethargic, and she dearly hoped that this holiday would restore her former vitality.

When she was not anxiously watching her mistress, Betsy was enjoying every moment of the journey. No doubt some would say the train was a noisy, smoky and uncomfortable means of travel, but Betsy had never been on one before, nor had she ever been out of London, and found the whole thing thoroughly exciting, something she would remember for the rest of her life and tell her grandchildren about one day. If only her mistress were interested in the journey, they might chat about it, but Nesta Bellingham showed by the withdrawn look on her face that she had no wish to converse.

A red-faced and excessively obese lady wearing a vast-brimmed bonnet edged with silk lilacs and a gown of a deeper violet hue was sitting with her lady's maid and a small boy on the opposite seats. Three or four times she attempted to engage Nesta in conversation, failing miserably, but she was obviously determined not to give up. She thought that the lady with the glossy black hair and deep amethyst eyes was quite the most mysterious and beautiful creature she had ever seen, for beneath the rolls and pads of fat the woman in lilac had a romantic heart.

She also loved to gossip. Who this intriguing young lady was she dearly wished to know. The lady was most properly dressed, in soft apple green silk, and her bonnet was quite the latest French fashion with its curling white ostrich feather bobbing in its brim. A single emerald on a fine gold chain hung round her slender white neck and her reticule was of white velvet, sewn most exquisitely with gold and silver thread.

The woman in lilac stared at Nesta far too long, realizing that she was being rude but finding her gaze drawn back time and again to the woman who sat opposite her in the carriage. Fortunately, the little boy who was travelling with her – her nephew – kept asking questions about the train; never having ridden on one before, he wanted to know everything about its workings, questions which the woman in lilac found increasingly difficult to answer, for she lacked a scientific turn of mind.

Once or twice, she said, 'Wait till we get to York, Benjamin, and Captain Maude will answer all your questions, I promise you,' but the boy, wriggling and squirming in his seat, his eyes darting everywhere, wanted the answers to his questions *now*. How could he wait until he met his uncle in York? He was only nine years old, and every hour of waiting seemed like a lifetime to him.

'Benjamin, sit still. Oh, do be still, my boy,' the woman in lilac reproved now and again, but without conviction in her voice. She really could think about little else than the mysterious lady who had sat throughout the journey with a stony expression on her face and without saying one word. How could she remain so silent? Did she not have something to say about *anything*? To the woman in lilac, who was a vigorous gossip, conversation was one of the most important preoccupations in life.

Finally, although still with a feeling of dissatisfaction, the woman in lilac, whose name was Annabella, Lady Blomfield, turned her thoughts to their arrival in York and the meeting with her other nephew, Captain Joseph Maude. She had not seen Joseph for four years; he had been abroad, serving with his regiment, and had only recently returned to his home in York. During that period young Benjamin had been a frequent visitor to Lady Blomfield's home in Chelsea, for Lady Maude – mother of Joseph, Benjamin and their sisters, Violetta and Marigold, now both married – was of a delicate constitution and bedridden. Lady Maude's husband had died during one of the battles of the Crimean War, and she had seemed to sink after his death, not wanting to live, taking permanently to her bed.

Maude Manor had become no place for a lively, spirited boy such as Benjamin to live and so he visited Blomfield House regularly. He found London an exciting and intriguing place, where he was allowed to explore reasonably freely in the stolid company of two or three of Lady Blomfield's dependable male servants.

During this, his latest visit, Benjamin had thrilled and shivered to the horrors and delights of the Tower of London, absorbed with fascination the scientific intricacies of the Observatory at Greenwich, journeyed repeatedly up and down the river Thames on every possible form of boat which could be hired, and been the guest of a close friend of Lady Blomfield's, the Countess of Alverston, who had found Benjamin stimulating and enjoyable company for her eleven daughters, seven of whom had not yet been found husbands. It would please Lady Blomfield immensely to have her dear nephew Benjamin married to one of the Countess's daughters, even if not one of them could be called a great beauty. But of course, that could not take place for many years yet, for Benjamin was still only nine years old.

Lady Blomfield had long ago relinquished all hope of Captain Maude's marrying. Joseph was a sturdy, active kind of man, forever on the go, who simply did not seem to find time for so much as a tiny divertissement with the fairer sex. She knew it was Lady Maude's dearest wish that he should marry into a good family, preferably a family which she, Lady Maude, knew well and liked. However, many of the young girls of Captain Maude's age group, with whom he had grown up, were now married and producing families of their own. True, Captain Maude's father had married Lady Maude a widow, late in life, but where was Captain Maude going to find a pretty and suitable young bride when he finally did decide that the time had come to marry?

Benjamin's voice interrupted his aunt's thoughts. 'Aunt Annabella, Aunt Annabella, we're here, we're here! The train is pulling up!' His lively, tanned face was full of anticipation. He was longing to see his brother again.

Lady Blomfield's maid began to assemble their belongings, gathering bags, gloves, reticules and parcels. She was a grey little woman who could pass unnoticed in a crowd.

The fact that the train was slowing seemed to break through Nesta's thoughts, for she looked round her as if she had suddenly wakened from a deep sleep. A little of the shadow lifted from her lustrous eyes.

'Betsy, are we here?' she asked.

'Yes, ma'am, we are. This is York, I do believe.' Betsy

lowered her voice, 'Leastways, that young boy over there says 'tis York an' he ought to know. From what he's been saying to his aunt, he lives here.'

Nesta did not reply. She was not interested in the noisy, flamboyant family which had accompanied them on the journey, although she liked the look of the boy's intelligent, lively face. His aunt, however, was another matter, definitely the sort of woman who stirred up tales and rumours, icing them with a good serving of her own imagination. People like her were to be avoided like the plague. Nesta wondered what the woman would say if she knew she had been sharing her compartment with the proprietress of a high-class brothel in the city of London. The thought brought a slight smile to Nesta's lips.

The train screeched its way to a halt as dark buildings came into sight. It was a picturesque little station, small enough to be friendly, large enough to border on elegant, and Nesta liked it instantly. The air was fresh and bracing; she liked that, too. How far away this place was from the smells and sounds of polluted London, where summer only increased the disadvantages of city life.

Porters rushed forward to greet the passengers, their stolid Yorkshire faces wreathed in smiles. How different it was from the station from which they had departed in London, where the men had seemed edgy and unhappy, unwilling to come forward to assist even a lady. If this was an example of the Yorkshire people then perhaps she would enjoy her stay here.

The woman in lilac, her nephew and maid were bustling past to the attentive accompaniment of porters. Nesta watched the woman's face beneath her exotic, over-decorated bonnet, noticing her eyes darting around the station. She was looking for somebody. While Betsy gathered their hand-luggage together, Nesta observed the other woman and saw her eyes light up as they came to rest on a man who had just entered through the station doors. He had wavy chestnut hair and a tanned face, a tan which showed he had been in some foreign clime for a considerable time. Everyone around him seemed to look pale, almost sickly by comparison. As he saw the woman in lilac he raised his arms and came hurrying towards her, his broad smile showing healthy white teeth. The man must be about thirty, Nesta guessed. He was very tall, with a proud military bearing, and he wore the smart, immaculate uniform of a Captain.

'Joseph! Joseph, my dear!' cried the woman, raising her own arms as they embraced, beaming at one another.

Benjamin thrust himself between them, throwing back his head and laughing, flinging his arms round them both, crying, 'Welcome back, welcome back, brother! I've missed you a great deal, yes indeed I have!'

'Benjamin, how you've grown,' the handsome Captain said. 'My goodness, you've quite doubled in size since I last saw you.'

'That is so, that is so,' the woman in lilac chattered merrily, 'has he not? And a lot of it is due to me you know, Joseph. I have fed him so well – you would not believe the size of his appetite! My goodness, my goodness.' She fluttered and blushed, fanning herself with one hand, seeming almost overcome by the Captain's presence.

He, for his part, looked immensely happy to have them back with him again.

'The carriage is waiting for us outside, Aunt Annabella,' he said. 'If you will both come this way. The coachmen will take your bags.'

'Oh yes, of course, of course, Joseph dear.' Aunt Annabella fussed, looking about her for her reticule before she realized that it was hanging on her wrist. Then she could not find her lorgnette, but that was soon discovered after a hurried search – it had fallen down the bodice of her gown. All the time she was twittering and expostulating, the Captain's eyes were on her, tolerant and amused, while Benjamin pulled on his brother's hand, saying, 'Oh, hurry, hurry, *do* hurry! I cannot wait to be back home. It will be so much fun now you are back, Joseph.'

The little party moved towards the station exit, gradually becoming lost to view. Betsy was saying something. Nesta turned round, taking one of the bags from her. She had not heard a word that her maid had spoken, so raptly intent had she been on watching the happiness and the closeness of the family who had now passed from view. She was being reminded all too poignantly of the happy family, mother and son, she had seen all those years ago at the soup-kitchen on St Thomas's Wharf. Then her spirits sank as swiftly as they had risen, and she was once more alone, an outsider, a motherless orphan with no one to love her. York station was not the friendly welcoming little place she had imagined but just like any other station with its cold bones of buildings, soot and dirt and clamour.

'Ma'am, *ma'am*. I asked you whether we was going to hire our own carriage or use one of the cabs outside?'

'Oh, whichever is easiest, Betsy. I'm too tired to think about anything at the moment.'

'Yes, ma'am,' Betsy sighed. She was steeling herself for a dull visit with an uncommunicative mistress and no chance for a pleasant gossip.

'Oh, ma'am, about the hotel where we're staying . . . .'

'Yes?' Nesta said.

'Well, ma'am, is it close by, or do we have a long way to go? 'Cause if the cabs have been taken up by all the other people what come off the train, we'll have to hitch our bags all the way by ourselves, won't we?'

Nesta had not thought of this. She seemed in a daze. What Betsy said was probably true; the station platform had now emptied. All those people who had been in the train had alighted and gone through the station exit; they were probably occupying all of the cabs waiting outside. Well, they had better hurry; perhaps there was just a possibility that there would be one left.

Picking up two of the bags, Nesta left Betsy to carry the others, and they made their way as quickly as possible through the station exit. Outside there was only one carriage but no cabs in sight. Nesta stared wearily at the scene. She simply could not go to all the trouble of hiring a carriage; everything was far too much of a burden for her at the moment. She had never felt so exhausted.

A voice called out, 'Excuse me, ma'am!' and it was some moments before she realized that it was she who was being addressed. The Captain, looking out of the carriage window – for it was his carriage – had seen the young lady and her servant standing with their bags and no cab to take them to their destination. He had told his coachman to delay until he had found out where the young lady was going.

Looking up into the Captain's face, Nesta saw that he had hazel eyes, thick chestnut brows and dark eyelashes, broad cheekbones and a thin mouth with deep, curving laughter lines on either side of it. She feared that he would think her odd, for she was slow to respond to his words.

He called out again, 'Ma'am, if we can take you somewhere with all those bags?'

'I – well, to be quite honest, sir, er, Captain, I have no notion where we are going. I believe you live here in York. I could not help but overhear on the train the conversation of your companions and I wonder if you could perhaps recommend a hotel to me or an inn of some kind where I and my maid might stay?'

The Captain grinned. 'Why, of course, nothing could be easier, ma'am. There is The George in Coney Street, or how about The Bell and the Rose – that is but a few doors away. If you require more luxurious surroundings, there is always the Station Hotel; that is nearer than either of the others.'

'Whichever you recommend, Captain. I leave it up to you.'

Captain Maude was as intrigued as his aunt had been by the pale, uncommunicative beauty standing before him. She seemed to be so preoccupied as to be taking little notice of her surroundings. Could it possibly be correct of him to surmise that she had journeyed here unprepared, without even having made enquiries about a place to stay? He feared she was not well – she might even faint in the street; pale she looked, and with deep shadows beneath her eyes. Accustomed as he was to his invalid mother, he believed he could discern all the signs of incipient collapse.

Being ignorant of the young woman's financial standing, Captain Maude decided to drive her and her maid to The George in Coney Street, which was a reasonably priced establishment. He would not wish to embarrass her by taking her to accommodation which might prove too expensive for her requirements. The George would suit her adequately. It was not far from the Shambles, that most attractive shopping area with its quaint medieval central street. She would only be a short walk from the Minster, a place he imagined she might have need of in her present state of mind. The river Ouse was not far away, where she would be able to walk up and down its banks and across its many bridges.

It was only a very short journey to The George, but Lady Blomfield intended to put every moment of it to good use. Immediately she had Nesta and her maid settled in the coach, she began questioning them.

'You are here for a holiday?' she enquired, tilting her head so that Benjamin was almost hidden from view by the ornate extremities of her bonnet.

'Yes, a holiday,' replied Nesta spiritlessly.

'You will find York a most attractive and picturesque little city,' Lady Blomfield prattled on.

Then she realized that in her excitement at actually having the intriguing woman in her coach she had quite forgotten the matter of introductions. She gasped, her cheeks going pink, and fluttered her hand up and down in front of her face, as if something urgent were about to happen and she must warn everybody. It was at that moment that the cord of her reticule broke. Beads popped all over the coach like dried peas from a shooter, necessitating everyone's attention.

Full of consternation that the short carriage ride would be over before she had even so much as found out the mystery woman's name, Lady Blomfield besought everyone present to ignore the beads, saying that they could be retrieved by the servants when they reached Maude Manor. Benjamin, finding it all a great lark, was bobbing up and down, picking up beads and pushing them into his pockets, his cheeks rosy from silent laughter. Joseph, too, appeared to be similarly absorbed, but had Nesta glanced up she would have seen his hazel eyes looking upon her questioningly.

'A holiday, you said. Was that right, a holiday?' Lady Blomfield went on, unperturbed by the commotion around her. Nesta nodded. 'And is it for a *long* holiday that you are here?' Lady Blomfield persisted.

'I really have no notion of how long I shall stay,' Nesta said coolly. 'I came on the spur of the moment.'

'So York has been recommended to you?' Lady Blomfield smiled broadly. 'Well, they say there is no fairer city, and I must agree with that. Since Georgian days it has been the social centre of the North, you know; second only to London for fine gatherings and grand occasions. Why, you will find so many jolly activities here that you will not have a moment to spare.'

Nesta must have looked alarmed, for Captain Maude interrupted.

'One is not forced to join in, of course,' he said. 'Miss... madam... er?'

'Bellingham, Nesta Bellingham, and it is Miss,' Nesta said with the smallest smile she could manage.

'Er... Miss Bellingham. There is plenty to do if one wishes to do plenty, and if one wishes to recharge one's energies, then York is also the right place to find peace and quiet.'

'I am glad to hear that,' Nesta said drily.

Betsy was smiling to herself. That woman in the loud lilac clothes and hat was quite the most persistent creature Betsy had ever come across. The way she was prying and questioning her mistress, and she a lady, too.

They were now in Coney Street and the coachman was calling out 'Whoa!' to the horses as the carriage drew up in front of the little inn where Nesta was to stay. In desperation Lady Blomfield put forward an invitation which, under any circumstances, she would never have proferred to a complete stranger, even such a dramatically beautiful one.

'Miss Bellingham, you *will* be our guest at Maude Manor? Oh please, do say that you will come! We have tea every afternoon for visitors, and I can send a carriage to collect you. Please do say that you will come!'

It was easier for Nesta to say yes than to fight the invitation. Half-lifting her head she replied that, yes, she would very much like to see Maude Manor. Perhaps Lady Blomfield would give her some notice as to when the carriage would come so she could be ready for it?

'Oh how nice, how very nice!' Lady Blomfield beamed broadly. 'I am so pleased, so pleased, my dear. I shall look forward to seeing you. Now if you have any problems just let us know and my nephew will be down here instantly to help you, won't you, Joseph dear?'

Joseph nodded, giving Nesta the same broad smile, which was obviously a shared family trait.

Captain Maude leapt down from the carriage to help Nesta out and then he lifted down her bags and helped Betsy to disembark. Taking Nesta's arm, he accompanied her into The George and introduced both her and her maid to the keeper of the inn, whom he knew well, saying that the ladies wished to have two rooms with as pleasant a view as possible.

The innkeeper was quite overwhelmed, Nesta could see, by the fact that it was Captain Maude who had escorted her. Bowing and rubbing his hands together, the man immediately ordered the preparation of two of his finest rooms for Miss Bellingham and her maid. Then, after ensuring that all was straightforward, Captain Maude gave a courteous bow to Nesta, kissing her hand lightly and repeating again that if she had any problems whatsoever she had but to get in touch with him and he would be at her side instantly.

'Thank you,' she murmured, a little colour in her cheeks, for he was quite the most dashing and competent young man. When he had taken his leave, she looked around, not quite so dazed as before. It was indeed a pleasant little inn, cosy, gleaming with polish and smelling of beeswax and herbs. She liked its old oak beams, polished to a high gloss, the French clock over the chimney piece, the paintings of horses and foxes which adorned the panelled walls of the hallway.

Nesta was suddenly assailed by a strong urge to go up to the room ordered for her, close her door and lie down on the bed, pulling the covers up to her chin, to hide herself in a warm cocoon of safety. She realized that merely to have got away from the club was not enough to soothe her frayed nerves; it would take more to calm and restore her. She needed peace, utter tranquillity, not to be badgered by questions, small talk. She was desperately tired, too; her body ached as if she had been riding a horse for long hours at a stretch.

The rooms were promptly in readiness, and soon Nesta was able to make her wish fact. Telling Betsy to unpack their valises later, she despatched her maid to her room, saying that she was going to rest and was not to be disturbed.

Nesta's room had chintz curtains and bedcover, and two massive portraits of men with severe-looking faces and sturdy bodies, dressed in the clothes of huntsmen. The sheets on the bed were spotlessly clean and smelt of fresh lavender. A pretty arrangement of early spring flowers stood on the oak bedside table. The wardrobe was enormous, dark and heavy, and would have accommodated the clothes of half a dozen women inside its cavernous recesses. The carpet was of a Turkish weave in bright reds and blues, and there were horse brasses along the chimney piece, gleaming and newly polished. Above her head, black oak beams told of the many centuries which The George had seen, and a lively fire danced in the grate, spitting and crackling as if it were trying to converse with her.

Half-smiling at this notion, Nesta began to peel off her travelling clothes. A china bowl and jug stood on the washstand, and she dipped her hands into the water, washing them and her face with the scented soap provided. A fluffy rose-pink towel lay nearby for her to dry herself.

After her ablutions, Nesta walked over to the solid bed

and sat down to test the mattress; it felt soft but firm. Within minutes she removed the last of her clothes, keeping on only her embroidered shift, and then turned back the covers. She rolled into the bed, covering herself quickly, and snuggled down.

When Nesta awoke eight hours later the room was pitch dark. For a moment she was disorientated, not knowing where she was. In the Crimson Club there was always a tiny light burning somewhere in her room, for she had a great fear of darkness. Had she not felt afraid now she would have leapt out of bed, but, instead, she huddled down, closing her eyes tightly against the blackness. Then slowly she began to remember that she was in York, at The George inn, that Betsy was in the room next door and that there was a little bell on the table at the side of her bed. Reaching out her hand, her eyes still screwed tightly shut, she shook the bell as loudly as she could; within moments Betsy was in the room and lit the lamp.

'Had a nice sleep, have you, ma'am? Certainly been in here a long time an' not a peep out of you. Feeling better, eh?'

'Yes, much better, thank you, Betsy. There must be something in the air here in York. I went out as if I'd been hit on the head.'

'Ready for your dinner now, are you, ma'am? Oh, there's some lovely smells of cooking coming up the stairs. I've been lying on my bed smelling them now for a good half hour an' wondering if you'd wake in time. Didn't fancy eating without you.'

'Well, I expect you'll have to get used to that sooner or later, Betsy, because I'm not here to make a lot of public appearances. The last thing I feel like doing is mingling with people. I just want peace and quiet.'

'Yes, ma'am,' Betsy said gloomily.

Betsy had been hoping that her mistress's spirits would lift so that they could embark on a jolly round of social activity, visiting and sightseeing, but it looked as if her hopes had been in vain. Still, after a few days' rest and quiet, perhaps her mistress would recover and things would brighten? She hoped so; she was far from being a natural recluse.

Now that Captain Maude, Betsy liked him very much; he seemed just the type to take her mistress out of herself, to treat her to drives around the countryside, to take her to a few of the local balls. That would be just the thing to give her mistress the lift she needed, and she guessed there would be some real nice gentleman servants at Captain Maude's home. She was longing to meet *them*.

'Shall I start unpacking your things now, ma'am?' she asked.

Nesta nodded and said, 'I'm not going down to dinner tonight, Betsy. I'll have dinner in my room. You can take dinner in yours or you can go downstairs and eat with the other servants. It's up to you. Take your choice.'

The thought of eating alone in her room was more than Betsy could bear, so she said that she would join the servants downstairs.

'Are we dressing special this evening, ma'am?' she asked.

'That will hardly be necessary if I am staying in my room, will it, Betsy? I'll just put on my robe, if you will pass it. And would you put more logs on the fire, it is becoming somewhat chilly. They say it's much colder up here in the North.'

'Yes, ma'am, some of the staff here was saying that they get snow, real thick snow, regular every winter, an' out on the moors the people in the little cottages get snowed in, with snow right up to their bedroom windows. Don't think I'd like that, ma'am. Imagine being snowed in with your family, stuck in the house for weeks on end, in the cold. How do they get food? That's not the life for me.' She shuddered.

'They're sturdy folk, these Yorkshire people, so they say. Hardy, used to the cold.'

Nesta pulled on her wrap and sat down by the fire to warm her hands. This was a cosy, inviting room; she would like to stay here for ever. Alone, in peace, never having to make any more decisions, untroubled by petty problems, not having to care about looking her best at all times, day and night. Just to sit here by the fire, snug and relaxed, having her meals brought to her on a tray.

Dinner that night consisted of superbly cooked roast beef, with a side-dish she had never before tasted: Yorkshire pudding, light and fluffy, made in a special way from batter and soaked in meat juices. Nesta thought it was so delicious that she sent Betsy to fetch her a second helping. There were also roast potatoes, crunchy on the outside, soft and fluffy inside. She left the sweet but had two pieces of cake, which looked and tasted like gingerbread but which Betsy said the servants called parkin. There was also an assortment of cheeses, and fragrant coffee to finish.

Had everything not been so excellently cooked it would have been a heavy meal, and Nesta ate far more than she normally did in the evening. Afterwards, she sat by the fire for an hour, thinking about nothing in particular, and then all too willingly retired to bed. Betsy lit a lamp for her in the corner. The fire was banked up so that its heat would last the night, and a pinkish glow lit the hearth. As the evening wore on, the sounds of movement and the comings and goings of the guests at the inn gradually faded away until a deep silence fell.

Nesta slept heavily, as if she had not been to bed for days. She did not awaken until eleven the next morning, when Betsy knocked on her door with a breakfast tray; steaming hot coffee, fresh poppy-seed rolls and butter, Yorkshire cheeses, ripe and golden, crisp curly bacon done to a turn, scrambled eggs and devilled kidneys. Realizing that she was ravenous, Nesta ate another large meal and then sat by the fire again, feeling a little more at ease.

After lunch, Nesta told Betsy to go out and explore the city if she wished. Betsy was delighted. Flinging on her cloak and her perky little hat with the feather in it, she called good-bye to her mistress as she clattered down the stairs. She was gone for two hours, and when she returned her cheeks were a bright rosy red and her eyes sparkled.

'Oh, ma'am, you really should get out! This is the prettiest little city you ever did see! It really is! Oh, the Minster! It's the most beautiful building. Oh an' inside! It's so huge an' old, ma'am; *so* old – you just wouldn't believe how *old* it is! The choir was singing, oh beautiful, like angel voices. An' I walked down the Shambles – that's what they call it, ma'am, the Shambles. They don't call it that because it's falling down. It's called after the butchers, 'cause once long ago all the butchers had their stalls down there. An' all the quaint little shops, all higgledy-piggledy.... Oh, you really should see it, ma'am!'

Nesta smiled at her maid's enthusiasm but felt no desire whatsoever to go sightseeing. While Betsy had been out, Captain Maude had called, leaving his card with the innkeeper when Nesta had refused to admit him. He had left a message, that his mother had invited her for afternoon tea; he particularly wished that she would come because he so much wanted to meet her again. Nesta had taken his card, which the innkeeper's wife had brought up to her, and asked her to convey to the Captain her answer: she would not accept.

She had thrown the card onto the fire, watching its edges curl and blacken, then turn to ashes. That chestnut brown hair and those hazel eyes of his, his laughing face; all conveyed such virility, such spirit – she could not take the strain of it at the moment. She felt he would rob her of what little vitality she herself had left.

Nesta spent that evening much the same way she had spent the previous nights, sleeping deeply again until midmorning. At two in the afternoon Captain Maude called again, repeating the invitation; Nesta again refused it. This ritual continued for four more days, until Betsy was all but lashing out at her mistress for her stubbornness.

'Ma'am, I don't know how you can do it! I've never seen anything like it before in all me life! How can you turn down that nice young man? Why, if it were me I'd be bursting to meet him again an' to see his beautiful house. I don't know *how* you can do it, ma'am.'

'Very easily, Betsy,' Nesta replied. 'I have not come here

to fraternize. I have come here to regain my strength, to think over things you know nothing about, Betsy. Now, if I might have a little peace? Perhaps you would like to go out again.'

'All right, ma'am.' Betsy sighed deeply, doing as she was bidden but shaking her head from side to side. If this way of living continued, her mistress might as well enter a nunnery; there was no point in living in the world if you just shut yourself up in your room, not seeing anybody. Why, in London her mistress was always surrounded by suitors, flattering her, smiling at her, bringing her gifts; more than one man was madly in love with her. How could she have left all that behind to shut herself away here in a strange room in a strange city? Some people were just beyond understanding.

On the seventh day, although she had fully intended to say no as curtly as before, Nesta astonished herself by accepting Captain Maude's invitation. While he waited outside in his carriage she selected a dress to wear; a beautiful tea-gown of rose-pink velvet trimmed with ruched violet silk, which matched her eyes perfectly. While she chose violet accessories to match, Betsy fluttered around her, giggling and chattering, her cheeks flushed as she helped Nesta fasten all the buttons and laces, then bringing out shoes and cloak, gloves and bonnet, from the massive, heavy wardrobe. Nesta decided against the pink pearls and wore instead the amethysts which had been her first luxury purchase and which had accompanied her through so much. When she was ready, she went downstairs and then climbed into Captain Maude's waiting carriage without a quiver of regret.

A radiant sun was trying to force its way through the dove-grey clouds, and occasionally the dark interior of the carriage was lighted by its rays, only to darken again moments later. Nesta felt almost a different person, as if she were not herself any more but someone else. It was a strange sensation, and she had not really come to grips with it by the time the carriage pulled up outside Maude Manor.

The young Captain had entertained her during the journey with interesting anecdotes about his home and his family. She had smiled and nodded, not at all interested in what he was saying but finding her eyes drawn to his, watching his mouth move as he spoke, noticing how he used his slender but strong and well-shaped hands, with their square, clean fingernails. What an excellent husband he would make for some young, pretty society girl, she had thought – if he were not already affianced or married. Then she had remembered his aunt's having said something about an absence from the country of four years; that seemed an awfully long time to leave a young bride, so possibly he was not yet wed.

As the journey had progressed, Nesta had found herself thinking that had she been anyone else, without her background, born into society maybe, she would certainly have considered him an ideal mate for herself. But how very young and innocent he was compared with her; she felt a hundred years old beside him, for all the experience of life he might have had serving abroad. What would he say if he knew of her origins, of what she was now, should she decide to confess everything to him? His face would become transfixed with shock and horror. He would draw back from her in disgust. His respectable, proud aunt would burst into hysterics if she knew whom she had invited into her home. But the family had taken Nesta for a lady and a lady she would be – in their presence anyway.

Lady Blomfield was dressed in the most ghastly shade of green Nesta had ever seen, and she wore an emerald necklace, grotesquely surrounded by the folds of fat on her neck. Her hair was elaborately coiled and ringletted round her face, and in the bun at the back of her neck were stuck two feathers of a matching green, which bobbed and waved as she moved. Draped across her back and over each arm was a shawl coloured acid yellow, which completed the eyesore that was her costume.

Lady Blomfield fluttered, blushed and gabbled her way through the first ten minutes, almost as if she had royalty in her presence. To some extent Nesta was flattered by her attentiveness, but she thought that her own lack-lustre response to her hostess's gushing friendship must make her appear cold and ill-mannered.

Benjamin's charging in and out of the room at various times helped to relax the formality of the occasion. Nesta considered him a welcome distraction, appreciating the fact that some of the attention was being taken away from her. She had never liked noisy children, after her early childhood amongst all the clatter and harshness of slum life where children ran wild in the streets, but Benjamin seemed a pleasant boy. He was also intelligent, and his colouring was like Captain Maude's, which made him physically very attractive.

Tea consisted of dainty iced buns, Madeira cake, delicate cucumber sandwiches cut so thin that they were almost transparent, and seed cake, a concoction which Nesta had never been able to stomach. Fortunately Benjamin dominated the actual tea ceremony, talking about his hobby, which was steam engines, and quizzing his brother about his life abroad. While Captain Maude was answering yet another of his brother's questions, the door was pushed open and Nesta saw a beautiful greyhound enter the room. He padded across the floor and lay down at Nesta's feet, looking up at her with limpid, appealing eyes.

'Don't feed him, please, Miss Bellingham. We're trying to train him. I'm afraid he has been thoroughly spoiled, and now at every mealtime he comes to beg at our feet. It really is such a bad habit. We must cure him of it,' Lady Blomfield said.

The dog had such soulful eyes that Nesta found it hard not to slip him a crumb or two. When she remarked on his slender physique Benjamin replied scornfully that it was due to his breed and certainly had nothing to do with his being starved.

'Do not be so rude, Benjamin,' Lady Blomfield said. 'I am sure that our guest was not suggesting that we have starved Horace. Now apologize to Miss Bellingham for your curtness.'

Reluctantly Benjamin did as he was told. Nesta accepted his apology gracefully. Afterwards there was an almost awkward silence until the servants came to bear away the tea trays, and then Captain Maude asked Nesta if she would like to see the conservatory, an invitation which she accepted gratefully.

'Plants were my father's love,' Captain Maude explained as they walked down aisles which were crammed with plants, shrubs and blossoms of every description and size. It was a vast conservatory, dome-shaped, and there was seemingly no empty space to be found. Captain Maude explained that his father's life's work had been the acquisition of plants, most of which had found their way into this conservatory at some time or other. His mother, he said, had shown no interest in horticulture. Her participation had consisted of voicing polite gratitude whenever his father handed her a bouquet of flowers.

His reference to Lady Maude reminded Nesta that somewhere in this beautiful old mansion house set on the wild moors there was an invalid who never ventured from her room and yet was the mother of this admirably vital young man and of the boisterous Benjamin. She found it hard to envision.

The conservatory air was heavy with the scent of greenery and of earth. Outside, a wind was rising, darting in and out of branches, swirling leaves along the paths, whipping against the windows of the house and demanding entry, but here in the conservatory it was warm, almost humid and very peaceful. Nesta would have liked to stay much longer, talking or just musing, but they had to return to the drawing-room, where Lady Blomfield awaited them. A servant was clearing up the remnants of a broken vase which Benjamin had accidentally broken. Lady Blomfield appeared not in the least perturbed by this mishap; she was careful, however, to instruct the servant not to say anything to his mistress about the breakage lest it upset her.

Lady Blomfield greeted them warmly. 'How did you like the conservatory, Miss Bellingham? I must admit that I hardly ever go in there. I have this frightful feeling that the plants are really alive, that they're watching me and will clutch at me with their long frondy strands!' She gave a tinkling laugh. 'You may think me a foolish woman but it is a fancy which I find impossible to banish.'

'I do like the conservatory, Lady Blomfield. It was so warm in there, and quiet. Certainly it has a marvellous collection of plants. I do not think I've ever seen so many at one and the same time.'

'Then you have not been to Kew Gardens, Miss Bellingham?' Captain Maude enquired.

'No, I have not. I know it must sound strange, since I do live in London, but somehow I just do not seem to have gone there.'

'One can neglect the place one lives in, I do know that,' Lady Blomfield said with a smile. 'Now, my dear, you will come and see us again soon, will you not? Next week we have the annual Spring Ball. I do hope that you will attend. My nephew will call for you at seven – that is, if you *do* decide to accept. You will be more than welcome here, and if you wish you may stay the night, as we have a multitude of rooms just longing for guests.'

Nesta was taken by surprise. She had expected to return to her hermitage existence at the inn, but here she was being invited to a ball, an event which was obviously one of the major social occasions of the year in York. Smiling, she replied that she would send word at a later date regarding her decision. Then she thanked Lady Blomfield warmly for a pleasant afternoon and for a delightful tea, said good-bye to Benjamin, patted Horace on the head and walked out to Captain Maude's carriage with her arm tucked through his.

When they were seated in the vehicle Captain Maude leaned forward to engage her attention.

'I have very much enjoyed this afternoon, Miss Bellingham,' he said earnestly, 'and I do hope that you will accept the invitation to the ball next week. I should be delighted, more than delighted, to be your escort, and if you would only say that you will come you will make me a very happy man.'

Nesta gazed momentarily into his piercing hazel eyes, which seemed to burn into her thoughts; then she lowered her gaze, her cheeks flushing. This young man made her feel so gauche, almost like a young girl again, not knowing quite what to say or do. She who had never been at a loss for words in her entire life found the experience disarming. She leaned back against the quilted seat of the carriage, as far away as she could get from those burning hazel eyes and the confident, lazy smile, feeling intolerably vulnerable while he was fixing her with his impassioned gaze.

She did not want to be forced into agreeing to come to the ball. If she said yes now, she would think about the ball for the next week, worry about it, fret over the possibility that she might feel completely unsociable by the date of the event. No, she could not accept the invitation. She had come here to rest, to be alone, to think in seclusion, to try to find some peace of mind. She had never liked parties and balls, finding them shallow occasions, with everyone starting out on their best behaviour and ending with too many men getting far too drunk. She would have to decline.

Drawing in her breath and raising her eyes with a complete absence of coquettishness, Nesta said, 'I should be happy to accept the invitation.'

CHAPTER THIRTEEN

After the passing of four more days Nesta began to feel more like her old self again. York seemed to have cast a magic spell on her, gently encouraging her to cheerfulness. She even set out to explore the city and found great solace from her visits to the Minister, whose atmosphere she found particularly potent and soothing. She liked to be there when the choirs were practising, and would sit and quietly listen to the sweet harmony, letting it ripple over her, healing her wounds. Afterwards, she would wander through the streets, browsing in the shops and taking in the pretty views, walking over the little bridges that spanned the river, looking at the goods displayed in the market stalls, taking tea in one or another of the little Tudor-style tea shops. She wandered round gown shops, hat shops and jewellers, buying a beautiful platinum Georgian ring embossed with rich blue enamel and studded with rose-cut diamonds.

Back in her room, Nesta held her newly beringed hand up to the light and watched the sparkling stones flash white-hot fire, imagining that it was her engagement ring, given to her by her Sun God. For a few brief moments she indulged herself in that poignant dream; then she closed her mind to all memories of the Duke of Malgrave. Dukes did not marry whores. The aristocracy did not accept such women in their midst (although the Prince of Wales himself was changing all that rapidly). But there still remained the staunch bastions of puritan society who would not countenance anyone but those of the highest breeding, the utmost respectability, in their presence.

Nesta's pride had prevented her from contacting James again. But she had to remember her vow to be true to both her mother and herself; she must make contact with the Duke of Malgrave in order to become involved, as she had originally planned, with his family. Until that time, Jenny's ghost would not rest in peace, nor would she know any peace.

Part of her wanted to stay in York now, for she had found it a charming place; a refuge, the first real refuge she had ever known. Although she had created the Crimson Club, it *was* a business establishment; there, she was involved in its daily organization and activities, and was more or less fully on call, day and night. She would say her own good-byes to York after the ball and would return to London, she hoped, refreshed, ready to take up the reins of her responsibilities again.

Nesta walked to the massive wardrobe and heaved open

its weighty doors. Inside was one of her favourite gowns; not a ballgown, but it was all the same extremely attractive: peacock green, rich but tasteful, and of a heavy, glossy silk trimmed with snowy white swansdown, which undulated gently against her shoulders and throat as she moved. With it she would wear a gold collar studded with green opals, which matched the colour of the gown perfectly, and white satin slippers and gloves. She would use her reticule of gold beadwork, fastened with its clasp of a solitary green opal.

The evening of the Spring Ball arrived all too soon. Nesta was called for promptly at seven by Captain Maude, resplendent in full dress uniform. He stepped back in stunned amazement at the vision Nesta presented to him, seemingly at a loss for words for a few moments before he complimented her on her outfit, saying that he had never seen her looking more radiant. It was then that she knew that the evening was going to be a success.

The lights of Maude Manor were gowing like fireflies on the moors; the French windows had been flung open onto the gardens; lilting waltz music floated out across the lawns, accompanied by the sounds of laughter and conversation. As the Captain led Nesta into the ballroom, there was a hushed silence, almost too long for comfort, when everyone noticed them, and then they resumed talking. Looking around at the assemblage, Nesta was momentarily dazzled by their finery and by the many candelabra which lit the room. There were no country bumpkins here. If she had thought that York society might be lacking in style, she was wrong. It was obvious that most of those present either shopped in London or had London fashions brought to them.

Lady Blomfield came hurrying forward to welcome them, arms outstretched. She was dressed in a crinoline of burnt orange satin with black velvet barred. From the hem up to the capacious bosom orange silk roses were entwined, giving the gown an undeniable resemblance to a flower trellis. Hiding a smile, Nesta went forward to take her outstretched hands to greet her. The black and orange ostrich feathers tucked into Lady Blomfield's coiffure trembled as if with emotion as she swept Nesta towards her. Then she raised her voice to present Nesta to the assembled company.

All faces turned again in Nesta's direction. She cowered inwardly. What if someone present recognized her, had known her in London? The thought made her stumble over her words as she greeted first one then another of the guests. Before long, however, she had no time for thought; Captain Maude was whirling her onto the floor. All the other men present seemed determined to dance with her, too, but the Captain monopolized her attention for the evening.

To Nesta's surprise she found that she felt secure in his arms, at home there. They danced well together. Nesta heard people saying what a handsome couple they made, and she was conscious of Lady Blomfield's eyes on them, admiring and more than a little thoughtful.

The cold buffet was a bounteous feast. There were massive silver bowls of punch with fruit floating on the surface and, for those who did not care to drink alcohol, a selection of fruit juices. Having eaten and drunk their fill, Nesta and the Captain returned to the dance floor, dancing until well past midnight. Then came the leave-taking. The Captain extracted a promise from her that she would see him again and asked her permission to call on her the next day.

Tired, but content, she was soon bowling home to the inn in the Maude's carriage. Betsy had left a lamp lit for her, and a fire quietly glowing in the hearth. Everything had gone so well; it had been a perfect evening. It made her wish she were the lady Lady Blomfield thought she was. If she were a girl of good family, her family no doubt would be invited to York to meet Lady Blomfield, preparatory to making the arrangements which would ensue when Captain Maude asked her for her hand in marriage, as she was sure he would do. Lady Blomfield had said repeatedly that she had never before seen her nephew so captivated.

'You mark my words, young lady, never have I seen my nephew so taken with a member of the fair sex before today!' Lady Blomfield had smiled, tapping Nesta on the arm with her fan. 'It's a good augury, my dear. Yes, a very good augury for you both, and for our family.'

Nesta had been sure Lady Blomfield was about to question her regarding her parentage, but fortunately another of the guests had interrupted at that moment. She knew that if she ever came back to York or decided to marry Captain Maude she would have to face endless intimate questions from Lady Blomfield – and from Lady Maude, too – and she wondered what she could tell them. If she were to say she was an orphan – which was quite true – they would want to know who her guardian was, who had brought her up. But, for the moment, she suspected that Lady Blomfield was so pleased and relieved to find her nephew paying court to someone that her habitual rigorous interrogation might be forgotten.

Before she sank into a deep sleep, Nesta actually contemplated marrying Captain Maude. If she sorted out her affairs at the Crimson Club, leaving it in the capable hands of Cathy and Amy, she could return to York, fabricate some story about her origins and marry Captain Maude; no one would be any the wiser. The prospect was very tempting indeed, and as she drifted off into sleep Nesta was seeing herself dressed in white silk, with a veil of Honiton lace on her head, taking the arm of Captain Maude to walk down the aisle of York Minster. It occurred to her that Jenny would smile on their union.

When Captain Maude arrived next day, as promised, Nesta greeted him in the sitting-room of the inn. Immediately, he launched into a frank expression of his feelings for her and his hopes of their future together.

Nesta listened with a half-smile on her lips, nodding her head now and again, her hands clasped gracefully in her lap. She was savouring every moment, indulging her dream. Freedom, a new life, the kind of life which Jenny would have wished for her, these considerations were drawing her like magnets. She was experiencing, for the first time in weeks, a sense of purpose.

'You are quite the most beautiful young woman I have ever known,' Captain Maude said as he took her hands in his. 'I can think of no one but you. When I wake, when I go to sleep, you are in my thoughts and dominate them totally. I have never felt like this about anyone before, not in the whole of my life. It is a totally new experience for me, Miss Bellingham, and one which, believe me, I am relishing to the full. My only fear is that you will go away and leave me alone. If you do that, Miss Bellingham, I do not think I could ever marry another.'

Nesta tried to interrupt him, but he begged her to listen a little longer.

'Miss Bellingham, I realize that you have only come here for a holiday and that I might appear to be taking advantage of your good will by besieging you with my feelings, but I assure you I am sincere in what I say. I would care for you most lovingly every day of my life. I would look after you and love you with all my strength. If you leave me, Miss Bellingham, you will make me the loneliest man in the world. No one could every take your place in my heart. You have shown me what has been missing in my life. You have made me want to settle down. Miss Bellingham, please tell me that I am not wasting my time.'

The Captain grasped Nesta's hands fiercely and his breath fanned her cheek. She bowed towards him, caught up in his ardour, not resisting when he kissed her forehead and then her mouth. She realized that he was easily roused, but he was so charming, so uncomplicated, and in his company she could forget her disreputable past and the strain of James's neglect. Here in York, she was accepted as a lady, which, but for an accident of birth, she would have been. Joseph was the first man who had thought her to be a gentlewoman, who knew nothing of her sordid background. He would love her just as she was.

There would be no questions, no recriminations, only love and safety in his arms. . . . She wanted to respond, and she did.

Oblivious of their surroundings, they kissed more ardently. Joseph murmured her name huskily, begging her not to leave him. His kisses were firm and fierce, and she felt an answering fire. When his mouth pressed against her throat, then lower, she sighed, tilting back her head in a gesture of submission. He was so lovable, and she was in desperate need of his unquestioning devotion.

'Nesta, my dearest Nesta, I have never felt like this about a woman before. You are adorable, so beautiful –' He clasped her breast, and she felt heat surging into her cheeks as his fingers slipped into her bodice. His breath rasped in her ear as she returned his embrace.

'You are very sweet, Joseph – I could – '

'Yes? You could what – ?'

'I could become very fond of you – '

'Only fond? No more?'

He took her lips again, more savagely, his tongue probing between her teeth. She could be happy here with Joseph instead of pining for the elusive James, *couldn't she*? She answered her own question immediately, and the enticing fantasy ended. Gently, she pushed Joseph away, aware of the hurt expression on his face.

'Forgive me,' he said. 'I was carried away – Now you are angry with me.'

'Not angry, Joseph. You must not rush me. I need time. I came here merely to rest. Can you understand that?'

'I think so. I am sorry, my dear.' He sighed deeply, pushing back his dark hair and straightening his cravat while Nesta smoothed her hair and gown. 'Nesta?'

'Yes?' She looked up into his bright hazel eyes.

'You know how I feel about you. I want to make you my bride – I want to take you back to Maude Manor as my wife.'

'Joseph dear, please do not expect too much of me. Who knows what will happen in time? But I must not be pressured. Just now I cannot cope with it – '

Smiling, Nesta touched his arm. What a charmer he was; if only they had met under different circumstances. If only her heart and soul were not torn by her attraction to James and her vow to Jenny. If she stayed here, someone would inevitably find out the truth about her and the delicate dream would be shattered. Joseph's life would be ruined, and hers; disgrace would fall upon them both. She did not love him but she did like him enormously, and she had no wish to wreck his happiness. She must let him down gently. So she spoke sweetly, making half-promises, begging his understanding, asking him to be patient with her.

If she were able to, she would stay, she said, for she knew that she could grow fond of him. No one was sorrier than she but she must return to London, and reality.

'You – you are betrothed?' he said, his face forlorn.

'Indeed, no. Nor am I promised to anyone.'

'So there is some hope for me?' He took her hands again, caging them so that she could not withdraw them.

'Give me time, Joseph, and there may be.' She hated to tell a lie but had not the courage to be more frank. Poor Joseph. He was so well-intentioned.

'What am I to do without you?'

'Come now, a few weeks ago you did not even know I existed and you were happy then, were you not? Well, so shall you be happy again. You will soon forget me.'

'*Never*!' he cried, leaping to his feet to pace up and down the room. 'Dear Nesta, you are the most unforgettable creature I have ever encountered. There is no way on earth I could put you out of my thoughts.'

'Dear Captain Maude, you have been so kind to me. You have no idea how much you have cheered me, and I truly wish that things could be as you would like them to be.'

'Might I visit you in London? Oh, do say yes, please!' he cajoled.

Nesta was in a quandary now. What could she say? There was no way she could invite him to call on her.

'You may write to me, Captain Maude, and I promise

that I shall visit York again in the near future for I have found it a most restful city. I would like to spend a longer time here and get to know it better.'

'I shall be waiting for that moment,' the Captain said, but he looked so glum and disheartened that it aroused her sympathy, making her want to draw him into her arms and say that she would stay. But she must harden herself. There was so much to do when she got back: she would never truly be free until she had fulfilled her vow to Jenny.

Uneasily, they took tea together making dispirited conversation. They had little more to say to one another and were awkward in each other's presence now. The time had come for Nesta to leave York altogether, for in some strange, indefinable way Jenny was calling her back. She was beginning to wonder how on earth she could have stayed away for so long.

CHAPTER FOURTEEN

Just as London had seemed a faraway dream when she was in York, so now did York appear when Nesta was back in London.

Cathy and Amy could not wait to tell her all the latest news, the best part of which was that they had had a visit from the Prince of Wales. He seemed to have enjoyed himself, but his aide had complained on His Highness's behalf that gambling facilities at the club were inadequate.

'Then we must put that right,' Nesta said firmly, her eyes gleaming. She was remembering the days when she had dreamed of knowing such awe-inspiring people as the Queen's son and heir. Earls, lords, dukes, she had yearned to meet them all, believing that they all must fraternize with her Sun God. During casual conversation James had mentioned the name of the Prince of Wales; it was obvious that he knew much about the Prince, things of an intimate nature which only a close friend could learn.

If Nesta wanted James back at the Crimson Club, then she must encourage those with whom he mixed to come there. If Bertie, as the Prince was known to family and friends, said that gambling facilities at the club were poor, she would organize something better: a new gaming-room.

One of the rear drawing-rooms could be put to this use. Nesta knew just the one to convert. Already she was imagining the plush crimson hangings on the walls, the Turkey carpet in crimson and deep, rich blues. The room would be sparsely decorated, however, for men intent upon gambling disliked being distracted, even by portraits of beautiful women.

For her own part, Nesta would never understand the magnetic attraction which gambling had for so many men. Whether they were ragged and drunken sailors making bets on whose pet rat would win a race or impeccably tailored gentlemen, their faces all showed the same rapt absorption, oblivious of everything but their bets. Although she had never felt that same enthusiasm, she realized that, in a different way, she was not unlike those men, for she had staked all she had on the Crimson Club and was just as obsessed as they with achieving a successful outcome.

As the days and weeks passed and the gaming-room neared completion, Nesta thought less and less of her brief, sweet interlude in York, but she did remember Captain Maude fondly. Had she not been Nesta Bellingham, had she been what he believed her to be, she would most certainly have accepted his proposal. She doubted that she would ever find a more suitable husband than he, and knowing he had fallen seriously in love for the first time in his life, she felt a pang of conscience. But she knew that she had not encouraged his advances. Poor Joseph. If he only knew the truth about her: that she was a scarlet woman. . . .

Nesta had put aside her regrets before and could do it again, with determination. What was the use of fretting for what might have been? She knew that she was not the innocent Joseph imagined her to be, and in facing this, she was being as much of a realist as ever before. Her course was set in another direction and had been so for years. She herself had chosen the cobbled, stony road with all its pits and troughs, and she herself would walk it, even though at the end of it there might be only shadows and bitterness – but surely no worse grief than that which she had suffered in the past?

It was Cathy's idea to make the opening of the gaming-room a Gala Night.

There were to be special terms for the gamblers, refreshments served free of charge, tickets handed out to all the winners during the evening so that they could claim a special additional prize – a crate of champagne. There would be gifts of gowns for all the girls so they would look their prettiest. Preparations for the festivities began weeks ahead of the opening so that everything would be perfect on the night.

Whether Nesta deemed it a presentiment or not she did not know, but she recognized a feeling gathering strength within her as the days passed and the Gala Night came closer. It was difficult, of course, to separate that from what she wished would happen; perhaps, after all, it was merely her own longing and not a genuine premonition. She only knew that, as the fittings for her new gown continued and the Gala Night drew nearer, she saw herself in the arms of the Duke of Malgrave.

They were dancing together in her own drawing-room to the distant strains of music from the orchestra hired to entertain the customers. She saw the scene so clearly, like a painting in front of her. She knew that if it did come to pass it would bring her total and utter bliss, the realization of her dreams – or rather the dreams of the little Meggie Blunt she had once been.

All that was required was for the Duke to appear at the Gala Night. He would see her and remember the night when Lord Trenton had gone berserk and attacked Carlotta. How close they had seemed that night, how well they had worked together; James had appeared to be every inch the stalwart, caring protector she desperately needed.

Looking back, Nesta saw that that night marked a turning point in her life. Before it, she had been single-mindedly pursuing success, checking her guilty conscience regarding her way of life in the light of her upbringing. Afterwards, she was to find her mind and heart struggling in different directions. Her heart wanted her Sun God, to love and cherish him all the rest of her days, whilst her mind remained ineradicably set upon revenge on the Malgraves.

Nesta looked at herself in the mirror. Clad in the froths of plum-coloured lace and silk of her Gala Night gown, she was a woman anticipating a meeting with her lover; when she took the gown off in order to work, she was Nesta Bellingham again. As she superintended the party preparations, discussing various aspects of the evening with Cathy and Amy, letting the other girls know what she expected of them, she was very much the efficient, well-organized business-woman, but alone in her bed, she was soft and vulnerable, staking all she had on the appearance of the Duke of Malgrave at the Gala Night.

She tried to reason with herself. Why should he come? After all, he had not seen her for nearly three months. Why *should* he come to the Gala Night? If he had wanted to see her he could have come at any time. He could have been at the club every night. What if he had married that milk-sop creature who seemed at long last to have given up plaguing Nesta about her morality, or lack of it?

The reformers had not been to the Crimson Club for months. Nesta had heard that they were besieging the Paradise Club now, driving its proprietor to distraction. They seemed to have had more success there, for some of the club's girls had actually given up their work and had returned to their families or taken up charity work themselves. She imagined that Lady Finchley-Clark was deriving immense satisfaction from such results.

Nesta realized with a start that James might have been a husband for some time now, that he and Jane might actually be on their way to producing a child. It was a thought which she had struggled to repress for months, an intolerable one against which she had no defence. She had consorted with other women's husbands before, of course, but if she wanted James at all, she wanted him entirely for herself. She would not share him with anyone else – certainly not with the vapid angel, Jane, Lady Finchley-Clark.

As she stood before her cheval glass at eight on the evening of the Gala, Nesta made a rash vow. If James did not put in an appearance at the club that night, she would eschew all plans for revenge upon his family.

Nesta's hands were bloodless with cold as she pushed back a strand of her hair, straightening the plum satin rosettes which framed her face and re-arranging the fichu of exquisite cream-coloured lace around her shoulders. The fichu had been designed to be removed with graceful ease, to reveal the *décolletage* of the gown, which gently lifted and shaped her handsome breasts, curving down to her hand-span waist before flaring out into the ebullient cage of her crinoline. Tonight she wore garnets round her porcelain throat, in her ears, at her wrists and on her fingers, their deep rich fire enhancing the milkiness of her skin. She was ready to meet anyone tonight, dukes, earls or the Prince of Wales himself.

From her room Nesta heard the little orchestra strike up the first notes of a Strauss waltz. The musicians had been instructed to play only Strauss and other light, cheerful music throughout the evening, after which they would be supplied with free champagne and a free supper. Nesta was nothing if not practical, having every arrangement organized down to the last detail.

At that moment a tap came at her door and Cathy entered the room, smiling broadly. She wore a cream crinoline of ruched satin, embroidered with cerise rosebuds; in her hair were entwined cerise satin ribbons, and there were pearls in her ears and at her throat.

'Everything is ready downstairs, Nesta love. Cor, don't you look a treat. That gown's something to stun the eyes. You'll certainly have all the men at your feet tonight, lovey.' Cathy dropped a kiss on Nesta's cheek, making her smile.

'That's not quite my intention, Cathy. I'm aiming more to have money dropped into my coffers and to have the Prince of Wales decide that he will be a permanent visitor here.'

'I know you are, lovey,' Cathy grinned, 'but it never hurts to have men at your feet, does it?'

Ignoring her question, Nesta asked if the champagne was on ice and if all the other last-minute arrangements had been taken care of.

Cathy nodded. 'Louisa says she's got a cold coming on, but apart from that everything seems to be fine.'

'There's nothing like planning ahead. Remember that, Cathy, won't you, when you have arrangements to make. Start well ahead, so that by the time the big day comes everything is just right.'

Cathy frowned. 'Don't talk like you're going to leave us, Nesta. You'll always be here arranging for us an' planning. How could we manage without you?'

'You managed when I was in York.'

'Well, we had to manage then, didn't we, 'cause you needed the rest, but we all knew at the backs of our minds that you was coming back, didn't we? That's what kept us going.'

Nesta remained silent, arranging a curl, putting a last pat of powder on her nose. If her secret plans did come to fruition she would not be remaining here as Madam of a brothel, but she had not told Cathy and Amy this. She had no doubt that they could manage things between them; they were capable girls.

Another tap came at the door. Amy entered, dressed in the palest green watered silk, froths of cream lace at her bosom and at the edges of her sleeves, peridots at her throat and in her ears.

'My, Nesta, you look a picture, lovey. You're going to sway 'em all tonight, you are.'

'I've already told her that,' said Cathy. 'Don't tell her any more, Amy, or it'll be going to her head an' it'll get so swelled she won't be able to get through the door.'

The three women laughed, aware that light spirits would break the tension they were all experiencing on this important occasion. Downstairs they heard the orchestra begin its third waltz and, outside, the clip-clopping approach of a horse and carriage bringing their first visitor of the evening. Cathy rushed to the window.

'It's the Earl of Brendon. Gosh, he's eager to get here, ain't he? I wonder who else'll turn up? We sent out so many invitations, we're bound to get quite a few tonight.'

'The only one we really need is the Prince himself,' said Amy shrewdly. 'Where he goes, everyone else follows like sheep. You could call him the Pied Piper of Hamlin, if you wanted, 'cause that's the effect he has. Once he takes to a place it's famous for ever.'

Cathy said, 'That's true. He never took to the Paradise Club, did he, an' I must say, it's had its troubles. It's on the downward slope now, from what I hear.'

Nesta lifted her hand. 'Now remember, girls, what I've told you. It's the Prince of Wales we've invited tonight, and if he comes you must treat him like the royalty he is. But you mustn't be so afraid that you make him think we don't know how to treat the higher-ups, because if he thinks that he won't want to come here again, will he? Remember he wants to relax and forget his cares. No doubt he'll want to gamble heavily, because that's what he likes doing, but don't crowd him, don't make him think he's being pressured in any way. Be relaxed, pleasant. Smile, laugh at his jokes – and that goes for his friends' jokes, too, however feeble they might seem to you. If he asks for anything unusual – ' At this remark the three women grinned, but Nesta recovered quickly, saying, 'No, I didn't mean that – I was talking about food or wine –

If he wants anything unusual, let me know at once. And don't gawk at him or make him feel his requests are outrageous, whatever you do, because that is just not stylish, and what we most want to put over tonight is *style*. Is that clear?'

Cathy and Amy might well have bridled at such instructions had it not been their adored Nesta who was giving them, but they respected her judgment and advice. Like two meek little girls they listened, nodded and promised to do exactly as she had said.

More carriages were arriving, so Cathy and Amy headed downstairs to welcome the visitors and take them into the gambling-room, where the first bottles of champagne were being opened. It was important that the evening begin on the right note.

'Are we the first?' said the Earl of Brendon. 'I hadn't realized it was so early. Is the Prince not here yet?'

'Not yet,' said Cathy, twinkling up at the Earl, who was a very close friend of hers, 'but he will be soon.' She was trying to hide the triumphant excitement she felt at the Earl's words, for it was obvious that the Prince did indeed plan to come tonight. As soon as she could she must slip upstairs and let Nesta know.

The Earl put his arm round Cathy, beaming down at her. 'Now where's all this free champagne that we've come such a long way to taste?' he teased. 'Didn't you know that's all I've come for tonight?'

By ten the room was filled with people, all in great spirits. The evening had been pronounced a lucky one, for more than half a dozen people had won quite large amounts of money at the tables; this pleased Nesta, for it was money well invested, she knew, as the lucky players would return to the tables again and again. It remained only for the Prince to come, but he was notorious for arriving at whatever time he wished (and, if things did not please him, for leaving just as abruptly).

It was after eleven when Amy came hurrying through the crowded room to whisper in Nesta's ear, 'The Prince is here! He's here! An' he's brought ever so many friends with him. How we're going to cram them all in the room I don't know!'

Nesta felt the heat rise to her cheeks like two hot hands placed on her face. How long she had planned for this moment, for the Queen's son to come to her club with all his friends, filling it with titled people, all of whom would look to the Prince to set his seal of approval on the venue. But Nesta knew that her heart was fluttering not entirely for that reason. Although he had received an invitation, the Duke of Malgrave had not appeared. If he had not come in now with the Prince of Wales she felt that it would be unlikely that he would come at all.

Another hour passed and still James did not come. Fighting off her bitter disappointment, Nesta had no choice but to respond to the Prince's attentions. He was plumper than she had expected him to be, and yet he possessed an astonishing charm and the most sensual eyes with which she had ever exchanged flirtatious glances. He made free with his hands, clasping her fingers and pressing them into her lap so that his knuckles nudged her thighs while he murmured flattering phrases to her. Smiling, Nesta responded charmingly, blushing and leaning against the Prince's arm. She was utterly heartbroken that James had not appeared, but she must be practical and not show it. The Prince's seal of approval could make her establishment the most successful and popular club in all London. She owed that much to the girls; she must think of them.

This was why Nesta was allowing the Prince to kiss her avidly, partially screened by his friends, at the moment when James walked into the gambling-room. He strode directly across the room to join them.

'*James*!' Nesta gasped, horrified by the steely expression in the Duke's blue eyes.

'Sir,' James said, bowing to the Prince, his manner icy, 'I believe you have something of mine.'

There was a stunned silence from those within earshot as faces turned to survey the scene. The silence lengthened, becoming acutely awkward, and then, to everyone's amazement and relief, the Prince slapped his hands on his knees and roared with laughter.

'James, you old goat, I do. But it is only on temporary loan. I have not forgotten what you told me. I came here to see for myself what was so intriguing about the lady, and now that I have, here, you may take her back!''

Not knowing whether to be shocked or to smile at both men's audacity, Nesta found herself being handed to James, who put his arm possessively round her waist.

Later, when everyone had gone home and Nesta and James were alone, he gripped her by the wrist, pulling her almost savagely to him.

'Would you have slept with him had I not come?'

'Do you mean the Prince?' Nesta felt her face burning. How dared James stay away so long, without a word, and then turn up expecting her to be waiting for him! 'What if I had? What is it to *you*? You have not come here for weeks! Do you think that you own me?'

'I came to see the woman whose beauty has haunted me – the one I have not been able to put out of my mind. *She* was not a whore!'

James thrust his face close to hers, his eyes icy.

'Then – then she was not me, was she, James, for we both know what I am,' Nesta stammered, but bravely, holding her back straight. 'I have never tried to conceal what I am from you, nor did I think I should ever have to do so.'

'The minute my back is turned, you think of bedding with another man – that is right, is it not? He would have been with you now, tearing off your clothes and touching you, had I not decided to come. It is true, you cannot deny it!'

'I honestly cannot say how far we would have got, James. He is a very attractive man, and he is not accustomed to being rejected. He might have commanded me to bed. . . .'

Nesta was attempting a feeble joke, but it served only to infuriate James all the more.

'He could not have commanded a lady, only a whore!' he said, grasping her wrist even tighter so that tears came into her eyes.

'If it is a lady you want, then you have come to the wrong place!'

James loosened his hold on her so suddenly that she fell against him with a little cry.

'Yes, I have come to the wrong place. You have never said a truer word. More fool I for being attracted to a harlot, a woman who sells her body to any man who can pay the price. Tell me, Nesta, tell me of the hundreds of men who have enjoyed your body. . . .' He stopped, his breath quickening, and then half-turned as if to leave the room.

'Do you think I enjoyed *them*? Do you think I couple willingly? How would you know, you who live a life of luxury, what it is to starve? My mother died of consumption and starvation in my arms when I was ten years old! I lived in a hovel where even rats did not come for there was not a crumb to tempt them there. I walked the snowy winter streets in bare feet – *bare feet*, James! How can you understand what I went through before I – I – ' She faltered, tears streaming down her face, her shoulders bowed.

'Before you became a common prostitute? No, I cannot, Nesta, for what decent woman would stoop so low? The ones I know would die rather than sell their bodies!'

James had his hand on the door knob, his face averted. Nesta could see only the cold, hard line of his mouth and jaw.

Knowing that she was going to lose him, she said, 'Before I did what I had to do to survive, I died a hundred deaths, James. No one can even imagine what I went through – no one. Had – had there been any alternative, I would have taken it – '

He flung her one contemptuous glance, then wrenched the door open and stormed out, slamming it behind him.

Sinking to the floor, Nesta plunged her face into her hands and wept.

When Nesta finally fell into a fitful sleep, it was dawn. She did not wake until midday. She felt gloomy and lethargic, but in an attempt to shake off her mood, she put on her smartest riding outfit and went round to the stables to collect Apollo. He was a beautiful chestnut stallion which she had acquired some two years previously, naming him after the god of the sun.

Apollo was, as always, delighted to see his mistress, neighing affectionately and nuzzling her. She gave him a sweet apple to crunch and then, when he was saddled up, mounted him and headed for Hyde Park.

It was a bright, sunny morning, and Apollo was in fine spirits. Trying to free her mind of James, Nesta concentrated on enjoying her ride and on seeing the society ladies riding alongside the ladies of the demi-monde who frequented this area of the park each morning.

She had often pondered on the strange name of this most fashionable of riding paces – Rotten Row. She had heard that it was a corruption of the French '*Route du Roi*' – 'Route of the King' – for it had been here that the Plantagenet kings had ridden in progress from the Palace of Westminster to their royal hunting forests west of London. She liked to think of them as she galloped along, imagining how they and their courtiers must have looked. They had been sovereigns who had brooked no interference, who had made the world their own by brute force.

It had been here in Hyde Park, in 1851, that the Great Exhibition had been held, and it was here, too, that the long curving strip of water known as the Serpentine, because of its shape, undulated its way along. Queen Caroline had ordered the river to be formed in 1731. For a time, before Hyde Park had begun to enjoy its present popularity and before the railroads presented an appalling alternative, it had had the grim reputation of being the most secluded place in London in which to commit suicide.

Rotten Row ran from Kensington Gardens to Hyde Park Corner. It was usually jammed with handsome men and women riding, driving in their carriages or strolling. It was one of the few places in the city where prostitutes could mingle with decent women. During the days of the Regency, fallen women had been banned from Hyde Park during daylight hours, but now they roamed freely, being welcome so long as they adhered to Park eitquette and wore the required fashionable dress.

Nesta smiled to herself as she rode, already feeling a certain elevation of spirit. Had she (or one of her girls) come into the park at this time of day on foot and attracted the attention of any young man, there would have been a public outcry and she would have been accused of, and prosecuted for, soliciting; but because she and the other members of the demi-monde were smartly attired and on horseback, nothing but admiring glances would be cast in their direction. Of course, it was also required that the women riders comport themselves with grace and composure, their backs held straight and their heads high, and they must follow the unwritten rules of the park.

Attire for the men on horseback nearly always consisted of a dark frock coat, with fitted trousers, an immaculate stock and the ubiquitous silk top-hat. The women wore bodices tightly buttoned to the neck with little coat-tails at the back which reached to the horse's saddle, long skirts tending to be voluminous and highly polished boots. Silk hats were tilted jauntily over their eyes. There were, of course, the eccentric few who broke the rules of fashion, often with panache, but in the main, the formalities were strictly adhered to by everybody.

Apart from the brash few who could be seen riding along the Row as early as seven or eight in the morning, it was not the custom to ride before midday. (The Liver Brigade, as the early morning riders were called, were renowned for their pasty faces and the slumped set of their shoulders, for it was not easy to maintain equilibrium whilst still under the influence of the dissipations of the previous night's revels.) Nesta herself had never ridden earlier than midday, and she usually stayed on horseback until around two, when she would return home.

It was unthinkable to ride or drive on Sunday, for on that day Hyde Park was the meeting place for respectable families who gathered after Church by the Achilles Statue. In high summer, ladies would seat themselves comfortably before the statue, their parasols protecting their skins from the summer sun, while male relatives and friends would stand about in gentlemanly fashion, monocles at the ready, while their daughters frolicked in lacy frilled bonnets and flowered dresses, and their sons in spotless sailor suits.

Nesta knew that some people were perplexed by her appearance, especially younger men, many of whom did not know whether she was a respectable young lady or a prostitute. This was one of the reasons she enjoyed riding in the Row: she could pretend to be and look every inch the lady, with only a few onlookers realizing the truth. Lady Catherine Walters, a low-bred girl of Liverpool birth, had risen to incredible heights in society after been seen riding in Rotten Row; her seat had been so admired that she was subsequently never at a loss for wealthy and generous gentleman friends.

Nesta rode in silence from one end of the Row to the other, not looking to her left nor to her right except to admire the scenery or to inspect the attire of another lady rider. She never fluttered her eyelashes nor sought to attract any gentleman; she was here purely for the pleasure of riding and for pretending, as she frequently did, that she was a lady of good birth.

Today she had every intention of acting the same way as she had behaved on all the other days, but fate was to forestall her. A petite blonde girl riding a few yards to her left on a satanic-looking black stallion, which seemed far too big for her, was suddenly flung into the most dangerous situation as her horse, for no apparent reason, took flight. It reared up on its hind legs before charging ahead at breakneck speed while the girl screamed and clung to the reins in terror.

CHAPTER FIFTEEN

Appraising the situation instantly, Nesta galloped after the blonde girl, gradually coming abreast of her and nudging Apollo towards the stallion, which was, by now, frothing at the mouth, its flanks heaving. Bravely, Nesta headed him off, proud of Apollo's immediate obedience despite what she asked of him, and then, leaning over at a perilout angle, she managed to grasp the reins of the girl's horse, but not without a struggle. The stallion seemed to know what she was about to do and put on an extra spurt, wrenching the reins from her fingers. Determinedly, she spurred Apollo on, making a second grab for the reins; this time she grasped them with all her strength and held them tightly as she rode alongside the stallion for quite some distance, crying 'Whoa! Whoa! Steady there, steady there!' in commanding tones.

Reluctantly, the stallion obeyed, slowing its mad pace. By now the girl was leaning forward in the saddle, clutching both reins and mane in desperate terror, her body racked with sobs, her throat raw from screaming. When the stallion finally came to a shuddering halt and stood head bowed, panting noisily, Nesta leapt from Apollo's back to help the girl down to safety. She was quite hysterical and began to scream again, her eyes wide and staring, her skin bleached of colour. It took Nesta some time to calm her.

A crowd had gathered, offering help, proclaiming Nesta's bravery. One voice rose above the others, causing Nesta to look up in stunned recognition as she stood with her arms round the sobbing girl. Whose voice could it be but his, her Sun God's? The hubbub seemed to fade away, as did the verdant surroundings of Hyde Park, the china blue of the sky. There was no one there but them at that moment as they stared at one another, amethyst eyes into blue.

Before Nesta had time to wonder why he was looking at the girl in her arms with such concern, the girl cried out, 'James! James! Oh, I'm so glad to see you!'

James stepped forward to take her into his arms protectively. 'I saw it all,' he said to Nesta. 'You saved her life. How can I ever repay such a debt?'

Nesta stood mutely, still shaken from her pursuit of the runaway horse, but her thoughts were gathering. Was this James's mistress? Slowly, her mouth curved into a wry smile. How ironical if it were so! Would it not be just like fate to deal her yet another blow? She did not know how she remained standing so aloof and composed when she wanted to break down and sob as the golden-haired girl was doing.

The crowd was dispersing, having seen the Duke of Malgrave take charge. Very soon they were indeed alone, the three of them. Sobs still racked the girl's body, while Nesta, saying nothing, stood waiting, feeling awkward and wanting to leave. The last thing she desired was to have an unfair hold over her Sun God. Last night he had made it more than plain that he despised her. She did not want him to feel obliged to say, 'I must repay you for saving her.' She did not want anything from him except what he freely wished to give her, and after their terrible argument, had it not been all too clear that he wished to give her nothing at all?

Nesta felt a little bubble of hysteria rising within her. Hastily, she turned on her heel, desperate to be away from this place before the sobs and the laughter broke through her control. But immediately she felt a hand on her arm; his hand.

'Wait!' James cried. 'Where are you going? Nesta, please do not rush away. If you could but wait a few moments until my sister has recovered.'

'Your sister?' Nesta almost gasped.

'Yes, my sister. Had you not realized that we are related?'

'Not . . . not in that way. I had not guessed,' Nesta

stammered. 'But now . . . yes, I can see the likeness between you.'

Scarlet suffused her cheeks. She felt miserable, totally embarrassed, longing to be back in the safety of her drawing-room.

She fast became aware of her appearance. Sweat was beading her brow. Her hair had become uncoiled and was snaking along her shoulders, and tangled curls were framing her face; her cheeks were rosy like a child's. Looking down, she realized that her riding skirt had somehow become torn during the ride, revealing a froth of petticoats beneath. Instead of feeling elated at the valorous deed which she had just done, she felt ashamed and discomfited.

Now the blonde girl was speaking, begging Nesta not to leave. 'Nesta – may I call you Nesta? Is that right – do I have your name right? Oh, how grateful I am to you! I was foolish. I wanted to ride Asmodeus. I was warned – everyone told me not to try it – but I think really that that was what spurred me on to choose him this morning. I see now that I have been very foolish. I could have been killed. And so might you have been, had you not rescued me so skilfully.'

Later Nesta was to wish that she had responded with brave and intelligent words, but instead she mumbled, 'Nothing. It was nothing. The least I could do.'

'You are a superb horsewoman, Nesta. Rarely have I seen better,' the Duke of Malgrave was adding, 'and now, before we take my sister home, may I introduce you to her properly? This is my sister, Ariadne, Lady Lansdowne. She has only recently come to stay with me in London. Now, will you not join us? Please, I insist,' he said, as Nesta began to demur. 'The grooms can bring our horses home. Our carriage is at the end of the park.'

The Duke clicked his fingers, and servants seemed to appear out of nowhere, taking hold of the reins of both Apollo and Asmodeus and leading them away, while the Duke shepherded Nesta and Ariadne to the end of Rotten Row where his coach awaited them.

Now that Ariadne had recovered somewhat, she began to chatter. 'I owe you so much, my dear Nesta! I really do! I am sure that as time passes and I recover from the shock I have just undergone, I shall realize that I owe you even more than I can possibly imagine at this moment. There is no doubt that you saved my life. I most certainly should have known better than to take Asmodeus, but, you see, I admired him so much and James did keep saying, "Take any horse but Asmodeus," and, well, I'm afraid I have always been the sort of person who must do what she is most forbidden. I know it is a weakness, but I doubt I shall ever overcome it and my friends just have to accept me as I am. You *will* be my friend, Miss Bellingham? Oh, I do hope so! Please do not deny me the pleasure of getting to know you.'

Dumbly, Nesta nodded, anticipating endless problems and embarrassments if Ariadne were to carry out her promise.

'I have only recently come to London,' Ariadne prattled on. 'You see, I am a widow. My husband, Lord Lansdowne, died exactly one year ago and I have been in deepest mourning, because although he was much, much older than I, he was a kindly man. I spent most of our married life nursing him. So I have just come out of mourning, you see, and have come to stay with James. And I fear that after all those long months shut away in the country, thinking about my poor late husband, in my desperation to be in the saddle again I forfeited much of my common sense in determining to ride Asmodeus.'

'That is perfectly understandable, Lady Lansdowne,' Nesta smiled, knowing how a love for horses can become an obsession. She herself had been riding for only two years and yet she was utterly captivated by Apollo.

'Perhaps we can meet and ride together regularly?' Lady Lansdowne continued. 'Indeed, I admit that I should feel a great deal safer riding next time with you beside me.'

The Duke, although noticing Nesta's uneasiness – for his sister was taking her at face value and obviously knew nothing about her identity – seemed not to be alarmed or concerned by the conversation. Nesta was beginning to think that he was either feigning interest or being cynically indulgent. Certainly one did not allow one's newly-widowed young sister, a titled lady, to mingle with a prostitute in Hyde Park, or anywhere else for that matter. Nesta was fully aware of this, but the Duke of Malgrave seemed to be ignoring the fact. She realized that his behaviour and their conversation and his inviting her back to his home all pointed to his accepting her as respectable. As respectable, in fact, as his sister.

Did he have some ulterior motive for doing so? Nesta wondered. Now that they were seated in his carriage and coachmen were whipping up the horses, she thought James looked rather smug and pleased with himself, as if he had accomplished some secret wish. But she had little time to ponder on his motivations, for Ariadne continued to prattle, telling Nesta about her life in the country and how but for her dear, late husband she would have been totally and excruciatingly bored with life. Now that she was back in the city, she said, she was determined to go to as many balls, dinners and dances as she could possibly squeeze into each week. She was seeing dressmakers and having fittings and ordering a complete new wardrobe. She also said that her birthday was May the 9th and that she intended to have a huge party, with all her old friends and as many of James's as wished to appear. Malgrave Manor was to be thrown open to them all. An invitation had, of course, been sent to the Prince of Wales, but whether or not he would attend she did not as yet know. He was very much a creature of whim, Ariadne said, smiling as if she knew him intimately.

By the time they reached Malgrave Manor, where James helped his sister and Nesta to alight, Ariadne had made a remarkable recovery. There was no trace now of tremors and hysterics in the girl whom Nesta had held in her arms in Rotten Row. Ariadne's face was still drained of colour, but her blue eyes were sparkling and her natural vivacity was returning. She seemed restless; her hands moved constantly, arcing through the air, adjusting her curls, her fingers splayed as she described some particular event.

Nesta wondered if she was always as animated, or whether she was suffering from shock. Whichever it was, she felt that Lady Lansdowne ought to rest for at least a day as the after-effects of such a frightening experience could be severe if one tried to ignore them. It became plain that James thought so, too, for he told his sister that she should lie down immediately. When she demurred, he insisted, and so, bidding them farewell, Ariadne went to her room, pouting a little.

Finding herself alone with James, Nesta tried to affect a relaxed air, as if nothing untoward had ever happened between them. They sat at a Louis Quatorze table with a silver tray between them, on which stood two silver-gilt goblets and a flask of Madeira. After drinking one glass of the wine, Nesta began to feel somewhat restored, her strength returning.

James was every bit as awesome to her as he had ever been; his vitality seemed to emanate from him in waves. Ariadne had a similar vivacity, but hers was brittle and nowhere near as potent as that of her brother. James, with his brilliant blue eyes and glossy, gilded hair, his muscular build and height, slim hips and flat stomach, had no less of a god-like aura than when Nesta – Meggie Blunt – had first seen him so many years ago. She wanted to reach out and touch him. She wanted him to take her hands and rain kisses on them, crushing her fingers with his mouth, and then kiss her arms, her throat, her neck, her lips.

Silently Nesta chided herself. She was letting her thoughts run away with her; she must not weaken. Last night he had made it clear that he abhorred her and all she stood for. He had not wanted her nor had he sought her before in the three months since their first coupling, and yet he had expected her to be waiting for him! He could not even guess at her feelings for him or the effect he had had upon her; she must never let him suspect.

Before she left Malgrave Manor today, she must make it clear to James that he owed her nothing for saving his sister's life. Or so her finer feelings told her.... But then she was possessed by another resolution, one which came straight from her childhood. She was forced to admit that never again would she be given a golden opportunity to infiltrate the Malgrave family – and put her secret plans into action....

At that moment, a bell rang in a distant part of the house. Instantly James was on his feet.

'I shall not be very long. That is my cousin's bell. She is an invalid. I must see what she wants.'

'Of course,' Nesta said, inclining her head.

When he had gone, she had time to look round the library. It was as beautifully appointed as the hall and every bit as perfect as she had imagined. It gleamed and shone, the linenfold panelling glossy as silk, the thick Turkey carpets rich in hues of green, crimson, wine, scarlet and gold. The wallpaper, which was the colour of ivory, was of Chinese silk with an exotic design of birds in flight and bulbous crimson peonies. The bookcases and shelves were crammed with books, beautiful leather-covered volumes, and she marvelled yet again at one man's owning so much. But there was no envy in her thoughts.

Nesta stood up and slowly toured the room, letting her fingers slide along the books as she read each title, reaching out to touch the sumptuous silk wall-coverings. It was wonderful just to be in the room, to be in Malgrave Manor itself. She felt as if she had lived here all her life and had just returned after a long journey. She knew that she was being fanciful and yet she felt as if the house had been waiting for her, as if it were welcoming her.

It was strange that from the moment she had walked over the threshold of Malgrave Manor, she had felt an innate sense of peace, as if the house were wooing her, telling her she had nothing to fear. She was being unrealistic, of course; it was simply that the past – all the years she had dreamed of coming here, of meeting the family, her mother's family – had caught up with her. She knew that she tended to unleash her imagination too readily, and that once unleashed it was hard to bring under control again. After all, how could this house, which was merely stone and wood and plaster like any other house, welcome her, speak to her?

In a few moments the Duke would be back. They would exchange a few more polite words and then she would return to the club – in the Malgrave carriage, no doubt. After that there would be nothing. No further contact, no more messages, no invitations to visit the manor as Ariadne had promised.

Perhaps it would be better that way. Surely once she was out of the house, James would speak to his sister, explaining things he had not been able to say in front of Nesta. Ariadne would cry out in stunned amazement when she realized she had been duped by a woman whom she had believed to be a lady. They would dismiss the fact that she had saved Ariadne's life, for how could they allow such an act to blind them to her origins when even she herself could not forget her lowly, sordid beginnings – and her all too immoral present life?

Nesta noticed a dainty porcelain figurine on the mantelpiece: a mermaid sitting on a rock in a stormy sea. She was combing out her long blue-green tresses, and her eyes were real turquoise. Nesta felt an immediate affinity with the statuette, for she, too, was neither one thing nor another. Mermaids were mythical creatures who lived alone, courageously, in the seas, fearing no one, neither man nor beast. Above the waist they had creamy white flesh, womanly in shape; below, they had silvery-green scales on a fish's tail.

Hearing footfalls on the stairs, Nesta turned suddenly. When the Duke of Malgrave entered the library she was standing by the hearth, her back to the mermaid. He did not speak at first and then apologized for his long absence, saying that his cousin was aged and an invalid, and that she liked him to attend her whenever possible.

'I'm afraid she has a somewhat tart tongue and will do

only for me what she will not do for others. It is very inconvenient at times, but it cannot be helped. Indeed, I confess that I derive a great deal of comfort from being able to help her when it is obvious that no one else can.'

'Your cousin?' Nesta enquired, not really asking a question but merely trying to be polite.

'Yes. Adelaide, Duchess of Malgrave. She was widowed some years ago and has since been an invalid.'

'How old would she be, if that is not an impolite question?' Nesta asked haltingly.

'How old? Now, let me see. Well, truth to tell, I have not counted it up, but she must be past eighty. She is a lonely old woman, that is the truth of it. She lost her only son when he was very young, and I don't think she has ever recovered from it.'

'Her only son?'

'Yes, Michael, the original heir to the dukedom of Malgrave. It was a tragedy; he died abroad in an accident. He was an only child. That is why, when his father died, the title fell to me, a very distant cousin.'

'I see.'

So the present duke was *not* close blood kin of hers but a very distant cousin. There would be no danger of incest between her and James. But was she not being arrogant again? She was about to leave Malgrave Manor, never to return, for it was plainly obvious to her that the Duke was now ill at ease in her company and wished her gone. Again Nesta wondered if he had married Lady Jane yet but decided against asking him. She would leave him with his two invalids, his sister and the old Duchess.

Adelaide, Duchess of Malgrave, the woman whom she had hated ever since Jenny had told her story as she lay dying. A bitter old hag with a tongue dripping malice and venom, that was how she had thought of Michael's mother all these years. The woman was still alive! It seemed incredible; she was past eighty and an invalid, without son or husband, attended by a distant cousin. In many ways, therefore, fate had dealt her a heavy blow, without Nesta's having to lift a finger.

Nesta found a spurious delight in knowing this. She burned with a need to meet her grandmother, to see for herself the harridan who had ruined her mother's life and who had set her, Nesta, on the road to prostitution. The prospect of coming face to face with her seemed so improbable that Nesta felt she must force herself to forget what had happened between herself and James altogether.

'Do you have only your sister to help you care for the Duchess?' Nesta asked. She waited tautly for his reply. She really knew so very little about his private life. 'What of – of your future wife?'

'She has not as yet helped me on that score,' James said.

Struggling to hide her dismay, Nesta dipped her head. So he was to marry Jane after all – how could she endure it? Clenching her hands, she asked when the wedding was to be.

'As soon as you say yes, my darling,' he replied.

Nesta stared at him incredulously, unable to believe her ears. 'You – you mean – ?'

'Yes, surely you have guessed? Forgive me, darling, for last night. I was not myself – it is just that I love you so much. I cannot bear to think of your other life, of the men you have known.' He pulled her into his arms, hugging her tightly. 'I confess that I was sick with jealousy when I saw the Prince kissing you; that is why I said those cruel things. Do you forgive me?' He gripped her shoulders, staring deep into her eyes.

'Oh yes, James dearest, I forgive you!' Nesta sighed, swaying against him blissfully. 'Do you mean what you say – you wish to marry me? You do not have to do that – I do not expect it – I – '

He put a finger against his lips. 'I love you, Nesta. I was brought up by parents who put love before all things, and I recognize the feelings I have for you. I have never felt like this about anyone before. I want you to be my wife. I want us to live together, to have children together.'

Nesta swallowed hard, closing her eyes, feeling a sudden sharp anguish. He spoke of a life beyond her imaginings, one she would give anything to live.

'What of your – your fiancée, Lady Finchley-Clarke?' she whispered.

'We were never suited. She is not for me. I suspected it all along – more than suspected it. She needs to be involved with charity work, helping others, as you know – ' He twinkled at her. 'I do not feel up to the same commitment.'

'She is the very opposite of you, my love. It was our parents' dearest wish that we marry, but I know that if mine had lived to see how Jane turned out, they would not have wanted us to do so. We are temperamentally unsuited to one another. I realized that on the day I came with Jane to visit you at the Crimson Club. Seeing you both together I could no longer avoid my doubts about our marriage. Since then, I have tried with all my strength to forget you – ' he laughed ruefully – 'but as you can see, I have failed most miserably. I forced myself to stay away from you for three months, but last night I planned to ask you to be my wife.'

Nesta's face was flaming and a wave of heat raged over her body, making her gown feel clammy against her skin. Where his hands grasped her shoulders they seemed to sear her flesh.

'James,' she gasped, her eyes lustrous with hope and joy, 'you love me – you truly love me!'

'I do, oh I do. Say that you will marry me, darling. Say it!'

'I will, oh I will, my dearest!' Nesta cried, before she had time to consider what her acceptance would mean. And then, biting her lip, she said, 'James, how can you want this? It will destroy your reputation. You will be cold-shouldered by everyone – Darling, I am – I have nothing to offer you. I am a scarlet woman, a lady of the night. You will regret it – Women will turn from you; men, too. You will not be able to endure it.'

James gripped her hands, looking deep into her eyes. 'Are you telling me that you are incapable of seeing it through? Are you telling me that you do not have the fortitude to become my wife, my duchess, to walk beside me publicly and share my life with me?'

'No, I am not saying that. I – I am thinking of you, my love,' she said huskily.

'And I am thinking of you, Nesta sweetheart. If we can share this, go through it together, we shall be all the stronger. We shall succeed, I know it. There are ways of getting round the more difficult aspects of the situation. For example, the Princess of Wales. She is not as straitlaced as her mother-in-law. I know the Prince well – we shall make sure that you are introduced to the Princess, that you become friends with her. I am sure you and she will like one another very much. That will get you your entrée into society. You will then be accepted by everybody.'

Nesta listened, astonished at his confidence. He had obviously put great thought into this. She asked him if this were so.

'Much thought, my dear. I have pondered on little else for months now, anticipating the day I would ask you to be my wife. This incident today, your saving Ariadne's life, merely precipitated what would have happened shortly anyway. It would not have taken me long to apologize to you for last night and my abominable behaviour.'

For the moment, little Meggie Blunt's scheme for revenge was put aside. It was Nesta Bellingham alone who responded ardently to the Duke's proposal. She felt strength welling up inside her, knowing that with James as her husband she could face anything, accomplish anything. Her past, present and future were, in fact joined at this moment. She was the child Meggie again, adoring her Sun God from afar; she was Nesta Bellingham of the Crimson Club, still besotted with her Sun God; and she was the prospective Duchess of Malgrave, mistress of Malgrave Manor, wife of the Sun God who had dominated her heart for ten years now.

Because of the powerful rush of feelings, Nesta had no difficulty suppressing her misgivings. She wanted James with a passion that shook her to her very soul. Yes, together they could face all censure, all disdain, making their way with courage and dignity, ignoring the hostility of those who would look down at her for her lowly origins. She had always believed that the people who matter do not mind, and the people who mind do not matter. It was one of Jenny's strongest beliefs, and it was hers, too.

Swept along by an upsurge of love and longing, she and James began to kiss again, his kisses gentle but firm, making her tremble in response. She forgot everyone, everything, in his arms; she could believe that life was sunny and beautiful again, without any ripples of grief or discontent, and that little Meggie Blunt and her harrowing childhood had never existed. Secure in the love of her James, she could experience heaven, or so Nesta imagined. Would it prove to be a fantasy? James obviously thought not as he led her to his bedroom where he took her in his arms again, telling her how much he adored her.

'I have dreamed of making you mine, darling, of marrying you and watching our children grow up. This was how I knew that I truly am in love with you, that it is not infatuation. . . .' He tilted her chin upwards with one forefinger. 'Oh those eyes – they are like jewels, and your skin is like magnolia petals. Did you know that, my darling?'

'No,' Nesta whispered, entranced by his passionate admiration. Few men had troubled to enthuse over her face, wanting only her body to satiate their lust.

His bedroom was some distance away from the others, but he locked the door to ensure privacy. It gave an added spice to their lovemaking, this feeling that they were secretly locked away together. The bed was wide, and they lay cushioned in its softness, kissing ardently.

'My betrothed,' James murmured as he caressed her neck, then slid his fingers inside her bodice.

She had flung her riding jacket over a chair, and soon her blouse and skirt were to join it, along with James's clothes. Then she lay happily naked, with James gazing down at her adoringly.

'My goddess, my beautiful alabaster goddess, that's what you are. But not cold like stone – warm, silken. . . .'

He nuzzled her breasts, her stomach and thighs. Then, breathless, they came together in a moment of almost intolerable bliss. Nesta's head twisted from side to side as she felt him move within her, hot and powerful. As before, it was as if he were all that had been missing for her to be happy. Only when he entered her body was she truly joyful, reminded of her destiny: to be his love.

'This puts ecstasy to shame,' James said between their kisses. 'Bliss, too. I had half-suspected it, but now I know for sure: I have been mixing with the wrong women.'

Nesta laughed. 'You are teasing me – You must have known many passionate women.'

'Not like you. There is something about you – a quality of innocent sexuality which is quite irresistible. Thank God it was I who captured you first!'

'Thank God,' Nesta echoed, knowing full well that she would not have surrendered to anyone else as she had done to him. And then there was no more breath left for conversation but only for the violent consummation of their loving.

Afterwards, they lay close, eyes shut, saying nothing for words were not needed. After they had rested, they made love again. The second time was even better....

Next morning, at eleven, a liveried manservant arrived at the Crimson Club with a package for Nesta. Inside was the exquisite mermaid which she had admired in the library of Malgrave Manor, and beneath it was a card which said, 'With all my love and devotion, James,' written in the Duke's large, expressive handwriting.

Nesta lifted the figurine out of its packaging and held it carefully in her hands. There were tears in her eyes. Her first gift from her Sun God, her future husband, for she had accepted him and they were now betrothed. He must have seen the look on her face as she was admiring the little mermaid when he came into the library. It was rare for a man to be so perceptive.

'How fortunate I am,' she whispered beneath her breath. 'How very fortunate.'

It was then that the enormity of what she intended to do struck Nesta like a blow to the heart. She clutched the little mermaid to her breast, tears in her eyes.

Nesta had barely slept the previous night after being returned from the manor. She had tossed and turned in bed, seeing her darling mother again dying of sickness and starvation in their hovel, seeing again the vile Jack Blunt attacking Jenny in one of his drunken fits of rage. She heard Jenny's dying voice telling her the story of the innocent Welsh maid-servant who had fallen in love with the young master of the house and who had parted with all she possessed for love of him. Such things could not, must not, be forgotten. Long ago she had made a vow to Jenny: she would keep it. She loved James, there was no doubting it; she loved him deeply and irrevocably, but he *was* a Malgrave and she had sworn revenge on the Malgraves for what they had done to her mother. If she forgot that vow now she would never know a moment's peace.

The instrument of revenge was in Nesta's own hands; she had it already. She knew what it would be, had known for some years. But she could not think of that now; later, after the wedding, would be time enough. If she pondered on the dreadfulness of what she proposed to do, she would possibly renegue, having lost the courage to go on.

'Oh, James, James, I love you,' she whispered, her eyes swimming with tears so that it appeared as if the little mermaid were actually immersed in the sea from whence she had come, the blue-green waters swirling around her as if unleashed by a storm.

CHAPTER SIXTEEN

What James had to do that morning was one of the most distasteful tasks of his whole life, but it was essential that

Jane heard the news from his own lips. He owed her that much.

Their relationship had cooled dramatically some time ago, for despite all her blandishments, her cajoling and pleas, he had continued to keep a distance between them.

'James dear,' she had said in a wheedling voice, 'I am sure that you will feel better soon. Many men are like this, you know. They become fearful when the marriage approaches and regret losing their bachelordom. I *do* understand, my dear.'

Her fingers had curled round his lapels as her baby-blue eyes looked up at him with understanding. How embarrassed she had made him feel with her condescending manner, for all the time he had known that she was barely controlling her animosity regarding his coolness, that her apparent patience could dissolve suddenly, leaving her red-cheeked and hysterical. There had been many such scenes, whenever he had attempted to explain that he needed time. Finally, having seen that she would get nowhere by wheedling him, Jane had given him the interval he needed. But he had subsequently noticed a strange look in her eye, which he eventually realized was contempt; his recognizing this helped to lessen the guilt he was feeling.

How could Jane claim to love him so passionately and then look at him with such scorn? On occasions he had seen the girl Jane might have been had she received a warmer, more indulgent upbringing, but she had been the victim of stringently disciplinarian parents. Long ago, spontaneous love and affection had been crushed out of her as if they were sins in themselves, and although she could touch him as she was doing now, when she urgently needed something, she had frequently flinched when he had so much as dropped a light kiss on her forehead. He could not even contemplate living with a wife who flinched when he came near her; their marriage would be a sham, she wanting all she could get by day, and nothing at night.

Today Jane was in the conservatory when James arrived

at her home. She was wearing an oyster brocade gown with a modest crinoline, ruched and gathered, with bunches of tiny silk violets nestling in the folds of the brocade; her sunny ringlets framed her face like goldsmith's work. She looked charming, someone to be adored and cossetted, a sweetmeat wrapped in pretty paper.

'James, my dear,' she said, hurrying towards him, her hands outstretched.

He saw hope and delight in her face, and his heart sank. The sooner he spoke the better, before this scene became a farce. As her hands were about to clasp his, he took a pace backwards, causing her to come to a halt with a perplexed look on her face.

'James, have you bad news? Is your cousin . . .?'

'Oh no,' he said, 'the Duchess is quite well. It is not that matter which brings me here. I wish to speak about us.' He paused, realizing that even these words could be misconstrued. 'Jane, you have waited very patiently for many months now, and I think you must have guessed that my feelings have not changed since our last conversation.'

'Not changed? *Not changed?*' she said, her voice rising on a tremulous note, alarm leaping into her eyes.

'My feelings are the same today as they were when we spoke last. I still feel strongly that we are not suited to one another, that I would only make you unhappy. I am not the man for you, Jane, for I am not the man you think me.'

'Oh, but you are, you are, James, *dear* James!' she cried, throwing herself against his chest, her gilded curls bobbing against his chin.

Gently he extricated himself. 'No, I am not, Jane. Please, I beg of you, do not make this more difficult for me than it is. It has taken all of my courage for me to come here today, but I wanted you to be the first to know.'

Jane took two steps backward, staggering a little, her mouth agape. At that moment she looked almost ugly. 'Th-the f-first to know *what*?' she stammered, feeling ice descend around her heart.

'I am to be married, Jane.'

There, now it was out, she knew the worst. James prepared himself for what must surely come.

'Who-who is the fortunate young lady? Do I know her?' Jane's voice sounded strangled.

'You have met her once or twice.'

James swallowed, suddenly realizing the enormity of what he was about to say. She would think him mad, suffering from a fever of the brain. He imagined her sobbing, pleading, clutching at him, pounding his chest in her anger and frustration. It was only for a few seconds that he contemplated her reaction to what he was going to say and yet it seemed like hours. Then, as the silence hung between them awkwardly, he spoke.

'The lady I intend to marry is Miss Nesta Bellingham of the Crimson Club.'

'You lie!' Jane spat at him hoarsely. 'This is some cruel joke! You have come here to taunt me. That prostitute! You are not going to marry that harlot! How can you even *speak* her name?'

James flinched. 'I can speak her name and I will marry her because I love her, Jane. It is as simple as that.'

Jane's face convulsed in shock. 'James,' she cried, 'you cannot, you shall not, I will not let you! You are mad to even consider it! This will be the end for you. The end, oh, the end, the end!'

She began to sob, and then, suddenly, she was only inches away from him, her hands clawing at his lapels.

'James, James,' she wept, 'don't let it be the end for us. We love each other, you *know* we do. We were made for each other. Everyone says what a handsome couple we are together. *Please*, James! Have I offended you? I know ... I know that I cannot respond to you as I should, but I will change, I promise you, James. I will work hard to make you a good wife, a *passionate* wife.'

Jane halted after saying these words, swallowing hard. 'If that is what you need in a wife, James, then I will give it to you. I will be like that – that *whore*. I will be like that for you in bed – If that is what you want, that is how I shall be. Look, look! I can be just like her!'

To his horror, Jane began ripping and pulling at the material of her bodice. The buttons spat across the room as she tore it open to reveal her high-necked lace chemise, which she proceeded to roll down until she stood half-naked before him, her pallid breasts freed.

'See, James, I can be just like Nesta Bellingham!' She gasped for breath as the realization of what she had done hit her, but she could not halt now.

'I can see by your face that I have shocked you, James, but isn't this what *she* does for you? Isn't this kind of thing why you want to marry her? Because she responds to you physically, because she is free of inhibitions? Not like me – I was beaten, accused of having lewd thoughts, when all I wanted to do was kiss my father. Did you know that, James? Did you ever guess what it was like being a little girl in my father's household, where even the most innocent gesture of affection was condemned as sin?'

'I had to comply, James, I had to, or else I would be beaten and shut in my room without food for days on end. I always gave in. I always begged Papa to forgive me. I used to kneel at his feet and beg him to take me back into his favour. Finally, he would, but not before I had been punished – and I had to *plead* for punishment or else he would say I was not truly repentant.' Jane stopped suddenly, sobbing, drawing in her breath with a loud hissing noise. 'He – he used to cane my hands, you know. He used to cane them until I fainted from the pain or screamed out loud, and then he would say I was not truly repentant and he would shut me in my room again. Once, when I had been particularly sinful, for some misdemeanour I cannot even remember now, he beat me with a leather belt across the back. I still bear the scars, James. Have you not noticed how I always wear high-necked gowns? If I did not, you would see the scars on my back and my neck.'

James was white with embarrassment and pity. This was the last thing he had wanted, this desperate confession. At last Jane seemed to have broken down the barriers which had stood between them all this time. Why, in God's name, could she not have done it years ago, when they might have worked out something between them, together? Now it was too late. Could she not see that? God in Heaven, how was he going to get out of this room and away from her now? Had he known it would be like this he would never have come; he would have sent her a letter, cold as that might have been.

'Jane, all this is unnecessary. Please, I beg of you, stop crying. Nothing can be done about us now, it is *too late*. I am to marry Miss Bellingham and that is all there is to it.'

Jane paused, her shoulders hunched forward, her eyes staring up at him, so distended that they appeared to bulge. Then she began to laugh hysterically, peal upon peal of screeching, raucous laughter which cracked against his ears like slapping hands.

'You are going to marry a *whore*, a brothel-keeper! You are going to marry a *scarlet woman*, a woman who sells her body to *anyone* who can pay her fee. *A prostitute*! *You are going to marry a prostitute*!'

Then Jane collapsed into another bout of laughter, which gradually subsided, leaving her ashen-faced and faint.

James helped her to a seat and settled her on it, standing by awkwardly, not wanting to leave her in this state and yet unwilling to call Jane's mother or her maid because of all the explanations which would become necessary. To his utter relief, Jane regained a little of her usual composure and plucked at his sleeve.

'Go away, James. Go *now*, before anyone comes. *Get out*!' she hissed.

When James got home he shut himself in his library; he remained there for several hours, struggling to cope with his feelings of pity for Jane and guilt over what he had done to her. The fact that he would never give in to her pleas or change his mind about Nesta made those hours all the harder to endure.

Instead of comforting her, the little mermaid standing on her mantelshelf seemed to be accusing Nesta: 'You are a pretender, a sham. You have the wrong motives for wanting to marry James. You want revenge on his family, but he deserves better. He is not vicious like the old Duchess; he would not turn a pregnant girl out into the streets – You really have no quarrel with him. Why, then, do you persist?'

Fortunately, Nesta did not have very much time for thought. The club had never been so busy, the gambling-room having proved immensely popular. Nesta had had to take on half a dozen new girls and was anticipating employing another half-dozen within the next few months. As always, she took extreme care to select girls who looked well-bred, even if they were not.

Now Nesta let Cathy and Amy know that she would shortly be turning the entire business over to them.

'To us, Nesta lovey? But what's this all about?' Cathy exclaimed. 'What are you planning to do? You're not leaving us, surely, an' just when the club's doing so well an' all? The Prince is here nearly every week now, an' the way he looks at you, Nesta, well, I reckon you could have him on a plate if you wanted.'

'Yes, Cathy's right, you could have him on a plate,' Amy chimed in. 'Right took with you, he is; that's obvious to everyone. All the girls were saying how his eyes light up when he sees you, an' he didn't bring no lady companion with him last time, did he? Spent the whole evening with you. You've made a real conquest there, Nesta. You should strike while the iron's hot.' Amy nodded her head vigorously, as if she were agreeing with herself.

Nesta told the girls to sit down and then she sat between them, looking from one to the other, remembering all the happy times they had had together and how they had cared for her when she was a half-starved orphan-girl. It would be painful to leave them, but she would soon have to sever all connections with the Crimson Club; one could not be a duke's wife and also be the Madam of a bordello.

Finally, she said, 'Cathy, Amy, my dears,' clasping their hands in hers, 'you have been like sisters to me and I'll never forget that, but there comes a time in everyone's life when they have to move on.'

'Yeah, but where're you going to move on to?' Cathy interrupted, frowning.

'Would you believe me if I said to a duke's house?' Nesta smiled.

'A duke's house?' Cathy repeated loudly.

'A duke's house?' Amy parroted, her mouth hanging open.

'Yes, that's right, my loves, a duke's house. The Duke of Malgrave's house. You remember him, don't you? He was here that night Carlotta was attacked. A tall, blond man with kind blue eyes.'

'Sure, I remember him, Nesta. He's a real handsome feller. You're a lucky girl. An' you ain't been telling us this, you've been keeping it a secret,' Cathy grinned conspiratorially. 'So you're going to be a duke's mistress? Well, that's a real step up an' no mistake, lovey. You've done well for yourself.'

Nesta looked at the floor before turning her face to Cathy, then to Amy. 'There is more to it than that. I would not give up the club to be anyone's *mistress*.' Before the girls could interrupt, as they were obviously eager to do, she added, 'The Duke of Malgrave has asked me to be his wife. He loves me and I love him. I think I have loved him for years.'

Shock flitted across Cathy's face and was as suddenly gone. She breathed in deeply as if she were about to speak, but then thought better of it. Endeavouring to smile, she patted Nesta's hand and seemed genuinely pleased as she offered her congratulations.

Amy, for once, seemed to be lost for words and squeezed Nesta's hand tightly, tears filling her eyes.

'Our little Meggie Blunt a duchess, well, did you ever!' she gasped eventually, having found her voice. 'Our little Meggie Blunt married to a duke, well, well, well! So he loves you, does he? Well, an' I thought he was dumb enough to marry that Finchley-Stark, or whatever her name is. Now there's a girl who don't ever take her stays off, not even in bed.' Amy cackled at her own joke.

'Finchley-Clark it is, Amy,' Cathy corrected her, unsmiling. 'But you're right about the stays. So he's come to his senses at last, has he? Well, an' about time. You could see a mile off he weren't suited to that cold-hearted creature. It would be like hugging an iceberg in bed. Now, when's the happy occasion to be, Nesta dearie? Let us know, won't you, so's we all can start choosing our dresses. . . .'

Cathy halted the prattle momentarily, for Amy was looking at her warningly, then she went on, 'Oops, of course you won't want your girls at the wedding, will you? I guess all his relatives will be there, lords and ladies, won't they? Oh, I hadn't thought of that. Can't be advertising your past, can you, lovey? We'll have to stay in hiding, won't we? Disown you, like, if we see you in the street in all your finery. We'll have to turn our heads the other way an' pretend we don't know who you are. Ain't that right, Amy?'

Cathy managed a shaky grin. She was going to lose the girl she had thought of as her little sister. But how could she say that to Nesta? You didn't douse a young bride-to-be with cold water!

There were tears in Nesta's eyes now. She had not thought telling them would be so hard.

'We'll have a party before I go,' she said. 'A real celebration, something to remember. Order the best champagne and whatever refreshments you think the girls would like and we'll have a real do.'

Amy exclaimed in delight, and then Cathy said hoarsely, 'What're we to tell the Prince of Wales when he asks for you, Nesta?'

Nesta shrugged. 'I expect I shall see him before I go. Leave him to me.'

'He'll be heartbroken not to see you here any more. In future when he meets up with you, you'll have to bow an' scrape an' be all pompous and proper, like, 'cause you'll be a society lady after the wedding. 'Twill break his heart if he can't ogle you like what he does when he comes here. Remember that night when he kissed you in front of everyone?'

Nesta gave a wry smile. 'I am sure the Jersey Lily will know how to cheer him up.'

'How could he prefer her to you, Nesta? Now you *know* that he's hardly looked at her since he met you. Brought her here once, he did, an' then after that he came on his own so he could be with *you*, didn't he? Take some cheering up, he will, an' that's for sure.'

'She's a handsome woman with those lovely big eyes and that titian hair. She has lots of spirit, too. She'll know how to comfort him,' Nesta said.

'Won't be the same without you here, Nesta.'

Amy sounded quite forlorn all of a sudden. Nesta reached over and gave her a big hug.

'It won't be the same without you, Amy, or you, Cathy, but we'll keep in touch, I promise. I'll call in and see you, and you can always write to me. And if you ever need help, just let me know.'

Cathy sniffed loudly, blowing her nose with the panache of a trumpeter. 'Well, all good things come to an end. I always said it an' I always meant it, an' it's true,' she said bravely, trying to put Nesta's needs first, as she had always done.

'Not really an end, Cathy dear. A beginning for us all. A beginning for the two of you running the club on your own and a beginning for me as James's wife. Oh, my dears, we'll not forget one another; we could never do that. We've had a marvellous friendship. I don't know where I'd be today without you – still in the gutter maybe. You'll be angels one day for what you've done for me.'

Nesta looked up, her eye catching the accusative gaze of the little mermaid.

'Traitor,' the little mermaid seemed to be saying. 'You won't be an angel, not ever. What you're planning to do will send you to hell and there's no mistake about that, Nesta Bellingham!'

'So you're going to be a duchess? That's a clever move, Nesta Bellingham, a very clever move. He's a rich man, Malgrave; he'll buy you all the trinkets you want, and you make sure you get as much from him as you can. Beauty fades, but diamonds never stop glittering; nor do rubies and emeralds! Store them all up, because you never know when you're going to need them. Men are fickle; they can change their minds and ditch you, just like that.'

The speaker, Lillie Langtry, clicked her fingers together and tossed back her mane of wavy auburn hair. She had huge, blue-violet eyes, which she used with the consummate skill of an actress, and Nesta always enjoyed watching her antics. They had often ridden together along Rotten Row, although Lillie was apt to be surrounded by men wherever she went, which precluded intimate conversation.

Nesta would never forget the day when they had been out riding with Lord Lonsdale and Lillie had stopped alongside the railing in Rotten Row to exchange a few words with someone she knew – a man, of course. She had barely said more than a few sentences when suddenly Lord Lonsdale had leapt from his horse, jumped over the railing and proceeded to attack her astonished friend. Soon a crowd had gathered round to watch Lord Lonsdale knock down his rival, who had turned out to be Sir George Chetwyn. (Sir George had let Lord Lonsdale overhear him saying that Lillie should be accompanying *him* instead.) It had taken the Duke of Portland and Sir William Gordon-Cummings some moments to tear the two men apart.

Lillie had never been bound by the dictates of polite society; she always did what she wanted to do. She was now giving Nesta what she believed to be sound advice. She did not care a fig for appearances, nor did she seem to know the meaning of discretion. She glittered with the jewels given to her by her admirers, one of whom was the Prince of Wales himself, and there was no hint of hostility in her voice as she advised Nesta, who had so often occupied the Prince's attentions of late.

Nesta smiled, 'Diamonds won't comfort you on your death-bed, Lillie.'

Lillie threw back her head and laughed out loud.

'That's true, Nesta, but they'll buy you a might of things that no man will buy you when you're old and grey and you've lost your charms.'

'I'll remember your advice, Lillie, don't worry,' Nesta said lightly, knowing full well it was not the diamonds, emeralds or rubies which she wanted from James, or from any other man. Her needs were very different.

Nesta and Lillie had much in common. They had both come up the hard way, although Lillie's straits had never been as desperate as Nesta's. It was true, however, that when she first came to London she had nothing but one very plain black dress to wear out in society. However, her profile and head, which was said to resemble that of a Greek goddess, her clear, blue-violet eyes and directness of speech had soon won her admirers.

Lillie's opening gambits were always of a controversial and unexpected nature. Men reared on women's inane flutterings and puerile simperings were at first stunned and then totally captivated by Lillie's words, from such unexpected questions as 'What are your spiritual beliefs?' to 'Do you think politics a lost cause?' Had Nesta wished to make the conquest of rich men her life's work, she would have studied the daughter of the Dean of Jersey in great detail, but now Lillie and she were about to embark on different paths. Lillie was fired with the thought of going on the stage and Nesta was about to marry the man she had loved since her childhood.

'You will come and visit me, and bring the Prince, will you not?' Nesta asked her.

'Of course, my dear. You'll need all the support you can get, marrying a duke! Titled folk can be the very devil when they want to, and you will have all manner of problems to contend with, take my word for it, Nesta. Now mind how you go.'

Leaning forward, Lillie fixed Nesta with her great eyes

and patted her on the cheek with a soft, white, jewel-bedecked hand.

CHAPTER SEVENTEEN

'James.'

The voice from the canopied bed was little more than a croak. James immediately bent over the bed to take the hand of the tiny, wizened woman who had spoken. He looked down at the sunken eyes, the fleshless cheeks and fragile jawbone, the hair as wispy and pale as the tuft of a dandelion spread out on the pillow, framing the ancient face. She was of a great age now, his cousin the Duchess, and she had been an invalid for years. Losing her son, Michael, so tragically had broken much of her spirit, and when her husband had died soon after she had seemed at a loss to know what to do; she had never really recovered from the debilitating despair of that double tragedy. James had not known her in her heyday, when she could make people blanch merely by glaring at them with her fierce black eyes. He saw her now as a broken, sick old woman, to be greatly pitied.

For her part, the Duchess felt for him as much as she could feel for anyone not born of her own body, and so she hid from him her vituperative side, the acid tongue which made her personal servants leave the house one after the other to be replaced by new maids who left similarly. Only one servant of long-standing remained: a timid little woman who always wore crumpled black and whose name was Margaret. The Duchess had long ago nicknamed her Maggotty. The cruel nickname had stuck, Margaret sometimes being called Maggott and other times Maggotty. For years, the Duchess had derived malicious pleasure from the use of that spiteful soubriquet.

In front of James, Margaret was always called Margaret and the other servants all received their proper titles; the old Duchess would speak in a quavering, faint voice and she would smile at her cousin and hold out her hands to him, asking him how his day had been and had he any news to cheer her as she lay on her sick-bed? He would do his best to remember snippets of gossip which might interest her and to tell her what was happening in the neighbourhood, to remember to pass on good wishes which her old friends had given him. Frequently he would bring her gifts, fruit or sweetmeats.

The old Duchess loved James a lot; in fact, almost as much as she loved herself. Only once before had she loved someone more than she loved herself and that had been her son, Michael. Occasionally she mistook James for Michael, although her son had had very dark hair and eyes, and a slighter build than James. Sometimes, she wanted so much for James to be Michael that she actually saw Michael's face bending over her and heard his voice speaking to her.

James never pretended to be what he was not, nor did he try to shake her from her dreams. He was a dear and tender-hearted, with only one glaring fault to her eyes: he had not married and produced an heir.

She gazed up at him now, remembering that he had said he had some particularly good news to tell her.

'I have chosen my bride,' James smiled. 'I do not think you will have heard her name, but she is an extremely handsome woman, with the most beautiful amethyst-coloured eyes and jet-black hair.'

Ever mindful of her longing to see James's heir before she died, the old Duchess said, 'What are her hips like, Jamie? Has she got broad hips, for child-bearing? You're after an heir, aren't you? Got to have an heir for Malgrave, you know. Look at her hips, Jamie!' The invalid's eyes sparkled. The boy had decided on a wife at long last. 'If she's got wide hips then take her. If she don't, then throw her out.'

James grinned. 'Oh, her hips are quite wide enough, I do assure you, my dear. But she has other qualities which are just as important. I shall bring her to meet you soon.'

'Now tell me who she is? The Duke of Coacham's

daughter? Lady Violet Ennerton? Now who else is unmarried, let me see – '

James dropped a kiss on his cousin's parchment cheek. 'I shall tell you all about her later. Now I must leave you, for I have an urgent appointment.'

The old Duchess's eyes glittered. She wanted so much to know all about the girl, but she reminded herself that this was James and she must not nag him. Without his daily visits, she would be a lonely old woman, shut away in this bedroom at the top of the house and dependent upon servants who despised her and who were so careless about carrying out their duties. Not like when she had been young, when no one had dared to disobey her. Then, servants, family and friends had all scuttled about like scalded cats to do her bidding. Now all she had was James, but he was enough, and she did not want to antagonize him. If he had chosen a wife then she would meet the girl and her family. She had become adept at acting, at pretending to be what she was not; no doubt she would be able to do it with the bride as well, certainly enough to satisfy James.

More than anything else, the Duchess wanted to see James's son before she died. It was a desire strong enough to overrule any emnity she might feel at having to share him with another woman. Before James left, she told him of her hopes. He smiled and promised to do his best.

She knew that she had been extremely fortunate. James was both generous and kind-hearted; because of this, she had survived an untenable situation, that of seeing her husband's and son's title going to a distant cousin she barely knew.

She had never been one to fraternize, not even with members of her own family. She had invested all her emotions first in her husband and then in her son. She knew that she was a difficult old woman and that, had the title gone to anyone but James, she would have been forced out of her home to live in the Dower House at the far side of the estate. It was a pleasant little house, well designed, but compared to the manor it was miniscule and far too modest for the requirements of a duchess who had been accustomed to magnificence all her life. If she had had to leave Malgrave she knew that she would not have survived very long, her heart would have been broken. She loved the manor. In every direction she looked it brought back to her memories of her son.

After James left, the Duchess thought back to a time over twenty years ago. There had been a girl, a Welsh girl – she could not remember her name now. Michael had been wildly infatuated with the creature, although she was low-born and just a serving-maid in the house. While he was on the Continent the girl had come to her to tell her she was pregnant, trying to accuse Michael of being the father of her child. The Duchess had sent the girl packing, adamant that Michael could not have done such a thing, that he was too innocent to have taken liberties with the girl. But when he had returned from abroad to find the girl gone, he had confronted her, asking for the serving-maid. No one knew where the chit was by then, certainly not she. Michael had been furious. Although no one else seemed to sense it, this altercation had ended their close relationship for ever. He had discovered his mother's part in sending the creature away; when she could not tell him where the girl was, he had thought she was lying. He had scoured London to find the girl; he had even written to her relatives in Bangor, but no one had seen her. After months of searching – during which he barely exchanged a word with his mother – he had become thinner, paler, so serious that weeks passed without the Duchess's seeing the smile she so loved.

She had tried to straighten things out with him. Tentatively, she had told him that the girl was pregnant before she left, that undoubtedly the child was someone else's and not his, that girls like her did not take any trouble to protect their honour. She wished she had not said anything, for Michael's rage had been terrible to behold.

'You told her to *go* and she was having *my child*? How *could* you have been so callous? How *could* you? Your own grandchild, and you did not care!' He had glared at her, gritting his teeth in white-faced fury. 'I shall never forgive you. *Never*! You are no longer my mother!'

He had stalked out and then ordered his valet to pack his bags. A few hours later he was on his way back to his friends on the Continent. Soon afterwards, he was dead, after a tragic riding accident.

The old Duchess shivered; she was feeling cold. It was time for her hot drink, and the coals in her warming-pan needed replacing. Where was that woman?

'Maggotty! Maggotty!' the Duchess roared. 'I want my drink. I'm cold, woman, where are you? Come here this instant!'

Red-cheeked, with her mob cap askew, Margaret came scuttling into the room and bobbed a curtsy at the foot of the Duchess's bed. She was a tiny woman, nervous and somewhat slow-witted. She was the last of a long line of servants who had attempted to serve the Duchess but who had found her demands and caustic manner unbearable.

The Duchess bellowed with fury, causing Margaret to start.

'You careless, clumsy creature!' cried the Duchess. 'You dug your nail into my leg when you were pulling out the warming-pan. See, you have fetched blood.'

Margaret looked as if she might faint. 'Oh, Your Grace, Your Grace! Forgive me. I didn' mean it, no I didn'.'

'What have I told you about your clumsiness, woman? How many times have I lectured you on using your body with grace and control?' The Duchess glared at Margaret, who shrank back in fear.

'Now, when you fetch my hot toddy,' said the Duchess sarcastically, 'don't forget that small, tapestry foot-stool just to the right of my bed, will you? I should be *most* disappointed if you do not trip over that and spill the hot toddy all over my bed like you did yesterday. And, of course, you must not forget to leave the lid of the warming-pan so loosely fastened that a hot coal escapes and burns a hole through the sheets. My days would be so tedious without these little mishaps to brighten them, Maggotty. Oh, and Maggotty –' the Duchess narrowed her blackcurrant eyes – 'when you iron my nightgown, *plea*se don't forget to leave it damp and unaired so that I get a nasty attack of rheumatism again.'

As Nesta stepped into the old Duchess's boudoir she was again assaulted by that feeling of past, present and future coming together. The part of her that had been little Meggie Blunt wanted to dash across the room and beat at the old harridan with clubbed fists until shock and terror brought on a seizure which would cause the Duchess to die. The part of her that was Nesta Bellingham instructed her to employ the utmost control, to go about her plans in a civilized fashion. The part of her that was soon to be Duchess of Malgrave, thus making this old woman a dowager-duchess, wanted to greet her as the relative that she soon would be.

James was at her elbow, a reassuring comfort. She wore a tasteful gown, mid-blue in colour, neatly tailored and edged with bands of dark blue velvet. On her head was a dark blue velvet hat, discreetly plumed with curving white feathers. Nesta had never looked more noble, and this fact was reflected in James's admiring expression.

Slowly, Nesta took those momentous steps across the floor of the old Duchess's boudoir towards the huge bed. Looking down into the midst of the pillows she saw a slight figure, wizened and emaciated, with a scant pom-pom of flaxen-white hair through which her pink scalp gleamed. Two frail hands peeped over the coverlet, glittering with jewels; on some fingers there were as many as four rings, all crammed together. The pallor of her parchment skin made her eyes seem all the more startling; they were inky sable, pulsating with life.

Nesta regarded the tiny stick figure with a feeling of shock. Was this frail, tiny creature her vicious, foul-tongued grandmother? She found it hard to believe.

Nesta's mouth quivered slightly as she looked into the old woman's dark eyes. There was grit and determination in those eyes, even the tremulous smile on the Duchess's face could not conceal that. Behind the welcoming expression Nesta sensed the harsh strength and indomitable will which still drove her ancient grandmother. Strangely, there was a feeling of recognition, too, similar to that which she had felt on entering the manor for the first time. It was an odd sensation and it stirred feelings inside her which she had not thought existed.

The invalid continued to smile up at her, revealing yellowed teeth which were nearly a century old but which nonetheless were intact. A slight turn of the Duchess's head revealed a thick collar round her neck, encrusted with diamonds, each one perfect, and matching earrings in the thin, pale ears which were so wasted that light seemed to pass through the lobes.

'Your Grace,' Nesta whispered huskily.

Before she could say any more, the Duchess smiled even wider, an almost joyous grin. 'Welcome, my dear! Welcome to Malgrave Manor. James has told me something of you – but not enough, not enough. I have been waiting so very long for him to marry, and now that the time has come no one could be more pleased than I.' The blackcurrant eyes narrowed. 'I can see why James chose you. You're a beauty, my dear, and there's something of his mother about you, I do believe. She was fair-skinned and raven-haired like you, did y'know it?'

'Yes, I remember her,' Nesta said dreamily, in a low voice; then she caught herself, but James seemed not to have noticed her slip. She had not told him how, as a starving urchin, she had taken soup from his mother.

The old Duchess chuckled. 'I can see you'll have fine, sturdy sons, my dear, and sons are what we need, you know.' Suddenly the old face was full of sadness as memories flooded back to her.

'It's been over forty years since a child was born in this house, my dear, and that was my own son. His name was Michael. Has James told you about him?'

Nesta nodded.

'We were so close, you know, my dear, he and I. In every way. His father was a taciturn man; he meant well but he had little to say to a young child and so retired more and more into himself. Naturally Michael turned to me for everything.'

The Duchess paused, plunging one heavily jewelled hand down under the bedclothes and then drawing it out, holding a heavy gold locket. 'This is my son, this is Michael,' she said, holding out the locket for Nesta to see.

For the first time in her life Nesta looked on the face of her real father. She saw the luxuriant black hair which waved across his forehead, just as her own did; she saw the fair skin, just like her own, and dark eyes, whose colour was impossible to discern in the miniature. Hadn't Jenny said they were very dark brown, almost black?

The face that looked up at her was sensitive and serious, totally innocent; he must have been only fourteen or fifteen years old when this painting was done, for he was attired in a schoolboy's collar and tie. His mouth was full, fine lines arcing on either side of it so that one imagined he would be more than willing to smile if only given the chance, if only he could forget for a moment the seriousness of his station in life. She knew why her mother had loved him. She could see her attraction to the handsome, boyish face; it brought out a woman's maternal instincts, her tenderness. When Nesta finished examining her father's portrait, there were tears in her eyes, tears which the old Duchess did not miss.

'I see that you are a girl who is capable of empathy,' she said, patting Nesta's hand. 'That is rare in one so young. He was a darling boy. He took all my love. When – when he died – ' the old woman's voice cracked – 'when he died, I wanted to die, too. What reason had I to live without my child? The little boy I had nursed and taught to walk; the little boy who said "Mamma" – his first word – to me. I think I shocked not a few people by looking after him so much myself. I did not want him to be reared by nurses and know me like some distant stranger. It is true to say I devoted my life to him from the moment he was born. I do not regret that. Had I not done so how much emptier and barren my life would have been! But now that James has chosen his bride I feel new hope,' she smiled, a nerve at the corner of her mouth jumping. 'You have got the family's colouring, my dear, the Malgrave family's colouring. That is good, for your son will be that much more like Michael.' Suddenly Nesta's hands were being tightly gripped by those of the old Duchess. 'Do not keep me waiting too long!'

Nesta was visibly shaken by the meeting with her grandmother. Seeing how white she looked, James took her to a seat in the library and ordered a servant to fetch them tea. Then he held Nesta's hand while waiting for her to recover herself.

'That poor old woman, lying in bed dreaming of her dead son – ' Nesta's voice broke. 'What a tragedy for her! Fate can be very cruel.'

'I feel the same, my love. I have tried to bring her as much happiness as I can in my own small way. She seems to like me, which is good, for it must hurt her to know that I, a comparative stranger, hold a title which should have been her son's and his son's after him. I was determined that she would not suffer, but I confess that I did not know what to expect when I first came here; I had heard so many tales about her terrible temper, her venomous tongue. She is obviously a deeply unhappy woman.'

Nesta did not answer for the moment. She was trembling and her head was beginning to ache. She knew why. Whatever the old Duchess had been like in her heyday, she was now a helpless and heartbroken invalid, frail and lonely. How could Nesta want to hurt her even more than she had already been hurt in the past? But then, how could she forget her vow of revenge without betraying her own mother, Jenny?

The conflict inside her was increasing and with it her headache. Part of the room seemed in darkness, the rest flooded with rivulets of light. Nesta had not had one of these attacks for a long time now, but she knew that she would have to lie down in a darkened room for some hours.

Placing a hand on her forehead Nesta explained to James how she was feeling. Instantly he told her that she must lie down in one of the guest-rooms. He would make sure that she was not disturbed until she felt better, and would send one of the maids to her with tea and one of the Duchess's headache-powders. Gratefully, Nesta let him take over, and soon she was lying in an almond-green guest-room, where curtains were drawn, as the thunderous headache gathered strength and threatened to consume her.

During the next half-hour Nesta fought the pain and lost. She was fighting also with her conscience. Before, everything had been so clear, so straightforward, but now that she had seen the sick old woman upstairs who longed to see James's son born before she died, it could never be clear or straightforward again. Nesta had had to fight not to let her heart go out to James's cousin. Under any other circumstances, she would have pitied the invalid and sought to help her in every way possible, but how could she relent? She had lived so long with her vow, her very just cause, that she had forgotten what life had been like before she had made it. It had been her lifeblood and sustenance since Jenny's death. What would support her if she did not have that?

Nesta put her hands to her temples, where the pain was beginning to course through her brain, a screaming blade cutting deep. Oh Mam, Mam, she thought, what am I going to *do*? How am I going to get through this?

At that moment a tap came at the door. When she called 'Come in,' a young maidservant entered with a silver tray. Placing the tray on the table at the side of the bed, the girl bobbed a curtsy and left. A cup of tea might help the pain. Then she saw the tiny medicine glass, spoon and powder, with a jug of water beside it. Adding the water to the glass, she stirred the powder into it until dissolved, then drank it in one swallow. As she had suspected, the potion was bitter and foul-tasting. Quickly she drank the tea to drown the taste. Then she poured herself another cup, but already she could feel the effects of the pain-killing draught, a swooning drowsiness overcoming her. Lying back on the delicate lace pillows, she fell into a deep, drugged sleep.

James took his tea with his cousin in her boudoir. She had some colour in her cheeks, and her blackcurrant eyes were sparkling more brightly than he had seen in many months.

'She's a fine girl. A good choice, Jamie. You'll have handsome children. You've done well. I thought when you first told me of her that there was something wrong – all that nonsense about my not having heard of her. It is obvious that she is a lady. Now tell me – who is she? With her air of good breeding she can only have come from the best stock.'

The moment had come. James put down his cup while the Duchess sipped noisily at her tea.

'I told you that you would not have heard her name, because she does not have a title.'

The Duchess's tea-gulping stopped instantly. 'No title? The girl has *no title*?'

'None at all. Nor has she any ancestor who possesses one.'

'Money, then – she has money?'

'No, I am afraid that she does not have any money, either.'

'Jamie, you are going to marry a commoner? How could you? Oh, how *could* you?' The Duchess's resolve not to interfere melted away. 'An untitled girl without connections, without money – what can she offer you? *Nothing*! You will regret it, Jamie. Believe me, you will regret it!'

The Duchess was thinking of her son and his love for the Welsh serving-maid. Was it a curse upon the Malgraves that their men should fall in love with commoners? A mere earl's daughter had been bad enough, but at least the Finchley-Clarks had been old family friends and they had money. This girl, lovely though she was, could give James *nothing*.

'I shall not regret it, because we love each other deeply. We are suited in every way. I knew that from the first moment I saw her.'

'She is a fortune hunter! Her head has been turned by your title and your money! Oh, Jamie, you must not do it! You must listen to me!' The Duchess reached out, gripping his cuff, her face ashen.

Gently James disengaged himself. 'She is not a fortune hunter, cousin. Far from it. Had she wanted, she could have had the Prince of Wales's attentions, but she chose me instead.'

'The Prince loved her?' The Duchess's eyes took on a different look. If the Prince of Wales knew her. . . .

'He has been pursuing her. She has resisted strongly.'

'That is a little more pleasing to my ears, but all the same, Jamie – ' The Duchess gripped her shaking hands. 'She will be the mother of your heir – would you rather not have a countess, a duchess – what of the Duke of Coacham's daughter?'

'She has buck teeth and smallpox scars!'

'But she is a duke's daughter! Breeding is everything when one is choosing a mother for one's heir!'

'Cousin – ' James was beginning to sound irritated, his patience running out – 'that is just it. She is going to be my wife and give me sons. You professed a great desire to see my son born before you die – do you still want that?'

'More than anything, Jamie! I have dreamed of it for years!' the invalid's voice quavered.

'If I do not marry Nesta, then I shall not marry at all.'

The Duchess gave a little cry of horror. 'Not at all? Not even Jane?'

'Most certainly *not* Jane!'

Tears rolled out of the old woman's eyes, but after a supreme effort, she managed a wintry smile. 'Do you mean that, Jamie?'

'Absolutely.'

'Then, then, you have my blessing,' the Duchess whispered.

CHAPTER EIGHTEEN

Nesta stood on the balcony of the Château des Reines, her hands gripping the balustrade. In front of her was a wide, curving arc of the brilliant, sapphire-blue river Loire, while, above, the sky was almost as blue and free of cloud. The brightness of sun and water was like a force demanding entry to her body, her eyes.

She had woken, only moments before, to find herself alone in bed. She was a bride of only two days' standing, but already her marriage was a nightmare.

Were she not suffering so deeply, she would be reproaching herself, for, in truth, all the blame was hers. She could not escape that fact, but she had hoped . . . well, she had hoped that she and James would be happy together, that their private life when they were alone in bed together would be ecstasy – as it had been before the wedding. She realized now what a fool she had been to think it.

They had had a quiet ceremony at St Margaret's Church, near Westminster, with James's sister, Ariadne, his close friends and a few of his relatives present. The relatives, who had come from distant parts of the country and even from abroad, knowing nothing of her life, had taken her at face value. James had told them she was an orphan, of a good family. James's closest friends, of course, knew who she was but they had not disappointed him. They had attended dutifully and had treated her like a duchess, which she now was.

Nesta would always remember the religious ceremony, for it had moved her deeply. When James had taken her hand to place the ring on her third finger a shiver had coursed through her body, as if she had been touched by icy breath. She was heavily enshrouded in exquisite lace veiling – the same veiling which had been worn by all the Malgrave brides since 1702 – a wreath of orange blossom on her head.

James could not see her face, or her expression, not until she turned back the gossamer lace from her face when the ceremony ended. Gallantly he bent down, his eyes slumbrous with emotion, to kiss her on her waiting mouth, his hands burning through the fragile satin of her wedding gown. She had wanted him to hold her in his arms for ever; she had wanted them to stay rivetted to that spot, holding one another close, never having to move, never having to think further than that moment.

But their guests had other ideas for them. Moments later they were standing on the church steps being showered with flower petals and rice, congratulations coming from all sides, and Ariadne was kissing them both, her face flushed, her eyes dancing. The photographer was setting up his equipment, darting here and there to arrange the entire wedding party in the most becoming poses and then returning to his tripod to plunge underneath the black veiling which concealed the rear of the camera and look through the aperture to check if the couple were fully in focus. It was a lengthy and tedious business, the long exposure time ensuring that the subjects 'caught' looked stiff and grim-faced instead of relaxed and smiling. It was the first time Nesta had had her photograph taken and she did not relish the experience.

More warm congratulations had followed. James's relatives had kissed her and wished them both every happiness. Some of them were similar in build to James and were blond like him; others had black hair and were slighter in figure – the French branch of the family, whom Nesta had not even known existed, and it was they who had given up this beautiful *château* to James and herself for the duration of their honeymoon.

The reception had been held at Malgrave Manor. As soon as she had arrived there from the church, Nesta had hurried up the stairs to the old Duchess's bedroom to show off her bridal outfit.

A new nurse had been hired to care for the invalid while they were away, and she had been standing by the Duchess's bed, patting her pillow, as Nesta entered the room. She was a tall, well-built, stout-hearted Yorkshire woman, kindly and much accustomed to dealing with difficult patients, which was why James had selected her.

'Come closer, come closer,' the old woman had croaked.

Nesta had obeyed. As she had hovered by the bedside while the Duchess looked her up and down and held out her hand to touch the soft satin of her gown, Nesta had seen another woman in bed years ago. A dying woman, wasted to a skeleton, a woman whose inflamed lungs had poisoned her whole body and eventually killed her, with the help of the beatings she had received from Jack Blunt.

If only Jenny could have been here now to see her daughter marry!

Nesta had had no one of her own to give her away, and so the task had fallen on the shoulders of one of James's closest friends, Lord Dunberry. Jack was a pleasant fellow, amiable and, fortunately, as lacking in snobbishness as James – which was probably why they were such good companions. All the same, Nesta had found herself longing for her father, Michael, to be there, to walk with her down the aisle to James's side. And, more than anything, she had ached to turn round and see Jenny sitting in one of the pews in wedding-guest finery, her black hair glamorously coifed, her face young and carefree again. . . .

Trying to suppress these haunting thoughts, Nesta had handed her wedding bouquet to the Duchess Adelaide, who had taken it in trembling hands, tears gleaming in her inky, dark eyes.

'My dear, how very touching. You have quite overwhelmed me!' The Duchess's voice had cracked as she had held the flowers to her nose to inhale their scent: roses, carnations, orange blossom, arranged amongst a froth of silver lace and a delicate cloud of fragile fern. 'I thought – when James first told me about you – that he was making a terrible mistake.' The Duchess had looked almost entreatingly at Nesta, as if to beg her indulgence. 'A nameless girl, with no title, no fortune. Can you ever forgive me for doubting your worth, my dear? I have been so wrong, so stupidly wrong. . . .'

It was the Duchess's tears which had moved her most of all. Nesta had known of the old woman's excessive pride and had noticed how she had endeavoured to welcome her as James's fiancée despite her misgivings. In the past few weeks, she had grown noticeably more frail, which was another reason why James had hired the nurse to be in constant attendance. If the old woman did but know the truth about her! Nesta had gone deathly cold all of a sudden, so that the nurse, seeing her change colour, had hastily brought a chair forward for her to sit down.

'I – I'll be all right in a moment,' Nesta had stammered while the nurse bustled round her.

'You came up those stairs too quick, Your Grace,' the nurse had accused in her stolid Yorkshire voice. 'After all the excitement of the wedding, it was too much for you. Sit there for a few moments an' gather your strength.'

Nesta had been all too willing to obey. The nurse had pushed a glass of brandy into her hand, telling her to sip the restorative liquid. She had longed to be able to blurt out the real reason for her distress, to seek the homely wisdom of the Yorkshire nurse, but she could imagine her shock and horror when she disclosed everything. The Duchess would have a seizure. An appalling scene would follow and James would never forgive her. To waylay their suspicions, she hid behind an obvious reason for ladies' feeling faint.

'I think my maid corseted me too tightly this morning. I seem to have put on a little weight since the first fitting of the wedding dress. It was something of a struggle to get me into it, I fear.' She had given a rueful laugh.

'I hope you won't adopt such tight corseting in future, Nesta, my dear,' the old Duchess had quavered. 'It is not good for babies, you know, to be tightly compressed.'

Fighting for composure, Nesta had promised to be careful on that score. Then, to her relief, the time had come for her to leave the invalid's room and return to the reception downstairs.

She had felt desperately alone as she walked into the room where the guests were merry-making. Anxiously, she had looked round for James, finding him just as he spotted her. As he hurried across to take her hands, she realized he was the only person in the entire room who truly belonged to her. . . .

What had followed the reception now seemed a blur. More kisses and congratulations, then James's whispering in her ear that it was time for them to leave. Shortly afterwards, she had changed out of the sumptuous wedding gown and put on her dark travelling suit and little feathered hat. Outside, their carriage had waited to take them to Dover, where they were to board a boat for the second stage of their journey to the outskirts of Paris and the Château des Reines.

Out in the Channel there had been no sign of the pleasant summer they had left behind; the clouds had darkened and a storm had hammered at the boat until Nesta believed she would die of sea-sickness. Fortunately, James had not suffered at all. He had spent the whole of the crossing placing cool cloths on her brow and holding her hand. She had felt miserable and ashamed at her indisposition and had begged him to leave her quietly in the darkened cabin, but he would not hear of it.

She had been deathly white and faint when they finally reached Calais, and it had been a relief to see the Beauricort's carriage standing by, as instructed. James had picked Nesta up bodily and carried her into the carriage and then tucked her up comfortably with sable coverlets around her knees. She had closed her eyes, intending to rest for a little while, and had fallen into a long, deep sleep, to waken in total darkness as the lurching halt of the carriage broke through her dreams. She had felt James's strong arms around her again as he carried her into the Château des Reines and then had known nothing more until next morning, when she had woken to see James bending over her, smiling.

'You're better now, my love? Yes, you do have more colour, but I insist that you spend the rest of the day in bed to recover your strength. We do not want you ill so far away from home, do we?' He had taken her hand and kissed it, his blue eyes filled with devotion.

'But I am quite recovered, James,' she said, only half-protesting, for the bed was soft and warm.

She had never spent a whole day in bed, doing nothing; it was a unique prospect, one that she intended to enjoy to the full. They had breakfast together in the bedroom, and then James had read to her, occasionally pausing to smile lovingly at her and squeeze her hand. Their lunch had been a light one: chicken soufflé, and then apricots in wine with fresh cream, with a fragrant Loire wine to wash it down.

After lunch, James had carried her onto the balcony and sat her comfortably in a sun-chair, handing her a wide, shady hat to protect her skin. She had begged him to take a walk along the river bank, as the exercise would do him good. Finally he had agreed, but reluctantly; he had strolled up and down the river bank so that they could wave to one another. The remainder of that day had passed just as pleasantly, until the time came to go to bed.

Nesta gripped the balustrade so tightly that her forearms and shoulders throbbed with pain. She did not know why she had behaved so strangely the night before. She loved James and she always would. She had wanted to marry him more than anything else in the world. For years she had dreamed of being his bride, but, when the time had come, as it had last night, she had not been herself....

James had dimmed the lamp by the bedside and moved towards her eagerly, pulling her into his arms.

'My darling, my bride,' he had whispered in her ear, kissing her hair and forehead, brushing his mouth against hers. 'I seem to have waited years for this moment, to have you as my wife and alone with me in bed. You always seemed to be a little preoccupied when we were at the club – '

'I – I did? I cannot recall feeling like that, not with you....'

'Perhaps I was wrong, but, anyway, who cares now? We are married and we have each other. Oh, my beloved, you are beautiful, adorable – I shall love you until I die. I want no one else but you.'

'I love you, too, James, more than my life....'

Nesta had felt uneasy, as if she were doing something wrong, something criminal. She had felt guilty, disturbed. Not wishing James to notice, she had fought the sensation, wrapping her arms round him and returning his kisses ardently. But the feeling would not be quelled; it had grown and become unmanageable.

First she had felt nausea, then dizziness; sweat had gemmed her brow. She had felt that she should not have been there, that she was committing a terrible wrong against James, who loved her. When he found out what she was about to do, he would reject her; he would never want to see her again. She would be an outcast, struggling to survive without his loving.... The thought had made her deeply frightened; to her astonishment and almost without knowing what she was doing, she had stiffened in James's arms and had turned her head away from his kisses.

'Nesta!' He had sounded surprised – and hurt, which had made her feel even worse. She had desperately wanted to be alone, to sort out her muddled and painful thoughts, the burden of shame like poison inside her.

'I – ' she had managed to speak, but what could she say? There had been no way she could explain how she felt without telling James the whole truth, and that was inconceivable, at least at this time when she was unprepared. The ensuing minutes had been torture as James had stared at her, puzzled and mystified by her coolness. Finally she had said that there was nothing wrong, and she had moved into his embrace once more, turning her face up for his kisses, revelling in the intimacy of being in bed with him. For a time, she had been able to respond, to shut out the convolutions of her guilty thoughts, the weight of knowing what she planned to do to her darling husband. James had caressed her breasts and kissed her shoulders, her stomach, then lower, and she had felt the fires beginning as of old, had curved up to meet his body eagerly. How lucky she was; how happy they would be – nothing was going to spoil their marriage. *Nothing*, she had vowed.

But Nesta had made another vow, many years before, as her mother lay dying in her arms, and that was to prove the stronger, whatever the adult Nesta now demanded of herself.

When James had moved gently against her, seeking entry to her body, she had frozen, paralysed with dread. She was about to betray him – she had already deceived him – after that, how could she relax and be his affectionate bedmate? Had she been callous, without conscience, she would have been safe, but she was not. There was much of her warm and sensitive Welsh mother within her, and that part would not be stilled. She was about to commit a dreadful wrong against the man whom she worshipped, because of a vow made long ago : how could she in all decency forget that?

James had tried to coax her into responding, hugging and kissing her, telling her that he loved her and needed her, but when he had tried again to enter her, she had been as frigid and unyielding as before. It had been a nightmare, no less dreadful to recall now than the actual experience itself had been. What had he thought of her icy lack of response, the manner in which she had pushed him away, a cry on her lips? She had wounded him deeply, she knew, and had disappointed him, too. How could she forgive herself?

Twisting her hands together, Nesta stared out unseeingly at the beautiful French countryside, the taste of ashes in her mouth.

She would remember his injured expression for the rest of her life, the pain in his eyes, the way his hands had slowly ceased to caress her. She imagined that death would be something like that moment: the gradual receding of the sun, darkness filling the vision, then cold, cold isolation. God forgive her but she had not meant to hurt him! And yet, to be true to Jenny, she must hurt him even more. How could she go through with it?

There had been awkward minutes as James tried once more to rouse her, but her own iciness had only increased. Finally she had had to draw away from him, unable to withstand any more intimacy. If she must be punished for what she had to do, then this surely was punishment enough!

Silently, James had turned on his side to sleep, but Nesta had lain awake for hours, thinking of Jenny and of her own ulterior motives for her marriage to James. Why had she flinched from him when all she most wanted in the world was to have him make love to her? What was so different now about their physical relationship save that they were legally married? She had not considered that the ceremony would have this crushing effect on her; she had thought everything between them would go on as before, until – until she told James her secret. . . .

She had counted on their having a blissful honeymoon before she told him. She knew now that she had been a fool. She loved James, idolized him – how could she betray her Sun God and behave as if nothing had happened? Her conscience would not allow it, and yet her vow to Jenny bore just as heavily on her conscience. In God's name, how was she going to solve it all? Nesta simply did not know.

At dawn James had woken her with his kisses, gently caressing her breasts. Before she had been properly awake she had been half-roused; her body had curved against his, ready for his lovemaking. As she had opened her eyes realization had struck and instantly all passion had ebbed. She had not been aware of having repressed it herself; it had seemed to happen involuntarily.

Instantly sensing her withdrawal, James could not conceal his deep disappointment. For a time he had continued to kiss her gently but ardently, whispering how much he loved her, his hand resting lightly on her breast, then on her thigh. Fear had welled up inside her again, and she had pulled back, thrashing out with her arms and beginning to shudder uncontrollably. It was as if a dark angel had landed on the bed between them, invisible and implacable.

'Nesta, sweetheart, tell me what is wrong,' James had pleaded.

'I – I do not know,' she had stammered. 'I think I must be ill.'

'I will leave you to sleep,' he had said, getting out of the bed in one sinuous movement and donning his clothes carelessly, as if suppressing anger. Then he had gone.

Nesta knew that she had hurt him and was ashamed. In truth, she did not want to cause him any grief, but she could not forget her vow to Jenny. She felt that her inner turmoil – being torn between the two of them, James and her mother – was going to destroy her. . . .

Hearing the door opening and closing behind her, Nesta turned. James was standing facing her, his arms laden with roses. Her heart broke at the wary expression on his face.

'Oh, James, they're beautiful! Thank you so much,' she said, inhaling their heavenly scent.

'Why don't you get dressed, darling, and we'll go down and walk through the gardens? I could describe them to you but it would take all day, and, anyway, the fresh air will do you good. I will send one of the Comtesse Beauricort's maids in to you – you must be missing Betsy.'

Betsy had remained at the Crimson Club to care for Cathy and Amy. Nesta had thought it wiser that way.

'Thank you, James. You're very kind,' she added, ashamed.

'With you how could I be anything else, my love?' He gave a smile, which made her feel confused and guilty all over again.

A few minutes after he left, one of the young French maids came in to help Nesta to dress. She was a dark-complected girl and not at all garrulous, as Nesta had supposed all the French were. She said very little as she brushed Nesta's hair, buttoned the back of her gown and helped her on with her boots, although Nesta had ascertained when she first entered the room that she could speak some English.

When Nesta was dressed in cream ruffled muslin and a wide-brimmed straw bonnet, with a muslin parasol to match, she sent the maid, Marie-Jeanne, in search of James. Moments later she and the Duke were walking down the steps of the *château* and out into the rose garden, where they were assailed by the perfume of hundreds of lush blossoms. As they walked along, James told Nesta some of the history of the *château*.

'It's called the Château of the Queens because it was begun by Catherine de Medici. A wing was added by Mary Stuart when she was married to Catherine's son, Francis, and the rest of the *château* was built according to the instructions of Marie Antoinette, so you can see that it has had connections with some quite notorious ladies.' He grinned, tucking her arm into his and squeezing it against him. Did he imagine it, or did Nesta flinch away from him imperceptibly?

'Three queens,' Nesta sighed. 'How beautiful. To think that three queens of France have lived in this *château* and walked through these gardens where we are walking now, James.'

'I dare say more than three visited here, my dear, for this has been a favourite retreat of the French Royal family for centuries. The Beauricorts bought it in 1805, and fortunately they have not tried to destroy its original beauty by adding any modern edifices.'

The sun was dazzling, and Nesta had to keep her lids half-closed against the glare. She tilted the picturesque straw hat down over her eyes, ensuring that it remained on her head by tying a wide blue sash around it and under her chin in a bow. Admiring her, James thought she looked every inch the carefree shepherdess, as Marie Antoinette herself must have looked when she was playing at herding her sheep in the Petit Trianon at Versailles. That tragic queen, who had been beheaded during the French Revolution, had come to stay at the Château des Reines when her opponents became too much for her, as they frequently did, he now told Nesta.

'It must have been her haven. I can understand what it must have meant to her coming here,' Nesta said with feeling.

James glanced at her, his blue eyes troubled. This was not how he had imagined their honeymoon would be. They were behaving towards one another with such detached formality that they might have been strangers or a strictly-disciplined couple of puritan persuasion who considered it a criminal tendency to indulge in emotion.

With a bitter pang he knew that it would have been exactly like this between Jane and he had they married. What had gone wrong? Had he in some way offended his bride? Desperately he searched his mind to find what he might have said or done in error during the past two days. Perhaps it had been the journey; some people, he knew, were very bad travellers, and Nesta had been upset by the sea voyage, the first she had ever taken. Perhaps that, plus the strain of the wedding, had robbed her of the glorious sensuality which he so adored?

How beautiful she was! James could barely take his eyes off her. But Nesta did look strained, and her cheeks were hollow. Against her pearly skin, her hair glittered like French jet. She did not seem willing to meet his eyes, so he had nothing but her luxuriant black lashes to look at, the shade of the wide-brimmed hat concealing half her face. She had a magnificent mouth; had it been sculptured by a genius it could not have been fuller or more shapely. She made the Mona Lisa look like a middle-aged peasant woman. He was determined that when they returned to London he would get one of the leading artists to paint her portrait for him – Millais, perhaps, for he would be able to do justice to her superb colouring.

They had reached an arbour where full-blown cabbage roses were entwined round ornate trellises, their fragrance eddying through the air like a balm to soothe the senses. They sat down on a rustic seat, Nesta inhaling the scent of the roses.

'I've always thought roses are like flowers from another world,' she said, pulling one of the huge blooms towards her face. 'Their colour and scent are so perfect, so faultless; surely they have been created by the gods.' Suddenly she began to remember, all too painfully, the china bowl covered with roses which Jenny had treasured.

'Gods? Not God?' James said quizzically, taking her hands in his and sensing rather than feeling the tremor that coursed through her body at his touch.

'If we are to believe in one, then why not more?' Nesta smiled, her hands lying in his without responding.

James was disturbed by her coolness. He had no way of knowing that she was thinking of the two gods who had shared her childhood; her mother's God, whom Jenny had taught her to worship, and her Sun God, who was now sitting beside her in the garden of the Château des Reines. Feeling only a sense of loss and, as yet, none of the bitter disappointment that would come later, James let her hands lie limply in his. Their honeymoon, he thought wryly.

How he had dreamed of being alone with this woman, of possessing her entirely, from the very first moment he had seen her at the Crimson Club. Her vibrant and alluring beauty had totally captivated him in a way no other woman's had ever done; he had wanted to make her his, knowing that taking her to his bed would simply not be enough. He had wanted everyone to know that she was his, untouched by anyone but him, and now that he had made this ambition fact, everything seemed to have gone wrong. There was a barrier between them.

However, James was still being borne along on the wave of anticipation and love which had carried him through the wedding. Being a bridegroom of only a few days he was ready to make every allowance for his new wife, but all the same he was troubled. Had he been too naïve, expecting too much? How would he be able to control himself when such passionate emotions were swelling inside him and all he really wanted to do was to take her in his arms, crush her to him and drown her with his kisses?

Nesta had tilted her sun-hat slightly lower over her eyes so that James could see only her mouth, and her hand still lay inert in his. To bring himself some small comfort, he began to imagine making love to her the way he wanted to do.

James saw himself leading Nesta back to their room. As he slowly untied the laces of her gown, she would be blushing and half-smiling, a languorous expression in her violet eyes. He would kiss her forehead, her cheeks, her chin, her lips and then her neck; his mouth would fall to her shoulders and then he would slowly begin to slip the bodice of her gown down to her waist, to reveal her beautifully moulded and heavy breasts. He would caress those magnificent breasts, and her nipples would flare beneath his tongue. She would be warm and voluptuous, curving against him sensuously, sighing in his arms, her eyes begging him to take her to bed. He would lay her gently on the silk coverlet and continue with his barrage of kisses, while her soft hands stroked his hair and framed his face as she returned his kisses. She would help him to push her gown down round her ankles, to unlace her petticoats and stays, to slip off her stockings and tiny satin slippers. Then she would lie naked on the bed before him, like Venus on some mythical and distant shore, her black hair rippling down to her waist, loosened from its pins and ribbons.

'Take off your clothes, James,' she would whisper, her voice husky with passion.

He would obey, divesting himself of coat and shirt, trousers, as quickly as he could, until they lay naked beside one another on the bed, her body like alabaster beside his darker form.

'The hair on your chest is gold, the same colour as your head,' Nesta would whisper to him. Then her eyes would go lower and a smile would curve her lips. 'But there you are dark,' and her hand would slip down to touch him where his hair was nearly brown, her fingers caressing him as if he were precious glass that might shatter.

'There is no need to be so gentle with me,' he would say. 'I'm quite tough really.'

And then he would pull her to him, his arms curling round her waist, his body shadowing hers as he leaned over her, feeling her gently part her legs as he did so. They seemed to be made to fit one another, their bodies moulding perfectly.

She would be soft and moist and silky, and he would sink into her as if drifting along on a voluptuous cloud. She would sigh deeply, her nails digging into his back, pulling him closer, as close as she possibly could against her body, whispering his name over and over again in his ear, telling him how much she loved him and wanted him, that they would always be happy together, blissfully happy, just as they were at this moment.

Her hips would curve against him as he moved in and out of her body; slowly at first, making her moan in her pleasure, then moving faster so that she would clutch him tighter and he could feel the sharpness of her nails in his flesh. Then, as she began to move almost convulsively against him, he would go slow again, prolonging the sensations they were both feeling. He was no insensitive lecher, taking a woman only to satisfy himself, for nothing would please him but to please the woman he loved. Alert to her every movement and response, he would mould with her needs as their bodies moulded together so well, ensuring that the experience of his lovemaking would remain with her, a beautiful memory which she would never forget.

Only when he believed that she had felt every possible emotion and response would he begin to show her what it really was like to be loved by him. If she had imagined that his eagerness would have made him too hasty, the loving over in just a few minutes, she would be surprised as he continued to move in and out of her body, bringing her to heights of passion she had never before reached, not even with him.

'James – ' she would say, and this time there would be surprise in her voice, astonishment even, and certainly admiration at his prowess. He knew she was a worldly woman and had had much experience of men, a fact which made him feel exceedingly jealous. He feared that, in many ways, compared with her he knew little of the world, but he felt himself more than capable of dealing with this.

James believed implicitly in the power of love. This was a legacy from his parents, who had loved each other, and him, deeply. 'Love can move mountains,' his mother had often said to him with a smile. 'It has a great healing power; it is the emotion which draws people more closely together than any other. No one can be a stranger if you love them; no difficulties are insurmountable if there is love.' And perhaps it was this all along that had told him that he would know instinctively how to deal with his new bride during their honeymoon and in all the days of their life together which would follow.

James still believed this. Love would weld them, make them inseparable, devoted to one another. He came out of his reverie. Looking at Nesta as she sat with her eyes closed against the sun's glare, leaning back against the rustic seat, her hand still cool and unmoving in his, he could feel the barrier between them, the barrier which *she* had erected. He realized that all his notions of their being happily married, of coping with any problems they might have, had always included their being close to one another, making love, sharing. If she by her own choice prevented this, it would deprive him of the cure-all, the great healer. He had never imagined her as prudish or cool in her emotions, certainly not with him. And until now she had never drawn back from him.

Basically, James's nature was generous and forgiving, but how could he control the searing passions which were coursing through him, the desire he had for her? How could he get through her barrier to show her that with their love they could conquer all? She must be shown that, and as soon as possible, before this coolness took root in her. He had seen it happen to other husbands and wives, and he did not want to make such a foolish mistake as to let any but the most enjoyable activities become habitual. Yet he would never, or so he imagined on that day, force himself upon her; that would be boorish and brutal, and he believed that he was neither of these things.

With the sun beating against them, its warmth penetrating their bones, and the pungent scent of the roses in the air around them, they sat on the rustic seat for some time, Nesta apparently totally relaxed. No onlooker would have guessed that the man sitting beside her was striving to quell virtually uncontrollable emotions and desires as he gazed on her beauty through half-closed eyes while trying to maintain a nonchalant manner. Nor would an onlooker have known how unhappy Nesta was feeling, sick and miserable, ashamed of herself, tortured by guilt, caught in an ineluctable trap of her own making. Whichever way she moved there would be pain, anguish, suffering – for at least two people. With all her heart she wanted to jump to her feet and fly from this place and from James before she did him any more harm, before she brought her revenge to its terrible climax. Powerfully she wished she had never met him, for then both of them would have been spared the suffering which must eventually come, whatever she did now.

CHAPTER NINETEEN

Neither knew how much longer they could go on; Nesta with her burden of guilt, James with his unalloyed desire to regain the marvellous intimacy they had once known. The languorous, sunny days did something to mitigate their dilemma, for as well as mellowing their spirits it enabled them to go out daily. They walked, sometimes round the estate, exploring every corner of it; they boated on the

Loire, Nesta leaning back, white muslin skirts carefully arranged round her knees, a wide straw hat with a blue ribbon on her head, trailing her fingers in the cool water, while James rowed, his powerful muscles straining against the silk of his shirt. Birds above them dipped and swooped in the blue. Occasionally a water-bird's cry would make them look round for the source.

These would have been halcyon days indeed had not Nesta been burdened with guilt and James desperate to regain what they had possessed before their marriage. The rowing, the walking and the exploring gave them both excuses to be weary, for Nesta to retire early and be asleep before James joined her in bed. It seemed, on the face of it, unlikely that two grown people who had enjoyed such ardent lovemaking once could now be so distant.

Remembering, James found it almost impossible to connect this cool, aloof young woman with the savagely sensuous girl who had captured his heart, body and soul from the first moment they had met. He wanted her to be exactly like that again; he had grown totally dependent on her responding in that way, which was why he had married her.

She had often told him that she loved him, and he had told her the same. Where now was that love? Did she regret marrying him? Perhaps the strain of becoming a duchess, knowing the social stresses she would have to face on their return to civilization, had served to frighten her, to make her cool towards him? But he had not thought her faint-hearted. No, he could never see Nesta being cowardly, avoiding her obligations. Having dismissed one train of thought, he would start all over again with a new one which would end yet again without an answer to her coolness being found.

James found lying in bed beside her every night intolerable; feeling the heat emanating from her body, hearing the rustle of her delicate lace nightrobe when she moved in bed, when she stirred sighing, occasionally making a little sound in her sleep, as if she were trying to talk to someone in a dream. He would lie awake far into the night beside her, revelling in the intimacy, pressing his naked body against her back or her side, whichever was closest to him, gently placing his hand on her thigh, slowly, so that she would not waken, and feeling the soft mount of flesh beneath his hand while he pulsed with longing, forcing himself not to invade her body until she was prepared to let him.

On the morning of the fourth day his control snapped. He had been out for an early morning walk, hoping to work off some of his energy, and now had returned, stepping into the bedroom just as Nesta threw back the covers and glided out of the bed. Thinking herself alone, she flung off her nightrobe and stretched sinuously. Then she heard rather than saw him, for his breath must have rasped as he strode across the room towards her. He pinioned her with his arms, forcing his mouth down on hers, clamping her lips to his.

Sensing what must come next, Nesta froze instantly, struggling to free her mouth, crying 'No! No, James! Not this way!'

Defeated, he let his arms fall to his sides. 'I cannot go on like this,' he said, and she looked away from him, almost shame-faced. 'Nesta – Nesta, listen to me! I cannot go on like this! How much longer must I wait?'

Reaching for her peignoir, Nesta struggled to smile, to shrug off the tension, but failed. How she longed to unburden herself to him, to fling herself into his arms and beg his forgiveness, to tell him everything, the whole of it. But she knew she could not, and because her burden must remain a secret, it seemed all the greater and heavier inside her. She was trapped by her own scheming, torn by her love of James and the love she bore her mother even now. She must either speak and break James's heart, ruining all her chances of their staying together, loving one another, or remain silent; either proceed to fulfil her vow to Jenny or abandon it for ever.

Much of it was the fault of that old woman lying in her sickbed in Malgrave Manor; *she* was the one who had turned Jenny out on the streets, condemning her to a terrible life and an even worse death, and it was she, the old Dowager-Duchess, on whom Nesta must truly exact her revenge. But she could not do it now without hurting James, hurting him irreparably.

But Nesta loved James crazily, irrevocably, and, to her dismay, during the next few months she discovered that she could have learned to love the old Duchess, too, had she not been the cause of Jenny's degradation and early death. . . .

The vow. Nesta could not go back on her vow. But she was beginning to realize that she was no longer the same person who had made that promise. James had shown her nothing but love and kindness. The old Duchess, once she had realized that she would lose James as she had lost Michael if she did not accept his bride, had tried her best to be nice to her. Their kindness only made what she had planned to do all the more terrible. If she spoke up now, she would destroy three people, herself included. Afterwards, of course, she could go back to the Crimson Club; she knew that, but what would her life be like without James? Without his love, she might as well be dead.

The panic which Nesta had been trying to control since the wedding ceremony – that moment of no return – took hold of her again. She needed all her strength to subdue it, to fight back the hysteria, the sensation of being crushed in a vise of her own making. Jenny had hold of one arm, James the other, and between them they were tearing her in two.

She badly needed the counsel of someone wise and knowledgeable, but who was there here? They were in a foreign country, where everyone spoke a language strange to her. She knew only a few words of French, although James had been teaching her in readiness for the holiday. There was no one she could turn to for advice so she must try to sort out this dilemma for herself, a task which was proving impossible.

A door slamming somewhere far away in the *château* told her that James had gone out. She could imagine how he felt, yet surely it could not be worse than her own anguish? But if she unburdened herself and told him the truth, he would be enraged. She tried to imagine him in a temper, fists clenched, eyes brilliant with fury, but she failed. He was so equable. She had never seen him lose control. When she told him her darkest secret would he lash out at her, beat her until she lay a crumpled bloody heap on the floor? Or would he become deadly silent, white-lipped, and shut himself off from her?

Nesta shuddered, pulling the flimsy peignoir round her body. She slumped on the edge of the bed, her knees weak, guilt enveloping her like a suffocating cloud. She could not even cry any more. Placing her hands over her face, she willed herself to weep, going over her deceit, but not even that was enough to free the torrent. She felt sick, dizzy, as if she had eaten bad food. More than anything in the world she wanted James's arms around her, his gentle kisses, his forgiveness. But she would never have that, not after she told him the truth. He would curse her and damn her to hell, and then he would turn his back on her for ever.

In the following hours, James exhausted his mount, galloping wildly for miles, not looking where he was going, letting the horse have its head. His body throbbed and ached for Nesta; there was pain deep in the pit of his stomach, between his legs, every part of him hungering for her. She had meant so much to him from the very first; no other woman had ever affected him as she did. To be rebuffed by her was the cruellest blow he had ever suffered. All the more hurtful and frustrating because he had never anticipated her being cool with him; he was unarmed against it and thus extremely vulnerable.

He had made her his bride, flying in the face of convention, making her his duchess because he loved her with a deep, raging passion, because he had felt all along that she was his kindred spirit. Before the wedding they had seemed inseparable, ecstatically happy in each other's company. Now she did not want him; she froze when he touched her, avoided his eyes. In God's name, what was he going to do? He groaned, wanting her with a desperate urgency.

Nothing, no one could ever satiate him as Nesta did. She was a palliative for his spirit as well as for his bodily desires. Now things had all gone wrong between them and he did not know why.

Returning to the *château* some four or five hours later, James found Nesta fully dressed, sitting on the terrace, the sun hat shading her face. He wanted to tear the hat from her glossy black curls and fling it into the river, to look into her eyes and find the truth in them, to crush her to him and make passionate love to her there on the terrace.

On seeing him she gave a half-smile, not meeting his eyes, turning her head a little to the side. He fought down the pain which her movement brought him. His Nesta, his beautiful amethyst-eyed Nesta, was averting her face; she did not even want to look at him any more!

'This is a beautiful view, fit for an idyll,' James said, forcing a smile. He poured himself some orange juice, which a servant had brought immediately on seeing him arrive. 'Do you not think so, my darling? Can you not see us as the gods on Mount Olympus, dining on honey-dew and peaches?'

'Yes, I can', Nesta whispered. 'You are Apollo, the sun god, and I am – Who do you think I am, James?' Her voice sounded constricted.

'Radiant Venus – who else, my love?' James downed a goblet of juice and poured himself another. 'Was it Whistler who said that to gaze at Lillie Langtry was to imagine one was dreaming?' Nesta nodded. 'Well, he has not seen you yet, has he, my darling? When he does he will not enthuse so heartily over her.'

'Lillie is a very handsome woman,' Nesta said.

James leaned forward in his seat and placed his hand over Nesta's. Her skin felt as cool and smooth as alabaster beneath his hot palm, and she flinched as if he had burned her. Nonetheless, he did not remove it.

'You have no rival,' said James, smiling at her. 'Not in Lillie Langtry nor in any other member of the Prince's coterie of beauties. If I had not chosen you for myself the Prince would have chased after you. After he met you he could talk of no one else.'

'Who told you that?'

'One of his aides. A man I know well because I went to school with him.'

'What else has this friend of yours told you?' Nesta lifted her brows inquisitively.

James saw that he had her full attention.

'Just that. I believe he wanted to know more about you, where you grew up, who your parents were and so on, but the truth of your origins seems to be one of your most closely-guarded secrets, for even I know so little about you, my love.'

'Do you need to know anything?' Nesta sounded a little haughty.

'No, you know that I do not. You know that I have always accepted you just as you are.'

Nesta was immediately shamed by his words, for he spoke the truth. It was one of the things that made him so wonderful in her eyes. That, and his assiduity were not only blessed, but rare.

'I know.' She smiled and to his intense delight squeezed his hand. She did not pull her fingers away until much later, when a servant announced that dinner was ready.

It was another brilliant repast, superbly cooked by Jules, the *chef-de-cuisine* of the Château des Reines. Jules's culinary arts were spoken of in rapturous tones; he was famed throughout France as one of her accomplished chefs. Many of his recipes had been used at the French Court before the deposition of Napoleon III, and some had been adopted by the Prince of Wales's cooks. For the bride and groom he had gone to great lengths to create new dishes for them, ones which appeased but did not over-laden the stomach.

Tonight Nesta had little appetite. She picked at her food, pushing it round the plate but pretending to enjoy it. Any other time how she would have relished the succulent meats, the buttery vegetables, the *gâteau Belle Bretagne* – a rich chocolate cake, layered with thick cream and decorated with icing and fresh cream, cherries, angelica and marchpane – which Jules had concocted specially in Nesta's honour. Nesta looked at it with longing, but her appetite was nonexistent. She found herself thinking of starving urchins, beggars in the street, who would rejoice over a mouldy crust of bread, and here, just for her and James, was all this delicious, rich, costly food.

The wines served throughout the meal were those of the Loire valley. Nesta sipped them, to give her hands something to do, to make it appear that she was actually eating. A delicious warmth undulated through her body. She glanced at James to find his eyes were upon her meaningfully. She blushed hotly, not knowing where to look, sipping at the wine to cover her confusion. Suddenly Nesta noticed the footman standing behind James's chair. The man seemed to be smirking; he was pursing his lips, trying not to grin. She could imagine his thoughts. He must be thinking about them in their newly-wedded state, imagining their bodies entwined, naked together in bed. Just like a Frenchman!

Hastily, she looked away from the man's leering face, for she, too, was thinking of lying in bed in James's arms, with his lean muscular body pressed against hers, his powerful arms caging her as if she were a captive linnet – his songbird and only his. Suddenly, desperately, she wanted to sing for him, to let herself be free and uninhibited in his arms!

The surging uprush of passion took her by storm. Surely he must know what she was feeling? Surely he must see? She believed that her desire must be stamped all over her face. She imagined herself whispering, 'Take me to bed, James, take me *now*,' and then she was horrified to realize that she had nearly said those words aloud, in front of the servants.

Her body was quietly but firmly taking control. Soon she knew she would be begging James to make love to her, pulling his golden head down to hers and kissing his lips. But that must not be! She could not let that happen. She knew now that she must force him to forget the happiness they had shared in the past, so that when she told him her secret he would not be doubly broken.

That was it – Nesta had her solution at last! If she could make him hate her, he would cease to love her. Then, when she had been true to Jenny, when he learned how and why she had tricked him, he would not be totally stricken with grief and despair.

She felt almost light-hearted at this brilliant notion which had so suddenly come to her. At that moment it seemed to her the only way in which she could keep faith with *both* her mother and James. Make him hate you first, she thought; make him turn away, loathing you, and then when he is hardened you can deal your trump card. Then you can keep your vow, but without destroying him. . . .

Nesta rose suddenly, a little unsteady on her feet, and instantly James rose, too, ever the gentleman. But she behaved as if he were not there and headed directly for the door, which he rushed to open. She pushed past him, making her way up to the bedroom, that beautiful, sea-green boudoir hung with silk and dominated by the magnificent sixteenth-century carved tester bed, which was to have been their blissful honeymoon haven.

Without summoning Marie-Jeanne, Nesta divested herself of her evening clothes and slipped on a nightrobe and peignoir. When James joined her a few moments later, she was sitting at the dressing-table brushing out her long black hair, her face impassive.

'You are not ill, my love?' James enquired, coming to stand behind her, grasping her shoulders with his lean, strong hands.

'Certainly not,' she snapped. 'I want to be alone, that's all. I need peace, can't you see that? I do not want to be pestered constantly. It seems that I can go nowhere, James, without your following me, hanging on my every word. Have you nothing better to occupy your time?'

She brushed her hair vigorously, not daring to look at his face, at the anguish which must surely be there. She felt his grip on her shoulders loosen and then his hands fell away.

Swallowing hard, summoning all her courage, Nesta said sharply, 'Well, James? Did you not hear what I said? I wish to be alone.'

'If that is what you wish, my love.'

He left the room soundlessly. Nesta heard the door close behind him, and then the brush dropped from her nerveless fingers as she hunched forward in her seat, her head dropping low. Such a tumult of pain seared her heart that she thought she would faint. How long could she keep this up, this heartless façade? Who would break first, she or James? Feeling as she did now, she was willing to place all her bets on its being herself.

CHAPTER TWENTY

James had arranged their itinerary before they had left London. He had wanted Nesta to see all the sights of Paris by day and by night: Notre Dame, L'Opéra, the Seine in all its moods, the Louvre, Versailles, St Denis, Montmartre and the artists' quarter, the magnificent Bois de Boulogne where the kings of France had hunted until Napoleon III had given it to the city and its people.

James had envisaged himself with his bride, holding her hand as they explored Paris together, gazing as ardently at one another as at the famous sights. Instead, the woman beside him was white-faced and subdued, barely exchanging anything but tart words with him, seeming to respond not at all to the heady atmosphere of the city of lovers.

James's disappointment was acute. This was their first holiday together, their honeymoon. Such a time could never be repeated, and yet, for some reason which was not apparent to him, Nesta was either bored or disapproving.

They had one more week to spend in France, and he did not think he could survive the days if they passed like this.

However vitriolic Nesta seemed, he still desired her; not even the sourest rejoinder could alter that. Even with her mouth tightly compressed and her brows raised haughtily, she was by far the most alluring woman he had ever seen. She had changed towards him – he tried in vain to be philosophical about it. Some people were uneasy away from home; perhaps that explained her attitude. If that were so, he had but to wait until they were back in London and she would be herself again. How he longed for that!

The couple strolled, ill-at-ease, round the medieval church of St Denis, viewing its elaborately-carved statues. Outside, in the brilliant sunshine Nesta noticed an old man sitting on the pavement surrounded by sketches and paintings he had made of the church. The man wore baggy brown trousers and had a face to match, his eyes wrinkled and sagging as if he had cried a lifetime's worth of tears. When he smiled up at Nesta, seeing in her a prospective customer, the smile did not lighten his face; all human misery was recorded there. The man had, in fact, lost his five sons, his wife and daughter during the past ten years; his wife from the fever, his daughter when she was knocked down by a carriage in the Rue des St Agnes, and his sons during the period when Paris had been occupied by Prussian troops and the Communards. That had occurred only a few years ago. Paris, which had believed herself to have outlived war, had been the scene of battles and cross-fire, destruction and pillage. The Tuileries, where the guillotine had stood during the Terror in the previous century, was laid waste by fire, as was the Hôtel de Ville. Even the sacred cathedral of Notre Dame had been threatened by gunpowder. The old man had sadly learned that nothing was sacred any more, not even God and the Blessed Virgin, not even life.

Nesta addressed him in her halting French, and he responded in his fluent tongue. James stood by prepared to translate, but Nesta managed to make herself understood. She liked the old man's paintings and sensed in him someone who had suffered, who had loved and lost as she had.

Carefully, Nesta selected two of the paintings, one each for Cathy and Amy. After paying the old man, she stepped back, trying to decide if she should buy another one. He thought she was about to leave and dabbed reverently at his black, pancake-shaped beret. He must be incredibly old, she thought, but there was still admiration in his eyes and she responded to it without hesitation, smiling broadly.

After they walked away a few yards, James caught her arm.

'The way you smiled at that old man, why don't you smile like that for me any more? You used to, you know; not very long ago, at that.' He tried not to sound reproachful.

Inwardly bracing herself, Nesta flashed him a look of contempt. 'You can't put back the clock,' she retorted, wanting to look away before the pain registered on James's face but unable to.

Nesta saw the kindly, humorous eyes which she had loved for half her life darken in unhappinesss. She saw him draw back, unsure of what to say next. Finally, when he did speak, it was to tell her that she was no longer the Nesta he had once known. He sounded perplexed but not accusative. Had he raged at her she would have found it that much easier to continue as callously as she had begun. As it was, it was requiring immense courage and fortitude for her to remain coldly acerbic. But she would do it; she had to – there was no alternative.

James remained silent after that exchange. They took a carriage from St Denis to Montmartre, Nesta sitting stiff-backed in her seat, hands tightly clasped in her lap. When they alighted, she did not allow her hand to remain in his one second longer than necessary. With the Mount of Martyrs – after which Montmartre was named – looming behind them, James and Nesta explored the lower streets and alleys of the artists' domain. Here, how different were the atmosphere and the scenery, with its rustic Bohemian flavour.

Here Degas had painted *The Dancing Class* in his studio; here Renoir and Van Gogh lived, all of them masters, all of them richly talented. Nesta walked staring ahead, except when something caught her eye, James silent beside her. All the while she was absorbing the scents and sights and sounds; the clamour of voices, sometimes quarrelling, sometimes gossiping; the bevies of prostitutes with their faces so heavily painted that their features were nearly obliterated – their eyes ringed with black, lips stained brilliant cerise, cheeks rouged so heavily that they looked like they were clowns.

There but for the grace of God go I, Nesta thought, taking in the brash faces and the bold stances of the women. Even her presence did not dissuade them from ogling James and swinging their hips at him provocatively. James seemed not to notice, however.

To harden her resolve, Nesta forced herself to remember her past and the old Dowager-Duchess. Because of her she herself might have been a strutting street-whore, tightly swathed in showy satin, her breasts half-exposed, her face lacquered with rouge and kohl, ready to lie with any man for a shilling, rutting in dark passageways, on street corners, behind bushes in the park, like an animal in heat. She had worked hard to better herself, to rise above street-whoring, and it had been entirely through her own efforts. Momentarily, Nesta thought of what had happened the year before she had opened the Crimson Club, then she pushed it from her mind.

Despite the burden of her secret, Nesta could not remain oblivious to Paris's persuasive enchantment for long. The city of lovers was not accustomed to indifference from those who visited it, and it seemed determined to show all its charms. Nesta marvelled over the mysterious three-thousand-year-old granite column in the square called the Place de la Concorde. It was inscribed with what James told her were hieroglyphics, the sacred characters employed in ancient Egyptian picture-writing.

'So this column is from Egypt?' she asked.

James nodded. 'Did you know it had a twin in England, on the Thames embankment?'

Nesta thought for a moment before replying. 'You mean Cleopatra's Needle, which was found in Alexandria?'

'Yes. Did you know that two jars were buried beneath the base of the Needle when it was erected? I only mention it because a friend of yours has her portrait in one of those jars, placed there for posterity.'

'A friend of mine? Who is that?'

'Mrs Langtry. It was the Prince's idea.'

'Burying a portrait of Lillie seems to me somewhat foolish. Surely it would be better on show?'

'I would rather London were filled with portraits of you, Nesta. Burying one of Lillie's will leave a little more room for others; few people can have been painted as often as she.'

There seemed to be a temporary truce between them as they viewed more of the Parisian sights; the recently finished L'Opéra, the Hôtel Dieu, the beautiful boulevards rimmed with chestnut trees. They dined at the Café des Deux Magots – The Sign of the Two Monkeys – a favourite haunt of writers near the Church of St Germain-des-Pres, and rode down the Champs-Elysées in their carriage, past the elegant mansions on the Rue St Dominique. They spent a day at Versailles, for one needed a day to explore it at leisure.

'Versailles was built as a shrine by Louis the Fourteenth, the Sun King,' James told Nesta. 'It was, at one and the same time, a pronouncement of his omnipotence and earthly powers and a grand declaration of his total disregard for his poorer countrymen.'

'And when the poor reacted, as react they eventually must, it was not Louis who bore the brunt but his grandson and his wife, Marie Antoinette. You see, James, I have been finding out a few little things on my own. Marie Antoinette was a Habsburg, daughter of Maria Theresa, and she had been raised to believe that the world was her oyster, that she could have whatever she wanted, that she could be as proud as she wished. Do you think it was really true, all that scandal about the diamond necklace that she was supposed to have ordered in the face of such shocked disapproval?'

'Such a thing does not need to be true. It is what the people believe that matters, and they believed she was guilty, guilty of spending millions of francs on luxuries while they were starving and in rags. Their destitution was such that even a modest show of wealth would have incensed them. Certainly when the Revolution finally broke out it was not only the fabulously rich who went to the guillotine; their servants, their estate-keepers and farmers, milkmaids and pigmen – all connected with the aristocracy – were beheaded with them.'

'I read that Marie Antoinette's hair turned white overnight when she was imprisoned. How she must have suffered, watching her husband go to the guillotine, having her children wrenched from her and not knowing what would become of them. Even if she had been the most selfish and extravagant woman on earth she did not deserve such a terrible punishment!'

'She was just that to the starving populace, my dear. In this palace and these gardens you see around you, there was employment for ten thousand courtiers, officials, servants and ministers of the king, as well as the royal family itself. Imagine the cost of the upkeep of those ten thousand people alone. Every year, one hundred and fifty thousand flowers were planted in the gardens.'

They were entering the Galerie des Glaces now. The Hall of Mirrors, with its view of the park, was a breathtaking spectacle. Here, glittering with jewels, their powdered wigs sometimes nearly half as tall as they were, and with their wide, swaying, panniered skirts, courtesans had danced with their lords, the dazzling spectacle being reflected by the myriad gleaming arched windows, the crystal chandeliers and candelabra which surrounded them. Here, too, were the vast frescoes by Le Brun depicting the victories of Louis XIV.

Outside again, Nesta and James strolled through the baroque gardens, admiring the magnificent terraces, the spouting fountains, like the Fountain of Bacchus, all of which were decorated with statuettes of nymphs and sea-gods with dolphins' tails. They rowed on the Grand Canal, which had cost a fortune to build and from which could be seen an awe-inspiring view of the palace, surrounded by its terraces, glades, vistas and groves. Branching off to the right of the Grand Canal was a smaller watercourse, which led to the parks and gardens encircling the Grand and the Petit Trianon.

James helped Nesta from the boat, holding her hand tightly. Then, as she stumbled on the little jetty, he scooped her up in his strong arms and placed her on firm ground. It was all over in a second, but she felt heat rush to her face, the response of her body betraying her intentions. Fortunately, he seemed not to see anything; there was so much to occupy their attention that her wildly beating heart and crimson cheeks seemed to have gone unnoticed.

Nesta forced herself to concentrate on the Grand Trianon, which had been built in the seventeenth century and looked like a massive, ornate, iced wedding cake with its facings of pink and white marble. Here, James told her, Louis XIV had come to be alone, in seclusion with his current mistress.

'I imagine that I would want the same if I were constantly surrounded by ten thousand courtiers and servants.' He smiled wryly.

Next was the Petit Trianon, where Marie Antoinette and her friends had gathered to be away from the staring crowds. Here, and in the little hamlet and the dairy nearby, Louis XVI's queen had dressed in the simple garb of a dairymaid or shepherdess, even having a flock of her own sheep to tend.

'People have not changed since then,' Nesta said. 'They are still the same, with all the milkmaids and shepherdesses wanting to be queens and all the queens wishing they could get away from the weight of their responsibilities.'

'You sound very philosophical, my darling.'

'It was merely an observation,' Nesta replied coolly.

That evening they were to dine with friends of the Beauricorts' at their *château* near St Germaine-en-laye. Nesta was looking forward to the occasion, for she would be able to relax her control in company and be more like her old self, without having to maintain that wearying façade she must keep erected when she was alone with James. Her nerves were screaming for release; she had little appetite these days and barely slept, continually waking with a jolt throughout the night as if something terrible had happened. Her fear and uneasiness in the dark had increased, so that there was little surcease from suffering and anxiety.

Marie-Jeanne was waiting with her gown in readiness when they returned to the Château des Reines. James disappeared into his dressing-room with his valet to prepare.

Nesta planned to wear buttercup-yellow silk brocade with necklace and earrings of yellow amber, black satin slippers, black lace fan and a yellow shawl edged with black tassels. Behind her ears, between her breasts and on her wrists she dabbed some of Monsieur Worth's very expensive French *parfum* which James had bought her a few days ago, when they had made an appointment to see Monsieur Worth to select a new wardrobe for Nesta.

When they were ready to leave, James took her arm to lead her outside to the waiting carriage. She looked and smelled divine, and he wanted to shout damnation to their dinner engagement and crush her in his arms. Indeed, he would have done just that if she had given him so much as one sign of encouragement, but nothing was forthcoming; she was as glacial as ever, so composed that she seemed almost frozen. James found her behaviour daunting, understanding now why men were driven into the arms of mistresses, why they needed so many other women to forget the chill of the marriage bed. The passionate nights he had spent with Nesta seemed a far-distant dream, almost a fantasy which he had concocted himself.

The Comte and Comtesse de Chailly were delighted to be entertaining an English duke and duchess, and they showed it.

The Comte was a small, painfully thin, ashen-faced little man, with a black moustache so small it seemed almost accidental and heavily pomaded black hair, greased and glossed so close to his head that he appeared to have an ebony skull. He wore a monocle, which Nesta looked at in wonderment, for not once did it so much as threaten to slip from his eye, where he had it carefully secured by a superior effort of muscles. On his immaculately arranged cravat was pinned an enormous diamond, and another diamond blazed on the little finger of one hand. He seemed to be wearing perfume, or was it some sort of flowery cologne? Nesta thought him a rather effeminate little man.

What her husband lacked, the Comtesse more than provided. She was of a burly build, with broad, fat shoulders thrusting from her low-cut puce satin gown styled in the very latest fashion. Her waist was tightly corseted and she had a particularly enormous bustle burgeoning from her hind quarters. She seemed to find breathing more and more of a difficulty as the evening progressed, gasping now and again, fanning herself furiously, dabbing at the beads of sweat that collected around her eyebrows and trickled down the sides of her cheeks and under her chin to mingle with the black hairs which sprouted there. Nesta considered her jewellery flashy, for she wore enormous pink pearls and garnets which clashed garishly with the puce of her gown, and she gave off a strong musky smell.

The Comte and Cometsse's son and heir, Gerard, was dining with them and there were four or five others in the party. Gerard was a handsome boy, about twenty-three years of age; he was dark, with flashing brown eyes and a roguish grin. Fortunately he had not inherited his parents' poor taste in dress. Nesta caught his eye on her more than once during the meal, his gaze lingering on her longer than was polite. She did not object to it, for James was engrossed in conversation with a sweet-faced young lady to his left.

Thinking her husband otherwise involved, Nesta responded to Gerard's flirtatious approaches, smiling at him coquettishly and tapping him with her fan whenever he became particularly outrageous. It helped her to forget the torment of the past few days, as did the heady French wines which were served with the sumptuous meal. Nesta knew that two pink spots of colour had appeared on her cheeks and that her eyes were perhaps shining too brilliantly, but she did not care. Why should she forego this opportunity to have a pleasant dalliance and enjoy a young man's open admiration?

When they had eaten, the gentlemen retired to smoke, while the ladies went into the withdrawing room to gossip. The matter of language did not present any difficulty for English seemed to be spoken, and spoken well, by more or less everybody Nesta had met thus far.

Although Nesta had not yet kept her appointment with Monsieur Worth to order gowns to be made for her in the very latest Parisian fashions, the ladies all admired her bright yellow dress with its slightly flared hem and ruched overgown gathered into a large bow at her lower back. The Comtesse asked if she might touch the fabric, for it was so beautiful; then everyone else wanted to feel the satin brocade, and they clustered round her excitedly.

'Have you met zis famous flower-girl?' the Cometsse wanted to know.

'Flower-girl?' Nesta said, puzzled, trying to think which famous beauty or royal mistress had begun life as a flower-girl.

'Ze lily, ze lily girl!' said the Comtesse, her plump, cushiony hands weaving through the air excitedly.

Nesta's frown cleared. 'Ah,' she said, 'you mean the Jersey Lily, Mrs Langtry.'

'*Oui, oui!*' cried the Comtesse. Ze Jersey Lily. She who has ze famous beauty, *oui*? Zey say her skin is like ivory, and her eyes a rich *violette, non*? Her hair is titian-coloured, *belle châtain roux*, like ze hair of ze ladies painted by Titian? Is it really true, such a glorious appearance?'

Nesta smiled. How rapidly Lillie's reputation had spread. Yes, she told her hostess, Lillie was as gorgeous as rumour would have it, and her hair was a true, striking golden auburn shade.

'I know zis Titian well,' explained the Comtesse. 'He is renowned for painting ze ladies with ze forms like Juno, is he not? A little like my own form, *n'est pas*?' the Comtesse simpered.

Nesta would have liked to say emphatically '*Non, non!*' but instead she smiled politely and agreed.

'Zey say ze Prince of Wales is head over ze heels wiz love for his Lillie,' continued the Comtesse, 'and so besotted wiz her zat he hardly sees his Princess at all zese days. And is it not also true zat the Queen's mother is furious wiz ze rage and turns her back on him?'

'At least that part is not true, *madame*. The Queen has had Mrs Langtry presented to her at Court, and Mrs Langtry has also been presented to the Princess of Wales, who seems to like her very much.'

'Ah, so ze Princess is wise like ze Frenchwoman, *oui*? We French women do not set up ze rumpus when ze husband takes a mistress. We are on ze dignity, cool and sensible. I am pleased to hear zat ze Princess is like we French ladies. Zat endears me to her. Ah, zese men . . . what shall we do wiz zem? If you had seen my husband in his youthday, ah, he was just ze same as ze Prince. . . .' The Comtesse shook her head from side to side. 'We women are too good for zem, and so zey must acquire ze mistresses, must zey not, to spare us? It is a strange *destin* for we mortals, *oui*? But I would not wish to change it.'

Nesta was receiving her first insight into what it was like living in a man-woman relationship where the man had normal appetites and believed his wife should be spared them, she being first and foremost a lady. The thought of such a passionless union made her shudder, reminding her acutely of how things might become between herself and James. It was a sobering thought, making her feel as if she were standing on the very edge of a precipice.

Fortunately, the conversation soon centred again on clothes. Nesta told the assembled ladies that she had an appointment to see Monsieur Worth. This brought cries of delight from them all; they told Nesta that she would not wish to return to the *Anglais ordinaire* dressmakers after she had been gowned by Worth.

'He is a marvellous man!' the Comtesse said. 'A little eccentric, but zen he is a genius after all. He wears ze, how you say, gaudy clothes – a bright purple jacket, a waistcoat embroidered wiz flowers. But he can be allowed his leetle oddments, for he is, as I say, ze grand genius.'

'Oh, he is surely zat,' said one of the dinner guests. 'He designed my wedding robe for me. It was white silk embroidered wiz ivory roses and forget-me-nots. Ze material had a sheen like pearl, and ze embroidery made it so heavy zat I could only move when supported on both sides by my attendants. *Belle, belle*!' The woman's eyes shone. 'He is a genius because he brings out ze hidden self – ze secret beauty – which shows only when one wears his clothes. He made me look like a princess on my wedding day.'

Nesta had little wish to be reminded of her wedding day, that evil hour when everything had begun to go so seriously wrong between herself and James, and so she was relieved when the Comtesse announced that it was time for the coffee and sweetmeats to be served and for the gentlemen to join them.

When the doors swung open and James and his companions entered, young Gerard de Chailly made straight for Nesta and sat down close beside her, his dark eyes fixed ardently upon her face. She was glad to see him again, for his unalloyed admiration was refreshing. She decided that she was going to enjoy his company, for here in this *château* was she not surrounded by those who would protect her reputation?

The Comtesse, for her part, seemed pleased that her

adored son was getting on so well with the English duchess, and so Nesta relaxed. It was Gerard who leapt to his feet to pour out her coffee with his own hands and who offered her a platter laden with the choicest selection of *petits fours*. Sitting down beside her again, he began to ask her questions about London. He said that he would like to visit England one day. Did she like Paris as much as she liked her home city, or could he hope that she preferred *his* country?

Nesta offered a diplomatic reply, which pleased Gerard immensely, as she had known it would.

'It is so good to see a beautiful new face like yours, *madame*,' he flattered openly. 'It can be so wearying seeing nothing but the same old features week after week, month after month.'

Sipping at the rich, sweet coffee, Nesta said, 'Why do you not come to visit us in London? You could stay with us at Malgrave Manor.'

'May I do that?' Gerard's eyes blazed. He leaned even closer to Nesta, almost as if he meant to kiss her.

'I would be happy to have you stay, M'sieur de Chailly. Why do you not ask my husband about it?'

'Oh, please, *please*, do call me Gerard! So I have your permission to approach you husband on that score? Oh you are *so* kind, as well as so *beautiful*!' Gerard raved.

'You have my permission – Gerard.' Nesta smiled winningly.

Gerard sighed, seemingly overcome with emotion at the thought of sharing the same roof with the Duchess of Malgrave. While he was silent, a drift of conversation reached Nesta's ears.

'Yes, it is a portrait of my great-grandfather, God protect his soul. He was guillotined by the mob during the Terror, his wife and three of his children with him. Two children managed to escape to England, and one of those was my grandfather. This very *château* was totally destroyed by the mob – they burnt it to the ground after looting it and stealing all its treasures. After the Terror was over, we rebuilt it, restoring every stone, every piece of wood and plaster, every castellation to its proper place.'

'It must have taken immense courage and determination, Madame la Comtesse.'

The voice replying was James's. How Nesta wished he was sitting beside her looking so ardently into her eyes — and yet, would she not freeze if he were?

'Our family has never been renowned for its cowardice,' the Comtesse replied proudly.

James and the Comtesse moved away and Nesta could no longer hear what they were saying, but their words had affected her deeply. The Terror. How far-distant the epoch seemed to her in this sumptuous and relaxed setting, and yet these French aristocrats, as the mob had sneeringly named them, must have lost grandparents, parents and other relatives during the Revolution. No one with a title or who had associations with a title had been spared save for the ones who had managed to flee France. Nesta shivered, her imagination reconstructing what it must have been like to have lived in those days, with men, women and children being dragged to the guillotine while the dispassionate peasantry looked on with total detachment at their appalling plight, some knitting, others gossiping, but none wasting tears on those who had titles. . . .

To look back into the past, to see death, agony and suffering, was like looking back into her own past, the time which Nesta so much needed to forget for the sake of her own mental health; yet every time she tried, she would be reminded of Jenny and the vow she had made. Not until that vow was fulfilled could her mother's soul rest in peace. But the price Nesta must pay for that peace — it was too much. It would destroy James, destroy her, and that poor old woman at the manor. . . .

Once again, Nesta became tense. She could see that Gerard had noticed the change in her, that he was concerned why she was no longer smiling. He wanted to know if he had offended her in some way, to which she answered that of course he had done nothing of the sort. It was at that moment that she made the decision. She could either become immersed in her inner turmoil and let it ruin the evening or she could put it aside and respond wholeheartedly to Gerard – if she could but succeed in forgetting it for a few hours.

Bracing herself, she forced a smile back to her face and looked squarely into Gerard's richly-dark eyes. The effect upon him was immediate. He poured some more coffee and, when he handed her the cup, let his fingers brush against hers. His skin was warm and dry. She realized that he was behaving with great impropriety, here in his mother's own drawing-room, and with a guest, too, but suddenly she did not care. Was life to be all seriousness and suffering? No! She must forget her misery, and Gerard was the one to help her do it.

When he suggested that they go out onto the terrace to smell the night-scented stock, Nesta willingly agreed, taking his arm and walking out with him through the french windows. The night air was balmy, and the stock smelled heavenly. Gerard did not release her arm even when they were alone in the darkness, and she knew that she should coolly step away from him to remind him that she belonged to the Duke, her husband. But somehow she could not. It was all so beautiful: the romantic, star-gemmed night, the flowers, the sounds of the fountains in the gardens and the proximity of this charming, attentive boy. She told herself that this dalliance was harmless, that nothing would come of it and so she could allow it to last just a little while longer ... just a few moments more, and then they would go back inside, keeping a respectable distance between them.

Nesta mused that if she had had a younger brother she would have felt towards him as she did toward Gerard. She conveniently put aside the fact that Gerard was certainly not responding to her as he would to a sister. ...

She might have succeeded in forgetting her trouble had James not stormed out onto the terrace some moments later. Nesta looked up, startled. She was sitting on the rustic seat and Gerard's arm was placed round her shoulders. His lips were about to caress her cheek when the french windows crashed shut behind James and he rushed to stand over them, white with fury.

Instantly, Gerard sprang away from Nesta, but it was too late. They had been seen.

'We are leaving *now*, madam!' James said through gritted teeth, his eyes pits of rage.

Stunned, Nesta stumbled to her feet, catching her hem in the heel of her shoes and almost falling. James did not move to assist her, nor did Gerard dare to do so.

Darting a venomous glance in the boy's direction, James gripped Nesta by the arm and almost dragged her to the french windows, his fingers cutting deeply into her flesh so she had to bite her lips to stifle a cry of pain. When she stepped on a rough stone and hurt her foot, James said nothing but continued to haul her unceremoniously into the drawing-room. He managed to assume a semblance of nonchalance as he thanked the Comtesse for her hospitality, saying what a delightful evening they had spent. Nesta managed to mutter her own thanks, although her mouth felt wooden. Did everyone in the room know what had happened? Did they think that she and Gerard had been – ? Shame hit her like a blow, and she wanted to sink out of sight of their staring eyes.

Then James propelled her from the room and out into the hall, where they were handed their cloaks. Once in their carriage, Nesta huddled down in the corner of her seat, shrouding herself with her cloak, not daring to look at her husband. His anger was a palpable force between them; she felt she could touch it if she were to reach out a hand. Why was he so angry? What had he thought she would do with Gerard? Surely he did not think that she would let him make love to her?

Cautiously, she gave him a sidelong glance. His face was still contorted with fury. He was staring out of the window on his side of the carriage as if he were alone, his shoulders rigid. It was the first time that she had ever seen him lose his temper, and she found the experience terrifying.

When they arrived at the Château des Reines, James

again took her arm in a vise-like grip, ignoring the startled servants who had assembled to take their cloaks. He hauled her up the wide carved staircase and then pushed her through the door of their room and flung her down roughly onto the bed.

Struggling for composure, Nesta tried to plead with him, saying that she had meant no harm, but he would not listen. Her pleas seemed to enrage him further. Pushing her down again as she sought to rise, he began to tear at the buttons of his jacket and shirt and then flung them across the chamber. As if it were all happening in slow motion, Nesta watched her husband undress; an icy feeling creeping over her skin like frosty, prickling fingers.

'So you can flirt with other men and look at them with promises in your eyes, but not with me, your own husband!' James growled. 'Do you think you can fool me? You are a wanton – it is true what they say about you. I should never have married you – All you wanted was my name! Now that you have it you do not even *pretend* to love me!'

Stunned beyond belief, Nesta gasped, 'But that is not true! None of it is true! How could you think that of me? You know I love you, you must know it! I could never pretend such a feeling, not with you – Oh, James!'

'You need no longer carry on with your play-acting, madam. It no longer has any effect on me. Now I am going to do what I should have done long ago – what I would have done had I suspected the truth before tonight.'

Nesta moaned, cowering back against the pillows, her hands clasped together entreatingly. She felt as if rough fingers were clutching her throat, squeezing it so hard that she could not speak. Everything was fast becoming a nightmare!

James, his voice cold and cruel, stepped to the bed and clamped his hand round her wrist. 'So it is not as I think – You really do love me? Then show me – *show me* – for I have need of proof!'

Nesta felt sick. Her head began to whirl. This could not be James speaking like this, not her darling James.

Unaware of her torment and confusion, James crushed her against the pillows, breathing heavily as if he had been running. She felt the full weight of his body upon hers and his knees thrusting between her thighs so that tears of agony fled from her eyes. Sobbing, she tried to resist but was overcome by the weakness of dread.

'Come tell me, woman, how far would you have gone with that boy if I had not come out onto the terrace and dragged you away?' James roared. 'Come, tell me the truth! I have to know! Tell me, *tell me*!'

'Not – not with – him – James,' Nesta managed to gasp. 'Only with you – you – I love you – you – James?'

'What is it? Have you so many lovers that you forget my name? Well, I am *James*, James your husband, madam – and do not *ever* forget that!'

'No – no – ' Nesta moaned, blinded by tears, unable to believe that this was James who was being so cruel to her.

James was kissing her throat roughly, bruising her flesh, her lips. He unfastened his trousers and flung them aside; then he was ripping open the bodice of Nesta's gown and pulling out her breasts to rain ardent kisses upon them.

'You were going to let that boy do this to you, weren't you?' James panted. 'You would let him – anyone – *have* you! Is that not true? Tell me, is it? *Is it?*'

'No – no, it is lies, all lies. . . .' Nesta gasped, daring now to look into James's eyes and seeing them so impassioned that they were no longer blue but black with a furious desire. It was useless now to struggle – this was not her beloved, sweet, kind James. This was a monster: a monster whom she herself had created by her foolishness.

'It is not lies – You cannot forget what you were – what you still are! Even now, married to me, you are still a harlot! Well, I shall show you what I do to harlots!' He tore at her gown again, ripping it from bodice to hem, and thrust aside the voluminous layers of petticoats to force open her legs with his. She found the strength to fight then, balling her fists and pummelling at his neck and shoulders.

'No, James, *no*, not like this!' she cried.

James was beyond hearing. His hands were like branding irons on her shoulders as he forced an entry into her body, ramming himself into her again and again, violently, so that the shock from each thrust jarred right through her. She screamed in fear and shame and anguish until he clamped his hand across her mouth so that she could barely breathe.

'Tell me now, madam, admit it! You are a whore, a whore – that is what you are, is it not? Nothing more than a *whore*!'

Nesta wanted to cry out that it was not true, that she had been faithful to him and always would be, but his hand was bearing down on her mouth so hard that her teeth were piercing her upper lip and she felt faint from the pain.

'You made me believe that you loved me so that you could be my duchess. Well, you will pay the price, madam! You will pay it! After this, there will be no more between us – no more, do you hear me, *do you hear me*?'

Sobbing, Nesta nodded, too frightened to reply otherwise. He was mad, her James was mad – and she had made him so! It was all her fault, all of it, God help her!

'And if you find it difficult to respond to me, madam, then imagine that I am that boy Gerard, or one of your many customers – then it should be easy! Whores are paid to respond, so respond to me now, *damn you*!' James rasped as Nesta continued to resist him. 'Pretend that you love me – *pretend*, damn you!' James's voice caught in his throat.

Nesta realized then that he was undergoing a violent conflict himself. She wanted to beg him to stop, just for a few moments, before it was too late, but the words would not come from her constricted throat. She was on fire, but it was the fire of agony and shock. She seemed to be burning, then freezing, and stifled her sobs with her hand.

James's assault upon her body seemed to continue for an eternity. It seemed as if she were being cut open, wounded; she was sure that she was bleeding.

A strange calm settled upon Nesta's mind; she seemed to be drifting away beyond reality, in a dreamlike trance. It was her mind's only way of coping with James's attack. The man she had loved and worshipped since she was ten had become a frightening, vicious stranger. The turnabout was too much for her to bear without total breakdown, so her mind drifted, making her feel as if she had been drugged. Her hands fell from her mouth limply, her body sagged; if James noticed, he did not show it. Finally, finished, he rolled off her and pulled the coverlet over himself.

Nesta lay as James had left her. She could not pull the coverlet over herself but lay still, as if paralysed.

CHAPTER TWENTY-ONE

By the time Nesta awoke, stiff and bruised, James had gone. Dawn was suffusing the bedroom with a peachy silver light. It was beautiful, but she was oblivious to it all the same. She seemed to half-remember that something terrible had happened to her – or had it? She tried to piece together the memory but became confused. Was it just a dream? And yet it had seemed so very real. A man attacking a little girl, who had screamed and fought to hold him off but was too weak to resist.

Tears came into Nesta's eyes. She saw the child so clearly in her mind, a thin child with long black straggly hair, not unlike her own colouring. A half-starved urchin. Then, focusing on the scene, she was assailed by a fresh outbreak of shock. She had been the girl. James had attacked *her*. Oh God, was it really true?

Nesta had suffered intolerably many times during her young lifetime. Even her birth had been brutal; her mother half-starved and in agony, alone in a field giving birth to her. For too long she had repressed her worst memories and experiences, but it could not go on for ever. As more painful happenings were added to them, they seemed to begin to overflow; unchecked, they could become an unstoppable torrent which would, inevitably, lead to her breakdown. What had happened the previous night brought her another step closer to that catastrophe.

Weak and dizzy but determined not to give in, Nesta tried to behave as if nothing unusual had happened. She breakfasted in bed, then rose and was helped to dress by Marie-Jeanne. Afterwards, she sat in a chair on the terrace, staring at the garden but seeing nothing, mute with misery.

She did not see James that day, nor did he join her in bed that night. It was dark when she heard his horse returning and she waited, half in agony, half in anticipation, before hearing a door bang in a distant part of the *château* and then silence. Next morning, James's valet came to tell her that the Duke was packing and preparing to return to London.

Shock made Nesta forget that one did not find fault with one's family before the servants.

'The Duke has told you we are leaving? But he has said nothing to me!' she stammered.

The valet looked extremely ill at ease, squirming where he stood, but gently and politely he repeated the Duke's message, saying that that was all the information he had been given and that he was very sorry but he could say no more. Perhaps if Her Grace spoke to His Grace? the man suggested tentatively.

When she was alone Nesta went out into the gardens, trying to find some solace amongst the rapturous scent of the flowers, their beautiful colours and textures. She crumbled rose petals in her fingers, lifted satiny blossoms to her nose, walked past border after border of brilliantly-hued blooms to no avail; there was no balm which could tranquillize her soul; but now, it was too late. Although she still felt shocked, almost stunned, she had an uneasy sensation that when the shock had cleared there would be something worse to replace it. It was how she imagined a vixen must feel after being wildly pursued by hounds until it lay panting and half-dead from shock and exhaustion.

There would be that blissful moment of relief when it was able to lie down to rest and then the incredible agony would come as the pack closed in to savage it to death.

These beautiful gardens, this very *château*, had been made for lovers. It should have been paradise for her and James; instead, it had been hell. Nesta did not know what to do, where to turn; there seemed to be no escape, and yet she must escape or be destroyed.

With slow steps she returned to her room to begin half-heartedly to gather together her intimate belongings. Marie-Jeanne silently helped her. It would not take them long; she had brought only a half-dozen simple gowns with her for the honeymoon, for James had promised her the visit to Monsieur Worth, where a complete wardrobe was to have been created for her. Now she would never see Monsieur Worth and never have the beautiful clothes. But feeling the way she did it did not matter – nothing seemed to matter any more.

Two days later they were back in Malgrave Manor. James had still not spoken to her; they had not exchanged one word during the journey. Nesta would have wept had she not felt barren of tears. She thought that James must be feeling very ashamed of himself, so much so that he was unable to find the courage to apologize. He did not meet her gaze once; his valet attended to her requirements during the journey, for she had as yet not chosen her own personal maid. She missed Betsy's earthy chatter and could have done with her company.

At least the old Duchess was pleased to see her, her face crinkling with smiles, her voice quavering, but her questions about the honeymoon were embarrassing intrusions. She wanted to know why they had come back so early. Had anything gone wrong? Had they not liked the Château des Reines and Paris?

James said little, his voice gruff. Nesta let him speak for her.

When Nesta was alone with the invalid afterwards, she gave her the presents she had chosen in Paris for her: a beautiful lacquered box, painted in crimson, royal blue and emerald green; a little silver replica of the statue of the Madonna that stood in Notre Dame; and a head and shoulders portrait of an unknown woman, painted by Edgar Hilaire Germain Degas, an artist whom Nesta loved for his powerful and colourful figures which were redolent with character and drama. She knew that the Dowager-Duchess would like them, too, and for the same reason.

'Well, my dear, these are beautiful presents.' The invalid's voice trembled, for she was quite overcome with emotion as her fingers traced the head of the painted woman. 'Her eyes seem to be alive – I imagine she is about to open her mouth and speak. Who is this Degas? I have not heard of him before.'

'I think his family is Bretonne in origin. His father opened a branch of the family bank in Paris and married a Creole girl. Degas himself is about twenty-five or thirty years old. He has been painting since about 1853, so I believe. He's one of the new-style artists that are being called Impressionists. I think his most famous painting is *The Dancing Class*. It was exhibited in Paris recently and it caused quite a stir.'

'Can he be commissioned? Do you think he would come to London to paint you and James and your son when he is born?' The old Duchess had blushed at the thought of the family portrait.

'I – I really couldn't say, madam. You would have to ask James. Besides, there will be quite a long wait, will there not, to get three of us in the portrait?' Nesta gave a half-smile, a little nerve jumping at the side of her mouth.

'Oh, you rascally girl!' The Duchess prodded Nesta's arm with one bony forefinger. 'It won't be long now before you're telling me the good news. I can tell, you know! One can sense these things when one gets to be my age.'

Nesta swallowed. Her throat seemed to have tightened so that she could hardly breathe. She could feel acid tears welling behind her lids. She must get away from this suffocating room and the Duchess's prying. As politely as she could she made her excuses and hurried to her own room.

If only Degas could come to London and paint the portrait of the three of them – herself, James, their son. *If only*. There was an old woman upstairs, barely alive, struggling to survive just long enough to see James's son born; longing, dreaming, for that day. If she only *knew*; if James *knew*. . . .

Nesta threw herself into a chair, her face in her hands. The burden of her secret was like a wooden yoke round her neck, a yoke with steel barbs which cut deep into her whichever way she turned. Her head was pounding; she was almost blind with the pain. She knew she would have to lie down. One of the maids drew the curtains and helped her into bed.

'Would you bring me one of the Dowager-Duchess's headache-powders, please, and some tea? That often helps.'

'Of course, Your Grace.' The maid bobbed a curtsy, hurrying away to do as she was bidden.

Nesta lay inert, not daring to move in case it made the pain worse, feeling it travel through her head, down her limbs, so that her entire body seemed to be one terrible aching wound. When the maid returned she mixed the headache-powder for her. Nesta swallowed it in one draught, after which she drank two cups of tea to drown its bitter taste. James was out; he had gone to look at some horses on a friend's Wiltshire estate, so she would not be disturbed. She could sleep in peace until she was better. Suddenly it was very important that no one should disturb her; she must rest.

Nesta woke sometime towards midnight. The room was pitch-black. She looked round in the darkness, terrified, sweat beading her body. Her stomach felt queasy, her body clammy, but at least the pain was gone. Closing her eyes hastily against the darkness, for she dared not look into it, she rang the bell at the side of her bed, huddling down beneath the covers while she waited for the maid to appear. The maid soon arrived, in curlers and slippers, drawing on a woollen dressing-gown.

'The light. You forgot to light the lamp,' Nesta said.

'Oh, Your Grace, Your Grace, forgive me, forgive me!' the maid stammered, remedying the situation immediately. 'Would Your Grace like a drink – some hot milk perhaps, or drinking chocolate?'

'I'd love some hot milk, thank you. I – I'm sorry to disturb you so late.'

'That's quite all right, Your Grace. I hadn't gone to sleep just in case you woke up wanting something. I was sitting in the chair in my room reading, waiting for your bell. I'll get your hot milk now, Your Grace.' The maid bobbed a curtsy and hurried off.

Nesta felt better now that the room was lit, although she had that curious sense of disorientation which comes when one has slept at the wrong time of day. But at least her headache had gone. The maid soon returned with hot milk sweetened with honey and a selection of fresh cakes and biscuits which the cook had made that afternoon. Nesta did not feel hungry, but the girl was looking at her so anxiously that she nibbled at one of the biscuits and washed it down with sips of milk.

'Can I get you anything before I go to bed, Your Grace?'

'No, thank you, Norris.' Then, as the girl moved towards the lamp, she added sharply, 'No, don't put the lamp out. You know I've always told you to leave a lamp burning in my room at night.'

'Yes, Your Grace. I'm very sorry. Please forgive me, Your Grace.'

'Of course I forgive you!' Nesta sounded more impatient than she had intended.

When Norris had gone, she decided to go to James's room. She flung on a peignoir and walked up and down debating whether she should. Perhaps he had stayed the night in Wiltshire? Well, she would go and find out for certain.

James's room was in darkness, but she could hear him breathing. Panic gripped her. As she stepped backwards to make a hasty exit, she caught her foot on a stool, turning it over with a crash. She stopped in her steps, her heart beating frantically.

'Who's there? Who's that?' James reached out, turning up the lamp by his bed. Seeing his wife, he leapt out of bed. 'Are you ill, Nesta?'

'No – I – I – ' She began to shake uncontrollably as he led her to the warm bed, tucked her in and slipped in beside her.

'Darling,' he whispered, 'what is wrong? Tell me!'

'Nothing – I – I just came to see if you were here.'

'Well, I *am*. What now?'

He gave her cheek a tentative kiss, making joy surge within her. How she wanted things to be as they had before their marriage! Perhaps they could be? Turning, she met his lips with hers, sighing. He responded by kissing her more ardently, repeating her name.

'Darling, it's been so long – How I've missed you! We should not let anything come between us – '

'I know, I know,' Nesta said. 'I don't know why I've been so silly. Forgive me?'

'Of course.'

There was silence for some time as they kissed. Nesta thought, it's going to be all right this time! It's going to be all right! And then as his hands slid down her hips and probed between her thighs, she felt a rising terror, the old terror which she had been foolish enough to think she had beaten. As soon as he felt her stiffen, his hand became still.

'So nothing has changed, Nesta?' His voice sounded choked. He was roused, he wanted her desperately, but she did not want him. Bitterness coursed through him, and angrily he gripped her shoulders, flinging her onto her back.

'You are my wife now. I can do anything I want with you, so it's no good fending me off. Are you trying to tantalize me, to drive me crazy by coming here and then going cold in my arms?'

'No! I cannot help this – I'm sorry, so sorry!'

'You expect me to believe that? I have only to think of

how warm and willing you were before we married. Remember when you kissed the Prince of Wales in public? Do you expect me to believe that you have become a puritan all of a sudden?'

Furious, and desiring her urgently, James moved atop her body, crushing her against the mattress, his mouth pressed heavily to her throat so that Nesta could not move. She sobbed in anguish but he did not heed her. When he took her, she grew even more rigid, but it did not deter him. He went on to the bitter end, driving into her body over and over, panting harshly until he had finished.

When he released her, Nesta slipped out of the bed weeping and rushed to her room, locking the door behind her. James did not follow.

The next few days passed much the same way. James and she were hostile strangers who did not converse, who never met at mealtimes, who never went anywhere together or sat in the same room with one another. He was out more often than he was in, and it was only through the Dowager-Duchess that Nesta learned what her husband was doing. Having become interested in breeding horses, James was going to buy two part-Arab stallions from his friend in Wiltshire; he had heard of two suitable mares for sale in Ireland, somewhere in the South, the old Duchess thought, but she could not remember exactly where it was.

'One of those florid Irish names, spelt nothing like how it is pronounced,' she said. 'Ballyglowry or Ballycoolly or some such name like that. Has he not told you? You like riding, do you not? James told me you had chosen a fine mount of your own before he met you. Apollo, is that not your horse's name?'

'Yes, madam, but I have not the heart for riding these days. I. . . .'

The old Duchess seemed to spring to attention, hunch-

314

ing her shoulders while at the same time peering forward piercingly.

'Don't like riding? You're not breeding, are you, m'dear? Are you? Well, tell me, are you, *are you*?' The Duchess's blackcurrant eyes positively throbbed with impatience to know.

'No, I am sorry, I am not, Your Grace. I am afraid you will have to wait a little longer for that.' She managed a twisted smile. If the old woman only knew the truth!

Nesta had put on a good face, visiting the Duchess daily, taking her little gifts, talking about the house, about James, about the latest gossip, as if nothing were wrong. She thought that she was managing well, that the Duchess had not suspected anything amiss, but this persistent talk of pregnancy and a son for James always cut through her. She would never grow accustomed to it; it always made her feel guilty and somehow criminal.

Later, Nesta went to her bathroom to soak in a hot bath to soothe her tortured nerves. After supplying her with towels, scented soap and bath oil, Norris departed, leaving Nesta to relax in the hot steamy atmosphere. She did not hear the door click open or notice James lounging in the entrance, his eyes glistening with desire. When he spoke, she jumped wildly, dropping the soap and trying to cover her breasts.

'Why cover them, my love? I have seen them before. You're my wife, remember?'

Leaning over the bath, James traced a finger across one breast while she sat rigid with shock at his nearness. She had never seen such lust in his face. Oh, if only things were as before! When his fingers plunged down into the steaming water to graze her thighs, Nesta almost forgot to breathe. With one hand cupping a breast, he allowed the other to explore between her legs, stroking her gently and then with more passion. She gave a little moan, and he leaned closer.

'James – ' she half-begged, wanting him to stop, feeling her mounting passion betray her.

'What, my darling?' He curved his finger inside her, as

far as it would go, and then, when he thought she was sufficiently roused, scooped her up out of the scented water and carried her into the bedroom.

'Norris – ' she cautioned.

'I have locked the door.'

The water's relaxing heat had removed her tensions. Nesta believed that if James made love to her now, it would be as rapturous as before they were married. All she had needed was to be truly relaxed. . . .

She lay back in his arms to let him kiss her. But first he reached for a towel to rub her dry. His hands felt strong and soothing on her limbs and breasts. Between each movement with the towel, he kissed her, and then, when she was dry, he took off his clothes and pulled the covers over them both. Again his hands explored her body, stroking her breasts, sliding deep inside her, cushioning her hips. How she loved him – More than anything she wanted to respond to his lovemaking, to find ecstasy in his arms.

He was between her thighs, thrusting into her, when Nesta began to panic. Such a wave of terror convulsed her that she felt as if she were in the middle of a terrible nightmare where a black demon was about to draw her into his arms.

Nesta cried out, 'No! No!' pummelling at James with her fists, and James withdrew at once, his face black with anger. Leaving her sobbing, he snatched up his clothes and stormed out of the room.

'James, oh James, come back!' she sobbed, but he had gone, closing the door behind him.

Nesta heard later from the servants that James had subsequently left for Ireland. He had not spoken to her since their last embroilment, nor had she sought him out. She was filled with remorse and guilt and shame, but there was nothing she could say to him now. He was expected to be away for a fortnight.

Nesta felt lost after his departure. How she would have loved to travel with him. She had heard that Ireland was a beautiful place, lush and green, and now that the dreadful famine had run its course, the people were beginning to farm again, planting their potatoes and cabbages and making buttermilk. She liked to keep up to date with reports of such happenings in *The Times* newspaper, which James read every day, for she always felt a deep kinship with the poor and downtrodden.

When she thought of her last scene with James, she felt sick at heart. How could she have fought him off like that? What must he think of her? She felt as if some fiendish devil possessed her and she was impotent to free herself.

Nesta's inner conflict had raged for longer than she could stand; she felt that she was approaching the snapping point. Her energies had evaporated. She slept late and then dressed incredibly slowly; sometimes she walked in the park, with Norris to accompany her, or rode in her carriage along the Serpentine.

Summer was over and autumn was fast making its impact known. The parks sported burnt-orange and gold and fading green foliage and the Serpentine was littered with dead leaves, black and glutinous on the water's surface. As she looked down into its murky depths she could not help but think of all the people who had committed suicide in this very river. But she chided herself silently: had she sunk so low in spirit that she could contemplate killing herself, jumping into those cold, dirty waters and not putting up any fight at all, letting the river carry her away, its water filling her mouth and lungs until she sank to its bottom, silent and unmoving?

Another week passed. Nesta could not bear her loneliness any more. She woke one morning knowing that she would go to see Cathy and Amy as soon as she was dressed. She went out alone, leaving Norris behind. She did not take one of the carriages, for she had no wish to let any of James's servants know her destination.

Nesta felt a nostalgic pang as she stood before the Crimson Club. Had it really been so dear to her, this epitome of her ambitions before James had come back into her life? Inside, everything was just as it had always been; lush, comfortable, well-tended. Her old friends were overjoyed to see her, as she had known they would be, and they kissed her warmly, taking her into the drawing-room which had once been her own private quarters, plying her with port and wafers, and besieging her with questions. It did not take them long to see how dispirited she was. They had known her many years, in every mood, but never quite so down as this.

Cathy kneeled down in front of her, taking her hands. 'Are you expecting, lovey?' she said gently. 'Is that why you're feeling so ill? Takes it out of a girl, it do, you know. Got to take care of yourself, put your feet up, drink lots of red wine – it makes your blood strong.'

Nesta felt a wave of embarrassment wash over her. This was almost like being cross-questioned by the Duchess. 'No – no, I'm not expecting!'

'Then what is it, lovey? Ain't things going how you'd hoped with the Duke? Got to give these things time, you know. He's been brought up different from you ... used to the high life an' everything rich an' fine. Had a quarrel have you, is that it?'

'We-we're not speaking,' Nesta confessed finally, feeling relieved at the problem's being brought out into the open. 'We – I – we went to some people for dinner while we were on our honeymoon and I, well, I'm afraid I encouraged a young man a little too much. James was very, very angry. Things have been bad between us since then.' Nesta's voice caught in her throat.

'Is he that type, then?' said Cathy, 'Jealous an' can't let bygones be bygones? Well, that's hard cheese, if you ask me, Nesta lovey.'

'There's a lot more to it than that,' Nesta said slowly. 'I think he's had second thoughts about marrying me. It's all gone so very wrong.'

'A bit late to have second thoughts now, isn't it?' said Cathy, as matter of fact as ever. 'If he was going to have those, he should have had them before the ceremony, eh? Can't back out once the deed is done. Not gentlemanly, is it, Amy?'

'No, no!' Amy was wringing her hands, aghast at what

Nesta was telling them. She was remembering Cathy's misgivings which, of course, had not been told to Nesta at the time – How sure her friend had been that the marriage was a dreadful mistake and would end disastrously. Cathy wasn't given to regular premonitions, but when she had them they were usually right on the nail. Now it seemed that again she had been correct.

'Where is he now, this Duke?' Amy said, her tone derisory.

'He – he's in – he's somewhere in Ireland. Ballagarry or somewhere like that. I don't know the name exactly. Buying horses. He's going to breed horses, you see.'

'An' a right little breeder he'll be, too,' Amy sneered, 'treating you like this. Got no right, he ain't! Once you makes a bargain you got to stick by it! These titled folk don't know when they got the whole world on their side, they don't. If he was here now I'd give him a right good smack in the jaw!'

'But it wouldn't help us,' Nesta said. 'I still love him. I love him so much that I don't know what I'm going to do if I can't mend our relationship soon. I'll – oh, how can I go on living without him!' She burst into tears.

Cathy and Amy rushed to her, putting their arms round her. They had never once seen their mistress break down like this before, not in all the years they had been together. If they got their hands on that James Malgrave they'd throttle the life out of him, they would! Cheeky swine, treating their Nesta like that. Those toffs were all the same, thinking they could do whatever they liked wth a girl!

Thanks to the ministrations of her two devoted friends, Nesta soon began to feel a little better. She hadn't been able to cry for months – the tears seemed to have been sealed inside her – and now that some of them were out she felt lighter, almost cheerful. She stayed with her friends for another three hours, and when she left they extracted her promise to visit them again soon.

'Come straight back here if he gives you any more trouble, Nesta lovey,' Cathy said, kissing her warmly.

'Come and stay here with us if things get too bad. No need to put up with that, you know, not while we're here.'

'Yes,' nodded Amy, 'leave him. Tell him where to get off. Show him you don't need him. That's the sort of treatment he deserves.'

Nesta kissed them good-bye, thinking what dears they were and how much she loved them.

After leaving the Crimson Club, Nesta strolled along the avenue until the river and the Tower came into view. She loved the Tower, despite its gory history: all those queens who had been imprisoned there, some of them beheaded – a reminded of how fickle men could be; how they could lift a girl up from nowhere, make her their bride and then knock her down. She shuddered, seeing the comparison with her own life. Not that James could ever be compared with Henry VIII. She gave a little smile at the thought and realized that her spirits were indeed much improved. She considered taking a cab back into the city but decided against it. It was a beautiful, crystalline autumn day; she would walk along the banks of the Thames for a while and then get back onto the main thoroughfare.

Some two hours later she walked into Hardingham Square, intending to cut straight across from there to Malgrave Manor. Seeing a particularly pretty garden, she paused to admire it, which was why she was standing half-screened by a golden beech hedge when the carriage drew up across the square and then two people alighted. Nesta glanced up out of curiosity and then froze on the spot, feeling as if the breath had been punched out of her.

James. Her James getting out of a carriage with a woman; a pretty blonde girl who was laughing up at him as he helped her down. He tucked his arm into hers possessively, smiling down at her as she looked dotingly up at him, and then they went up the steps into one of the big houses which edged the square. The door closed behind them with a terrible finality.

Shock had paralysed Nesta's wits and it took her a few moments to realize who the woman was. But this was not the rigid, sour-faced girl who had harangued her with talks of morality, decency and respectability when she was mistress of the Crimson Club; this was a relaxed and laughing girl, who seemed miraculously to have shed her inhibitions.

It was none other than Jane, Lady Finchley-Clark. The woman to whom James had been betrothed before he met Nesta.

Nesta pressed a hand to her forehead. Could she be mistaken? James is in Ireland, she told herself, how could he be here, too? But it had been James, there was no doubt of that! She had carried the searing image of her Sun God in her mind for more than half her lifetime. No one else was so tall, so strong, with that glossy, gilded hair, the adorable smile. No, it was James. James who supposedly had gone to Ireland to buy horses but all the time was here in London seeing another woman behind her back and, from the look of it, on intimate terms with her! *That* woman – that stupid, pompous woman! Nesta wished it was anyone else, even a common trollop, but the prudish Jane.

But Lady Jane no longer looked puritanical. She glowed; she had *blossomed*. What had changed her so? With a sickening heart Nesta thought she knew: it was James who had wrought this miracle. He must have been meeting Jane for quite some time, which was why she, Nesta, so rarely saw him now.

As full realization hit her, Nesta knew that she was going to be very ill. She had not even time to look round to see if anyone was watching her before she leaned behind the golden beech hedge and was violently sick. Afterwards, she felt no better; she was shivering with cold and still felt nauseous. Panic was bubbling inside her -- she had experienced it before but this time she knew she had no strength to control it; things had gone beyond the limits of her endurance.

Escape, she must escape! Feeling a scream beginning to mount in her throat, she clamped her teeth tightly together. She wanted to lash out, to destroy, to tear up the beech hedge beside her and rip off all the heads of the flowers which a few moments ago she had been admiring before her world had turned into hell. Clamping a hand over her mouth she began to run. She would get her reticule at the manor, put some money in it and go away. Yes, she must get away!

Nesta burst into the manor, not looking to right or to left, ignoring the startled butler who opened the door to her. Within minutes she had searched and found all her loose change. She did not have as much as she thought – a few sovereigns, that was all – but it would be enough to take her away. Where, as yet, she did not know. Had she not felt suffocatingly hot from running, she might have decided to take one of her cloaks, too. As it was, she rushed from the house, wisps of hair coming loose from her chignon, wearing only a gown.

Outside on the avenue, she hailed a cab, and it was at that moment that she knew where she was going.

'York. Take me to York, please!'

'York?' coughed the man, 'I don't go to York. This ain't the bleedin' railroad, y'know.'

Nesta struggled to recollect which station she had used to get to York, but she could not remember. There was only one word in focus in her head, the name of the place where she had once taken refuge.

'I want the station. The station which will . . . where there will be a train to take me to York,' she called up. 'Please, please, hurry!' she pleaded.

She had to get away; the London air was stifling her. She pulled at the buttons of her collar, tearing them open, and rubbed her fingers across her throat.

Grunting, the man jerked his horses' reins and the cab lurched forward.

Nesta sat stiffly in the train seat, tight as a coiled spring, unable to relax. She must get to York – she had friends there; everything would be all right once she got to York. Captain Maude would be there and – and – what was his brother's name? She tried to remember but could not. And his aunt. She could remember nothing about her except that she had been kind, in a blustery sort of way, and that she had deplorable taste in dress. But that did not matter. Once Nesta got to York, the Maudes would look after her; she would never have to worry about anything again!

How hot it was in the carriage. Nesta felt as if she were burning up. She pulled her collar open even more, startling the tubby little gentleman dressed all in black who sat on the opposite side of the compartment. He gazed at her in horror; it seemed to him that she was about to undo all her clothes. She did not notice him. All she could feel was the burning heat, the lack of air, her longing to scream, to shout, which she managed to suppress only because she knew that in a few hours she would be with Captain Maude and his kind family. *Safe*.

Nesta stumbled out of the compartment at York station. It was a chilly, autumn day in the North, far colder than in London, but she was oblivious to this change in temperature. She must get to Maude Manor as soon as possible, otherwise the terrible mounting pressure was going to consume her. She could not control it much longer; it was all the time growing inside her, pressing against her skin like a myriad spider's legs, probing, wriggling, irritating, so that she knew that only a scream would release it.

'Maude Manor, as quick as you can!' she snapped to the cabbie waiting outside York station.

Shrugging, he flicked at the horse with his whip and they were off.

The journey seemed interminably long. Taut, Nesta sat on the seat, hands tightly clenched in her lap, teeth gritted together. Joseph was going to put everything right, she knew that. Oh, how she longed to see him! She would be safe with him. *Safe*.

The carriage finally rolled to a halt, and then the cabbie called down, 'We be 'ere, ma'am,' in a gruff, Yorkshire dialect.

Nesta leapt down, trembling with anticipation. Then she looked around, unable to believe her eyes.

'Cabbie, you have brought me to the wrong place, the *wrong* place! I asked for Maude Manor!' Nesta's voice rose on a note of hysteria.

The man, who had been in the act of turning his horse, gave a shrug. He was impatient to be back at the station and picking up more fares. He had no time to waste speaking to emotional females.

'Didn' y'know, ma'am? Burnt down it wahr a while back. Burnt reet down t'ground. That's why ye can't see it.'

'A fire? Oh no! No! How could that *be*?'

'They said it wahr started by 'Er Ladyship. Invalid she wahr. Must've been careless with 'er candle in the beddin' and it caught light. Burnt t'death she wahr.'

'And – and the rest of the family? What of them?' Nesta gasped.

''Er son, the liddle 'un, he wahr burnt with 'er they do say.'

'Oh, no, no!' Nesta wailed, digging her clenched fists into her mouth. 'Burnt? Oh that's terrible – I cannot believe it!'

The man shrugged again. 'Believe what ye like, ma'am, that's 'ow it wahr. Cap'n Maude 'e tried t'get 'em aht, but 'e didn' mek it. Driven back by yon flames 'e wahr. On t'staircase when t'fire overtook 'im. Bruk both 'is legs 'e did. Crippled for life they do say. Now I gotta be off. Cahn't sit 'ere all day gawpin' at nowt. Got fares waitin' back at yon station.'

Whipping up his horse, the man set off at speed.

The breaking-point for Nesta had finally come. This was as much as her tortured mind and body could stand. They were dead, bright young Benjamin and his poor mother, and Joseph had been horribly injured. The thought of their dying agonies was more than she could endure in her distraught state. The blood ebbed from her head, leaving her a sickly white colour. When she fell to the ground, there was no one to see her or to rush to her aid.

CHAPTER TWENTY-TWO

Time passed, the dying light of day shrouding the moors in a purplish grey mist which rose rapidly, eddying round the body of the woman lying on the ground, nudging at her with fingers she could neither see nor feel. The earth cooled beneath her, chilling her limbs, and the dampness penetrated her clothes. There was no sign of her regaining consciousness, and it was getting darker by the moment. A wind was mounting, buffeting the grass and the inert form. If she remained where she was, she would probably freeze to death by morning. This was to be her fate after all, dying alone of the cold, just as she had almost died as a child. Not in the murk of a London backstreet but alone out on the Yorkshire moors, in a place she barely knew but which she had regarded as a haven.

The man was driving the dog-cart at a furious pace, eager to be home by the warmth of his daughter's fireside. The Yorkshire nights at this time of year were very damp and never failed to chill him to the bone although he had grown up in the extreme climate of Hungary.

The lamp was swinging to and fro, its rusty hinge protesting. His daughter always insisted he carry the lamp with him when he went out on his journeys, for now that they were reunited she had an inordinate fear of his getting lost. His eyesight was none too good these days; nonetheless, by the light of the lamp he saw the humped, inert body lying at the roadside, and he slowed the dog-cart down. A drunk probably, but what he was doing out here on the moors alone? As the man peered closer at the body, he saw the curve of shoulder and hip, and realized that it was a woman lying there in the twilight.

Muttering beneath his breath, the man pulled the cart to a halt; as he stepped down, tentatively reaching out to touch the woman to see if she was dead, a thunderclap proclaimed rain was about to start, and then the downpour began. He could not make out much in this foul weather. Whether she was dead or not, he could not leave her lying there, poor soul.

How would he raise the woman? He did not ponder on it too long, for there was nothing wetter than a moorland deluge. Puting one arm beneath her head and one under her knees, the man half-dragged, half-heaved her into the cart, laying her along the seat and covering her with a rug. He held the lamp over her face to see if there were any signs of life. He had never seen any living person so deathly white; he thought that she was already dead, that he had come upon her too late. He was overcome by a feeling of despair for his work was healing the sick, and when he was unable to do that, or when he failed in his work, he was always deeply affected, as if part of himself were being lost. Putting the lamp back on its hook, he whipped up the horses and speeded along the road as fast as he could to his daughter Magda's farmhouse.

The storm was insistently battering at the walls of the farmhouse, the byre and the stables beyond. The animals had scurried for cover and were now huddling in their sheds. The rain was lashing down like barbs, stinging the man's face as he hammered on the farmhouse door and summoned his daughter's husband out to help him with the body.

'A woman dead? *A dead woman?*' gasped his daughter, coming to the door, her hands tucked beneath her apron for warmth. 'You're not bringing a dead body in here! Put it in the outhouse.' She turned to her husband. 'Do you know who it is, Josh? One of the locals, is it?'

Josh turned back the rug covering the woman's face, peering closely at her in the light from the door.

'Nay, lass, it's nob but a dead body. Strange female by t'looks on it. Ah bain't seen 'er before.'

The two men carried the body to the outhouse and were laying it out on the old, scrubbed pine table there when Nesta moaned, a shiver running through her body.

'God in heaven, she's alive!' the old man cried. 'Get her in the house, Josh! Quick, quick as you can! Wrap her in that blanket. Keep it wrapped right round her.'

As rapidly as they could they carried Nesta into the living-room of the farmhouse. The old man's daughter fetched heated bricks from the hearth, wrapping them in cloths to place them alongside Nesta and at her feet while he chafed her hands, occasionally lifting up one of her eyelids to see how she was faring.

Josh stood in the background, his mouth agape. An almost dead woman, and a lady by the looks of her clothes; and brought to his house at this time of night. This was a queer turn of events and no mistake! He didn't know her face, but she did look like a lady; there must be someone searching for her somewhere. He wondered if she had been robbed of her money and then flung from a passing coach, but then he saw her beaded purse hanging from her wrist and heard the clink of coins inside it as she moved her arm and opened her eyes for the first time.

'Now do not be frightened, *kisgalamb*,' the old man said soothingly. 'You are in a safe place and we shall take care of you. Just lie back and rest and be quiet. . . . Be at peace. Lie back, breath deeply, slowly, and all will be well. Can you not feel the peace stealing through your body? The peace and the calm and the tranquility. . . .'

The old man was stroking Nesta's forehead and looking deeply into her eyes, and as he did so she felt the calm overtaking her, travelling through her tortured mind, which had broken out there on the moors. How peaceful she felt, as if she were drifting away on a smoothly undulating river.

When she woke, she found herself tucked into a narrow bed laden with coverlets, and she could feel the heated bricks pressing into her sides and her feet. There was a small oil-lamp in the corner of the room, and by its glow she could see the old man sitting hunched in a chair, keeping watch over her. Suddenly she was filled with a feeling of thorough safety. She must have made a sound, for he rose immediately, coming to her side.

'How are you feeling, *kisgalamb*?' Gently he stroked her forehead, then took one of her hands in his.

'Better, I think,' she said haltingly. 'I don't know what happened. I had a shock, a terrible shock, out there on the moors. I – I wanted to die.' She turned her head away, unable to look at him.

'The mind knows when it has had enough, when it can take no more, and then it takes its own rest, whatever else the body wishes to do. You have been through a great ordeal. I can see that in your face. You have suffered – for years you have suffered, and your burden has grown heavier and heavier, until it has become like a cross on your back which you cannot support alone.'

Nesta looked back at him, stunned. 'That is it – that is it exactly!' she gasped. 'How did you know? How could you tell?'

'I have spent all my life helping people who have reached the breaking-point as you have, *kisgalamb*. I know these things from experience. In my life I have seen hundreds of faces looking just like yours.'

'And what have you done with them?' Nesta asked, willing him to tell her what she must know. She was sure that he would have the right answer, although she as yet did not. How safe she felt in his presence. He could help her; she knew it.

'I did my best to heal them, little one. It was not always possible, and not always as well as they would have liked, but in the main with success, I think.'

The old man stroked her hand; his skin felt like crinkled hessian against hers. He had a battered face, as if life had dealt him many blows; his brows were fat and bushy and very white, his eyes a mellow golden brown. He had very little hair left on his head, his scalp being very pink. When he turned round later she would see that he had a little fringe of soft white hair just above his neck. Perhaps he was an outdoors man, for his face was dried, tanned by years of sunshine and wind. He wore an old, very threadbare black suit and a baggy, collarless countryman's shirt, with a coarsely-woven scarf knotted at his neck.

Nesta was about to ask his name and why he had come to live here in York, of all places, when, suddenly overcome by total exhaustion, she slipped away into sleep.

The wild, moorland storm split the night, drumming against the windows, driving at the doors and the walls. Lightning sliced through the black and murky air, and, following it, deafening explosions of thunder. Nesta, however, heard nothing. Oblivious to the hardness of her pallet, tucked up warmly in the bare, serviceable room, she slept as if she had been starved of rest for an eternity.

Next morning when she awoke, the room was suffused with a peachy light and Magda, Josh's wife, was bending over her, holding a plaited rush tray on which stood a steaming mug of thick, black tea and a slab of freshly-baked bread iced thickly with butter and honey. Thanking her, Nesta took the tray and leaned back against the hard pillow in its rough linen case.

'Fresh morning,' Magda said. 'The storm's blown itself out. It was just as if old demons were abroad on the moors last night. We get the brunt of all the weather up here. We've no shelter at all.'

She had tucked her large red hands back under her apron, which seemed to be her favourite place for them, and looked down at Nesta with something like pity in her tawny eyes. She was a big woman, quite tall; but for her rough farming clothes, she might have been stately. Her hair was very pale and fine, secured into a tight knot at the base of her skull, and over it she wore a gaily coloured scarf in a triangular shape, knotted at the back beneath the bun. Her apron was intricately-embroidered in red, blue and yellow silks, an elaborate flower design, which Nesta realized must have been her own work.

Seeing Nesta's eyes settle admiringly on the apron, Magda smiled and said, 'Embroidery is second nature to us Hungarian women. We like to sew flowers and leaves on everything. I don't have my folk-costume with me – I had to leave it behind in Hungary – but if you could see it you would know what I mean. I spent many months embroidering it, and I embroidered Papa's jacket and his cap as well – We had to leave those behind, too.'

Sipping at the hot tea, Nesta asked her why they had had to leave their clothes behind, why they had rushed away from their homeland so quickly.

'It is best not to speak of it,' Magda said, 'for it only revives the pain. To leave one's homeland, to become an exile, never to be able to go back, this is a terrible thing: a suffering which lies with you for the whole of your life, like a great stone in your breast.'

She walked to the window, looking out at the freshly-laundered scenery. 'Papa took it worst of all, for he was, and is, a great patriot. His family have lived in Hungary for generations. The uncertainty of life there, the military occupation and dictatorship, the Austrians taking over, it was all very upsetting. The strain of it killed my mother.'

Magda turned to look at Nesta, who was holding the mug of hot tea in her hands and listening intently.

'My mother was a jolly, laughing woman, always cheerful, always believing in God and trusting in His protection. She would quote to me from the Scriptures. She would say, "To the pure all is pure," and "Trust in Jesus and you will never hunger," and "The Lord is a rock in the time of one's needs." She did not falter in her faith, even at the end.

'In many ways Hungary is still backward. Nearly a quarter of the babies born die in infancy. I had two sisters; they both died before they learned to walk. My mother took their deaths particularly hard. Papa, he had his work to do; he was always busy helping others, healing the sick, consoling those with troubled minds. By the time he realized that my mother was very seriously ill it was too late for him to help her. He was stricken then; he knew that he had devoted most of his time to others, all strangers, and neglected my mother. She died in his arms. I was about twelve.

'I remember kneeling at the foot of the bed, watching the life ebb from her face, her hands fall on the coverlet. Papa bending over her body and sobbing, begging her to forgive him for neglecting her. Then he took me in his arms and he made a vow. He swore that if it was in his power he would never let anyone suffer again as my mother had suffered. Since that day, he has kept his vow to the best of his ability, working sometimes by day and by night to help the sick and the distressed. He travelled widely on the Continent, learning more about the arts of healing, the new ideas and techniques. Meanwhile, I married Josh, and he is good to me; solid, reliable, which is what I need. When Papa is tired from his work he comes here to rest, and the local people visit him then to be healed.'

Nesta put down the empty mug of tea. 'If I hadn't been seen by him last night I would have been dead now, frozen in the storm.'

'I doubt it was an accident he found you. He has an unerring instinct for discovering people in need. I expect God had His good purpose for putting you there and for making Papa find you. There will be a reason for it, you will see. It is all part of the great embroidery of life. At birth each babe is given his needle and his skeins of silk; what he sews with them is the destiny he makes for himself. That is what my mother always used to tell me. Some, she said, will work untidily and with impatience, cursing when they make a wrong stitch or stab their fingers on the needle. Others will get deep delight from executing something beautiful and will work at it hard and lovingly. Others will give up halfway. That is just how life is, exactly like that.

'Well, I must go back to my work now. The animals must be fed. Although we start in the morning at six there is never enough time to get everything done, and this bad weather does not help to make things go easier. The light gets shorter and shorter at this time of year, until we are working for much of our time in the dark. You cannot tell a cow that needs milking to come back at another hour when it is lighter.'

Magda flashed Nesta a lop-sided smile which stripped ten years off her age.

When she had gone, Nesta snuggled down into the bed. Out on the moors, staring at the space where Maude Manor had once stood, she had reached the nadir of despair. Now she could sink no further. From the moment she had regained consciousness in this house she had felt lighter, easier somehow. The old healer – she did not know his name yet – filled her with a quiet contentment and a feeling that he could help her in a way no other man could. He was wise and skilled; instinctively she knew that. It showed in his eyes, which were at one and the same time old and yet ageless. She knew absolutely nothing about Hungary and its people, its history or its present troubles; not that any of that mattered at this moment. Destiny had brought her to this place, and for a purpose.

A few minutes later when the door to her bedroom swung open and the old healer entered, a sweet smile on his face, she was ready for him. He took her hand, still smiling.

'Now, what I want you to do this morning, my dear, is to relax, to imagine that you are drifting through clouds, that you weigh nothing at all. And to help you with this feeling, you are breathing deeply now, in and out, slowly and deeply. In a few moments I shall count backwards from a hundred. When you are ready you will close your eyes.'

He began to count. One-hundred, ninety-nine, ninety-eight, ninety-seven, ninety-six, ninety-five, ninety-four. When he reached ninety-three Nesta closed her eyes, a deep, pacific feeling overcoming her, as if someone were carrying her soul in gentle palms.

'That is good, good,' nodded the old man. 'Now, together we are going on a journey, you and I. You will be the traveller, and I shall be your companion. Wherever you go, however distressed you are, I shall be with you, so you need have no fear that you will be overcome. And you may speak to me when you wish. At any time feel free to speak.'

'Yes,' Nesta answered, in a low, sibilant voice.

'Today we are just beginning, so we will not go very

far. Certainly on this day and on every other day we will never go farther than you are able to go at any one time. Never shall we go beyond your strength or your capabilities. Now, I want you to tell we what worries you most of all in the world.'

'No love,' Nesta moaned, as if in pain. 'To be without love.'

'Is that what troubles you *most* of all?'

'Yes. Being without love.'

'Can you tell me when you were first aware of this feeling?'

'Always. Always I've felt like this.'

'Now I am going to take you back over the years until you are a child again. Now, you are a child of five. Can you tell me what you are feeling?'

A smile curved Nesta's lips. 'Mam – Mam is holding me on her knee. I am so warm and cosy. Mam loves me. I love Mam.'

'That is good. Now if you would like to stay there, being five again, for a few moments, you may. Take as long as you like to remember that warm feeling.'

The old man leaned back in his chair, watching the happiness radiate from his patient's face. It was at times like these that he felt as if he had the power of the gods, but he was never arrogant enough to consider himself equal to the omnipotent. A gift had been given him to use during his lifetime for the benefit of others. That was all there was to it. It was simply a fact of life.

When he had asked his new patient her name the previous night she had not been able to remember who she was. He was not overly concerned. She had received a shock of some kind and had been exposed to the wrath of the elements. That was more than enough to make her confused and forget her identity. He would only begin to be concerned if she did not remember who she was after a week or so. To remind her now that she could not remember who she was would only add to her uncertainty and bewilderment. If necessary, he could make her remember, later, when she was in a deeply-relaxed trance, after she had unburdened some of her suffering. To force her into doing it now would be tantamount to heaping coals under a cooking-pot which was already boiling over. What he had to do was to lower the heat, quench the fire and remove the coals; the boiling would be reduced to simmering and finally to stillness – so that the fragile liquid in its equally fragile vessel would be as calm as a woodland pool on a summer's day.

Nesta woke to find Magda standing by her bed with a tray of chicken broth and a mug of steaming hot milk.

'It is not morning again, is it? I have not slept right through the day and the night, have I?' Nesta gasped.

'No, indeed not. Papa left you to your dreams. He said you needed them. You have only been away from us for an hour or two, that is all.'

'I had a beautiful dream about my mother.' Nesta smiled. 'I dreamt I was a little girl again, sitting on her knee. But it seemed more real than a dream. I can't explain it.'

'There's no need to explain it to me.' Magda shrugged. 'My father has been giving people beautiful dreams for many years.'

Late that afternoon the old man visited Nesta again. This time he told her a little about himself. 'You will have learned from Magda that my name is Jaroslav, but that is a clumsy name for an English tongue. Call me Jaros – all my friends do. My surname is not particularly important.

'Now we are going on our journey again, *kisgalamb*. Remember that you may feel *only* what you want to feel, only as much as you *can* feel for today.'

Lightly he touched Nesta's forehead, beginning the backward count. This time her eyes closed before he had reached the number ninety-five.

'Now you will relax deeply,' he said. 'Your muscles are growing heavy. Your eyes are growing heavy, and you cannot open them. Your hands are so heavy you cannot lift them. Your legs are heavy; you cannot move them at all. But you can hear everything I say and you can speak to me, too, if you want to. Now, my dear, can you tell me your name?'

'My name is – ' Nesta paused, her face convulsing as she struggled to think. 'My name is – is – ' She sighed, falling silent.

'What do you see when you try to think of your name, my dear?' Jaros asked.

'I see flames. A terrible fire. A child is dying in the fire – screaming, screaming. It is terrible, terrible.'

'Who is the child? Is it you?'

'No. A young boy called Benjamin Maude. He lived in Maude Manor, just outside York. I came back to see his brother, Joseph, but the manor had been burnt down.' Nesta's face screwed up again and she sobbed, a lifetime's worth of tears demanding release. The old man let her cry, nodding to himself, knowing that when she had shed some of the tears she would be closer to being healed.

'Yes, I know about the fire and how Maude Manor burnt down, my dear,' he told her when her tears had begun to abate a little. 'We were all very upset about it. Now, tell me what else you see when you try to think about your name.'

Nesta was silent for quite a long while, her head moving from side to side.

'I don't deserve it.' Nesta began to weep again. 'I don't deserve my name. It isn't really my name. I shouldn't have that name. My name – is – is – Meggie Blunt.' Suddenly her voice was childlike again; she was a little girl once more, with a little girl's voice.

'Tell me about Meggie Blunt,' Jaros said.

'Meggie Blunt is always hungry. She has only one dress to wear. A ragged, dirty dress. She has bare feet and nowhere to wash. She lives in a dirty, wretched hovel . . . in a slum, in Rats' Castle, in the Rookery, near St Giles's in London. She has nothing except a beautiful mother who loves her deeply, but her mother is poor, too, and she has a cough. She is always coughing. And when she disturbs Jack Blunt in the night when he is trying to sleep, he beats her into silence with his fists.' Nesta's voice cracked.

'Jack Blunt is Meggie's father?'

'Yes, he is. No, no, that's not right. No, he is her stepfather. Yes, that is it, her step-father. But she did not find that out until too late.'

'Too late for what, my dear?'

'Too late for little Meggie Blunt to be saved.'

'Now that is wrong you know, my dear. It is never too late to be saved. You and I together can save little Meggie Blunt, I promise you that.'

'She thought her father wanted her; her own father wanted her body as he wanted her mother's.'

'How did she feel about that, my dear?'

'Scared. Terribly scared and ill.'

'And did anything come of this wanting?'

Nesta's head began to twist from left to right, from left to right, over and over. Her hands rose, clawing at the air, her eyes flew open. '*No!*' she screamed, the scream racking her body, splitting her throat. '*No, don't do that, Da! No, Da, please, please, no! Please, please, no! No, not that. No, get off! Get off, Da, don't touch me like that, Da!*' Sobbing and pleading, she twisted on the bed until Jaros began to speak soothingly to her.

'It is time to wake up now, my dear. When I count to five you will wake up and you will feel refreshed and bright and happier than you have felt for a long time. Now listen – one, two, three, four, five.'

Gradually the racked muscles loosened themselves and the twisted face relaxed. Nesta's eyes closed and she lay back, breathing deeply.

'Now, sleep, my dear,' whispered the old man, touching her forehead lightly with his crumpled hessian hand before pulling the cover gently up to her shoulders and tiptoeing out of the room.

Next day they began again, the same as before. Again little Meggie Blunt took over Nesta; again she took her straight back to the hovel in Rats' Castle and Jack Blunt's assault. And when it became obvious to Jaros that she was growing over-stressed he relaxed her again and told her to choose the happiest moment she could remember and that moment would be hers again. Obeying, she returned at once to being five years old and on her mother's knee; that was how Jaros left her, allowing her to spend as long as she wanted in that happy moment in the past before she fell into a deep and natural sleep.

Days passed. Each time Jaros asked Nesta to return to the time of her worst ordeal she returned to that day when she was being attacked by Jack Blunt. Gradually, as one week, then two weeks, then three weeks passed, the horror diminished. Her tears lessened as she came to terms with her subconscious memory of the rape. Jaros explained to her carefully how returning to times of stress whilst in a trance ensured that she could face up to her past under its protection.

'But I do not know how reliving suffering can heal you,' she said, puzzled.

'Is it not true that you had forgotten about your stepfather's attack, pressing it down into your inner mind and closing the door on it?'

Nesta nodded.

'While your outer mind appeared content with that arrangement, thinking it a very good one, your inner mind was very unhappy about the whole situation. It didn't like to be keeping such an unpleasant secret, it wanted to let it out. In its attempts to get out it affected all of you; your inner and outer mind and your body, your physical wellbeing. Now, tell me, my dear, if you have had symptoms such as these: severe headaches, sudden illnesses, unexplained weariness, nightmares, either great tearfulness or an inability to weep, to let out the poisons. Ah, I can see by your face that you have suffered some of these.'

Nesta was staring at him in astonishment. 'Oh, yes, at some time or another I have experienced all of those things. Especially the severe headaches.'

'You see, we are not only what we appear to be on the

surface. When we are adult we think we are big and strong and that nothing can touch us. But at all times we are also the child we once were, the infant, the baby; the unborn baby, too. All those past people that we once were are still a part of us, and all the sufferings they endured are still with us. But the ones we cannot face up to are battened down deep in our inner mind. Do you understand what I mean, my dear?'

'Yes. It is true that sometimes I have felt a child again, starved, alone, cold. But I have upbraided myself, telling myself that I am not supposed to be helpless and childish now,' Nesta said. 'For much of the time I have succeeded in pushing away little Meggie, who wanted to take control of me again, but it has been a hard struggle and I have not always succeeded. I had to do so much which was against my upbringing – do things to survive which would have broken my mother's heart had she known about them.'

'But how many hours have you spent struggling to push down little Meggie, who wanted to appear again? All those energies, spent straining to keep her in check. The mind can only stand so much tension, so much strain. If the inner mind is burdened with terrible, secret memories, anything can set it off-balance; great shock, upset, an experience such as you had out on the moor when you found that Maude Manor had burned to the ground, and your friends with it.'

'And what would happen if I looked back on those past tragedies without being in a trance?' Nesta wanted to know.

'You could not do it, my dear. Have you not tried to do so in the past, and has there not been a terrible inner struggle which has made you exhausted and ill? The trance is like a caul, a protective shell inside which you can face everything with the minimum of trauma.'

'What is that word "trauma"? I have never heard it before.'

'It is a German word meaning a wound, but it has come to mean an experience which has marked a person deeply, so that he – or she – carries the scars of that experience around with him for the rest of his life. Just as you have done, my dear.'

'I see,' Nesta said wonderingly, beginning to understand something about her innermost self. Even in her dazed state when Jaros had first found her, she had been struck by the knowledge that he epitomized a truth which it was necessary for her to face. She had sensed all along that she could trust him, believe what he said, learn from him and be healed. She relaxed, lolling amongst the pillows, for she was still weak and Magda had insisted that she stay in bed.

('You're not missing much, my dear,' Magda had said heartily. 'Outside, it is demons' weather. Such a howling and a lashing you have never heard or felt in your life.')

'Think of a wound, my dear,' Janos continued, linking his fingers together and caging one knee in his palms thoughtfully. 'Think of a festering wound which will not heal. Over the top of it there is some semblance of healing, but underneath, out of sight, the blood is poisoned. If the wound is on a finger, then the finger throbs and aches and so you know that things are not right with it. That is what a trauma is like. The mind is a delicate blossom: after harsh storms gust against it, it conceals its worst injuries deep below; outside the petals continue to wax and bloom and look delightful, but underneath there is a worm in the bud.'

Nesta smiled at the flowery analogies which Jaros seemed to love but which never failed to make her realize exactly what he meant. To learn about her innermost mind was like learning about another person. It made her realize how very limited her self-knowledge had been in the past. Now she was learning about her other side, facing herself as she had been as a baby, an infant, a child. Gradually, with each session which took place with Jaros, she was facing all the injuries and the damage done to the infant and the child Meggie Blunt, coping with them again under the protection of the gentle state of trance into which Jaros put her at the beginning of each healing period.

Many of the things which she learned shocked her. Things she had never guessed at, not even in her most enlightened moments. The greatest surprise was to find out that she, even as a new-born infant, had been angry at being cold and hungry, with never enough milk coming from her half-starved mother's breast. How she, in all her innocence, had silently raged at her mother for not having enough food to give her. Being unable to speak, Meggie the infant had repressed her rage, like so many other feelings which she had been unable to deal with. Her rage had grown as subsequent traumatic events had taken place until her anger was a driving force, which demanded her attention constantly. She had even, before her birth, experienced some of her own mother's agony and suffering as she had lain, cold, starving and lonely in the field near London, immobilized with pain and shock. So deep had Jenny's sufferings been that they had been transmitted to the unborn infant she was struggling to bring into the world. Last of all in the process of healing through which Jaros took her, she relived her own birth struggles, all the time protected by the gentle trance.

Nesta lived in a constant state of wonderment, telling Jaros that she felt like Pandora, who had opened the casket, letting out all feelings, emotions, trials and triumphs. 'But unlike Pandora, there is so much hope where all those pains and struggles used to be,' she said.

Nesta was much stronger now, and Magda had let her get up for the past week, helping her down the wooden steps into the warm living-room, where Josh had piled up logs in the hearth so that a crackling fire burned merrily. Magda had placed a woven wool rug over the most comfortable armchair by the hearth. There Nesta would sit, with her feet on a padded tapestry stool, staring into the flames or chatting to Magda as she worked at her chores about the house. Sometimes Magda would hand her the great wooden cooking-bowl and Nesta would beat eggs in readiness for a cake, or cream black treacle and butter and rich, dark brown sugar together in readiness for Yorkshire parkin.

All Hallow's Eve passed, and Guy Fawkes' Night (a night when Nesta stayed in, not wishing to think of all the Guys being burned on bonfires throughout the country, memorials to Guido Fawkes, who had tried to blow up the Houses of Parliament along with its King, James the First). Nesta did not want to think of flames or fires or of anyone burning, for however much Jaros had healed her and taken away the extremities of her pain, he could not deprive her of her sensitivity, her warm and caring heart. Her ability to empathize and her generous spirit remained, as strong as ever.

She was ready now to face herself, Nesta Bellingham, for little Meggie Blunt had been exorcized for ever, and along with her her traumas. Now Nesta was Nesta alone; now she could face up to her present life and her vow to take revenge on the sick old Dowager-Duchess reclining in her bed at Malgrave Manor. But most of all, from morning until night and throughout her dreams, she thought of James.

Nothing could eradicate her love for and devotion to James, and in her new altruistic state she could face, but not without bitter-sweet pangs, the knowledge that she had lost him for ever. She was healed by Jaros's inspired care, but it had happened too late for her to keep her adored Sun God. It had been little Meggie Blunt, embittered and bent on revenge, who had lost James.

Nesta could look back on those feelings which had once been all-consuming, driving her with a barely-manageable passion, for Jaros had assured her repeatedly that one thing more than any other would allow Jenny to rest in peace – and that was her own daughter's spirit being at peace.

'The feeling you had that your mother could not rest until she was avenged was, in fact, your own spirit telling you that *you* could not rest until your grief and misery had been avenged,' he explained carefully.

'I realize that now,' Nesta said, feeling a new maturity. 'My mother was, above all, a generous-hearted woman.

She would not have wanted me to live through any more agony than I have done already. If she were here now she would be hugging me and kissing me and telling me to be happy, to look upwards to the stars and not down to the earth. I can see that now.'

Jaros was beaming, one knee caged in his palms in his favourite position as he rocked backwards and forwards, smiling with pleasure, in an almost gnome-like merriness.

'That is right, my dear. How right, how right! Look to the stars, look to the stars! You have made the right choice.'

Tears slid out of Nesta's eyes, but they were tears of happiness as much as of grief.

'If only I had met James after meeting you, Jaros,' she said in a low voice, staring into the flames, her hands linked together tightly, almost as if she were afraid they might shake if she loosened them.

'But it is never too late, *kisgalamb*,' Jaros said, drinking in the vibrant black and amethyst beauty of the girl who sat before him. He felt that any man who deserted Nesta Bellingham was an abject fool who would regret his folly for the rest of his life. A tender-natured girl, with a heart of fire and flame, who had now shed her burden of ice: such a woman was one to warm a man's bed through the long winter nights, to walk hand in hand with him in the spring, to ride on horseback beside him in the summer days, to sit by the hearth as autumn drew in, staring into his eyes, her own mellow with love. Her very presence had made him realize what a lonely old man he was and how much he missed his dead wife.

Although Nesta was now healed, she would always have a particularly poignant look about her, an air of delicate tragedy. But, as Jaros knew from past experience with his other patients, that would gradually diminish, especiallly when they had dealt with the very last hurdle of all.

'I was only fifteen. The man who had been visiting me regularly, keeping me, was going to leave. He was going to marry someone else,' Nesta told Jaros. 'It was a few weeks after he had gone that I found I was expecting a child.' Nesta's mouth trembled even though she was under the protection of the healing trance. 'I was at first very alarmed and then dismayed, remembering my own birth or as much as I knew of it then – being born illegitimate. I did not want any child of mine to be born without a father, without properly-married parents. Those were my worst fears; giving birth to a child and raising it on my own.

'I was seldom ill, but a friend of mine, Molly, visited me and she had a heavy cold. She looked feverish and so I sent her home, telling her to stay in bed until she was better. But I caught the fever and I dragged myself to bed, unable to summon anyone to help me, living on my own as I did. I lay in bed with that fever for some three or four days, and when it reached its height I lost the baby. I remember – oh, forgive me for saying this – I remember the feeling of relief and gladness which washed over me. One poor child would be spared the suffering and agony of being illegitimate, of being raised without a father. In a way, that lost baby was myself, for I had suffered the same stigma; I could not endure seeing any child of mine suffering the same way that I had.

'I was in a daze, alternately feverish and then cold with chills; when I was finally able to get up on my own I had lost two or three weeks of my life. Later, I called a doctor, and he examined me. He told me –' Nesta's voice faltered – 'he told me that I could never expect to bear another child. That I had had a deep infection inside me and that the scars would prevent me from ever conceiving again.'

Tears rolled out of the corners of her eyes as she continued. 'That was the dreadful secret I kept from James. I know now that there is no hope that we can ever be together again. It is better that things remain as they are, that he has gone back to Jane, for she is everything I can never be. She will give him the son he needs, to inherit his title and his estates.'

Jaros sounded quite snappish when he next spoke. 'Has

all I have taught you in these past two months been wasted, *kisgalamb*?'

'Wasted? How do you mean?' Nesta asked.

'Have I not told you about the power of the mind, how miracles can be accomplished, how *all* parts of the body and the mind can be healed?'

'Yes, but. . . .'

'Then why do you doubt that this is so?'

'But I do not doubt it. You have told me and I believe you. I have seen for myself how you can heal and make better a person's mind.'

'And what of the body, *kisgalamb*?' Jaros leaned very close.

'The body? That also? But I do not see. . . .'

'*All* things are healed, *kisgalamb*. The mind *and* the body. *All things are healed.*'

'I must appear stupid, but you mean – you mean that I might be able to have a child one day.'

'That is what I mean, *kisgalamb*. I have seen it happen. People have come to me who have had no children and who desire one, two, or even three or four, and after my treatment they have had them. It is a miracle, but a simple one. When the deep stress is removed, one merely has to tell one's innermost mind that one wishes a child and it is so.'

Nesta's cheeks were a rosy pink, her mind soaring with excitement. 'So you mean – I shall be able to have a child one day? Is that really true? Can you really tell me that, Jaros, and mean it?'

'One, two, three, four, five, or even six. Did I not tell you so? The healing goes very deep. *All* things are healed.'

Nesta began to cry then, but this time she shed tears of total happiness.

The catharsis was now complete, Jaros told her; he had done all that he could for her. The rest was up to her own mind's healing processes, which, unhampered by neurosis, could do their work as God had intended that they should.

Nesta had noticed a slow improvement all the time that

she was receiving treatment. She felt lighter; her dreams were more peaceful; she slept deeply, falling asleep instantly, and woke feeling bright and ready for the day ahead, whatever it might bring. The crisis was over and she was healing. Totally, she hoped, just as Jaros had promised.

It was at this time that Nesta had a visitor. She was sitting by the hearth sorting out bruised apples from unblemished ones in readiness for pie making when Jaros answered the knock on the door and stood back to let in the young man who was walking slowly, using sticks. It was Captain Maude! Nesta jumped to her feet, scattering apples everywhere.

'Joseph!'

She ran across to him to help him to a seat by the fire. His face was glowing from more than the exertion of walking into the farmhouse from his dog-cart.

'My dear Nesta. I heard about you from Magda – She supplies us with eggs, you know. I have been living at a friend's house while I convalesced. I am much better now.' He grinned bravely.

'Joseph, it must have been a terrible ordeal for you! When I heard about the fire, it made me so ill to think of – of poor little Benjamin and your mother. I am so very sorry. Words just do not seem enough.'

'I tried my best, but the staircase gave way when I was on it – I thought I was going to die, too. In a way, I wish I had.' He looked away, his face grim.

'Oh, you cannot truly mean that!' Nesta touched his arm, deeply moved. 'You will be yourself again soon – See how well you are walking now, almost like your old self – And then you will go back into the army and – '

'But I no longer have the heart, Nesta. Is life worth living when those you love most are dead? Can it be endured alone?'

'My mother died in my arms when I was a child, Joseph. I loved her more than life itself, but I went on. There really is no alternative, you know, my dear. You will love again – ' Nesta smiled at him comfortingly.

'If I could only be sure – sometimes I feel so desperately alone. I have dreams about the fire, the flames, the smoke, my brother and my mother calling me to help them, and I cannot move, my legs are wooden – It is unbearable.'

Nesta took his hand and squeezed it warmly. 'The dreams will fade. You will recover. I have been through similar ordeals, and here I am all in one piece – ' She smiled. 'Jaros is a miracle worker, you know. He will be able to help you.'

'Do you think he could? Myself, I doubt that anyone can help me, except – '

He looked into Nesta's eyes, his own hungry and pleading. She knew what he was going to say, and in a strange way she felt content. She could be of use here, helping poor Joseph, who had gone through hell just as she had done. She would care for him, cheer him, perhaps come to love him one day. . . .

When Joseph had gone, promising to return very soon for another visit, Nesta decided to write to Cathy and Amy. She felt capable of that now. They would have been worrying about her disappearance; she ought to let them know where she was.

As she sat writing the letter, pausing now and again to chew the end of the old, battered quill pen which was the only writing equipment Magda could offer, she realized what a furore she must have caused by vanishing. But it had been for the best; certainly for James. He was a duke; he had money and power behind him. Now he would be able to marry Jane and they could have the son they deserved.

She did put down the quill pen, feeling a heaviness descend upon her, thinking of the son she might have borne James had life taken another course. She knew now that she was needed here, very much needed, but even so, to say good-bye to her Sun God was like killing part of herself. But it was the most loving act she could do, to free him. In time he would forget she had ever existed. . . .

She gazed out of the farmhouse window across the

moors, leaning her elbows on the scrubbed pine table where Magda made her pastry. She had grown to love the moors during her two and a half months' stay at the farmhouse, and she knew them in all their autumnal moods. Now winter was drawing in, and they had a closely shaven look, as if hundreds of cows had been feeding on the stubby grass. The bracken was a dull, dark brown; the heather, which had been a glowing, rich purple on her arrival, was now the shade of winter beech leaves. The skies were as dull and heavy as dirty pewter, the dingy metallic light making the house gloomy, necessitating the use of more candles and oil-lamps.

The harsh, shroud-like greyness was bathing Nesta's face as she looked out across the unfenced land; the gloom seemed to have seeped into her very soul, permeating her body and mind with an ineradicable misery. Nothing Jaros said or did, no miraculous healing process could cure her longing for James, which was a perpetual ache in her heart. Where he was concerned, she would always be little, half-starved Meggie Blunt, yearning to bathe in the rarefied light which emanated from her Sun God.

Resting her elbows on the scrubbed pine table, Nesta placed her forehead in her palms and closed her eyes. She thought of James in the arms of Jane, kissing and caressing her as he had once done to Nesta, making her his bride, looking forward to the arrival of their first child. Stinging tears forced their way out from behind Nesta's lids to roll down her face and arms onto the wooden table.

Her James – her own beautiful, handsome, generous James – married to another woman. Oh, she had failed him, she knew that; she had failed him dreadfully, and she could only hope and pray that his memories of her would in time become happier ones than they certainly must be at the moment.

How he must hate her! For her he had defied society; for her he had cast caution to the winds; for her he had been willing to risk all that he had. And in return, what had she given him? Only suffering and pain.

The tears continued to pour from her eyes in a ceaseless flood. No punishment was bad enough for what she had done to James – and to that poor old woman in her sick-bed. Would she survive the shock of Nesta's disappearance, the long wait before the divorce and James's marriage to Lady Jane and the birth of their son? Divorce proceedings could take quite some time; certainly too long for an old, sick woman to wait.

Fresh guilt stabbed at Nesta. She had been so absorbed in her inner self during the past months, thinking of no one else save herself, and James. She would write to Cathy and Amy and ask them to find out for her how the old Duchess was, how she was taking her disappearance. It was the least she could do.

Nesta was learning to help Magda around the house and on the farm. She had Joseph, and she believed that she could find a spurious happiness with him. He needed her, and it was bliss to be needed. It would be nothing like what she could have had with James, but gradually she would adjust.

First, though, she *had* to know if James were happy. If that were not so, then her sacrifice would be in vain. With this thought in mind, she added a postscript to her letter.

Whatever you do, do not let James know where I am, but tell me how he is. Find out in secret for me, but do not let him know that you are acting on my behalf. You can soon find out from his companions how he fares. I shall only be truly happy when I know that he is happy, when he and his Jane are married. (At this point she blinked back tears.) *Please keep me informed and let me know when they are married. It is better that he forget me completely, but I can only bear the pain if I know for sure that he is happier in his new life.*

At the Crimson Club, as Cathy read Nesta's letter to Amy, their faces became masks of astonishment.

'Here, Amy, how's she got hold of this, then? What's got into her head? Her James marrying that Jane. What gave her that idea?'

'Crikey, don' ask me! But what a relief to know she's safe. That's a weight off me mind. Fancy her going to York, of all places!'

'What are we going to do about James? She's asked us not to tell him, but how can we keep silent knowing what we do? How in God's name she got that idea he was hot for Lady Jane I dunno. He'd sooner swive a polar bear than her, if you ask me. Don't say how she got the idea, do she?'

Cathy and Amy were quite adamant that James was not planning to marry Jane, Lady Finchley-Clark, for that young woman had married Sir Gordon Geoffrey-Smith, an associate of Dr David Livingstone. She and her new husband had already set off for Northern Rhodesia, where they were to help with the missionary work there. James Malgrave had been best man at the wedding.

When Cathy and Amy had heard this they had looked at one another knowingly. 'Missionary work'll be the right thing for her an' no mistake,' they had said. 'Sort her out good an' proper that will. Take all her po-faced, hoity-toity manners over to them poor savages an' confuse 'em right an' proper, she will, telling them all their normal feelings is wrong. Can't you just imagine it?'

They'd had a fit of giggles at the very thought and then collapsed into a kind of sobriety as they visualized the fate of the bemused and innocent natives when Her Ladyship got to work on them.

Cathy read the letter again and then she looked at Amy and said, 'She asked us not to tell him, but she's labouring under a misapprehension, ain't she? He ain't going to marry this Lady Jane at all, is he, so he certainly won't be happier, will he? He'll have no one. Last time I saw him riding by in his carriage he looked all white an' haggard an' drawn an' proper ill. All that searching an' looking for her that he's been doing, an' all those people that he's sent out scouring the country for her an' not one of them turned up with her hide-away. Why didn't we think of York?'

'Would we have told him if we had known for sure it were York? At the time he'd behaved real bad to her, hadn't he? She was very unhappy, wasn't she? We'd've thought it was for the best if she wanted to go off on her own an' please herself. It's a free world, you know.'

'Yes, that's right,' Cathy agreed, 'but we know now he's very unhappy, don't we? We know he's been living in proper misery since our Nesta went off. Shown that he loves her, hasn't he? Proved it. Not looked at another woman, has he? Just spent all that money on trying to find his Nesta. An' then there's that poor, sick old Duchess. Been real ill since she heard the news, ain't she? Doctors do say she's fading away an' won't last much longer. What about her? She'd be real happy to see her James's wife back again, wouldn't she? You know how she doted on Nesta.'

'That's right,' Amy nodded vigorously. 'We've *got* to tell him, Cathy. Now, this very minute! It's no good humming and hawing over it an' thinking what's right an' what's wrong. He's desperate. thinking he's lost her for good, an' she's desperate, thinking she's lost him for good. We can put it right. We can mend it! Hey, don't that give you a thrill to think that, Cathy lovey?'

Amy gripped her friend's arm tightly, her face radiant with excitement.

Nesta had grown accustomed to the gentle, peaceful round of life on the farm and Joseph's regular visits. Magda and Josh were so good to her, although Josh was a man of very few words; he called his wife 'lass' and that seemed to be one of the main words of his vocabulary. 'Yes, lass,' and 'No, lass,' he'd say; sometimes, 'Give over, lass,' if she talked too much and he wanted some hush. Occasionally he'd say gruffly, 'Do 'urry up now, lass,' but that was rare, for Magda was usually ahead with all her tasks and didn't have to be prompted.

The farmhouse was run very efficiently, and after Nesta had helped with the lighter tasks – feeding the hens, stamping the pats of butter with Magda and Josh's own trademark, a bumble bee, preparing vegetables for the next meal, or mulling cider or ale for warming drinks for the farm labourers – she would spend some time walking on the moors, loving them in all their moods. Warmly wrapped up in one of Magda's massive woolly shawls, a pair of her fleece-lined boots and one of her much-darned dresses, Nesta would roam the moors, watching pewter skies turn to murky blue and then back to grey, watching the shadows of clouds scudding across the moors at her feet so that land and sky seemed to be inverted.

On one such eerie day when the sun had come out quite sharp and yet thin, and its butter-yellow light was thrusting out between grey clouds, Nesta watched the reflection of the clouds moving along on the moors in front of her, thinking how like running sheep they were, blown and tossed by the wind. Her eyes followed the clouds to the furthermost point of the moor, in the direction of York city, and it was then she saw the lone horseman silhouetted against the eerie yellow and grey light.

Nesta knew that a storm was brewing, one of those savage storms when wind would tear at her hair and lightning would bifurcate the sky. She ought to get back to the farmhouse quickly, before the weather broke and she was drenched. The man should be returning back the way he had come, too, or he would be caught in the storm. It was quite a ride back to the city.

Before she began to turn back, she watched him, but he did not turn his horse; he just sat there, staring hard across the moorland, and she stared back. Had the butter-yellow light not been so bright in her eyes he would not have looked so densely black against the sky and she might have realized who he was all the sooner. When she did recognize him, it was as if the sun were shining in her own heart; it felt as if it were trying to burst out of her breast. She began to run towards the horseman at the same moment that he urged his horse on towards her.

YASMINA'S DAUGHTER
By Corinne Childs

PRICE: $2.50 LB838
CATEGORY: Novel

A NOVEL OF A MOTHER'S TURBULENT LEGACY

Yasmina was a robust and strongly independent woman, struggling to survive as an exotic dancer in a two-bit traveling show. Physically ejected from her only source of income, Yasmina became the housekeeper of farmer Oliver Broadbent and his several children. She soon married him, but became trapped in an environment she despised. The rest of her life she struggled, and passed a legacy of wisdom and torment to her daughter, Victoria. But Victoria, too, was destined for denial and heartbreak before she could practice the wisdom of her mother.